OLD AS THE HILLS

LAND MYSTERIES
BOOK THREE

CELIA LAKE

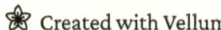

ABOUT OLD AS THE HILLS

What would you risk so others could live?

It is the early months of WWII and Rathna already has an idea of how bad it might get. If she can make the final connections she needs to create a new portal in a matter of weeks rather than years, she might just be able to get a few more people out of Germany's ever expanding grasp. But she's also been asked to take on a new apprentice. Rathna has no idea whether he'll be willing to help, if she can trust him, or if he can trust her enough to do what needs to be done.

Her husband Gabe has a challenge that will use every single one of his skills and then some. He's been charged by the Council to coordinate magical responses to the war, not only in Albion itself, but among the many esoteric and occult groups of Great Britain. His own apprentice is brilliant, in a different way than Gabe, but this project will ask everything of them both.

Together, Gabe and Rathna have built their lives to bend their passions, talents, and magics to making things better for the world around them, including their three growing children. Now their war work is going to separate them, certainly for months, possibly for much longer. As they tangle with ancient magics, seeking new ways forward, there are more unanswerable questions, tremendous risks, and a few glimmers of hope.

Old As The Hills follows Gabe and Rathna's adventures from the autumn of 1939 through the summer of 1940, a time of desperate plans to save lives and hold back invasion. It is full of ancient fae magic, the power of place, urgent witchcraft rituals, and unexpected encounters. The Land Mysteries series explores the Second World War in the magical community of Albion and is best read in order.

Note: While *Old As The Hills* does not end on a cliffhanger, the last chapter does pose a particular and urgent question, answered in *Upon A Summer's Day*. If you don't care to be left hanging for a little, pick them both up on June 21st, 2023.

CHAPTER 1
NOVEMBER 6TH, 1939 AT THE PORTAL KEEPER GUILD HALL

Rathna was glad she'd had nearly a week's warning before this meeting. It had given her time to plan, time to consult, and time to figure out what needed to happen if she went forward. Fundamentally, she was beginning as she meant to go on, even if that was not entirely what the young man she was meeting was expecting. Especially since it was not entirely what he was expecting.

There were things he would know, of course: Rathna was a Portal Keeper who had finished her own apprenticeship nearly twenty years ago now. She had taken on two successful apprentices, both fully established and tending portals themselves. Her marriage and children were recorded in the Gold Book that listed all the lines of the Great Families of Albion.

And yet, all of that was the most superficial sort of information. Her husband wouldn't stand for that, chaotic and glorious magpie of a man that Gabe was. Nor would Richard and Alysoun, his parents. Even her children wouldn't. Well, at least the elder two. Avigail, at seven and three-quarters, certainly had opinions, but she did not have as much experience of the world to argue from yet. That would certainly come.

Rathna had chosen the setting for this conversation carefully. She wanted Ferdinand Howard to be off balance. The young man knew what to make of a parlour, a library, or an office. Rathna could have had her choice of those. The country house of the Portal Keeper's Guild had plenty of parlours and offices, as well as four separate libraries. She could have chosen the Guild Hall in Trellech, or even invited him out to Veritas, the Edgarton family estate in Kent. Instead, she'd chosen the Guild estate's orangery.

It did not, in fact, contain orange trees of any sort. For the last century and a half, since the Guild had had the space, they'd used it to nurture and tend the saplings intended for portals. Only a few would thrive, but the trees were grown pair and pair, as was required for their eventual vocations.

Rathna enjoyed taking her turn to tend and encourage them when she had the chance, with both fertiliser and magic. She found the place restful, in a way she'd never been able to explain, but that Gabe understood. Trees had quite simple desires compared to the rest of the world, and they were fundamentally honest about them.

She'd chosen it because it was unusual, and she liked it. But also, the orangery was cosy, even with a brisk November wind outside. The heat radiated up pleasantly from pipes under the floor, making Rathna feel properly warm. She'd even discarded the wheat-gold shawl that went with this dress on the chair at the tea table.

The rest of her outfit, well, that was a particular statement as well, and she'd selected it with Alysoun's advice firmly in mind. She had decided against a saree, but her emerald-green silk frock was cut very much like one, flaring out from a fitted bodice to a broad draping skirt. The golden embroidery around the hem, collar, and sleeves picked up the theme, brighter than most people in Albion would choose to pair, but striking.

Rathna, though, was making a point. If Ferdinand Howard had a problem with her Bengali heritage, she needed to know immediately. If he wanted someone traditional in the ways he understood tradition, she needed to know that. She kept her own learned and chosen ancient traditions, now in three distinct forms, but she suspected Howard only knew much about one of those sets.

Precisely on time, she heard leather-soled shoes coming down the polished marble of the hallway. She turned, having placed herself where the light shone through from the glass roof above. She took her time, the way she'd learned from Alysoun and Richard, making every movement matter, not rushing anything. "Good morning, Apprentice Howard."

Rathna had seen him before, of course, at a conversational distance. He'd been a sworn apprentice for two years. He was two months from turning twenty-one, and decidedly handsome by current standards, with blond hair and bright blue eyes. She suspected he might still fill out a bit in the shoulders, but not by much, and he seemed to be more or less comfortable with his height. That was about Gabe's height, a head taller than Rathna. He wore a navy pinstripe suit that - these days - she could identify on sight as coming from the second best tailor in Trellech. Along with it, he'd selected a silver-grey tie and pocket square, anchored by a moonstone tie pin. It made his house at Schola easy to read, even if she hadn't spent hours with his file over the past few days.

Owl House produced swots, as many people liked to point out. Many of them spent their days lost in their books or their aspirations of knowledge rather than more practical work. But Rathna had come to know a number of quite effective Owls over the years, including Lord Geoffrey Carillon. She'd test young Howard, and see what he did with a situation he hadn't already studied.

What he made of her house, that was perhaps the more interesting question. Rathna had found enough of a place for herself in Seal House, the most liminal of the seven. She hadn't gone in for their more common arts and magics, though she wouldn't be surprised if Rowena did. Their eldest daughter had taken to the house magics like, well, a seal to water, delighting in playing with them, and she was only a third year. Somehow already a third year. Both at the same time.

Rathna was wearing her guild token, as she usually did, with the cast gold portion of the disc resting against her skin, just slightly warmer than anything else touching her. The lemniscate on the visible side had an aquamarine for her Schola house in one half, and the labradorite that shimmered and flashed with the portal energies in the other. Both echoed the deep green of the frock and the gold of the embroidery. She'd hung it on a thicker golden chain than most did. It was one of the little touches that her parents - their memories a blessing - would have read as all the visible signs of success and security they'd craved when they came to England.

Howard came within a foot or two, just the right amount of polite distance. He made a sharp and precise bow, and when she extended her hand, palm down, he took it carefully in his own and made a precise kiss over it. "Magistra Edgarton." As he straightened up, he looked her in the eye, which was a good sign. The very Continental manners, his own heritage on his mother's side, those were more complicated to read correctly, especially at the moment.

"A pleasure." Rathna offered a smile. No reason to be harsh about any of this, and again, beginning as she meant to continue was the thing here. "Do let's have a seat. I gather you prefer coffee. My husband does as well. He approves of this roast." She didn't expect other people to like tea the way she took it when she had a chance. Rathna gestured toward the table. Howard hovered by his chair until she was settled, then took his own seat.

She nodded at him. "Do pour for yourself, the cream and sugar as well." There was a little decorative tower of plates with biscuits. She'd brought the orange-scented shortbread from Veritas, where Cook had a touch with them. Rathna poured from her own pot, inhaling the spices of the chai masala before she added her own cream and a dipper of honey. There was talk of rationing, starting soon, but a childhood of scarcity had taught her a great deal about enjoying things while she could.

Only when all of that had been sorted did she continue. "Our goal today is to see if you might suit as my apprentice and if I might suit as your apprentice mistress. I am, to be up front about it, nothing like Master Fortnum. I respect him, his work, and his training, but we have decidedly different styles and approaches."

On the other hand, beggars couldn't be choosers. Davis Fortnum had been called up for war work, and it wasn't suitable for an apprentice. They'd sealed the portals against those in Germany and Austria and Czechoslovakia, of course, each in turn. But layering additional protections without damaging the portal connections was fiddly, delicate work that needed extensive experience. More to the point, it didn't generally allow for extended explanations.

"Magistra?" Howard looked up from his own cup, now a medium brown with the cream. It was not a particularly informative reply, even if it was suitably polite.

"It must be both of our choices, of course." She wondered, all of a sudden, if that was what hadn't been in the file - or one of the things - if he'd been given a choice about going into the guild in the first place. She gestured slightly with a hand, the gleam of her wedding band and betrothal ring catching the light. "I've read your formal records with the guild, and of course, I've talked with Master Fortnum about what you've studied so far. But I would like to hear from you, directly, about your experience and background."

"Background, Magistra." He gathered himself up. "My father is Francis Howard, of the Wiltshire Howards. Mother is German." Rathna couldn't tell if that slight pause were deliberate or simply a needed breath. "She's lived here for many years, since before the Great War." He wasn't tentative about it, at least. He must have known she'd know, and she respected the way he rode that delicate line of protective defensiveness that Rathna used herself. Telling people the distasteful thing up front meant they couldn't claim it was kept from them later. "I have two older brothers and an older sister. I'm the youngest by five years. The others are all married and established."

Rathna nodded. "A good start, though I am more interested in who you are than who your people are, in the more genealogical sense. Though, of course, our parents shape us in all sorts of ways."

He nodded once, as if thinking about saying something and deciding against it. He governed his impulses, then.

That was useful information. Gabe would have asked, almost certainly, unless the duel of the conversation would go better if he refrained. "You have children, Magistra, from what I read?"

"I do." She leaned back a little to tug the shawl over her shoulder from the back of the chair, partly for effect, and partly to keep the draught off her neck. She'd have to check the charms on the glass when they were done. One of them must have loosened beyond the tolerance of the insulating cantrip. "Why do you ask?" He wouldn't have overlapped with any of them at school. Rowena hadn't started until the autumn after he left Schola.

"Pardon, Magistra. Your family comes up in conversation from time to time." Which it might well, especially among the Howards. Those weren't people Rathna knew well. The Wiltshire line of the family didn't directly hold the land magic, but Rathna didn't know the Devon side of the family much better, for all she saw them at the obligatory rituals and social events. They had to make an appearance, since Gabe was his father's Heir in that as in other things. Also, Alysoun always appreciated both company and an arm at that sort of do.

"My husband? His parents? Morah Avigail, her memory a blessing, who trained me?" The phrase came to her as naturally as always, but she saw it hit him oddly. Another thing he hadn't expected, then. And of course, he would never have known her beloved apprentice mistress, who'd given her a home from the time she was fourteen until she married Gabe.

Avigail Levy had died eight years ago, not long before their youngest daughter had been born. She'd lived to a grand old age, surrounded by children and grandchildren and great-grandchildren, and died content with her life.

Rathna missed her every day, and three or four times more on Friday evenings.

Howard had the grace to blush. "The first two, Magistra. And your children. They weren't sure what to make of Magistra Levy beyond the fact she was respected by the guild." No, the Howards wouldn't know what to do with a woman who'd gone to Schola, but who'd made her life among the Jewish community in Spitalfields. Those with magic who lived there, like Rathna and Morah Avigail, kept to the agreements of the Pact, but otherwise lived lives intertwined with those without it.

Rathna nodded and Howard went on. "Lord Richard Edgarton has held the title since his father's death in 1901, and the lands are widely considered to be flourishing, both agriculturally and magically. He is, as I am sure you know, both a Captain in the Guard, and a respected Magistrate for nearly as long. Lady Alysoun Edgarton comes from the Forsythes, though the family has been a bit attenuated in her own generation." Her brother, expected to continue that line, had died in South Africa.

He took another breath, as if needing a moment to figure out what he should make sure to mention. "I have heard many good things about Veritas. The architecture, as well as the current health of the land." That, now, held a hint of hopefulness, that this wasn't going to just be a dull and rote recitation of known facts. Rathna knew the architectural magics were well up to snuff; Gil Oxley had lived at Veritas for five years now. His chosen partner, Magni, had been Richard's own apprentice master. When he'd finally retired from the Guard, their house just outside Trellech had been a bit much for them to maintain. Gil was still one of the foremost experts on architectural magic, and just as busy consulting as he chose to be. Howard hesitated. "And you have three children with your husband."

Ah, he was entirely unsure what to make of Gabe. That put him in the same company as most of Albion, so it wasn't anything to be ashamed of. And they could tackle the matter of the children quickly enough. "Our eldest, Rowena, is at Schola, in her third year in Seal House. Anthony is in tutoring school. Our youngest, Avigail, is very almost eight, as she would tell you."

She saw a moment of the flash of consideration, and she went on. "She is named for Morah Avigail Levy, my apprentice mistress, yes, her memory a blessing. They have a custom, a longstanding tradition, among their people - she was Jewish - that you do not name a child for someone living. But she died knowing I would have another daughter, and that I would name her Avigail." It was a particularly tender point. If he were a bigot about her own parents, that was one thing. If he were going to be an antisemite, that was even less tolerable. Best to know now, so she could declare her refusal and be done with the question.

Howard nodded once, then considered his options, showing no further reaction to the matter of Morah Avigail, negative or otherwise. "Your husband, Magistra, is the eldest child of his parents, and Heir to the land magic for that part of Kent. He's considered gregarious and charming." He stopped before saying more, and Rathna suspected Howard had come across a story or two from women who thought that charm meant he could be seduced. Which he couldn't be, not like that, certainly. "Attentive to the land, Magistra, and my family respects that."

That much was certainly true, though it left a lot out. She'd never met anyone who loved the land as much as Gabe did, not even his father or Geoffrey. However, the way

Howard had danced around things gave her an opening to challenge him and see what he did with it. Rathna was no duellist, but she'd married into a family of them, and she'd been looking for a chance to see what he did when he was pressed.

Rathna turned her hand over. "If you think the most important thing about my husband is that he's Heir to his father, you are missing a great deal. Try again, please."

CHAPTER 2
THE ORANGERY

Rathna settled back to see what Howard made of the challenge, picking up her tea. Gabe was going to laugh and laugh when she got home tonight. That was all to the good. He'd been increasingly worried lately, little twitches he hadn't been able to explain. Not that the war didn't give an excellent reason for nerves of all kinds.

He did something she hadn't expected. "The portal at Veritas is made of local sandstone, isn't it?"

"Quarried a few miles away, yes." Rathna nodded. "You've not been through it, though, I believe."

Howard shook his head. "No, Magistra. I've not done much with any of the sandstone portals, so I was curious. I saw in the notes that you've refined the tuning."

Ah. She had, but explaining that was a trifle delicate. "A gift for my mother-in-law." Alysoun suffered from pain that came and went, though mostly it came and stayed. Rathna had tuned the Veritas portal over months and years to make travel as gentle on Alysoun as she could. "Within the tolerances and scope, of course. There's a fair bit of flexibility, especially with a private household portal."

Howard nodded slowly, as if that were some interesting piece of information he was now filing. "Your husband, Magistra, is a Penelope. I am afraid I don't quite know how to appreciate his skills there." Howard didn't sneer, but he was clearly dubious about what the Penelopes were. Interesting and quite telling about his family's attitudes in general.

The Penelopes did tend to pull an air of mystery about them like a cloak. Even Rathna felt that, and she'd been married to Gabe for approaching two decades. They had their own jargon and their own codes. Aunts Mason and Witt had been firmly included as members of the family from when Gabe was tiny. They could signal each other like a couple who'd been in each other's pockets for half a century, because, in many ways, they had.

Though they were rarely actually in the same office. Aunt Witt was a force of order and precision, and Aunt Mason was a swirling mote of chaos, nearly as much as Gabe was. Lucy Doyle, Gabe's own apprentice mistress, was much more along Witt's line, and Isobel, his current apprentice, seemed to lean that way as well. It worked very well as a principle of assignment, working the polarity, so long as it didn't send them and everyone near them round the bend.

"What do you know of the Penelopes?" They could start there.

Howard frowned. "They work closely with the Guard." It was a faint sort of answer, and he seemed to know it.

"Yes, but that is not why they exist." He looked up at her, and Rathna took some pity on him. "We solve a particular category of problem, one that takes a specific, quite uncommon, flavour of magic. And we must be extremely skilled at our work to do it without causing more problems. There aren't many people who can even attempt it and we have a long apprenticeship." Gabe had, over the years, persuasively convinced Rathna how essential the Portal Keepers were, and how skilled any of them who made it through an apprenticeship had to be. Not that other people really appreciated those skills, they just complained when the portal didn't work as expected.

Howard nodded, hesitantly.

"The Penelopes solve problems on a vastly larger scale. Any sort of problem. Someone comes up with a new approach to magic, and it backfires. They are the ones to solve it. An elderly alchemist locks themselves in their lab, and - well, we all know what can happen there." She didn't need to spell out that particular horror. There'd been another case in August that had seen extensive coverage in the papers about the need for better safety options. "They assist the Guard with investigations. The Penelopes can chase the thread of a particular magic through portals. They can figure out where someone was standing when they did something criminal, determine the cause of death in collaboration with the Healers, and much more."

"Magistra." Howard nodded again, slowly.

"They hold the depth and breadth of what magic can do in their hands and heads. And they turn it uniformly to helping people out of trouble, as much as they can. The Penelopes are experts in a dozen different kinds of magic, though they do in fact pick specialities. They work with each other closely, borrowing a cup of cleverness or expertise whenever it's needed. They can't let their egos get in the way, or nothing would get done. So when I tell you that Gabe had the shortest apprenticeship in the Penelopes in three centuries, finishing when he was twenty-one, it tells you a bit about his range of skill."

"Shortest...." Oh, there was a burst of jealousy there, though he tamped it down quickly. Not quickly enough for someone who'd learned from Gabe and Alysoun and Aunts Mason and Witt how to spot that sort of thing, but quickly. "May I ask what his specialty is?"

"Magic that affects places. Architectural, but also the land magic. He hadn't quite intended that, but they do keep asking him, because he's Heir to his father and has been for so long. The two work well together. He's a terror in an alchemy lab, but much more to the furnishings than to himself, thankfully." Gabe had a very real appreciation for the safety precautions that mattered. Thankfully. Or the marriage would probably have done her in.

Gabe was impulsive, quick, and didn't hesitate, but he was also often absolutely right about what needed doing and how. A burst of intuition with thumbs, and rather longer reach than a toddler. She half-smiled at it, and then held the moment. Let Howard puzzle over that. It would do him some good.

The young man across the table from her was quiet for a long moment. "This is not what I expected, magistra. Perhaps, would you be so kind as to instruct me? In what I should be considering."

That had the first real solid of promise she'd heard yet. "Master Fortnum has given you an excellent and deliberate grounding. But the way I teach expands from what is known to be true to what might be possible." She lifted her fingers, calling a charmlight wordlessly. "I learn a great deal from my husband." She sent the burst of magic and vitality off toward a pair of the trees that could use a little more help. "Before I met him, I was a trifle rigid." Also terrified of stepping out of her assigned place in society. "May I ask what your parents think of your apprenticeship?"

It mattered, whether he was here because of some obligation, internal or external, or whether he honestly felt a pull toward it. She could teach the skills of tending portals, but she couldn't teach the desire to do so. Portals went at their own speed. She had not put Howard off yet, but she also hadn't heard that spark she wanted from him, some desire beyond it being a respected profession and specialty.

Howard cleared his throat. "I'm the youngest. It's known to be an honour, to be asked to apprentice here. It is work, yes, and my family does not generally need to do that." Rich as well as posh, then, not that the two always ran together, especially these days. "They don't entirely know what to make of me. They aren't upset that I chose to apprentice, but it would...." His voice faded out.

"It would be complicated if you didn't continue."

"Yes, magistra." His manners remained impeccable, though he had flushed, his cheeks going pink. It was one of the downsides of being quite that fair.

"Do you want to continue?" That was another question he definitely hadn't expected. His chin came up, there was a flash of utter confusion on his face. She went on, more gently. "If you do not wish to, this would be a, shall we say, decorous way to end your apprenticeship. A public good reason."

Howard didn't hesitate. "Mistress, I'd like to continue, if it is possible. I don't feel I know much at all yet, but what I have learned so far, I..." He stopped and looked away. Ah. He had feelings about it then, and it was beyond him to show those feelings, certainly to her. She could indeed work with that, given a little time. Probably also an application of Gabe, to shake things loose.

Briskly, she went on, saving him from the awkwardness. "Well, then. I believe in giving my apprentices my best. On that note, you may want to talk to Mhairi and Petrus about what to expect from me before you make a formal commitment. You'd not have met them, I suspect, other than perhaps very much in passing. Mhairi's up in Scotland, and Petrus has been deeply involved in the adjustments to the Plymouth portal the last two years." She reached to one side of her teacup, where her journal waited, and pulled out a small cream coloured card. "Their full names, so you can write by journal. They know you might write tonight." The magical journals were tremendously handy, and the guild had made them a requirement for all members and apprentices in 1925. It had vastly simplified everyone's lives.

"Magistra." He barely hesitated, then reached for the card. "What will they tell me, magistra? About your training?"

"That I'm fair minded. Patient, as long as someone's doing their best. Though they both saw me tear strips off someone who wasn't. He was an apprentice at the same time as Petrus." She glanced up, arching an eyebrow. "He shaped up." It had, however, been the talk of the guild for a good six months. "That I get ideas and I want to try them out."

Howard nodded, cautiously. "May I ask, magistra, does my family background bother you?" Ah, that was quite brave of him, if he was as earnest as he seemed.

"Your mother? Or your father's people?"

"Mother's, mostly. The white paper that came out from

the British government last week." He had the good grace to look worried. That paper had laid out, in quite plain language, what was happening to Jewish men and women in Germany, and to anyone who opposed the Nazi government. Even quite minor offences could get one thrown into a work camp, perhaps never to emerge.

"The question, on the whole, is what you value and what you choose. You have a choice here. It is a limited choice because of circumstances beyond your control." She hesitated, then decided to give him the gift of knowledge. "I had not taken an apprentice recently because I have been working on something complex."

"Magistra?" He leaned forward, though. That was promising.

This was the crux. She had to decide which way to go with this, whether to tell him what she was working on, or wait until she figured out if there was a faint chance he might actually be able to help. She chose the former. He should have as many choices as he could be given. "Your oath on the Silence, not to share this with anyone I don't designate? It is related to the war and security."

He didn't hesitate, making an oath on the Silence and his magic. She wondered what flashed through him. The Silence oath brought a moment of greatest fear to the one taking it, what should force them to silence if they tried to break it. What could break a spirit, if pressed at, and shatter a mind into pieces. Whatever his was, only a flicker of it showed on his face, but of course she wasn't as adept at reading those signs as some people she knew.

Rathna went on, keeping her voice even. "I have been working on research and some trials to see if we might establish a portal far more quickly than we have in the past. A matter of months, maybe weeks, rather than years.

You know the Fatae tales of them springing up overnight, yes?"

Howard's eyes had got wide. "That's impossible." It came out clipped and quick, before he flushed again. "Pardon, Magistra."

"No one has been able to do it since the Pact." The Fatae portals were different in so many ways from the ones humans had learned to make from them, perhaps most obviously in how they grew. "But we said it was impossible to create them across water, and the ones on Samson Island and in the Hebrides are doing well enough. A bit touchy in bad weather, but predictable about it." Once one had solved one mythological problem, others seemed decidedly more within reach. Though someone did have to sail out and bang on those island portals with a metaphysical hammer on a regular basis to make them behave.

Howard considered that, and he had the patience to hold his tongue while he did. Finally, he said, "May I ask about the results so far?"

"An excellent question." It was, and she was generous with her praise for a number of reasons. "We've made two. The process can't be forced in the trials we've made so far. The portal that results isn't terribly stable, but you have plenty of warning before it collapses. You can't take much ferrous metal through it, certainly not much worked iron. It takes focused magic, trained skill, and raw power. As well as, well, convincing the local water or stone to do what you wish."

"Not trees, magistra?" Trees were the other form of portals they could make, which was impossible to forget in the orangery.

She shook her head. "I haven't had luck with trees." She

suspected it was because it was tricky to find paired trees in an otherwise suitable location.

Howard considered again, reaching for his coffee. Rathna matched him with a sip of her chai, charmed to still be the perfect temperature. Then, slowly, he asked, "If you made one, what would you do?"

"Ideally? You know of the kindertransport? Getting children out of Germany. Jewish children, in particular, but anyone who'd be at risk for their lives. Innocents." She gestured, twisting her fingers in the air. "It could be abused all sorts of ways. Though it wouldn't permit the passage of anything like automobiles or cars, or probably even rifles. Even the axles on a cart are iffy. And there are other complications."

"Other complications, magistra?" He was leaning in again. Good, she'd done a fine job of hooking his interest.

"May I ask, have you visited your mother's family in Germany? Are you familiar with the portals there?"

"I— pardon, magistra, but I need to know why you're asking." He stammered, flushed, and looked down. She waited until he looked up again, not quite meeting her eyes.

"To anchor the portal, you must tie it into the existing Fatae portals. The more recent ones, since the Pact, won't do, and of course, all the portals on the Continent are Fatae made." They had nothing like Albion's Portal Keepers, who were a gift and consequence of the Pact made in 1484. "You do not need to go there or to open the portal between the two. You need them for alignment." And it would work for only portals the creator knew well enough.

She'd worked out that part, painstakingly, with Thesan Wain, Astronomy professor at Schola and now a close friend. Thesan was a year younger and had her own particular brilliance in her chosen field. It had taken them all of one summer hols, and regular work through the next school year, to do the mapping. She let the question she'd asked sit.

Finally, slowly, he swallowed. "Does that mean that's why you'd take me on, so I could help with it?"

"The question of whether or not I take you on is, shall we say, distinct from your choice to help here. On the other hand, it is the research I am working on, and if you apprentice with me, I will continue working on it, with or without your help."

Howard nodded slowly. "Do you have other questions for me in making your decision?"

Rathna shook her head. "If you wish to agree, we will need to talk in detail through your training so far. You will need to work through some of the basics with me again, so I can figure out what we need to cover. A tad tedious, but a return to the essential skills never did me any harm, or anyone else I know." She spread out both hands. "We could give it a trial, for a couple of weeks, a month or two. See how we do."

Howard nodded, carefully. "And the etiquette, magistra?"

He was so careful about that. It was, on the whole, endearing. Certainly, it was a great deal better than the alternatives. "You may call me magistra or mistress, as you prefer, for the moment." Rather than the more intimate form, with her first name attached. "We will see about it after that."

"Magistra." He nodded. "Howard, or apprentice, as pleases you, for now?"

"Certainly." Rathna had expected formality from him. He was decidedly from the sort of family - both parents - where that would be the most comfortable for him. "Write to Mhairi and Petrus tonight. See what they tell you. If you wish to make a trial, we can begin tomorrow by signing the papers. I'll make it all right with the Guildmaster."

"Magistra." Howard swallowed once, hard. "I expect that will be my answer."

He really didn't have much choice, no matter how much she wished he did.

CHAPTER 3
NOVEMBER 6TH IN THE MINISTRY QUARTER

Gabe opened the door to the meeting room, leaned his cane against his thigh, and blinked. "So I should tell Isobel we might be a bit?" Isobel, in the hallway behind him, was a year or so out from finishing her apprenticeship. She could certainly start processing the materia they'd collected this morning and do it properly without his supervision.

Aunt Mason snorted, and Aunt Witt arched an eyebrow. They were seated facing the door, with Witt in the centre of the three seats on that side of the table and Mason to her right. Witt looked entirely proper, as always, while Mason's hair was up in a remarkably tidy bun compared to her usual. She was setting out her pen and notebook.

Gabe glanced at Isobel, and let his mind shift over to a more professional mode. "Back down to my workroom, Isobel, and get a good start on the sympathetic resonances. I'll be down when," he turned back to the room, considering the number of chairs and the coffee and tea service. "Eventually."

"I should get a sandwich for you from the canteen if it

gets on for lunchtime." Isobel had taken a step back when he paused, pushing a bit of her blonde hair back behind her ear from where it had escaped from her bun.

"Please." If it were a substantial sort of project, he'd both need to eat and forget to eat. "And for yourself, mind."

She laughed, turning away. She was wearing the near enough standard uniform of the Penelopes, as he was. In her case, that was a black skirt, dark green vest, and a white blouse. Like his, the cuffs were a bit splattered. They'd had a bit of a problem with the ink earlier, and there was a small rainbow of delicate pigment droplets like dots of embroidery. Ah, well. No help for it. He didn't have time to go change. He'd grabbed his jacket on the way up here, and it hid most of the staining. It was rather artistic, actually. Rathna would approve of the bright colours.

Instead, he stepped inside and took his place, nodding at his two aunts by choice. They both looked particularly well, which suggested they knew what was going to get proposed here and approved of it. Mason had looked decidedly worn when she'd been out at the house on Saturday. Now, she had a better glow to her skin, rather than the more ashy pale brown she'd had then. He hadn't seen Witt for a week. She'd been busy with some research. She had smudges under her eyes, but her cheeks were rosier.

He checked to see that they both had sufficient tea to be going on with and poured himself a coffee. The decent coffee, not the canteen. "You're softening me up." Gabe said it half-teasingly, half to see what other information he could get out of them. Now it was time to get himself settled and focused on the task at hand, not the dozen other things on his mind.

"We want your brain fully engaged, and I gather you were out early." Witt waved a hand. He and Isobel had been on duty overnight, and they'd got called out at half-five, which his seniors clearly knew.

"All sorted now, other than the analysis. And Betts had a grand idea for simplifying some of that. She wants to talk it through with you, Mason, when you get a minute. Not urgent, but interesting." Mason smiled at that. Those were the best conversations, the ones that fuelled them all.

Witt and Mason were largely retired from field work these days; they were both in their seventies and had declared that was what younger bodies were for. But they'd kept on coordinating the work as the senior most active Penelopes. No one - not the Ministry, not the Guard, certainly not their juniors - had wanted to argue with them. They didn't miss much, and Gabe found it immensely reassuring, especially at the moment.

Before he could say anything else, he heard footsteps on the stone tile work, and he took his seat to Witt's left. Right as he was properly settled, in came two men he knew by sight, and one woman he didn't. He felt a faint shiver, the sort of thing he'd need to track down and follow to its root when he had a moment.

Cyrus Smythe-Clive was the head of the Council. He looked appropriately resolute and formal in a deep purple robe that was striking against dark hair and strong features. Malcolm Rolls was beside him, wearing a black robe over his suit, steady. He was the usual Council liaison to the Guard and Penelopes, so Gabe talked to him regularly. He thought the woman was Hespasia Wallace, one of the senior department heads of the Ministry Outside the Borders. That was curious.

He was fairly sure he knew more about Smythe-Clive these days than the man knew about him. Gabe had the advantage because Alexander Landry, also of the Council, was a close connection of Gabe's family the last few years. But Alexander had kept that connection quite private, far more than his alliance with the Carillons on a number of matters. It likely meant Smythe-Clive only knew the public things, and Gabe could do a great deal with that. Gabe nodded once and let the senior Penelopes take the lead.

Witt, in specific. The Council didn't know what to do with Mason's tendency to associative thought - or Gabe's - and Witt's order and behaving to expectations was a much better choice to lead here. "Council Members, Minister. Please have a seat. Tea?" None of the three Penelopes moved. After a moment, Rolls went and got cups, bringing them back for the other two before gathering his own. He was the decidedly junior member, then, though he was fifteen or so years older than Gabe himself. One didn't ask the experts to fetch your tea. It started the negotiations on entirely the wrong foot.

"We appreciate your time." Smythe-Clive got right down to business. He was in control of himself and the setting, but Gabe could see the minute tell of his nerves about something in this situation. "We have a particular challenge at hand, and we do not know if the Penelopes are the solution. We are quite sure that if you are not, you will have an idea who is." He glanced around from his place, across from Witt. "I assume there's a reason you have Penelope Edgarton here, in particular."

"Your request for this meeting mentioned the land magic. Edgarton is our choice for such matters, due to his own familial commitments and his long-standing interest in the land and all who live on it." Witt was clipped and precise. Gabe inclined his head once. All three of them knew who he was, he was sure. Heir to his father, entering middle age himself, and established as an expert in his field, even if most people weren't quite sure what that actually meant. He, himself, felt for the land magic, almost instinctively. There was the bubbling surge that always responded in Trellech, that this was land, but not his to particularly tend.

"There are several matters since the start of the war that have come to the attention of the Council and the Ministry." Smythe-Clive went on without hesitation, though he was choosing his words carefully. "On the one hand, we have numerous reports of esoteric organisations from Britain seeking to lend their energies to occult protections of the land." That meant folks not counted as magical by Albion's standards. Certainly no one who'd made their promise to the Silence at twelve and was now bound by it. Gabe knew perfectly well that people dabbled. It was a significant part of the work of the Penelopes, to tidy up the mess when it went wrong.

"The Society of the Inner Light, and all that?" Mason was the one who spoke up, a bit surprisingly. "They're sending out letters every week." She glanced at Gabe and arched an eyebrow. "Two people I know are getting them." Ah. One of them was his mother, then. The other was probably Doyle, his own former apprentice mistress. She liked a bit of esoteric literary analysis as a hobby.

Smythe-Clive nodded. "Exactly so. Good, so I don't need to explain the context. We don't want to stop them, mind. We instead need to make sure that whatever they get up to neither goes against the Pact, nor causes problems for those who are doing our own work on the magical front."

That raised half a dozen questions for Gabe, and he pinched the skin between his thumb and index finger to keep from saying anything. He hoped Witt and Mason appreciated his self-restraint and containment. Fortunately, Witt asked one of the most demanding questions immediately. "And on the other?"

"We have verified reports of the Wild Hunt riding in the opening days of the war."

There was dead silence in the room for a good minute. Focus was no longer a problem. Gabe's mind was rapidly whirring through the implications. He desperately wanted to discuss this with half a dozen people. They'd not sworn him to secrecy. Everyone he wanted to talk to was either on the Council or sworn as an analyst to the Guard or under the same oaths. Even his wife. He had an idea what Mason and Witt were working through as well.

When no one spoke, Gabe finally leaned forward slightly. He could feel something spinning now, the sorts of magics that changed the world. "That would be a Council matter, surely?" By one count, each of the Council was a twenty-first part of a sacred king. They were ennobled and enjoined by the Pact to handle those matters that needed negotiation between humans and the Fatae, after the Fatae had retreated to their own magical realms.

Smythe-Clive spread his hands. "Yes. And no. We have no one available who can travel widely who can be spared for this. And no one who has the range of skills. We have duellists, alchemists, ritual specialists, experts in protective magic, illusionists. But we need, we think, someone who can be a dozen things, and do them well."

Well, that was Gabe, in a nutshell. "And able to pass between magical and non-magical society easily. Comfortable with both." Which he was. He lived and breathed a life woven through the magical community's heart, half a dozen ways. But he also delighted in a day at the British Museum Library, or a lecture on the latest natural history in London, or even listening to a skilled mechanic go on about the wonders of an automobile. And he could wander agreeably through London's markets and drive a suitably hard bargain, without drawing much notice. Or he had, before the war began, and he hoped he would still when it ended. Not that he said any of that.

"Exactly." That was Wallace. She had a remarkably pleasant voice. "The Ministry and Council are willing to provide support - staffing, equipment, all that - for a suitable person to take the lead on it. We do not know where to send someone. That is the first part of the task."

Frankly, for a Penelope, that was an average Tuesday. Gabe considered saying so, but a look from Witt made him subside. Witt made a series of precise inquiries. They were all about clarifying what that support meant in practical terms. Gabe didn't follow all of it, but he thought it meant half a dozen analysts and secretaries, an alchemist on tap, and high priority draw on materia. Ah, no. Not just for this project, the materia, Witt was making short work of arguing they should also get priority for other projects of national interest.

In a different time, Gabe would have found the negotiations fascinating. He always did. This time, though, he was trying to decide what it meant, how he would tackle it. Mind, none of them had said that he would. He could think of a dozen reasons he should be the one to do it, and rather more that made that complex.

For one thing, it would likely mean a lot of travel, and even with the portals, he'd be away from home far more than he preferred. For another, nothing about this was simple, and a lot of it was potentially dangerous. Not so much physically, he could take care of himself there, but magically. Arguably spiritually, if the various things he'd picked up about what the Germans were up to on the magical front were valid. He'd be in the midst of it.

When Witt wound down, Wallace looked amused and surrendered with good grace. "That's about what I expected we'd actually come to." Clearly she knew Witt's measure there well enough.

Smythe-Clive cleared his throat. "I assume you have someone in mind, Penelope Witt?"

Witt didn't look at him, she didn't need to, her fingers had brushed his in signal under the table, and he'd already replied. "We are glad to assign Penelope Edgarton to this matter, as well as his apprentice Isobel Thomas. We'll consult about the analysts and other staff once we have the full brief on what you have in mind."

Gabe smiled cheerfully. Oh, they were going to have questions; he knew that. He wanted them to.

It was Rolls who first cleared his throat. "Pardon, this might require quite a bit of travel and ..." He gestured with his chin. "I know you use a cane, routinely."

Gabe didn't bother to glance at it. "I do. I can, however, ride anything with four legs, rope myself up to climb a mountain, and run a good few miles without tiring if I've got the right boots on. I can fight a duel and best near anyone except the top duellists of Albion, and I'd give them a fair run. I have acknowledged expertise among the Penelopes in architectural and structural magic, with a decided sideline in those magical effects touching on the land magic. I can identify most native plants, animals, reptiles, and fungi, and more importantly, I know the limits of my knowledge. My ritual skills, formal and informal, pass muster with several acknowledged experts of Albion, and my wife's knack for sympathetic magic has transitive properties."

He considered and added a smile. "And I am no longer nearly as impulsive as I was in my youth, which means I give Mason and Witt somewhat fewer white hairs every year." They both laughed at that, uniformly, from his right, and the tension in the room cracked. It meant Gabe went on. "My ankle's not as sound as some, but it's more a question of pain than a limitation of movement. I have a great deal of experience working through it."

Smythe-Clive considered. "What's your duelling standard, then?"

"I look forward to my matches with Isembard Fortier, and we're evenly partnered. I think I'm currently ahead by three bouts, but I picked up a new trick on a trip to India two years ago that I've been improving." Isembard was the Protective magics professor at Schola, well known to the Council members. He consulted for them, and Isembard's brother Garin had been on the Council for years. And it was a connection Gabe could make clear, because Rathna and Thesan were known to collaborate. "I don't advertise my skills generally. It's such a bother when people try to rise to the challenge when you had something else to be doing."

There was a silence again, this time more amused. Good, the way he'd gone at that had hit exactly the right note.

"All right." Smythe-Clive wasn't going to argue. That was good. "Let's get down to the details, as we know them at the moment. Malcolm, you have the materials?" The other man produced a stack of folders from a satchel and handed them out. Gabe thumbed through them, paused ten pages in, glanced at Mason, and got a nod. They'd be here for a bit, but this might just be captivatingly interesting.

CHAPTER 4
THAT EVENING AT VERITAS

"I have something serious to ask you." Gabe said it clearly as soon as he pulled back from kissing Rathna hello. He'd been later than he wanted getting back. It was past seven.

Gabe had written, of course. He wasn't careless about that if he had any choice. But he'd assumed he'd find Rathna downstairs, chatting with his parents, Uncle Gil and Uncle Magni, or whoever was about. He hadn't expected to find her standing by the window, like she was as full of nervous energy as he usually was.

"Your parents are out for the evening. I already asked for supper up here." Rathna hesitated, and that wasn't like her either. "I have something serious to ask you too. Avigail first? She was missing you at tea."

"Asking her something, being asked something, bedtime? Give me a hint, please?" Gabe could generally parse Rathna's commentary better than that. The events of the day had him more than a little off his game. Part of him was still caught up by the implications of what he'd agreed to take on, as if it had unsettled his sense of north.

"Bedtime. You go, love. Read her a chapter. I'll make arrangements about supper, and I wanted a couple of things out of the library. I wasn't sure when you'd be back." She shooed him off with a wave of her hand, and Gabe went.

Half an hour later, he came down, restored to his proper place in the ecology after having read their youngest a chapter of her current book. It was a rather fabulist tale that drew on folklore and natural history. The author, a Thalia Morgan, had quite a knack for a turn of phrase that both delighted children and gave the adults something to think about. It was a particularly neat gift. This was the latest of hers, and Gabe was enjoying it quite a lot.

Rathna was sitting, this time, at the small table they kept for private meals. That was more often breakfast or a working lunch, but it served just as well for supper. She was pouring tea as he came in. "I thought you wouldn't want wine, at least not right now."

Gabe shook his head. "A complicated conversation, and I'm not sure what you're going to think about it. I'm not entirely sure what I think about it."

Rathna nodded, pausing to brush her fingers over the back of his hand. "You first? Me first?"

"Ladies first is proper, yes? Even if Mama isn't here to stare at me." Gabe settled in. "Also, I haven't eaten since half a sandwich at two, and it'd let me get a few bites in."

His wife snorted. "Fair." She did, in fact, let him get a good minute of eating in, enough to begin to take the edge off. He hadn't forgotten to have tea, not exactly. But he'd been busy pulling things from the library, after he'd sent Isobel off to continue the analysis she'd been doing under some further supervision. He certainly wasn't sure how to talk to her about this, and absolutely not before his wife.

Once he'd paused, Rathna cleared her throat. "I had a decent conversation with Ferdinand Howard." Somewhere in the middle ground, then, not as easy as Gabe had hoped, in an optimistic phase, but not horrible, either. "He's writing to Mhairi and Petrus, but I expect we'll sign the papers on trial basis in the morning."

"Did you ask about the portals?" This was the tricky part of talking through things, as they had done in depth as part of preparing. There were so many ways the conversation could go once the other party was actually involved.

"We talked about my research. He asked if I'd want his help with it. We didn't get beyond that. He doesn't know what to make of me." Rathna tapped her finger on the edge of the plate, then nudged it closer to Gabe, and he took another half sandwich.

"You did get him off balance, then. Good. What did you think of the rest of it?"

"I think he loves his mother, and isn't sure that's permitted." Rathna came out with it quickly. She must have been thinking about it all afternoon. "He's cautious about her. Of course it's delicate."

Gabe nodded. They in fact knew more about the Heinrichs, Howard's mother's people, than he likely expected. That was thanks to both Geoffrey Carillon's earlier connections in Germany, and Geoffrey and Alexander's particular adventures in Berlin four years ago. Proud people, fond of their traditions, magically competent, but - as Geoffrey had put it once - perhaps a bit more focused on themselves than on others.

That Dita Heinrich had married an Englishman, even one of such excellent family as the Howards, had apparently been something of a scandal. And it wasn't entirely clear why she'd been so insistent, not from the visible information. Geoffrey hadn't been able to decide, still, whether she'd been deliberately escaping her family, or whether it had been an unexpected love match. Or both. Both was always a possible answer.

"But you think he knows the portals?" Gabe offered this carefully.

She nodded once. "He didn't say. And asking him to help is a huge question. Of course, he'd feel loyal to his family. Both sides of it. But I think he does. Or maybe he knows one somewhere that's still neutral. I made it clear I'd be working on it, if I took him on."

Gabe let out a rush of breath. "How soon?" That was the question. Was she going to go charging off to the Continent now, in a month, in the spring? The war was changing every day, and he knew - they both knew - that the window where she could do any good was shrinking.

"Not yet." Rathna let out a long breath. "Early spring, probably. Even if he'll help, we can't do much before then. It's a lot of outside work, it has to be. I'm not sure we could do it anyway until the ground begins to thaw. Even if the rest of it works, and I still have to sort some of that out." She glanced down, then met his eyes again. "You're sure?"

That was enough to get him to stand up and come around the table, going to one knee, the weight on his good ankle. "I have the good sense to be terrified of what might happen. But I also know how much you want to do something that could truly help. I know how brilliant you are to figure this out. We need that. I'm confident you won't take any undue risks."

"No more than you do." It was what they'd said for all their partnership. He climbed out of windows, flung himself off horses, had tremendous duels with magic buffeting back and forth, descended into mine shafts, and a dozen other things. He took risks, he always would, even if he did his best to measure them and make every bit of the risk count.

Now, it made him flinch, just once. Her hand immediately came to cup his cheek. "And that would be your part, then?"

Gabe nodded, just once, turning his cheek to kiss her palm. "What else about yours? What can we do to help?"

"I need to get him to trust me, and I don't know what's going to do that. I can hear it, the little ornamentation in my head, not quite getting the overtones to ring." She did like music for her magical refinements. "There's nothing there now that's blocking it, it's just not…" She gestured with both hands, an open but unaligned space.

"So we hope that he'll come to trust you and open up to you." Gabe let out a long breath. "And begin with what you can. What does that look like?"

Rathna had a list. Of course she did. She was organised and systematic like that, not Gabe's chaos. "I need more time to talk to Gil. I'd like to see if Magni can evaluate Ferdinand's skills, the duelling and protection things, or recommend someone to do it. There's a lot of gear to think about, and much of it's going to be tricky to get." Seeing as how it was in high demand for the war effort.

"You've got lists. We'll work through them. Call in favours. Do you have—" He hesitated. Rathna was going to do this, whether she had permission or not. "Do you have any idea about permissions?"

"The Guild's going to back me if I can figure out the locational anchors. And we probably could do something with Switzerland, if we had to, it's just not as well positioned. We confirmed it this afternoon. The liaison to the

Army wasn't any too happy about it, when we brought up the idea a month ago, but he can't stop us."

The current man in charge was rigid, even by Army standards, and Gabe thought that wasn't going to work out well for a lot of people. Major-General Gospatrick had been a great deal more reasonable, his father said, but the Army did eventually enforce retirement on senior officers. Rathna went on. "It helps that there isn't a military application. If it works, we could get Healers to more places, though. Or get them out quickly."

"Well, there's just you who has the trick of the work. And not so many who could go over." Her former apprentices might grasp the work, but Petrus was needed just as much in Plymouth, and Mhairi was expecting and couldn't travel much, certainly not in possible battle conditions.

"So. I have to go." Rathna hesitated, then reached for his hand. "Help me?"

"Always." He pushed himself up, then, to tug her to lean against him. There'd be more of that later tonight. His stomach picked the worst time to grumble - or perhaps the best, because it made Rathna giggle.

"Eat. Sentimentality and pragmatism later." It was one of the many unending things he loved about her, that she understood how to balance things. He smiled and kissed her before going back to his chair.

Again, she let him get a bit of food, then she murmured. "Yours?"

"The meeting at eleven ran to past six." Gabe took a breath and looked up. "Cyrus Smythe-Clive, Malcolm Rolls, Hespasia Wallace - she's senior in the Ministry Beyond the Borders. And Aunt Witt and Aunt Mason."

"And you." Rathna considered. "And you were their choice, obviously."

Gabe nodded. "And I could see why once we heard the details. They got a two-line summary, that it was something about the land magic. And obviously, well."

Rathna waved a hand. "Half a dozen reasons why they started with you, only one of which is about Richard."

Gabe felt his mouth quirk up. "Well. Who I am in other ways, also Papa's doing. Do you have things to tell Mama about how the conversation with Howard played out?"

His wife grinned, and Gabe was glad to see her eyes dancing with amusement. He liked it much better when she was smiling, even if they were talking about difficult and complicated things. "Quite a few, and yes, she'll be delighted. And she'll probably want some distraction in the next day or two. I gather tonight wasn't in the original plans. Magisterial social obligation of some kind."

That meant a death or some other sort of crisis, or Papa wouldn't have had Mama come along. Something with social expectations, as well as practical ones. "She'll be glad to hear, I know." Right, he'd had a chance to gather himself.

Rathna settled back in her chair, just waiting patiently, though she added. "It's not going to explain itself, Gabe."

"Long and short of it is that they want someone who can take a look at all the different threads of magic and attempted magic going on, and make sure no one messes things up horribly." Rathna was about to say something, and he held his hand up. "Council doesn't have the right people for it, which I had the sense not to bring up in the meeting, but I definitely need to talk to Alexander. Geoffrey as well, he'll have good ideas." Geoffrey was Lord in his own right, but he'd done extensive Intelligence work in the last War and since. He landed solidly in the generation between Gabe and his parents. But the Carillons' own children were more or less of an age with Gabe and Rathna's, and that made a bond.

His wife nodded slowly. "I assume there are briefing papers?"

"There are. And they didn't have me make any additional oaths about it. Usual restrictions." He wouldn't have taken it if he couldn't share it with Rathna, honestly. There were tasks where he would have, but not this one. To make it work, he was going to need to draw on every bit of skill and knowledge and expertise he had any connection to.

"How dangerous is it?" It was a fair question, and he knew he'd have to answer it.

Gabe set down his fork. "There are verified reports of the Wild Hunt riding at the start of the war." He stopped, letting her react to it. It wasn't a thing to rush. "Not public, not yet, but if people keep going on about astral workings and going out in the dark at night to do rituals that might or might not work, someone's going to notice something. Pact or no, Silence oaths or no. That's part of why they're rather worried."

He was understating the worry. The more they'd got into the details that afternoon, the more visible it had been. It wasn't just the threat of wild magic, unknown magic. It wasn't the uncertainty about what magic Germany and the occupied countries might bring to bear. It was that the Council were terrified of losing control of something.

Gabe hadn't been able to ask what. But he knew well enough how to work with something that had its own mind. He'd done it with horses, he'd done it with duelling, he did it inside his own head, working through and with and inside his impulses, day in and day out.

His wife was watching him, reading it, he was sure. She always could, with him. From very early on, she'd traced his own throughlines as surely as she followed the lines of magical flow that were her life's work. "And you need to figure all of it out. Well, that's a proper sort of challenge for you. And Aunts Mason and Witt think you can do it?"

"They do. They're helping, obviously. And I think it made them feel a lot better about things, like we're doing something, the Penelopes, that only we could do. They need dozens of skills, in a couple of people."

"Well, that does describe you, love." Rathna considered, then picked up her own fork, going back to her own meal. "Both of us gone quite a lot, though I assume you'll still be back here sometimes."

Gabe nodded. "We need to talk about that."

CHAPTER 5
LATER THAT EVENING

Rathna watched Gabe. She'd had a rather more solid lunch than he had, almost certainly. He generally forgot to eat in the first flurry of a new assignment, and this was a vastly larger one than usual. She gave him a moment or three, nudging the cheese plate closer to him. When he had settled down into nibbling, she asked, "Have you spoken to Isobel about that?"

"You first. Ideally, you and Mama and Papa first, we'll see about that." Gabe hesitated. "There's something in the back of my head, dancing, about what she might do with it."

"Well, people will tell a young woman a lot they wouldn't tell you. Especially one who's as good at looking innocently curious as Isobel is. I'm sure she's got significant skills in chatting up older women over a cuppa." Rathna liked Isobel, honestly. Of the three apprentices Gabe had taken on this far, she was the one Rathna would pick for something like this wide-ranging assignment.

She'd been asked, a time or two, if she were jealous. Not by Alysoun or Richard, or any of their closer set. But others had asked when she and Gabe made the rounds at the more bohemian and eclectic social parties in Trellech. If Isobel had wanted, she could have had half a dozen artists begging for her to be their model and their muse. She had the sort of blonde English beauty that caught the eye, but with a depth to her that meant people kept looking.

Isobel came from a farming family up in Yorkshire, and had an instinct for charmwork Rathna expected was rather more rare than Isobel realised. More than that, she had a gift not just for accents, but for language in general, in particular picking which register to use when.

In fact, Isobel and Gabe could go through half a dozen registers in the space of four or five sentences, chasing each other around in mode and formality. And Isobel was sharp enough to keep up with Gabe's wide-ranging focus. Rathna just sat back and laughed, when people asked, when she could.

No, she didn't resent Isobel, or worry about what Gabe might get up to. For one thing, the worst impulses around abuse of power and inequality had been trained out of Gabe very early, by half a dozen people besides his parents. And for another, all she had to do to be certain of Gabe's affections was look at him. He was whole-hearted, loyal as his father, and he never did manage to keep much from her, anyway.

Which made her certain something else was going on for him, some uneven spark in his reactions, stuttering up and fading. Certainly not under his conscious control, but as if some part of him were working furiously on it. Rathna was still considering that point when she heard a gentle chime, just loud enough to register. Rathna glanced up to a thin row of lights. "That's your parents. Shall we go downstairs?"

"I don't know how tired Mama is." Gabe hesitated, and that wasn't like him at all. He had an easy and loving relationship with them, unlike many of his peers in age and station. He trusted them, and he leaned readily into their skills and experience.

Rathna ran through what she knew of Alysoun's day. Gabe's mother had lived with exhaustion and pain that came and went on no particular schedule since he was tiny. Exertion and going to one of these obligatory social outings were always worse, and more so on short notice. Rathna had been able to tune the portal here, but she couldn't do that for all the others.

"Let's go ask her. She'll be glad to see you, anyway." She always was, and Richard would be as well. Despite them all living at Veritas, it was remarkably common for the four of them to go a couple of days at a time without all being in the same room. They had busy lives, given the various cases, assignments, social obligations, and personal amusements they got up to. It had been true before September, and it was even more true now they were at war.

Five minutes later, they'd acquired after-dinner drinks, and had settled in their usual chairs in the library. Rathna thought Alysoun was looking tired, but thoughtful. Rathna's own commentary was brief. "I believe Howard will turn up tomorrow, willing to make the apprenticeship oaths. A trial, though, to see if we suit each other. He spent the beginning of our conversation entirely unsure what to make of me." It had been the part they'd known, talked about, though of course they couldn't be sure how it would actually play out. No plan ever lasted past that first contact.

Alysoun snorted. "Well played, then, dearest. Well played. I'd love to hear how it went when you've got a minute to breathe, but not tonight." Her gaze flicked over to

Gabe, who had his hand on Rathna's, like he wasn't sure how to stop touching her, and certainly didn't want to. Rathna smiled back. Alysoun was generous with her praise and with her shared joy when things went well, but it felt like something special every time. She was incredibly fortunate in her in-laws, and she kept finding more reasons why.

She lifted a finger slightly, pressing it against Gabe's hand, and he sighed slightly, shifting to focus a bit more on his father. "The meeting this morning was with Aunt Mason and Aunt Witt - and with Smythe-Clive, Rolls, and Hespasia Wallace." His parents placed the names immediately. Gabe dove into the heart of it. "The Wild Hunt's been seen. They think they need someone to figure out all the moving pieces, all the people doing magic and trying to do magic."

"And likely, what's coming from overseas, or via agents here, in Britain and Albion." Richard saw the core of it immediately. Of course he would; his Guard training led to that, inexorably. And that was the crux of it, wasn't it, that there were the two sets of people, magical and non-magical, sharing space and not, all at once. What threatened one of them might be nothing to the other, and that went both ways.

Gabe inhaled sharply, and Rathna paid close attention to his hand on top of hers. It wasn't that any of his nerves were particularly obvious, though it was likely his parents had noticed as well. But that tremulous set of nerves, that wasn't much like Gabe. Nor were the few stumbles of clarity earlier over supper. Something about this had caught at him, more than he'd expected. "There's a budget, supporting staff. My choice, along with Aunt Witt and Aunt Mason, of course."

"Well, you'd be unlikely to go against their advice if you

hadn't won an argument about it." Alysoun sounded very amused at that. "You have more sense."

Gabe ducked his chin. "Just so. The Council doesn't have anyone who can do all of it, apparently. My guess is that Alexander is closest, but he's said himself that - well, for one thing, he's obviously himself, half a dozen ways round. Magically, his background." Alexander was half Egyptian, half French, and wherever he was, he stood out. "And of course, he's got other things he's needed for."

Alysoun considered that, taking a moment to do it, and Richard held back on whatever he'd been about to say to give her the space. When she spoke, it was careful. "What's giving you pause, Gabe?" It was one of the things Rathna most appreciated about Alysoun, about both of them, as a model of how to raise children.

They respected Gabe as a grown adult, with different and equally potent gifts to their own. They weren't threatened by it even if they were sometimes baffled. Well, given Gabe, regularly baffled. But they trusted his instincts, and a remarkable number of times they had trusted them even above their own. This, though, this was bigger than most matters they'd tackled as a family. They all knew it.

"I don't know. Not enough." Gabe twisted his other hand over. "I need to talk to Alexander, obviously, find out what else he knows that he can share. I'm certain he's not told Smythe-Clive much about us, as a family. I mean, first of all, he'd have checked, and second, the way they both reacted."

Richard nodded once, picking up. "Well, the Penelopes are rather mysterious. The Council's seen you as my Heir, respectable enough, good sense of the land magic. They know the lands here are thriving, but I don't know how much they attribute to you, rather than me."

That at least got one of those flashing smiles out of Gabe, and Rathna squeezed his hand. He was so eager for his father's approval, even though Richard was as generous with it as Alysoun, if in a more reserved mode, and Gabe did a great deal worth approving of. "Sir." That was Gabe teasing with the formality, and the twitch of his hand settled a little. "It will mean - well, it'll be challenging. The scheduling. And for Avigail in particular."

Alysoun picked up on that quickly. "How long do you think you have in the planning, both of you?" She glanced at Rathna first, since at least Gabe would still be in the country, and could make it home by portal, at least semi-regularly.

"I did get permission this afternoon, assuming we can work out a few details. I can hope Howard might come around to being willing to help, but even if he doesn't, there are some other possible sites further south. I can't imagine we'll be ready to go before March, and we need at least a bit of a thaw to work with. I'm confident we can make things work, but getting the materia, getting other staff together, training them. That will take time." She'd batted around ideas, with Richard and Magni, in particular, as well as with her own guild. Both of them had long experience with planning similar enough sorties for the Guard.

It meant everyone looked to Gabe, who held up his free hand. "They'd like us to get a move on, but obviously, we need to do some preparation. Mama, do you by chance already have a running analysis of the Society of Inner Light letters and anything else like them?"

Alysoun laughed, amused. "Oh, that came up? Yes, I do. I'll make a copy in the morning and add a few more notes in the margins. Lizzie's been cross-referencing a few specifics to reports in the Trellech Moon and a few of the more likely journals. You'll want to check with her."

Gabe inclined his head, but he was smiling a little when he looked up. "Aunt Witt gave me the hint. And I've scheduled some time with Doyle tomorrow afternoon, if nothing actively explodes."

He hesitated, then. "It will mean a lot of travel. Other people's schedules, as well as whatever emergencies or urgencies - or whatever we call them in a time of war - come up. Needing to stay places until I can visibly get a train out to keep up the proper show." The situation was changing fast, and Rathna could only assume it would continue to do so. She turned her hand under his, to thread her fingers through and squeeze, and he squeezed back.

Alysoun nodded. "It's good you settled back here, really, rather than insisting on staying in London." They'd spent the earliest years of their marriage in a flat there, not least to be near to Morah Avigail. They'd moved back properly after Anthony was born. Rathna had to admit that having a generously sized nursery and Nanny to go with it had made balancing their various complex lives much easier. "Avigail's old enough to understand a fair bit. How do you want to talk to the children about it?"

"Not yet, I think, the details. But letting Avigail know we're working on big projects, we'll be around less." Rathna spoke nearly before she thought about it, but she knew it was the right answer. "She's the one still here, and - well. We can pass letters to her, but I'd rather not tell her difficult things by letter without someone else handy."

Rowena and Anthony both had their own journals, and were actually remarkably reliable at writing most days, even if it was only a few sentences. "And we'll go out and talk to the others as soon as we can." She glanced at Gabe.

"Together. Sort that into your diary, please, in your planning. Tell them enough they don't worry if they don't hear back as quickly as usual."

Gabe smiled at her. "This is where I'm going to need a reminder, I'm sure." Calendars and diaries and appointments were not a gift of his, though he'd go to the things if someone reminded him.

Alysoun shook her head. "At any rate. We are here for the duration, and while Richard might be on call for any number of reasons, he is not in the field as regularly. And there's Nanny, and the rest of the staff, and Gil and Magni around the place to keep her occupied with interesting questions." She glanced toward the door. "When will you tell them?"

"Tomorrow. Evening." Gabe let out a long breath. "It's Isobel's birthday tomorrow. I don't want to keep her late. The others had something planned, too." A bit of a prank, a bit of a treat, as the Penelopes usually ran to.

"Right. I'll make sure I'm handy by teatime." She sounded relieved, honestly. Mornings were not Alysoun's best time, but the outing must have been more of a strain than some. Gabe must have realised the same, and he looked uncertain again.

"Come, give me a kiss. No, doing the set-up right matters here. Give me a day to work on it, and I'll have a timeline for you on what else I'll be able to get and who you want for staff to start."

"You are entirely under-appreciated, Mama, by nearly everyone." Gabe obligingly stood to go and kiss his mother's cheek, and nod at his father, then held out his hand to Rathna as she kissed both of them gently.

"You two enjoy the time you have together. Make the most of it." That came from Richard, and it made Rathna blush. Gabe's parents made no secret of their ongoing plea-sure in each other, but that was a tad more explicit than usual. Not that she was arguing. It was a solid sentiment to build on. Whatever happened from here, she didn't want to regret any time she could have had with Gabe, when they had the chance.

CHAPTER 6

NOVEMBER 7TH IN GABE'S OFFICE, TRELLECH

Gabe opened the door to his office at half-nine, carrying a basket. Isobel was already settled at her desk, tucked into the corner. It was a good-sized room, at least. He was sure Mason and Witt had helped him land in an office that not only had its own attached workroom, but plenty of room for him to pace. It was convenient when he had apprentices, as there was space for them as well without crowding anything.

"Happy birthday, Isobel." He deposited the basket on her desk with a flourish. "A variety of things to amuse and delight and educate." He gestured. "I'd invite you out to Veritas for supper, but it's Diwali starting Thursday. Come out on Saturday, like you did last year, but we'll find another time for a birthday supper?" She came out to Veritas every fortnight or so, for a meal that wasn't out of the apprentice refectory, and a chance to get outside in the country, pet a cat or two, and see what new books Gabe and his parents had acquired.

Isobel glanced over, smiling, before she was distracted in peering at the basket. "Thank you! I enjoyed it last year.

All the lights and the colours and the patterns." It was one of the festivals Rathna - and now the rest of the family - made a point of celebrating. A bit more light and joy and abundance in the world never did any harm, was how Gabe's mother put it. Gabe dropped his own bag by his desk, scribbling a note to Rathna and his parents and his father's secretary before he forgot.

"Go on, open the rest of it." He settled in his chair, leaning his chin in his hands. At the top was a small tin, with biscuits, Isobel's favourite from Cook. Below that, though... First, she pulled out the small wooden case, and then the books, below. He watched her blink at the books, thumbing through a couple of pages, before she glanced up at him. "One from Rathna, one from Mama, one from Papa, one from Aunt Mason, and one from Aunt Witt. You know we want to keep building up your library."

It was an interesting trick, making sure she had the resources to excel in a way she wouldn't become prickly about. Gift-giving occasions were very convenient that way. Gabe had instituted three: her birthday, winter solstice, and the anniversary of her apprenticeship since it fell in early June. The arrangement was that on those days, she wouldn't worry that what they'd found for her was too much. His, now, he expected she'd squawk about, but it was well past time. And if the new assignment went as he expected, she'd need them.

She pulled the case over, running her fingers over wood polished smooth as silk and made of good solid British oak. Then she opened the latch, then the lid. Her eyes went wide, her fingers simultaneously opening to push it away, and then contracting to draw it closer.

"You should have a set of your own. More so, after yesterday." He knew exactly what she was seeing. The box held a set of working stones laid out each in its place, with the little delicate wood tool to use them. They weren't all gem quality, but a wider selection than she'd used before unless she'd borrowed Gabe's.

"I can't. This is..." He could hear the vowels broaden, the way her voice changed when her control slipped enough.

"It is my responsibility to see that you have all the tools you need for your apprenticeship. And you're going to need them." Gabe flicked his hand, palm up. "You haven't asked about yesterday."

"I know better." She swivelled in her chair, tucking a foot under her other leg, covered by her split skirt. Just as quickly, she'd gathered herself up. It was one of the things Gabe liked most about Isobel, her swiftness.

"We've been handed a tremendous task. Me, you. Half a dozen support staff to start. Likely two secretaries and typists and four analysts, plus an alchemist, but Witt's still sorting out the precise details." He'd stopped there on the way in, of course.

Isobel nodded, then pulled a notebook over. "And what will we be doing?"

"There's magic moving in the world, in new ways and in old ones. It's our jobs to figure out what's going on, the moving pieces, and which ones we need to worry about." Gabe felt his finger twitch. He wasn't making light of it, exactly, but he knew he was skimming the surface here. He was also sure Isobel would call him on it. Rathna, last night, had looked at him, and left it for later. Tonight or tomorrow, probably.

Isobel tilted her head. "And that means what, exactly?" Gabe, despite himself, smiled.

"That's the first question. On the one hand, we have

what Albion is doing in the war. Much of that we know, can find out, or can approximate. Not least because I know a great many people, and a number of them can be provoked into being usefully informative." Isobel snorted at that as Gabe went on.

"But there are a number of groups interested in bringing magical and ritual practices to bear, who are not of Albion. The old lore might or might not be relevant, Bran's head and Vortimer's parts buried at the ports to prevent invasion. And who knows? Some of their magic might work - the gods, such as they are, are outside the Pact, after all."

Isobel's pencil twitched, and she made a couple of notes before looking up. "And the other workings?"

"Might work, might fail, might cause difficulties for the rest of us. We care about that last one most, but all three might be relevant." Gabe spread his hands.

"That already seems like work for an army of analysts, not half a dozen people." Isobel had it right.

"We are what there is. We can call on experts, as we see fit, and that apparently includes anyone on the Council. So if we do need to arrange a proper negotiation with the Fatae, it is within the grounds of possibility." Mind, he really desperately wanted to talk to Alexander about that part of things, about what the range of potential even looked like. It was one of those topics the Council never discussed, and Gabe had only theories and wisps of intuition to work with.

Isobel glanced up at him again and made several more notes. When she looked up more steadily, he went on. "And then there's whatever Germany is doing that might need to be countered. There are already discussions about an agency on the British side, non-magical, to counter some of that in propaganda, if nothing else. Astrologers and ritualists and all that. I have a source who might be able to get some information about who's in the midst of that, and whether they're competent." Gabe had no idea who Geoffrey Carillon reported to, when he was doing Intelligence work. But he knew there was someone, and that they could likely arrange a bit of useful information.

Isobel scribbled half a dozen things, paused, and added three more. "And? There's something else you're not saying."

There it was. Gabe wasn't even sure how she'd figured it out, except that she was as gifted with those flashes of knowing as he was. It was why she'd apprenticed with him. Him and not someone else, that was. The Penelopes had decided that she was skilled at the stubborn, gruelling application of time and focus. What she needed was the example of Gabe's bolts of inspiration and the internal self-assurance to follow through on her own. Applied diligence was the kind of thing Gabe could do when it suited him, but had never been able to sustain if he got bored. It was, however, good for him to have a model of what that could do, sitting there and arguing back.

He respected how she'd stuck with it, reshaping herself over and over again to be what was needed. Much the same way Rathna had, and quite possibly more deliberately and consciously. He wanted, more than anything, to make sure that work paid off, that it gave her the gifts and joy and blessing she richly deserved.

"I don't know. Honestly, I don't. Just that there's something deep here, something with layers that I don't understand. Implications. You've seen enough code work, now, that it's not just deciphering the words, it's figuring out what they mean in this context, what the connotation is.

It's going to be dangerous, but I don't know in which ways it will bring danger. Just..."

Just that sense of a flash, of something sharp and unknown. It could be a scythe or a knife or the flash of a snake's fang, or something else entirely. That was the bloody annoying thing about intuition and symbol. Sometimes a knife was a knife and sometimes it was a hint of something else entirely. It was like that shiver he'd felt, when they first laid out the project, and it nagged at him that he didn't know what he was feeling or where it came from.

Isobel hesitated. "How do we start, then?"

"That's why I'm going to be working late tonight, and tomorrow, and - well, I'll be home and out of the office for Diwali, but reading things there, too, most likely." He let out a long breath. "The other part of it is, Rathna has a lead on something important. And if she can pull it together, and things there don't utterly collapse, she's likely to be on the Continent come spring."

Isobel let out a low, fierce whistle. "Both of you. All right. Where do I come in?"

Gabe considered. "We're going to need to go to a number of places, and play a number of roles, most likely. We can get you identity papers that will suit, but you're going to need the right sorts of clothing and backgrounds prepared."

"To match you or something else?" There was a flip of a page, and more scribbling in her notes.

"Both. I'm well enough known that I can't pass for something entirely different. Minor aristocrat, known to have an interest in wildlife, and such, married an Indian woman, very progressive or questionable, depending on your politics." Rathna had come to enough lectures with him, and they certainly knew a number of people in London. "We may need to send you off on your own. Charming innocence, that can play very well with some of the esoteric orders. A niece, maybe, where I'd take an interest, but not direct family."

"How likely is it that they're going to want to do something untoward?" Isobel wasn't the duellist Gabe was - few people were - but she could hold her own in a number of situations. She had a deftness with boot, knee, and applied charms that went a long way.

"Depends on the group. We'll talk through all of it before we send you off to do anything, but I want you to do the background reading on a lot of them. And then work out how to keep it all straight. Which ones are some splinter of the Golden Dawn, or the Rosicrucians, or who took some sliver of the Theosophists sideways, or - well, there are still some spiritualists active who aren't scams, them too. They all have their own jargon, and you need to be able to pass for someone interested."

"We're going to need a cork board. A big one." There was a space on the wall they could mount one; they had before, though it blocked half the window.

"If you'd go sort that when we're done here?" Gabe tapped his fingers. "I want you to pick up training in the Guard salle again. I'll ask who would be best right now." Kate Lefton might do, and if not, she'd know who would. There was a trick in it, for someone like Isobel, who had to rely on swiftness and cleverness, rather than strength and bulk.

"And the projects we were working on?" Isobel pulled over a notebook to peer at it. "There was that set of warding, the safe and the room. That potentially cursed bracelet. And that tracing for the Guard."

"Loft's got the Guard work. I've an appointment to talk it through with her this afternoon. And I think we've given as much as we can to the other two. Doyle had a thought about the curse, or rather if it's not a curse, what it might be. I ran into Althorpe on the way in. She wants my thoughts on a bit of materia work, plan to sit in on that." He glanced at his watch. "An hour from now, she said she'd come here."

Isobel nodded, scratching a few notes to herself. Then she leaned back. "Before we get entirely distracted, what should I tell my parents? My brothers and sisters?"

"We'll be on research for a bit, yet. A few weeks, at least. But there will probably be field work, sooner than later." He hesitated. "Here's the thing. There are verified reports of the Wild Hunt riding at the start of the war." Early September, that had been. "Quiet enough I hadn't heard of it. The Council's getting us the full details, but I gather it may take a few days."

Isobel frowned. "That's. That's out of season." There were choices in the seasons, but all the lore Gabe had ever heard had it at the liminal points, May Eve and All Hallows by whatever names they went by, or perhaps the solstices or some saints' days. But no one had confirmed the Hunt riding in Albion in ages, he'd checked. All the lore from earlier times stacked up in certain ways, but that was far less of a help than it should have been.

"A time of great risk to the country. And I don't think they actually touched the ground." Which was an entirely different sort of diplomatic problem, as he understood it. "I don't think they took anyone, but again, no details yet."

"So. Tell my parents I've got important work. I'll see them and write when I can, do a bit more now, because later is going to be much worse." Isobel looked up, suddenly stubborn again.

"You don't have to. You could bow out." Gabe felt he had to make the offer.

"It's my land too. Got to do my part."

There was, after all, nothing he could say to that which wasn't entirely hypocritical or outright wrong. Gabe nodded. "Right. I want you to go pull things from the library. I have a partial list and I'll have more when you get back. I need a bit more time with the catalogue lists." That would keep them busy today and into tomorrow, just figuring out what sources to lean on first.

CHAPTER 7
NOVEMBER 22ND IN LONDON

Rathna had not expected the commotion on the street. She had arranged to meet Howard outside the Natural History Museum in Kensington. A fortnight into their trial of his apprenticeship, he still wasn't at all sure what to make of her. He was polite, of course. She was, at this point, certain that he wasn't capable of making himself be rude without excellent reason. However, he had not unbent at all. They were still "Howard" and "Magistra" to each other, "Apprentice Howard" if required by the situation.

She hoped today's excursion might give her some sense of what interested him. The museum itself was a cathedral of learning, of sharing the mysteries of the natural world in a way that enthralled and delighted. When they'd lived in London, she and Gabe had come here often. He knew far more of the curatorial staff than she did. Of course, she mostly cared about the geology. Gabe loved the stones and minerals, but he was just as fascinated by plants and trees, animals and birds of all kinds, fossils, reptiles and insects.

Rathna's goal today - besides seeing what Howard was

like in a different setting - had to do with some geological research. The Portal Keeper's guild had its own reference specimens, of course, but she was interested in consulting the geological maps near Dover, and what the minerals nearby might imply about the portal there. She'd also like to ask for some geological references for the Netherlands and for Switzerland, and that sort of delicate request was best made in person.

She'd come to the museum via the Spitalfields portal, then the Tube from Aldgate East to Earl's Court. She assumed Howard would take the Bedford Square portal, and she certainly wasn't ready yet to see how well or poorly he dealt with Spitalfields. Not a place he likely knew at all, given his background. Besides, she'd wanted to check on one of Morah Avigail's great-nieces, who'd taken in a refugee child, and how they were getting on.

The plan had been that she would meet Howard on the steps of the museum. She was a minute or two early, and she'd assumed she'd have a moment to gather her thoughts. He'd been precisely on time, but never early, so far.

Instead, there was a tumult on the museum steps. She heard it, more than saw it, at least at first. There were shrill sounds, the way a pack of hounds sounded when they were hunting, uncomfortably eager. Rathna couldn't make out any words, not clearly, but it was not remotely a pretty sound. It wasn't even the honest, forthright sound of a pack doing its proper work. There was a nastiness she did not like at all.

It was the flashes of colour that caught her eye. Half a dozen shades, bright teals and burgundies, a vibrant green with a flash of yellow, they all went by, circling and shifting. She saw flickers of white, too fast for her eyes to focus on, moving oddly, not like hands or cloth. Mixed between were pale skin, dark hair, one flash that was more red-auburn, and two different shades of golden blonde.

Once her focus settled, she made the moving shapes into a pack of women, all perhaps in their mid-twenties. They were circling and buffeting someone in the middle. An instant later, she realised it was Ferdinand Howard, his hands raised as if to protect himself. He was wearing an impeccably tailored great coat of black wool, his Homburg knocked askew on his head. The flashes of white sharpened into focus as white feathers. The pack of women was jabbing them at his coat, anywhere they thought one might stick.

Rathna made her way up the stairs, briskly but with dignity. She pitched her voice to carry the way she'd heard half a dozen of her chosen family do, drawing on all the strength of conviction she could manage. "Ladies! Whatever do you think you're doing?" She couldn't check on Howard. She'd have to assume that a stiff upper lip and his breeding would carry him through for the moment.

The half-dozen women stopped and wheeled as one, as if they were considering rushing forward at her now. They were like bacchants, wild women, for all they were properly dressed in tailored day dresses and coats, leather shoes firmly strapped to their feet, and their hair coiffed under their hats. "He's a coward." It came out as sharply as a krait striking. One of them stepped forward, braver than the rest. She was a hair taller, a hair louder. "We all must do our bit."

"Yes, of course we must." The agreement unsettled them, and Rathna could see a ripple of confusion. "Did you ask this young man, or did you just swarm around him?"

"He's a healthy young man, not in uniform!" One of the

other women picked up the cry, shriller and sharper. "Shame! Shame on him, and all like him!"

Rathna took another step or two, bringing her five feet away from them, but on the same step, so she was no longer looking up. "There are such things as reserved occupations. Men who are serving, but not in uniform. Women, as well, for that matter." She let her hand flick down at her own outfit. It was properly professional by non-magical standards, a fitted frock under a camelhair coat. "This man is assisting me. An engineer, working on an essential project." She raised an eyebrow and waited. The space was as important as what she said here.

Howard's eyes widened for a moment, but he didn't move. He was brave enough, really, and steady in himself, to have not made things worse. The women chittered around him, a flurry of passing comments back and forth. The leader wheeled back, but the rest didn't move. "How do you know? You could be..." There it was, the little racist sniff. "Anyone. And he's too young."

Rathna shrugged. She'd seen and heard far worse. And they were, for better and for worse, out in a very public place. "I could be." She drew herself in, as steadily as she could, the way Gabe and Richard and Magni shifted when a duel got serious. "At the moment, I'm someone who could get a senior Minister on the telephone and report interference in essential war work." She didn't bother with the comment about age. Anyone who actually looked at the reserved occupation charts and understood what they meant would realise there were professions where age was not at all relevant.

They had no idea what to do with that. Their leader took a step forward. "Prove it."

Rathna tsked, loudly enough they could hear it. One of

the women retreated slightly, as if Rathna had hit the perfect disapproving note, the one Nanny or some teacher had used. "Will I bother a very busy official just on your say-so? No. But we have an appointment with one of the curators. Come watch how he greets us, if you like." It was messy and annoying, but it was what she had. Curator Lawson would make sure they weren't troubled further. "Come along, Howard."

She set up off the steps, angling past the knot of women. Howard took a step back, then fell into place behind her, slightly to her left, on the far side of the women. He didn't say anything, just tucked his hands behind his back.

Rathna went along the way Gabe would, as if she were certain that nothing would stop them. Acting as if was sometimes all she had. She imagined herself as an arrow flung with speed and accuracy and skill. That would land as it ought. Odd, she didn't usually think of Gabe in flight. He was more about the ground, like a horse or fox or something of the kind.

Someone held the door open. As soon as she was inside, she blinked several times to let her eyes adjust, then changed trajectories to aim directly at the man waiting for them. He was in his fifties now, more active in his youth, in a well-fitted navy suit. "Curator Lawson, pardon the delay. We had a moment outside. I do hope we didn't keep you waiting? This is Mister Howard, who is assisting in the project I mentioned." Lawson wasn't magical, but he'd been tapped by the guild some years ago to be of assistance when they needed it. A bit of an endowed grant here, a titch of access to mineral specimens there, and their appointments received every possible bit of assistance the museum could offer.

"Mrs Edgarton, of course, a pleasure to see you again. And your assistant, of course. A pleasure, Mister Howard, I'm Theo Lawson. Come along, please, out of the crush. I have tea waiting in my office. Rather brisk out today, isn't it? Not nearly so bad as, what was it, Iceland in '24, but this is England, isn't it? Not nearly so glacial." He chuckled at his own joke as he escorted them off to the staff hallways. Rathna caught a glimpse of the women, still in a pack near the door, as they turned the corner. She plucked a fluffy white feather off the back of Howard's arm as they walked and shoved it deep in her pocket.

The meeting itself went well. She was pleased to see that Howard settled into the work promptly after accepting his cup of tea. They chatted about the Dover materials, and Rathna was able to inquire about the other two locations. Lawson went off to pull the necessary volumes, leaving them in a cubicle to make the notes she needed. Or, in her case, make magical copies, which was decidedly more efficient.

When Lawson returned, he left them with the maps for the Netherlands, and for Basel, and she made copies of those, as well. Howard didn't ask about them, not a word, but he tucked the sheets away with the others. "We'll go through them later." After a suitable pause, they took their leave.

It was past one when they left the museum, thankfully without further challenge. She'd been trying to decide what to do next, and had decided on the family townhouse in Trellech. "Come along, we'll see about lunch." Howard didn't ask where they were going, or where that lunch might be, but was quiet as she hailed a cab. "Bedford Square, please, the south side of the square."

It wasn't until they were at the portal, going through to

Trellech, that Howard looked at her, baffled. She simply smiled. On the other side, she turned away from the guild-halls of the crafting quarter, toward the posher residential streets. "The Edgartons have two townhomes in Trellech. One is still inhabited by my grandmother-in-law." She considered, then added, more quietly. "She refuses to acknowledge I exist."

It didn't sting. Not anymore. Not since Rathna knew perfectly well that it meant the rest of the family had been spared the Dowager Lady Edgarton's disapproval at short range for obligatory holiday visits ever since Gabe had brought Rathna home to meet his parents. Richard called on his mother, of course, but neither frequently nor for long.

"We use the other when we need to spend a night in town. Charlotte and her family live a few squares down." Gabe's sister was cheerfully married, and the backbone of her husband's business of alchemical perfume work. They found it easier to be in Trellech and close to his suppliers, though.

Twenty minutes later, they were settled in the library with lashings of sandwiches, a few pastries, and plenty of tea and coffee. She'd given Howard a chance to wash up, and she'd done the same upstairs. Rathna set out her own plate, letting him choose what he wanted. Before he ate, though, he cleared his throat. "Magistra Edgarton, thank you for earlier."

She nodded at him. "You are my apprentice." She then chose her words carefully, now. "Seeing to your well-being is part of that. A pleasure, as well as an obligation."

Rathna caught the shift of his lips. Not something Davis Fortnum would ever have said, though he'd have gruffly dealt with that kind of angry chaos more loudly, but in much the same way.

"Weren't you scared?" There, it burst out of him with almost no warning, the way Gabe blurted things when his self-restraint had finally snapped. She was, in fact, impressed that Howard had managed for so long.

Rathna considered. It was an excellent question. "Before I answer that, are you hurt? Is there anything that needs tending?" He shook his head, but took an obedient sip of his coffee. She went on. "Leverage."

His eyes widened at that. Definitely not an answer he had expected.

"I wasn't born to any of this." She waved a hand at the house, its solid bulk and history. "Ma and Baba were servants, originally. An ayah and a lascar. They were born in Calcutta, both of them, though they met in London. They came, both of them, to make a better life. And it was good, for a bit. A lot of love, which is more than you can say for a number of families with houses along this street." She said it that way deliberately, expecting it might hit hard, and she saw him shift, just for an instant. "But I've learned."

"They listened to you. Enough." He wasn't grudging about it, and that gave her a great deal of hope. Instead, he was curious, perhaps even a touch in awe of it. "You, you." He flushed again, and ducked his chin, then partially covered his embarrassment in a bit of sandwich.

She let him. She didn't need to hammer this point home now. "I've dealt with a number of difficult situations over the years. This one, where I do not care what they think of me, that's rather easier. I cared about you, and about us getting on with our work. And if what I said deters them from surrounding another young man, well, that's all to the good. Shame sticks like clay, and it's as hard to wash off. It does no one any good, almost all the time."

That got Howard to look up again, sharply. He took another bite, a bit more coffee. "You have been very attentive to my preferences, Magistra." This was cautious, laying out the logic of it. "And you have not pressed me, about—" He glanced down at the portfolio on the floor by his chair, leaning against the table. "You wanted those maps for a reason?"

"I have permission to make an attempt at a portal this spring, if the war does not change too much, and if I can get the necessary materials together."

Another bite, another sip, another swallow or two. "Why two different maps?"

"It depends on you. Basel would be our best choice if we cannot link to a portal further north." In Germany. "But it presents a number of challenges. We'd be at the southern tip of the Black Forest, with difficult terrain. And quite a lot in the way of legends and lore to contend with, which always complicates things. Both people's reactions, and the tales of where that lore comes from."

She knew that the Fatae agreements were different in Germany - and in the rest of Europe. There was no such thing as the Pact there, not something clearly laid out, in mutually agreeable terms. Instead, it was piecemeal and unbalanced, depending on who'd had the most potent leverage when whatever local agreements there were had been made.

Howard nodded. She took a bit of food in the silence that followed, a good two minutes. It was enough for half a sandwich and some chai to soothe her. She was deeply grateful for Cook pulling the right sort of thing together on no notice. Then he cleared his throat again. "And the northern site?"

"There is a spot in the northeast of the Netherlands that would do very well. A water portal, not stone, which might be both more flexible and faster. But to make that work, I would need a known portal within two hundred and fifty miles."

"Berlin." He knew the map well, and the distances. He swallowed hard, this time from emotion. "Oh."

She didn't ask him to help. She wouldn't pressure him. That wouldn't do what she wanted, for one thing. Instead, she continued with her lunch. Rathna had a great deal of practice doing that when in the middle of a complicated conversation.

"You called me an engineer." This time, the curiosity was back in his voice.

"It's the closest thing to what we are. And, as I pointed out, a reserved occupation without any limit on age." She looked up to meet his eyes. She had come to realise he'd come to the apprenticeship through a twisted road, and he was only now beginning to understand how much.

"What would you ask me if I were willing to help?" His voice stammered. "With Berlin, I mean."

"Have you visited your family there, since you apprenticed? Do you know the portal?"

"The family one, yes. There's quite a bit of lore about it." Howard met her eyes, then looked down at his hands. "I could never go back, if I did."

Probably not, no, though it was impossible to have any certainty about that, given the state of the world. She didn't respond to it. Instead, she said, "You wouldn't need to open that portal. They've likely locked it, or put in other protections. We just need to align with it. I can show you the process, if you like, tomorrow, so you know what would be needed."

Another duck of his chin before his voice was softer still. "Magistra." Then, in a rush, like Avigail ready to burst with something she had to say. "Please, if you'd prefer to use my forename."

"Ferdinand." She said it as gently as she could. "And you may use mine, as appropriate."

"Mistress Rathna." Then he swallowed hard. "I was there last summer. And I spent a good bit of time trying to understand it. It feels different from the ones here. Even the older Fatae portals, though I haven't spent much time with those yet."

That was a fine day's work, and then some. She smiled at him, letting her approval show. "I should have a word with Cook. When we're both finished with the meal, we'll have a look at the geological maps, shall we?"

CHAPTER 8
DECEMBER 4TH AT VERITAS

Gabe woke with a start, rather earlier in the morning than he'd meant to. He lay there, hand clenching at the sheet for a good dozen breaths, until his heart stopped racing. Only then did he gather himself to see if he'd disturbed Rathna. She was curled on her side, facing away from him, breathing evenly.

Good. She needed her sleep. His had fled. If the dream hadn't done it, the shock of waking up would have. Instead, he eased himself out as gently as he could. Not, however, as gently as he'd needed to. By the time he came back from his dressing room, wearing his riding gear and carrying his boots, she'd rolled over into the empty space and was blinking sleepily at him.

"Going riding. Back for breakfast. Go back to sleep, love." She made a muzzy noise and buried her head in the blankets. Gabe managed to restrain himself from brushing her hair back into place. It was very tempting that way.

The ride gave him a chance to clear his head. It was brisk, but not as chilly as some of the weather predictions were suggesting would be coming. His current mare, Meliora, was as much a joy to ride as Invicta had been when he was younger, but she took a little longer to warm up and settle into her work. Much as he did these days, honestly. On the way back, they took several fences, flying over them easily.

He was back in good time for a quick wash and then breakfast with Rathna and his parents. She raised an eyebrow at him, and he said, amiably. "I'm meeting Alexander to talk about something." He'd arranged it while the bath was running. For a wonder, Alexander actually had a morning free, rather than the snatched hours they'd been working around. "I'll be in the office by, oh, eleven. Probably."

His father snorted, amused, and thankfully didn't press. His mother raised an eyebrow, but didn't ask. At least, not right now. He was quite sure she would tonight. He managed one more quick kiss for Rathna. "I should be home for tea with Avigail. I'll write if I won't." He then went off to check his satchel one more time, running down the little list he kept inside his notebook. Journal, pen, pencil, notebook, working stones, his potions kit bag, he'd wound his pocket watch, he didn't need a different cane. Not for Trellech, certainly.

Twenty minutes later, he was knocking on the door of Alexander's townhouse. It opened, to make it clear Alexander was in Egyptian mode today. He was wearing the deep black robe he favoured at home, down to his ankles, with an overrobe of a red-coral, rather than his usual blues. Gabe wondered about that omen.

"In. Cyrus wants me to come by this afternoon, so clarify what you do and don't want him to know as appropriate."

Gabe grunted. That was an additional layer of complication. "Something specific on your end, then?"

"Bloody awful dreams, emphasis on the bloody?" Alexander gestured Gabe into the library. Gabe had been here a number of times now, but the impact of it never failed to make him want to stop and figure it all out. It wasn't just the books and the scrolls, though there were plenty of those. It wasn't just that the jewel tone leather bindings stood out against ebony shelves like the depths of the night sky, or the range of writing methods visible on the spines. Or the fact there were half a dozen alphabets just on the nearest shelves. It was also the weight of the warding, how it echoed in Gabe's head.

Gabe wanted desperately to unpick it, using every tool he'd ever learned as a Penelope and a few he made up for the occasion, but that would first of all be rude. And second, no matter how brilliant he was, he was sure he'd not manage it. Not without a fair bit of help. Instead, he nodded, setting down his satchel as he took the guest chair in front of the fire.

"Here, read that." Alexander passed a letter, printed and imprecisely folded. Gabe knew what it was, one of the Society of Inner Light letters. He flicked through it, the one that had been posted this morning. Alexander had particular resources, then, to get it this fast. The core of it talked about the role of mediumship, and how it could be easily abused, about the stresses and 'unbalanced forces' of the previous week. In Gabe's long experience as a Penelope, that meant someone fooling around with things they didn't understand, and it was going to cause trouble.

Gabe looked up. "Do you believe this bit about the veil being thinner right now?" He'd been soaking in that kind of comment from a dozen different esoteric and occult groups, all of whom often shouted their thoughts on the matter.

"Which veil?" Alexander rubbed his nose. "Coffee?" Alexander, blessings on his name, had as much fondness for the stuff as Gabe did, though he made it in the Egyptian manner. Gabe nodded and waited for a cup.

"The dead, the year's death, the Fatae. So many choices." Gabe looked up then. "Has the Council had word of the Wild Hunt again?"

Alexander made that ambivalent gesture with his hand. "Nothing certain. An increasing number of hints. What was your most recent report to Cyrus?"

Gabe reached into his bag, and pulled out a copy, handing it over to Alexander while reading the letter in his hand again. He was not at all sure about some of the language, the whole thing about visualising a Master - a figure of light and illumination - to connect with, and ask for help. Gabe had learned to build his own help, one way or another.

Alexander finished skimming through. "Cyrus has been sharing freely, then. Good." He sounded as if he'd not quite allowed himself to hope.

"I could just send you copies as well." Gabe offered it a bit cautiously. They'd been playing a careful balancing act for the last month. It had been complicated by the fact Alexander had been here and there, in Albion and outside the borders, on almost no notice. He rubbed his face. It had only been a month, it felt like at least six already. And yet, a month was bringing them barrelling closer to the spring thaw, and when Rathna might well be gone. Probably would be gone, though her apprentice was still deciding how much he was going to help.

The balancing act, right. He was more scattered in his

head than usual this morning, and that wouldn't help anything at all. He took another sip of coffee, and another, willing it to work its particular enchantment. Gabe was reporting directly to Cyrus Smythe-Clive, as head of the Council. Alexander, another of that particular tangle of obligations, was consulting on the side. "Does Smythe-Clive know you've been talking to me?"

"Probably not. He hasn't asked." Alexander flicked his fingers and accompanied them with a toothy smile. "He knows better."

"And you're not going to tell him. Right. I'll send you copies. It's a mess, to be honest. A lot of supposition from certain quarters about Arthur returning in triumph in Britain's darkest hour. Nothing that's shattered yet, no one caught up in truly damaging magical rites. But I can feel the currents around every corner, lurking, and more as we go on. This, for example. Thanks. I'll have a copy on my desk by the time I get there." He handed it back. "There's odd news out of the contacts in Germany. Did you know?"

"Yes, but which parts?" Alexander reached for a cup of tea waiting on the table for him.

"The back and forth on whether they're visibly supporting astrology at the moment. You know and I know that some of it is total bunk. And at the same time, some of it is entirely relevant and important for magical work."

"They do seem, shall we say, unusually indecisive about which parts they're listening to. I did hear they're banning astrological calendars and public profiles and all that. Which doesn't surprise."

Gabe shook his head. "No, it doesn't. But they're not banning it outright, either. Does Geoffrey have a thought there, do you know?"

Alexander put back his head, chuckling. "He does, yes.

We've told you a bit about the Heinrichs. The parents lean into the land magic in the older German forms. Seasonal rites, not all of them pleasant, but traditional. Sepp, the oldest brother, well, he mostly likes an excuse for a party. Or an orgy." Something complex flickered across Alexander's expression for a moment, the sort of thing where asking wouldn't do any good, Gabe knew. "The younger, though, he's in with a mess of people with ideas. Some of them Indo-Aryan, some of them more distasteful than that. If you don't already have a bibliography, Geoffrey and Lizzie can likely share."

"I'd appreciate that." Gabe agreed. "What do you think of how it's actually working for them?"

Alexander tapped his fingers together. "We have a very different relationship to the land magic and the Fatae than they do, and I don't know Germany well enough. I wonder, though, how angry the land is, or will be. Or how angry it's been since the Great War. They had more active fighting than we did, of course. Much more."

"And then all the political constrictions, the Great Depression, all that." Gabe winced. "Right." He took a breath and let it out. "This morning."

"A dream?" Alexander leaned back, and Gabe knew the older man well enough now, had duelled him often enough to read that visible casualness as anything but.

"And you did too." Gabe couldn't decide whether the tiny approving nod was reassuring or terrifying.

"Mine wasn't particularly informative. I'll put some time into work in the Keep. Today, tomorrow, Thursday." Alexander grimaced. "Before Thursday, I hope." He routinely spent the second half of the week out with the Carillons at Ytene, and Gabe knew Alexander hated to disrupt that particular ritual of his life.

That left it to Gabe to explain. "It wasn't entirely like other dreams I've had, the potent ones." Such as the one that had changed his life in March of 1918. He'd woken from that, knowing that if he kept going as he was, he'd be dead at the age of eighteen. Before the end of July, a few bare months away then. He'd done something else and twisted up his fate. He'd chosen what had looked and felt like dishonour for years until Rathna had helped him untangle everything.

He rarely talked about it these days. He hadn't ever told Alexander the story, just his close family. Alexander was new enough to their nest of allies, as Geoffrey put it, that a lot of things simply hadn't come up.

Now, though, Gabe thought it might be relevant, and he wasn't going to stint on relevant information. "When I was eighteen, I had a dream. A massive black snake rearing up to strike and swallow me. I went out riding, and my mare…" The times he'd said it out loud didn't make this any easier. Rathna wasn't here to buffer it with her calmness and certainty and perspective.

He went on, keeping his voice as calm and studied as he could. "I knew if I stayed on Invicta's back, I'd be dead by the end of July, somewhere in France or Belgium. Not here. Not Albion. If I fell, I'd live. I fell, but my ankle's never been the same. It's healed. All the Healers said so." But it still hurt, somewhere between an ignorable constant ache and a searing sharp pain. It depended on the weather and what he'd been doing and some mysterious calculation he still hadn't worked out despite all his collected data.

Alexander had almost said something at the start, but then he leaned forward, listening intently. "And last night was like that, and unlike that? You're older now. What do you make of it?"

"Rathna has made a persuasive argument - we have a bibliography - about how it was something about the land magic catching me, but needing to pull the vitality for it from somewhere. Me, in this case. And you've heard her theory about the Silence being a living container, with her own needs." Like the eruv she'd lived inside, with Aunt Avigail, her memory a blessing over and over again. A container for the community, a space within which they moved freely and different rules applied.

Alexander nodded, now more distracted. "Moment. Tell me about last night, while I look for something. And I'd like the bibliography, of course, if you're willing."

It wasn't quite an order. Alexander didn't give orders to Gabe. Gabe had noticed and appreciated that. It was an instruction, a hope. That they could work on the puzzle together, if Gabe laid out the pieces.

"Last night had something of that quality, though I did not fall from Meliora this morning. Thankfully." He wrinkled his nose. For one thing, that had felt like an insult to Invicta, back then, and to his riding skills, and he was vain about both. "But there was a snake in it, somewhere. Maybe a dragon? I don't know about the imagery. Far larger than a custos dragon, though, even the older ones." He'd seen them a few times at a distance in the banking vaults. But they rarely got taller than a horse, and perhaps twenty yards in length, including the tail. The dragon, thinking of that moment in the dream, brought back that shiver of something that would change things once again, like feet over his grave, only it might not mean that. He repressed a little twitch of his hand, glad Alexander was distracted.

"Go on?" Alexander was thumbing through books now. He'd crossed the room so quickly and quietly Gabe had barely registered it.

"An iridescent green, more like a peacock than anything else I could name. I didn't see it for long, then there was mist, being in a deep wood, one I knew and didn't know. Not Kent." He was absolutely sure it wasn't Kent. Not that he'd been in every bit of woodland in Kent, though he'd made a fair try at it over the years. But he knew what Kent hummed like beneath his feet, and this had not been that.

"Somewhere you have been?"

"That doesn't narrow down Albion much." He considered. "Albion, though, yes. Not the Continent, certainly not India." He'd done enough travel there to have filed the harmonies there inside his head into a different category. "Southern England, probably. Wales has that overtone harmony, and Scotland has the..." He didn't really have the proper words for it. "Spaciousness."

Alexander turned around. "One of these days, in a future in which we have leisure time, we really must get you to articulate that better. You and Rathna. It's clear you know exactly what you're talking about, and if we could cross-reference it with the demesne lands and the geology, I think we'd have something potent." He then turned back to the shelf, plucked out a book bounded in bright wheat-gold leather, and brought it back.

The image on the page was an illumination, done by hand in an early book. Likely printed not much before 1484, though Gabe was not remotely the expert on that sort of thing some people were. Aunt Mason, Geoffrey, and even Alexander had him bested there, and he was glad to admit it. He considered the image. This was not one of the stumpy dragons of some illustrations that looked much like a confusion of a crocodile. Gabe had seen them in the flesh, more than a bit too close, actually. This had the long sleekness he'd seen in his dream, something sinuous, but with the great wings sweeping back like the custos dragons writ large.

"Like that, not that I got a precise look at it. Dreams, so unruly that way." Gabe nodded.

Alexander grunted and gestured. "Read, then."

Gabe took the book carefully, only now considering why Alexander might have something of the kind. He didn't go in for natural history as a rule, not like Gabe did. And much as the man loved books, he wouldn't keep something he'd never use. He'd find a better home for it. He skimmed the text, instead, blessing Aunt Mason and his mother for making sure he was as literate in Middle English as anyone in Albion.

It talked, metaphorically, about the green dragon being the creature of the Fatae, of the strength and potent magic of the green land, furling and unfurling with the seasons. Stalking, perhaps, might be the better word. He didn't quite touch the page, running his finger along the words, before he looked up, blinking. "Am I reading this right? About how it is a symbol of, how do I translate this?"

"The green does suggest certain things, of course." The green of the Fatae, but Gabe had thought that perhaps too pat and simple an answer. And certainly, the shade of green didn't help with other questions, why a dragon, why now, or particularly why him. "You must have done your own research on serpents, long since."

That made Gabe snort, despite the seriousness. "Come on, Alexander, you know me better than that." Then he considered. He was not an expert in Egyptian lore, but he certainly knew the power of the uraeus in their symbols. "What do you think of snakes and dragons?"

"That I'd certainly rather not be bit by one." At another

time, the comment might have been as sharp as the jab of a fang, but Alexander laughed at the end of it, easing it. "I respect them, like any sensible man who sees the power there and doesn't want to die."

Gabe could read enough of what Alexander wasn't going to say, that they were a symbol of sovereignty, of power and the protection of that power, that Alexander did not have the standard reactions of Albion to serpents. At some point when they had leisure, in some distant future, that would be worth coming back to. Instead, he shifted directions. "This does not help me decide what to do about it, you realise. Seeing as how the symbol did not come with a set of instructions, wishes, or even quests."

"You are no Celt, but the legend of Lleu Llaw Gyffes." Alexander let his voice trail off. "He of the skillful hand. The cognates to Lugus, to the Britanno-Roman Mercury. Consult with Geoffrey on that point. You are skilled in multiple directions."

Gabe looked down, more to hide his expression than anything else. "May I borrow this? The metaphor is unusually - well. Dense."

"And you want your mother and Mason to have a look. Yes, yes. I will find you a suitable book box." Gabe would have to run it back to Veritas before doing anything else today, but he could do that. He didn't want to entrust it to anyone else or to his office.

"How do I explore this?" The book suggested a direction, but vaguely, in the mist.

"Read. Keep your eyes open." Alexander shrugged slightly. "That's what we all do, you know that, unless we get lucky enough to strike on an answer."

Gabe had to snort at that. It was true. He'd hoped that

with age would come more certain knowledge, but no. His esteemed elders were all just better at faking their sureness, until the evidence and results of their very real skills caught up.

CHAPTER 9
DECEMBER 28TH AT VERITAS

R athna and Gabe had, after a long conversation with each other and with the rest of the family, decided to wait until the Solstice festivities were over before having the necessary and complicated conversation with their children. For one thing, it had taken until the last week, just before the solstice, for Ferdinand to agree to help with a portal that connected to the Heinrich portal outside Berlin. And Gabe had been doing more research than active engagement with his own concerns.

That was going to change in the coming year, even the coming month. They both knew it. They'd been simultaneously confronting the implications and not really talking about them. Rathna couldn't blame Gabe for it. She wasn't talking about it either. They both knew the reality, and until it had got closer, they could just let it sit there. Looming.

Now, though, they were tucked into the library, the heart of the household. Rathna had let everyone know they had an important conversation to have at luncheon. Now, Alysoun was in her usual chair, with Richard beside her, and Rathna had claimed the sofa. Rowena had settled straight and tall on a pillow on the floor, her long dark hair in a gorgeous braid down her back. She looked confident in a way Rathna had never been at that age. She also had her nose in a book, until they were ready to begin, and that was as much like Rathna as any of Gabe's family.

Rowena had been doing brilliantly at Schola. She had a gift for the Seal House's liminal magic, and Rathna had vastly enjoyed their conversations now Rowena was home for the holidays. Their eldest daughter had all of their best qualities, mingled. Gabe's quicksilver mind mixed with some of Rathna's steadiness. She thought Rowena might have a gift for the portal magic, too, and she hoped, well. She hoped she'd be able to explore that more thoroughly sometime.

Anthony was off by the shelves across the room with Gabe, asking him a question about something in another book. They were peering at something, a diagram or illustration. He was bright, both intellectually and in appearance. He had Gabe's lighter skin, but it was his eyes that made her come back to that adjective, with their clear sparkling blue. Rathna loved watching him with Gabe.

In truth, she loved watching Gabe with all three of their children. He met them absolutely where they were at the moment. He uniformly treated them like intelligent people who just needed more information about the world. And he had their own childlike glee about discovering something new and sharing it. He wasn't the adult to go to for steadiness or the daily planning of making sure there were enough clean clothes or a schedule to the day, but that was why Alysoun and the household staff and the nannies and governess had been such gifts.

And Avigail, well. Avigail was on the sofa, nestled in

against Rathna's side, entirely content to be there. She was the quietest of their three, the one who watched most without speaking. It hit Rathna, again, as it had been doing since she first met with Ferdinand, that Avigail was near enough the age Rathna had been when her own mother died. When she'd been left more and more alone, before she'd had that interview with Morah Avigail, her memory always a blessing in her second year at Schola.

Whatever happened to Rathna, Avigail would have family, and not just in distant Bengal. She had Gabe; she had Alysoun and Richard. She had her Aunt Charlotte and her cousins. She had Gabe's adoptive Uncle Gil and Uncle Magni, though they were both getting on into their eighties now. And there were Aunt Mason and Aunt Witt, the Penelopes, and the larger close circle of the Carillons and their children and the Leftons, and theirs, and all the others.

Rathna had to keep telling herself that, because there was this vast gaping pit inside her, about the terrible risks she'd be taking. She'd woken, more than once, shaking with it. Four times in the past fortnight. She had never been the risk-taker, not in her marriage, not before that. She'd always clung to what was safe, what had been tested and reviewed.

She wasn't going to be able to do that. She wouldn't have Gabe with her, so she could borrow his instincts and his absolute gift for timing and when to lean forward. She wouldn't have Alysoun's confidence and good sense, or Richard's honour and stability. And she'd be worrying, all the way, about what it meant for the children.

Gabe caught her eye, and murmured something to Anthony, before they set the book on the table nearby, and came over to join the rest. Anthony settled next to Rowena and spoke up. "Mama, you look worried."

"We have something serious to talk about, love." Rathna slipped her fingers into Gabe's hand as he sat down, his other arm going around her back. She'd cheerfully put up with him fiddling with the end of her braid if he needed to fidget. At least at the moment. He'd needed to fidget a lot, the past months. "Papa and I have both been working on very important projects, and we need to talk about what it means for all of us as a family."

This was not, perhaps, entirely what Rowena had expected. There was the sharp look up, then down and away, as she calculated. Avigail had gone still against her side. Anthony glanced from one of his sisters to the other. "Can you explain more, please?"

Gabe picked up smoothly enough. "You know we have both been very busy. We make it back for tea with Avigail, much of the time, but we are working very hard on different things." He glanced up and caught something from his mother's expression. "We waited to tell you until now, because we wanted to talk about it in person, now we're through all the holidays. And because we weren't entirely sure about some of the timing, not until the last week or so."

Anthony nodded, solemnly. "Are you working on things together?"

"Oh, no, love. Unfortunately, maybe." Though there would have been no way both of them could go to the Continent. That was too much risk, entirely too much. And Gabe was his father's Heir, and Anthony was too young to hold the land magic without a regent. Rathna didn't want to continue that train of thought at all. It was all horrible. "Separately. Your papa is working on a project here in

Albion. But I am working on one that, if things don't change too terribly much in the war, means I will be overseas in the spring. As soon as we can do things outside again."

"Where, overseas?" Rowena looked up, and she was weighing things, doing the maths.

They'd had had a long talk, several of them, over the past week, about how much detail to give the children. Gabe had argued - cogently, brilliantly - for honesty. But also for telling them that they had to keep it private. It wasn't as if the children weren't used to the idea that some information wasn't to be shared. Richard talked about his cases, sometimes, with both Alysoun in her role as analyst, and Gabe, for his professional opinion. They were careful of that, around the children, but of course some general topics spilled over.

"Family only. Aunt Mason and Aunt Witt, Uncle Gil and Uncle Magni. Just them, unless we say otherwise. Not your cousins, or anyone at school, even your teachers. If you get questions, you send them to Papa or to Grandmama and Grandpapa. And use the extra charms for privacy, in the journals, all that." The cousins were growing up in a different sort of house, with people in and out all the time. While Charlotte and Lewis could be trusted, their children weren't trained in confidentiality the same way. It was more complicated there.

"Of course, Mama." Rowena nodded immediately, echoed by Anthony.

Avigail peered up at her, sideways. "Me too, Mama."

Rathna leaned to kiss her head. "Of course. And you don't see as many people yet." Then she took a breath. "I'll be in the Netherlands, likely." It was the best option for their choices - an area that didn't have a portal near, but where they thought they could establish one. There was a whole plain that flooded regularly. Connecting to water would be easy and they could anchor it in the bedrock.

"Do you have to go soon?" That, oh, that was Avigail, and it cracked Rathna's heart.

"Not just yet, dear one. But in the spring. Maybe the beginning of March, maybe April. It depends on the weather."

There was silence then, as all three of them thought about it, in their different ways. Anthony leaned back on one hand. "What will you be doing, Mama? Something with a portal?"

She nodded. "We think we might be able to make one, much more quickly than usual, and use it to help people escape." They had been determined, as parents, to be honest with their children, even if the war had made that incredibly complicated. "You know how people who are Jewish, like Morah Avigail was, and her family, have been leaving Germany and Austria, if they can. How we helped children come here, the kindertransport."

They'd sponsored a full eighteen children, helping connect them with families who would take them in, and give them homes. Of course, Rathna wasn't Jewish, and neither was Gabe. They couldn't exactly offer the children a Jewish household. Nor could they navigate around the challenges of the Pact and the Silence, and being a decidedly magical home. But they could help ease some of the money worries, and make sure they had suitable clothes, and a toy or two, and someone to check on their interests.

Rowena nodded. "So you might help more people be safe." Something in that had decided her.

"That's the hope. It is a very big thing to try to do. No one's done anything like it since the Pact." Humans had gotten the gift in trade of making portals, of some of the

Fatae healing techniques, half a dozen great magics, in exchange for other concessions. It had changed the bedrock under their feet, in ways Rathna thought they were still learning about every day.

"And Papa?" There was Anthony.

Gabe shifted a little against her. "I'm staying in Albion. But we are working on, hmm. How to put this." He let them see him thinking, saying out loud what at other times might have been a flurry of thoughts through his brain. At the end of which, he'd come out with some extraordinary statement at the end of the process that was simultaneously correct and baffling. "You know that many different people want to help the war effort, with magic and prayer as much as anything else?"

He waited a moment to see them nod. "Isobel and I, and some other people, are trying to figure out all the patterns of what people are doing that's having an effect. For good and bad. We're going to have to start meeting up with people. I don't know when, yet, or how often I'll be doing that, but I expect - well. It will be often, probably. I'll sleep here, when I can, and I'll have my journal. But I might take longer to write back, and I might not be home when you're awake much, Avigail, love."

Avigail grimaced at him, and snuggled tighter against Rathna's side, fingers digging into her stomach a little and the folds of her dress. "You're gone a lot now." It was grumpy, but Gabe reached out to brush her fingers.

"I know. And I'll make a point of seeing you. Or leaving notes. How's that? But it really is important work, and someone has to do it. That's me." The cheerfulness was a bit forced, and they all knew it.

Rowena coughed. "Papa, don't." She was old enough and sure enough of herself to call her father on his failures, now. That was a whole stage of parenthood Rathna had not anticipated at all. She'd never dared with Morah Avigail, not remotely.

Gabe folded immediately and spread out his free hand again. "I don't like that I won't see you nearly as often as I want, which is always." There, that was much more honest. "But it's also a truly interesting challenge. And you know how I like those. Aunt Witt and Aunt Mason don't think there's anyone else who could do it as well as I can."

"And you want them to be right." Anthony looked up now.

"Life works better that way. We all know that." It provoked Richard into a chuckle. They'd been very quiet. Gabe nodded at his father. "And Grandmama and Grandpapa will be here, and the others. Plenty of people to teach you things and listen to you, and write letters. And me when I can."

That was, clearly, a somewhat easier potion for them to swallow than Rathna's absence. When there were no more immediate questions, Rathna cleared her throat. "Anyway, that's why we wanted some time, just the immediate family, for the rest of the holidays. We want all the time we can get with you right now, before you go back to school, Rowena, and to your tutoring house, Anthony. And maybe we'll get some time around equinox, but if we don't, I don't want..." She hesitated, then forged forward, feeling Gabe's hand on her shoulder, steady and certain. "I don't want to regret it."

There was a silence again, a weightier one. Finally, there was Avigail's voice, a bit wavery. "Are there proper prayers and offerings, Mama?"

"Well. We might have a lot of obstacles. I think we should tidy up Ganesha's shrine, and figure out plenty of sweets for his offerings, don't you? And clean and tidy the lararium, as well." They'd had both for all their marriage. "And there are some prayers from Morah Avigail's people, for all sorts of reasons, and we can look and find what fits best."

She wasn't at all sure there was a proper prayer for trying unfathomable acts of magic. She supposed that if anyone had them, the people who had built the great Temple in Jerusalem might have one. And she could ask Morah Avigail's grandson, now well established as a rabbi, who considered her one of the family.

CHAPTER 10
FEBRUARY 5TH, 1940 AT SCHOLA

"Oh, merciful gods. You don't have rampaging angels with swords stalking about the place." Gabe let out a breath from the doorway of Schola's salle. He hadn't realised how much metaphysical aggravation he'd been carrying around. Two of the three men seated in the salle snorted. Isembard looked baffled for a moment, before settling back into a complicated exhaustion.

Gabe made his proper bow then, waiting for permission to enter the salle. "May I have the freedom of the salle, Professor Fortier?" Isobel, just behind him and to his right, made the same request, half a beat later.

"Come in, make free, both of you." Isembard said, with a wave. He stood from where he'd been sitting on the bench along the wall, pressing his palm against the whitewashed plaster behind him. Gabe felt the wards close up behind him, smoothly and securely. "My office, shall we? I have the makings for tea."

Gabe gave a slight salute, then encouraged Isobel over as the other two men stood as well. "Gentlemen, my apprentice, Isobel Thomas. Isobel, Professor Fortier, of course, you know." She'd had him as a student, though only for general physical skills, not his particular magical speciality. "Alexander Landry of the Council, and Lord Geoffrey Carillon, who holds Ytene. Sorry we're late. I lost track of time this afternoon. Isobel had to roust me out twice."

She made the proper bow and murmur, and Gabe was pleased that the formal manners were coming easier to her. She hadn't grown up with them, and they could be baffling, as Rathna complained on the regular, still. And better yet, she wasn't cowed. These were impressive people, in a number of ways, but they were also particular allies.

Isembard Fortier was Professor of Protective magics, and Schola's champion in many ways. He was as attuned to Schola's magic as Gabe was to Kent, or Geoffrey was to the New Forest. His wife Thesan, the Astronomy professor, was also a particularly good friend of Rathna's.

Geoffrey himself looked surprisingly at home in the salle, for all he swore he didn't duel. Alexander's comfort with the space was much more to be expected. He'd taught here for two years, as well as having trained Isembard himself. Gabe duelled both Isembard and Alexander fairly regularly, when their schedules permitted, to keep his own skills as strong as possible.

They'd agreed to meet here because it was term time, and Isembard couldn't get free and away for long. But Gabe had also, in the few days since they'd arranged this, wanted desperately to know if a particularly attention-demanding bit of magical work had stretched this far.

A handful of minutes later found them settled in Isembard's office, supplied with decent tea. The office was also, thankfully, warmer, with a fire in the fireplace. It had been a bitterly cold January, the worst on record, and February wasn't looking much better. "Explain yourself, Gabe, would you?"

Isembard might look at ease, but he had always reminded Gabe of one of the great cats. He'd had a chance to see tigers in the wild on their last two visits to Rathna's extended family. There was something about the lazy energy of a tiger sure of its next meal in Isembard. He was getting up into his fifties, and Geoffrey half a decade older, with Alexander grizzled and nearly seventy but still active, but all of them wore it comfortably. Age had made them efficient, not less effective.

"The latest round of the Society of Inner Light has the membership working with a particular visualisation." Gabe flipped through the notebook he'd set aside for this project and read out loud. "I quote: 'Let us meditate on angelic Presences, red-robed and armed, patrolling the length and breadth of our land. Visualise a map of Great Britain, and picture these great Presences moving as a vast shadowy form along the coasts, and backwards and forwards from north to south and east to west, keeping watch and ward so that nothing alien can move unobserved.'"

"Oof." Isembard suddenly looked very tired, and Gabe was sure, all in a moment, he was dealing with some other complexity.

Beside Gabe, Isobel shifted a little in her chair, making her own notes with the little scratches of her fountain pen. She was here to observe and see what she picked up. Gabe had encouraged her to ask questions if she had them, but she tended to keep quiet when she was unsure of her footing. He couldn't argue with it as a working rule, and so he didn't fuss her about it, beyond making sure his debriefing after was always thorough.

"No. Nothing like that here. I haven't felt the brush of anything of the kind." Isembard let out a long breath, as if he'd been consulting with some local deeper magic.

"I've got a contact in the Hebrides. I suspect, though, they'll say they feel it." Gabe offered that easily enough.

"And Schola isn't, because no one without magic remembers we are here." Alexander gestured broadly. "I think you're right, but the confirmation would be very helpful. It also has implications for the protections."

"Mason's got someone in the Orkneys, too. And we should check the Isle of Man, and ..."

"Making a note, sir." Isobel piped up beside him. "Channel Islands, Hebrides, Lundy Island, Isle of Man, Orkneys, Isles of Scilly, Shetlands, Isle of Wight. And Ireland, too. Might as well find out what they know."

Gabe snorted. Their brains worked in rather different ways, but he'd noticed she'd run them down in alphabetical order, as the Penelopes held them. "Just so. Pass it along to Witt and Doyle, would you, while we talk?"

"Sir." Isobel subsided into the notes for a moment. She wouldn't need to write more than a few sentences. Witt was expecting something of the kind. And she had the proper diplomatic connections to Ireland, which was neither under the Pact nor part of Albion, whatever the non-magical politics looked like.

"Isembard, is there some other issue here?" Gabe wasn't sure he was the person to press this point.

"Not the way you mean." Isembard ran a hand over his face. "We found out last night that one of our recent students had been killed. It's not public. He - well. Thesan's taking it hard, and so am I."

Geoffrey, interestingly, added a comment. "In

Germany." That meant Intelligence work of some sort, then.

Gabe cleared his throat. "His memory a blessing." He'd picked the custom up from Rathna long ago, and it often seemed the kindest thing he could say. Alexander, he knew, had customs about the name living on mattering, and the memory. "And may the memory touch you kindly." That bit extra, because he could not have carried that particular weight with anything like that amount of grace.

Isembard nodded once, not curtly, but closing the conversation off. "I'll pass it along to Thesan." Then he swept back into business. "Nothing like that here, but I'm quite sure the Lady of Schola wouldn't have that sort of incongruence. Is that the word I want?"

Alexander nodded. "It's a different mode than we use, in half a dozen ways. I could write a paper, had I world enough and time." Certainly, people in Albion held with angels, in their various forms. But it was not a mode anyone well-trained would pick as a visual for the entire country. Too many people had practices where angels played no part. And more than a few knew enough of their history to remember how chaotic Edward Kelley had been for the magic of Albion. And for England, for that matter, though that got less space in the history books.

It had been one of the key case studies of Gabe's train-ing, actually. He'd spent weeks exploring how to unpick the garbled ritual magics that had gone into Kelley's attempts and frauds and counterfeits. Gabe nodded. "We've noticed odd spots around places. Mostly but not entirely London. A couple of things near the usual sorts of stone circles, people attempting rituals or wardings, but they've mostly faded out quickly. The Tower of London, where people think the White Hill is, and Bran's head. The ones that haven't, they're small and private homes or gardens." Gabe shrugged. That was not a particular worry for his work.

"That brings me to the other question. How much does this angel nonsense interfere with the Pact, Alexander?" Part of that agreement, a key part of it, had to do with humans agreeing to avoid messing with matters of the Fatae. This was perilously close to that line, depending on the nuances of reading fifteenth century legal Latin and its various glosses.

Alexander was the one to look tired now. "We have no particular signs of a direct problem, but a number of issues to keep an eye on. I'm off to Yorkshire when we're done here. Matters are unsettled. That's the only way I can put it."

Geoffrey had been rather quiet. "I've noticed that effect in the New Forest. It's too much in winter still for most of the more obvious signs to be visible. And there's some pulse of something, down near the southeast. Or more there than anywhere else. Highcliffe, Christchurch. Non-magical, not of Albion, at least. You might go visit, Gabe, and see what you think." Geoffrey held the land magic for the north of the New Forest, in the ordinary way, but he'd also taken on the duties of regent for the southern half. It was a lot for one man to pay attention to. And Geoffrey's own Heir, his eldest son Edmund, was still at school.

"Any additional info you can get me?" Gabe wasn't sure how far he could press here.

"I've heard rumours of several groups. Not the expected place for them. I'd have thought London, too. And yet, this predates the war, some of it. Some Rosicrucians, one of the Golden Dawn offshoots, something about an esoteric theatre. Mostly middle-class, that lot, with time to spare before the war, but Rufus has heard of a more mixed group. He'd be willing to see if they'd welcome him. That one respects the Horseman's Word." Rufus Pride was Geoffrey's head of stables, and an excellent man with a horse.

"Please, if it's not a bother. Though I suppose you'd like to know what's up."

"I'd certainly like to know who we might run into on a dark night. It's hard to keep the place safe, between the war work, the blackouts, the Home Guard, and who knows what else. I putter around keeping my ear out, but there are places I can't show my own face."

Geoffrey made light of it, but he did look the perfect slightly daft aristocrat, complete with monocle. More to the point, he sounded like one. Gabe had made a point of having other options, but he'd had his adopted aunts and uncles to help. He didn't dwell on that; Geoffrey knew his skills and limits, Gabe knew them as well. They didn't need to discuss. "And nothing of the Fatae?"

"Not of any particular note. The land seems happy enough, but of course, we're quite aware of the coastline." If there were any kind of attempt at invasion, it would almost certainly come to Hampshire and the New Forest, and to Kent, first. Gabe and his father had the same set of worries. Only part of the land they held was coastline, with the rest held by Lord and Lady Thanet, just outside Canterbury. They dealt well enough with Gabe's father, thankfully, though both of them were more overtly political than the Edgartons.

"We've been toying with ideas for warding. Stones, something of the kind. I've been trying to figure out the Vortimer legends, what seeds of truth they have in practice, in my spare time." Gabe nodded at Alexander. "You'd mentioned that set in the Council Keep. Something attuned to particular events, if we can describe them precisely enough, magically."

"I'll ask Thesan for her notes. She laid out most of the alerts in use here, these days." Isembard gestured at the castle proper. "And we've laid out a set for each of the Houses."

Something in that surprised Alexander, who raised an eyebrow.

Isembard spread his hands. "I hope we won't have a bombing raid hit us directly. I'm doing a fair bit to avoid it, besides the usual island protections." Those had been in place since about 600 AD, but they had been designed and tested against dragons rather than aeroplanes or submarines. "We want to know where the students are, which building. We're training them to touch a panel by the door of the Keep or their House, as they come and go. It maps - well. It maps onto something we can check, that should hold."

Gabe was not wrapped in the mysteries of Schola, and he was glad to leave that particular tangle for other people. But he nodded. "Whatever she can share, we'd be grateful. I've got maybe a month where I can consult Rathna, too, as she's got time."

Isembard and Geoffrey made simultaneous quiet noises, then looked at each other. Their wives were actively doing any number of things for the war effort, just as every man here was, and Isobel as well. But Thesan and Lizzie would be working where they were, in a place they knew, with all the protections that came with it. Gabe nodded once. "We'll - well. It matters."

"If that's where we are, let me run you through a few things, Gabe? I want to see if you can pick up that new approach to reading signatures." Alexander stretched slightly, and Gabe felt more than saw Isobel react to it. Alexander didn't exactly look harmless, but he had a knack for not looking nearly as terrifying as he was. This time, he'd shifted from apparently relaxed to intently focused without moving a muscle.

"Both of us?" Gabe wanted Isobel to pick this up, and he was sure he couldn't teach it half as well. He'd almost caught the knack the last time they'd tried, and Alexander thought this new approach would work better. If it did, it would make Gabe and Isobel's work vastly easier.

Alexander had managed to pick up a new trick eighteen months ago for seeing how oaths bound and crackled through someone's magic. Someone who could read that, could map, more or less, what they'd touched. Or what sort of person had done the magic. Gabe had only been able to read the land magic oaths last time, but that only made sense. It was the part that came easiest to him, it always had. With Geoffrey, Alexander, and Isembard here, he'd be able to try his hand at a much wider range.

"Both of you. Ready to see me keep your apprentice master on his toes, Mistress Thomas?" Alexander was cordial, now the essence of etiquette.

Isobel, to Gabe's great amusement, snorted. "I do that on the regular, Council Member, but I'm always glad to share that task. I'm under orders to make sure he stays busy from higher powers than himself." Witt and Mason, clearly.

"Come on, come on. If you can pick it up this time, we'll stop by a bookshop on the way into the office." It was an entirely practical sort of bribery. The three older men chuckled as Isobel grinned and got up, moving to the door and waiting for Isembard to arrange the protections in the salle.

CHAPTER 11
MARCH 3RD AT VERITAS

"Talk to me about something else, Gabe." Rathna was fussing with things, and she knew it.

Tomorrow, she would meet Ferdinand and two others in Trellech. Two of their party from the Guard had gone ahead to set things up and put together a campsite. They'd take the portal to Paris, then to Basel, so she could get readings for both, then to Amsterdam. It wouldn't be enough for what she needed. She still needed Ferdinand's feel for the German portal near his family's home to anchor it properly. But every point counted.

From Amsterdam, they'd take a train to Groningen. There, finally, someone would meet them with a carriage and supplies for the last leg of the trip. They were aiming for the south side of the Dollard, a bay that sat on the northern coast, a mile or two south from the tip of the bay, which had something of a tendency to flood. It would be two or three days of travel, depending on if they made their train connection and if the weather held.

They'd be a bare two miles from the German border, such as it was. That put them forty or so from Oldenberg and sixty from Bremen. A hundred and twenty-five from the nearest portal in Amsterdam itself. There was no quick way out if anything went wrong, not by land. The Guard had promised a ship that could plausibly cross the Channel on the northern coast. But even that was a faint hope if anything significant actually went wrong.

She shivered once, turning her back to the rest of the room as she went through the top of her dresser one last time. It was only after a moment that she remembered the mirror. Before she could turn around, she felt Gabe behind her, his hand hovering, then he murmured, "Bright lady." Still one of his favourite endearments for her. He bent to kiss her, once he was sure he wouldn't surprise her, and his arm went around her back, hand cupping her hip.

Rathna peered at the image in the mirror. "Talk to me, Gabe. About what you're working on." She lifted her free hand. "In a minute."

"Bed, then. A bit of talking. Other things. I'm not wasting the opportunity." The hand on her hip didn't squeeze. Gabe wasn't gauche about his affections, but he leaned into her, before giving her space to step back and come to bed. Their bedroom. The last time for who knew how long, if they were successful. She couldn't think about if they weren't.

By the time she joined him, Gabe had settled under the sheets. He'd somehow stripped both dressing gown and pyjamas off, leaving them over the stool on the far side of his bedside table. She did the same, more tidily, and turned back to bed, to see him watching her avidly as he pulled the sheets back for her to slip in beside him. He'd charmed them warm, bless the man.

"You spoil me." It came out sharper than she meant. Rathna didn't want anything sharp tonight.

Gabe didn't appear to notice. He tucked the blanket up over her shoulder and settled on his side, where he could see her face. "As much as I can. Always." He hesitated for just a moment, as if weighing what she'd do at the touch, the way he did with an unsettled horse, then brushed his fingertips against her cheek. "You're all a tangle. With excellent reason."

"How are you so calm?" It clicked for her, then, that he was. He'd had that restless uncertainty, the little stops and starts, for months. Thinking back, in the last week, as she'd launched into her final preparation, he'd gone still. The way he did when he duelled, when all his focus was on one thing, and one thing alone.

Gabe didn't answer her, not then. He brushed his fingers along her cheek. "What have I been up to? The Council meeting on Wednesday was a shambles, but an informative sort of shambles." He'd been invited up for the first time to make a report to the full Council, all of them who were available. They'd not had a chance to talk about it, and after all, it wasn't the sort of thing Rathna could help much with directly. Alysoun was far more deft with the dynamics, Richard and Magni with the strategy.

"You and Mason and Witt, yes?"

"And Isobel, though she kept quiet. We were in the public rooms, of course. Only those chosen few get to go in the bulk of the keep." Rathna had been there enough times, for the solstice presentations with Gabe's parents, for a bit of the dancing and other festivities. She'd been cordially ignored by most of the Council, which was better than coming to their particular attention.

"And?" Rathna didn't try to force herself to relax. That never worked, not ever. But she could slow her breath, let herself slip into feeling the room sing, the way she heard a portal. She'd attuned herself, over the years, to this room. To this manor house. Even before they'd lived here all the time.

"Huge row between the Fortiers. I gather they were due. Alexander wasn't remotely surprised." Livia Fortier was perhaps the most dangerous of the Council members from Rathna's point of view. She had exceedingly sharp and nasty ideas about proper marriages for the Lords and Ladies of the land.

Alysoun had quipped once that it was at least partly because Livia thought she'd married beneath her own family's heritage. The Fortiers might have come over in the Norman Conquest, and had a long history of service to the Crown, then to the Council, and always to the land magic. That wasn't nearly good enough for the Alveys, as one of the First Families, who had a history that went back to Roman Britain, like the Edgartons.

She half-shivered again, but this was a familiar sort of fear and distrust. Livia had never acted against her, neither directly nor through gossip and innuendo, not like some people had. But if Livia ever realised that Rathna's parents hadn't had magic, not as Albion counted it, there would be chaos.

There was no denying Rathna's own magic. It had been strong enough at twelve that she'd been plucked out of the London orphanage and sent off to Schola at thirteen. It had run deep and clear and potent enough that when Morah Avigail had come looking for any prospective apprentices, Rathna had been the only one selected out of three years of students. And her magic had served her well, ever since. It coiled around her hand, like a spinner worked with wool or silk or flax. Rathna had learned to give it shape, and she was confident in her skills as a Portal Keeper, with all the magics that went into that.

"And?" Rathna met Gabe's eyes. He was still quiet, in a way he almost never was. All of him was focused on her. That was part of it. She liked him being able to pay attention to so many things at once. And it was certainly a joy, watching him with the children. He had an unerring ability to keep track of their favourite things of the moment, without getting hung up in what they'd liked best last week or last month. Always in the moment, except when he deliberately dove back into history and precedent.

"I talked about them with Alexander, after. His townhouse, that's why I was so late back." Gabe shrugged one shoulder. "He says they have a marriage made of constant challenge and competition, even though they play on somewhat different fields. There are few better fighters than Livia."

"And Alexander would know. Being one of the others."

"Just so. Though as he says, age and experience still give him the edge." Alexander was a decade or so older than both Garin and Livia. She'd have worried he was getting too old for duelling and keeping his own skills sharp, except she'd seen him duel Gabe regularly, as well as Isembard, Garin's younger brother.

"What was the argument about?"

"She wants to go and fight. On the Continent. And on one hand, she might do some good, but on the other, it's generally a problem to send any Council Member into combat. At least without a specific good reason that supports the land magic here." Gabe spread out his hand. "And we don't exactly have that. I gather she thought about arguing her way into your little band of people, but she got talked out of it."

Rathna grimaced and then shifted, to bury her head against Gabe's chest. His arm immediately went around her back, one of his long legs stretching out against hers. "Hey." He murmured it into her ear. "You know the people going with you are fantastic. Hand-picked. Papa and Kate vouch for them all. Both their skills and their attitudes."

Two women Guards, who wouldn't have been able to enlist, and two men who'd chosen to continue serving in the Guard but who were delighted to have this assignment. They'd been training together since January. Even Richard had proclaimed them entirely up to his standards. They'd be meeting two more from the Netherlands, to help with the supporting magical work, local knowledge, and to lend vitality if needed. And generally to monitor what was going on while Rathna and Ferdinand did the work. A modest sortie party, as it went.

"Kate went through it all with me. Back when they started training." Kate was one of the steadiest of the Guard captains other than Richard, with an eye for solving complicated problems. Rathna had liked her since they'd first met, not long after Gabe had dragged her home in the midst of a costume party to meet his parents. "I know we've done everything we can."

"You have. Everyone else has. You've done all the preparation possible." Gabe swallowed hard. "Papa, and Geoffrey, and Alexander, and Isembard, and Giles, and - all the others we've consulted. They all made it through the Great War. No two wars are the same. You know what Uncle Magni says about that. But as much as any of us can be prepared, you are. You all are."

Rathna nodded slowly, just breathing in the way Gabe smelled, since she couldn't seem to pull herself away from his chest. He wasn't broad-shouldered, he never had been, but everything there was muscle and strength. He smelled like the woods around Veritas, with a hint of sharp herbs from his favourite cologne, and the faint scent of old books. She breathed it in, let out a long breath, and then finally settled on her back. "Why are you so calm? You've been so - not. Something in the meeting?"

"Before that. I think." Gabe rearranged a couple of pillows, pressing up against her side, and draping an arm over her waist above the sheet. "I think I was bouncing all over because I didn't have a good sense of the whole picture. Caught in the trees, not seeing the whole forest, not for a long time."

That made sense. Gabe had an amazing talent for pulling together dozens of different details into a swirling, cohesive whole. She'd seen him do it, over and over again. "And now?"

"I don't know. Coming into spring, something snapped into place. The land is waking, and that matters. I've got plans to go walk the bounds in the New Forest with Geoffrey, see if he picks up some of the same things I have here, without hints."

"Keep yourself busy?" Rathna said it hesitantly.

Gabe pushed himself up on his elbow, slipping his hand to brace on the other hand as he bent to kiss her. He took his time with it, all his best attention, and she let her own hand slide into his hair, wanting to soak it in. He finally pulled back, intense now. "You need to go. To save any lives you can. And prove that you're utterly brilliant to anyone who might ever have doubts, for the rest of time." He tilted his head. "Prove to them all that you're magically much more terrifying than I am."

He was ridiculous, but it made her smile. She tapped his cheek. "You'll be all right without me?"

"I'll manage. This is important. What you're doing. What I'm doing. Both of us. I'll miss you, every day, every time I get a chance to think about it. But we'll have the journals. I'll let you know how things are here, anything you want to know."

"If the mirabiles come out in the woods." They had been seen in the greening of the woods around May Day, the last decade, remarkably reliably.

"Tell them where you are, wish you home safely when it's time. I'll tell the bees all your news. All the country customs you tolerate."

That made her laugh and tug him down. "Not just tolerate, you. I had no idea I'd end up here, but..." But there was nowhere she wanted to be but in this bed, with Gabe. In his life, for all the wild tears he went on, all the chaos he sometimes trailed in his wake. She wanted his laughter, his quickness, the way he never looked at her without his love shining out. "Send me off properly."

Gabe threw his head back and laughed. "No lingering aches tomorrow. Everything else is permitted?"

"Everything else is encouraged." She had no idea what she'd get out of him, if it would be charms and enchantments that made her moan with desire, or that left her quivering in dissolute pleasure. If it would be comforting or energetic. Whatever it was, she trusted he'd read her, what she needed, and give her his all. He always had.

She could hold on to that, whatever the future days held.

CHAPTER 12
MARCH 6TH IN THE NEW FOREST

"What are you trying to sort out, sir?" Isobel caught herself before Gabe could say anything in reply. "Pardon, sorry, not that." He expected her to apologise for overstepping. She had a tendency to do that, even when she hadn't. Instead, she shook her head as if to clear it. "I know what you're working on. My question is about the mode."

"The mode?" They were in the New Forest, about at the midpoint, having borrowed horses from Geoffrey for what could pretend to be a pleasant ride. They were skirting well away from the towns with better connections to the outside world, like Brockenhurst.

"You're..." Isobel pulled her mare to a stop, and Gabe did the same. "You were all over the place, sir, before. And then you were settled. And now you're not, again, but it's different. Is it just Mistress Rathna being gone?"

"You don't have to use the title, you know." Gabe knew he wouldn't win this particular battle with Isobel's formality, though he was going to utterly treasure the moment she referred to him just as Edgarton. Whenever that came.

"Sir." That was amused and disapproving, both, and she didn't bother to comment further. "What I can't make out is why it's different. Obviously, you're worried."

"I am. They were likely to get to Donnart today if all went well, she hasn't had time to write much. They got held up in both Basel and Amsterdam, people wanting to be difficult about the papers, and then they needed a bit of quiet with the portals. Which was, you know, midnight or something like that." Gabe pulled his cap off his head, and ran his hand through his hair. Then he reached back to arrange the braid so it sat tidily and wouldn't be too obvious.

He kept to the old custom of Albion, that hair held power, and kept his long. The length of it was tucked down the back of his shirt again. Isobel did the same, but it was far more common for women than men, even in this era of curls and waves and even a fringe. He might well need to cut it if they had to mingle more, but he hoped not.

The mare he was riding stamped once, and he grinned. "Up for a bit more of a ride? I was thinking to circle by Burley, see what I feel. Or - hmmm. Depends on your stamina."

Isobel stretched slightly. "Which means we're going to be out for hours, if I say yes."

"You do know me." Gabe grinned, cheered, a bit despite himself. "We're in Bolderwood, now. I'd like to go down to the Naked Man."

"Pub, landmark, or someone who really ought to reconsider his choices, seeing as how it's early March after the coldest winter in near a century?"

. Gabe let out a barking laugh. "Landmark. A particular tree, in this case. Stump of a tree." He gestured. "If we make a large circle, it's about a twenty-mile ride. Though there's a good pub on the way back, Rufus says. We can stop in there for a pint and something to eat."

"So, five hours or so at a walk. This is one of your fiendish plans to get me comfortable doing an extended trot and canter, isn't it?" She was a perfectly reasonable rider, about Rathna's current standard, but she needed to build stamina and confidence. Not everyone had to match Gabe's skill. Or his father's or Geoffrey's or Rufus's. On the other hand, it was the lot of a Penelope to need to get places quickly that were not handy to a portal. And seeing as that was how he'd met Rathna, it often had unexpected benefits besides.

"It might be. You know how I like to have a thing that's useful in half a dozen ways." Gabe waited to see what she did with that.

Isobel let out a long, beleaguered sigh. He'd felt a lot better about her insistence on the formal title when she'd started doing that. Quite early on, though, he was fairly sure it was after Doyle had a talk with Isobel. His own apprentice mistress had opinions about Gabe and what was good for him, as was right and proper. And Mason and Witt would have left that bit of education in managing the chaos that was Gabe to Doyle. She had first dibs. "All right. I'll cope."

Gabe had been about to ride off, but he tightened his legs, without really thinking about it, and shifted his weight. The mare he was riding backed up until he was parallel to Isobel. "You could stay at Veritas, you know."

He'd managed to completely wrong-foot her. Delightful. Glorious, in fact. One of the things he liked about her very much as an apprentice was that he had to work for that.

"I couldn't. It's not proper." Her voice had gone breathy.

"You're my apprentice. We've been in far more improper places." They were at what, five months in a tent or a bothy or a rundown cottage on cases at this point if he added it all up. "And it's not as if there aren't plenty of other people around the place. The guest rooms are on the far side from mine. The food's better."

"That's not a high bar to get over." The refectory wasn't horrible, but they were cooking things that had to hold for a long meal period and an unknown number of people eating. "You can't just invite someone like that."

"Yes, I can. Mama suggested it a while ago, actually, but up until now we've mostly been working from Trellech. If you're out at Veritas, we don't have to wait for that portal unless we need the office." His logic was impeccable.

He could see Isobel was thinking about arguing with him. "If I say yes, what am I in for?"

"Lots of discussions in the library. Plenty of working through notes. Probably me blowing up the workroom once a fortnight or so. You can help. That's about my current average. You can watch me duelling, and we can keep getting your skills up. Without having half the Guard watching." There had been a tremendous amount of that. It soaked up all the spare time Gabe might have once had.

"That's an incentive." She didn't like being watched, Gabe had discovered. He didn't exactly care to show off his skills, but he didn't mind informed viewers.

"And a very nice soaking bath. I mean, the ones in the suites are fine, but there's the Roman bath. You have to pry Mama out of there with a stick some days. Nothing better after a long day in the field."

"You're not making this easy. No one will, I mean." She ground to a stop.

"Half the Penelopes have entirely unusual sorts of

personal arrangements. More than half, I haven't actually counted up recently." He shrugs. "This one is actually terrifyingly traditional. It's odd we don't have you live with your apprentice master or mistress, like most apprenticeships."

"Because," Isobel pointed out, "of all those unusual arrangements. Also, the usual difficulty of finding a spare bedroom that isn't covered with books, turned into an alchemy laboratory, or whatever it is Mason does with paints and inks. Or something else."

"She also has a darkroom and a stillroom. Though, admittedly, only by sacrificing what used to be the box room." Gabe nodded and said. "Talk as we ride?"

She got her horse walking, and Gabe fell in beside her. They were on one of the smaller paths, and just had to keep an eye out for the local livestock. "Will it help you if I'm there?"

That was a very clear-eyed question. Gabe nodded once. "It will. I mean, I'll try not to drag you out of bed, metaphorically speaking. I'd just bang on your door or something. But some of my best ideas come at odd times."

Isobel looked him up and down. "All right. I'll have to pack my things. Not tonight, even if the bath is tempting. Tomorrow."

"I can get someone to come by the apprentice dorms with a cart. Ten?"

She snorted. "Nine. We'll have a full day's work. If that's not a bother for them." Her voice got an odd note. "I'm not—"

"The apprentice rooms have staff. Just a bit different. You know we make sure everyone's treated well, that they can get the education and training to move on to other things if they want." He felt more than a bit embarrassed sometimes at the sheer number of staff Veritas employed, but many of them insisted they'd rather be there than elsewhere. They did treat people well, and the work was varied, with everything from Mama's parties to Papa's magisterial duties to Gabe dragging people home to talk with them at length.

"How much managing your files am I in for?" That was also an excellent question from her, really. And not one of his good skills.

"I could, in fact, use someone to make sure I'm not late for half a dozen meetings a week. And that the stacks of files on my desk get reduced over time rather than toppling." Finding things in files was, at least often enough, exciting. Putting them back was decidedly not.

"Still." Gabe watched her, thoughtful now. She'd certainly shaped herself into a distraction to get him to settle, and he had no idea if she'd done it deliberately. Isobel wasn't exactly disapproving, but she saw a shape to the thing that he didn't quite, and that was exceedingly interesting. "All right."

They rode along in agreeable silence for a bit, first at a walk. They picked up a comfortable trot once they got over the road that cut through the New Forest, and into the woods beyond. The ground was smooth enough they could have a reasonable canter. It meant they pulled up to the Naked Man at about one.

"So, landmark, then. What was it?"

Gabe pulled up his mare to a tree stump covered in ivy. It had been a massive tree, once upon a time, but a stump as long as Geoffrey had been alive, and then some. "A gibbet, when it was still standing. For smugglers and highwaymen, so the legend goes."

He heard the footsteps before anything else and forced himself not to turn with his usual reflexes. He did make it obvious to Isobel, and they'd not said anything that might cross the Pact. There was a man behind them, wearing a uniform, but by himself. "Afternoon."

Gabe nodded back. "We were out for a bit of a ride." He didn't give his name. There were plenty of reasons not to. "I've been by this grand old former tree a few times. I wanted to show him off."

The other man grunted. "Moving on, then?"

"Oh, got to get the horses back in time for their tea." Gabe knew how Geoffrey made use of the slightly foolish aristocrat mode, and he could certainly do the same thing. "They're some of Geoffrey Carillon's. He was kind enough to lend them." He didn't use the title, as he was reasonably sure this man was not Albion.

"Ah." That got another grunt. Also not informative. "Heard a bit about him." He looked the mares up and down, but without a particularly trained eye. "Isn't that rather far?"

"Thought we'd make the most of it when it wasn't actually raining." Gabe shrugged. There was something about this that was odd. Or rather, several things that were odd, and he wanted to count them up properly. "We should get on." He'd hoped to have Isobel get a sense for the land here, but they could pick some other location for that. Perhaps they could circle back that way after the pub. "Ready?" That was directly to Isobel, of course.

"G'day." It was gruff, uncompromising. Gabe waited for Isobel to get her mare going. They kept it at a leisurely walk until they were well away.

"Was that as queer as I thought it was?" Isobel's voice was conversational. "What was he up to?"

"He was in uniform. I've heard rumblings - so has Geoffrey - about Brockenhurst being used for things. It's on a train line, the roads are decent. We weren't too far away. But what they'd want with that bit of clearing, I've no idea."

"And you wanted me to do something there, didn't you? Blast. Why do people have to be so, so pervasive?"

The tone in her voice, that mix of baffled annoyance, made Gabe laugh. "It's a rather large forest, and yet, you keep tripping over people. Come on, pub, and then we can circle up back by the Knightwood Oak, and see if we have more luck there."

"How do you know all this?" Isobel picked up a slow jogging trot. She was getting better at riding to it, excellent.

"Flung myself on Geoffrey and Rufus's superior knowledge. I don't need to know everything in the world. I just need to know who does." It was, in fact, one of the keys to what any Penelope did. They all knew a great deal, but no one knew everything, and he had no shame in asking for expert advice. Especially, particularly, when it came to local magic.

The trick, always, was figuring out who was actually an expert, and who was pretending to be.

CHAPTER 13
MARCH 7TH NEAR GRONINGEN

Rathna took a deep breath. They were here, actually here, after four days of travel and three uncomfortable nights in transit. Here was, well, a bit of formless farmland. It flooded fairly regularly, but at the moment it was dry enough underfoot.

There was a hut off to one side, their home for the next weeks or months, possibly more. Not a large hut, mind, and that was going to be an interesting challenge. The Guard were already looking at striking tents in the lee of the house, where they'd be protected from the wind off the bay and the ocean, further away. Rathna was getting a sense of the land in the quieter ways. Each to their own work. She had to keep telling herself that.

She was glad to be here, but she'd learned things from the travel. Ferdinand had been quiet, but steadfastly polite throughout. She was glad he had turned out that way. She'd been spoiled by her travels with Gabe, who met every unexpected moment with delight rather than irritation. One of the Guards with them, Lucas, had got more and more frustrated at each delay. It never helped, and certainly not when Rathna was relying on a number of favours in many directions.

Ferdinand had been a help there, taking the man off to round up some more food and drink for their train trip, and coming back with quite decent meat rolls. She was travelling. It was a war. She would not worry too much about where the meat came from, or that it certainly had pork. Rathna avoided beef, and anything from pigs or shellfish when she could, but she'd deliberately avoided making oathed commitments about that. There were times when that kind of choice wasn't an option.

And here, well. It would mark her in complicated and quite possibly dangerous ways to stand out like that. More than she already was. The other members of their party, bar one, were all nearly as pale as Ferdinand, though Beth had red hair, rather than blonde or brown.

The exception was a cousin at one or two removes of Elizabeth Mason's, with the same brown skin, with a tad more yellow to it than Rathna's own. Grietje was maybe thirty, thirty-five at most, with the sort of vigour that suggested she rambled or biked across vast distances for amusement. She thankfully spoke impeccable English as well as Dutch, and apparently also German and French. She'd taken over as their local contact immediately on meeting them in Groningen with a cart.

Rathna closed her eyes for a long moment, reaching to hear the land under her. This was the part she hadn't been sure about, couldn't be sure about, until they were actually here. There was only so much the geological maps could provide, because, well, geologists weren't looking for the same things at all. And for another, even if there had been some Portal Keeper here, in the past, they'd have felt the land differently.

Here, she had to feel her way through the water, the way everything around here was affected by and tuned to the water. It was not a bog, but it was not solid, either. There was something up to the northwest she couldn't make sense of yet. Rathna just listened, let everything be still around her. Yes. She could do this. If they could align things properly. It would hold.

Better than the trials in Albion, perhaps. The water had reach, and this land was used to the water. There was a flexibility here that might do very well. It had a hum to it, a little motif repeating, ebbing, then rolling in stronger again. She half-sang it under her breath.

When she opened her eyes again, Grietje was standing in front of her, just waiting. Rathna must have looked foolish. There was no elegant way to do that kind of deep magical work sometimes. But Grietje wasn't mocking. She waited until Rathna focused on her. "An orientation, magistra?"

"Rathna, please do. And yes. Have I been holding you up?"

Grietje's eyes danced. "Aunt Lies told me you would say that. No, not at all. The tents are up. Let me show you the hut?" They walked together to the hut, which Grietje had arranged. There were two tiny bedrooms, each with two single beds. Rathna's bag was at the end of hers, and Grietje gestured at the other. "If you don't mind my taking the other bed? Constance said she preferred the loft."

There was indeed a small loft over the kitchen area, but Rathna had gathered Constance liked smaller enclosed spaces. "Whatever suits you both best." Rathna gestured. "Honestly, I'm surprised we're not all in tents."

"A bit of a foundation is good, against the water." Grietje gestured off toward the bay. "This is sturdy. We have a fireplace. If it rains very hard or gets cold again, the Guards can sleep on the floor. We can store the supplies there." A small covered hutch area in the back had held the winter's firewood, and by now, in March, there was plenty of room to store the crates of supplies. "Nelis or I will go to Groningen every fourth day for mail and supplies. Fresh milk and cheese and whatever else is needed."

Rathna nodded. "Shall we gather everyone else up, then?" This kind of information was something everyone needed to hear more than once. They were isolated, a bare two miles from the German border. They'd need to be prepared for a range of problems.

Five minutes later, they were settled with beer and cheese and bread, as the near enough equivalent to tea time. A stew was cooking over the fireplace. Nelis had apparently started it that morning, and it smelled honestly delicious. "We begin with safety then, Magistra, if I may."

Rathna nodded her agreement, but Grietje began somewhere Rathna hadn't quite expected. "The Fatae walk here. I have had it explained to me, more than once, that you are not at all familiar with this. You do not know the customs. You should not be out in the dark. You do not know the safe ways of being in the dark."

Rathna considered that. "What sort of dangers?"

"Go no further than the necessary." There was an outhouse, five yards or so from the hut itself. "The hut and the ground around to the brush, is warded. But no further."

Everyone else was silent. Rathna had expected this, or at least something like it. And she had experience in India, where things were much the same, where people had to keep the folklore, the ancient customs, in mind. That was how to avoid giving offence, or being cursed, or something else unwanted.

"What manner of Fatae, and is there anything in particular to do or not do?"

"Here, in specific? There may be Börries. They are like a dog, a, what do you call it. Hell dog?"

"Hellhound. Like some of our moor legends, then." Rathna supplied the word easily.

"So." Grietje went on. "Like a large poodle, their eyes are fire, and they walk, so. One side, then the other." It was like a horse who paced, the two right legs then the two left. "If you see them, it is best to be still. Don't blink. Let it go by, as it will. It may have other creatures with it, headless calves or dancing juffers."

The first one, Rathna could make sense of. Before she could ask about the other, Ferdinand spoke up. "Pardon, but what are those, the dancing juffers?"

"They are, they are ladies. Witte Wieven. Also widde juvvers." Grietje shifted, leaning her elbows on her knees. "There are the white ladies and the black ladies. The white ladies are - you have white ladies, ghosts, yes?"

Ferdinand nodded. Rathna supposed he came from the sort of family home that had them. Grietje went on. "They wear white, often torn or dirty dresses, and they may come three together. They are Fatae, elves, near enough. We do not know how they name themselves. When they are kind, they may help with harvest or babies. But they can also steal milk, tempt men into death from their lusts, lure men and women into the swamp, steal babies. One does not know what they want on any given night."

"We do not have the skills to bargain with them. Staying away - and polite - is definitely the safer thing." Rathna glanced around and saw the others nodding. "Are there others?"

"There is the Zwarte Juffer, the Black Lady. She wears

119

black, she looks like a woman mourning, weeping and wailing. If you see her, you have this tale too, I think? Someone in your family will die soon. Let her pass, if you do see her." Grietje considered. "You have shapeshifters in Albion, yes? We have them too, nachtmerries and weerwolven." Rathna could make out the language there well enough.

"And the wards will hold against them?"

"Oh, yes. They are very good wards. Nelis and I know our work well." Grietje seemed proud of that. "There are questions? No? Magistra, then, the project."

Rathna laid it out, thoroughly. The first step, which might take days or even a fortnight, was to find the ideal spot for the portal, which would mean testing the flow of the surrounding magic. Then, they would need to begin constructing it, making it out of will and magic and stones to shape the frame, shaping it bit by bit. The Guards were here to make sure they were not interrupted.

They had permission to be here, to do this work, from the Dutch government, but still, it was delicate. From there, they would align the portal, and with any luck, open it. If that worked, when they did, they could bring people across the border and whisk them to safety, or open it perhaps to one of the portals deeper in Germany.

That led to a few questions, but by and large, they would have to get settled into the work to figure out the next steps in detail. The survey first, everything else later. Once they had all had a quite tasty stew, Rathna checked that it was permissible to look at the stars outside, from outside the hut, and went out. The others were talking, getting to know Nelis and Grietje better.

Rathna looked up into the dark. Everything was a little off where she expected it to be, but not so much as all that. She found it soothing to know where she was in relation to the cosmos. Tiny, insignificant, but located in space and time. Rathna traced the lines of the constellations, over and over again, like working prayer beads through her fingers.

She heard the step behind her, and the sound of the hut door closing quietly. "May I join you, Mistress Rathna?" Ferdinand spoke quietly, not disrupting the calm out here.

"If you like, yes. Or did you have a question?" Privacy was going to be in short supply for the duration. They'd need to talk about how to signal they wanted it or needed it.

"Not exactly, mistress." He waited to see if she'd say something, then he went on. "Does it scare you? The Fatae, being right there? Without the Pact?"

Ah, that was what had got to him. "You've been to Germany. They are much the same, the Fatae are not bound except by what local treaties and agreements were made. This is no different. India is no different. Albion is unusual, in how that happened. And the places the empire has touched more heavily."

"India." She looked up, because his tone was utterly neutral, to see him testing it. When she smiled, he relaxed.

"You had told me what it would mean to be here. But it was not real until..." He gestured back at the front room of the hut. "Mistress, I am afraid I will do something wrong."

Ah, there was the crux of it. This was a young man who had always done things right. More than that, he had always known what the right thing was. His crisis of identity was, honestly, right on time. And, to be fair, this was not a bad time for it to fall. The survey work, he was entirely competent at, they'd done that together already.

"First, you follow Grietje's instructions. Ask her more, in private. If you are not sure how to do that, I will let her know you might ask." She was certain Grietje would be willing. She might tease, a little. Grietje was decidedly Aunt Mason's cousin that way, but she would tell him what he needed. "And as to the work, you listen to what I tell you, and you ask questions if you are not sure about anything. I will ask you questions as well, to make sure you understand."

"Mistress." That was a tad more relaxed, as if giving him the guidance was a help.

She nodded. "You know the surveying and you're excellent with the details. The feeling will come, and we are not relying on you for that here." She was confident if he kept going, he would grasp it. That might not be on this trip, and she couldn't see out into the future, not at all, but she knew it was something he could come to trust.

"You seem as if you know, mistress." There was a careful note in his voice now, leaning into it. Being willing to be a tad more vulnerable. She had not pressed him on that, for all she thought it was necessary to make a proper apprenticeship work. It wasn't something she could rush, and he was in a very different position than she had been, or than Mhairi and Petrus had been.

"I do have some experience." She smiled at him, as she said it. "Though, may I ask? Why did you apprentice, originally?" There were a great many possible answers, and she did not know which ones were true for him.

Ferdinand gathered himself up, like a bird settling his feathers. "They asked, and I did not have another particular focus." There was a tiny silence, then he added, "It seemed interesting."

Which said something, and nothing, all at once. Rathna let her own pleasure at the work show as she said, "It is. Or at least I think so. What did your parents think of it?"

"A bit surprised. They don't - they don't understand

what I do. I am the youngest. They did not have expectations for me. There is respect for the Portal Keepers, though they complained, before the war began, about my hours. How it keeps me from the various parties and balls and galas and events." His voice wavered slightly on the last words, and Rathna rather suspected he didn't care too much for them. She was fairly sure the Howards would arrange a suitable match for him, one way or another, but in the meantime, there would be the illusion of choice and the obligation to make one.

Rathna nodded. "The social obligations. I manage by only going to the most necessary ones, or the ones I will actually enjoy. And when there is not a war, when I am not at some remote portal to tend it, it is easy enough to arrange things. I do what is needed, come home and change and go out." He could have a hope of a reasonably ordinary sort of life, after the war, as much as any of them did.

"My parents think it a bit queer, maybe. Not that Mama would say it that way. Portal Keepers are known to be a tad, um."

"Many things." Rathna snorted. "Demanding. Odd. Too mystical for our own good. Obsessive. Not around." She waved a hand. "Especially when we're younger, and more able to do the travel. I am, on the whole, grateful to have stretches where I am not living in some small cottage or bothy or what have you. But at the same time, what we do matters tremendously. I like knowing I have done my part to make it work. Done my work well, so people can rely on it."

She was fairly sure that if Ferdinand felt any of that, he had not yet begun to articulate it to himself. Davis Fortnum almost certainly had assumed it, the way he assumed Ferdinand drank tea. Because it was what people like Davis did.

Not an evil man, not even bigoted. But, in Rathna's eyes, a tad short-sighted on a number of fronts. "Gabe explained something to me, not long after we met. He was the Penelope assigned to assist, up in Glencoe, when the portal stopped working."

"I read about that, but some of the records were sealed. Some kind of interference?" Rathna did like how Ferdinand did his research, when he had a chance and perhaps a bit of a prod.

She nodded. "There was a court case, that's the sealed part, people had been illegally mining a magically load-bearing mineral seam." She heard his sharp inhale as he put together the seriousness of that. "Gabe pointed out that the infrastructure of Albion relies on us. More than trains or roads or barges or anything else. There are only so many portals, and back then, even fewer of us to tend them." They'd got their numbers back up over the past fifteen years or so, but only after a great deal of effort.

"My parents just assume the portals will work. That it is, well. Routine work. Respectable, because the magical talents are noteworthy, but something like one of the people working in the Halls of Justice."

"Who work quite hard, mind. But no." Rathna glanced at him, to find him unreadable, and went on anyway. It was as good an opportunity as she was likely to get to start him thinking about this. "We have a particular - and uncommon - gift for this strand of magic. But that doesn't make us better people, or more worthy in any way. It does mean that we should know our value, and decide what we are going to do with it. Do we turn that gift to service? Or to selfishness or idleness and waste?"

There. That would do very well to get him working on that particular challenge. He took a long breath and let it out, then he murmured. "May I think on that, Mistress Rathna?"

"Of course. Let me know when you'd like to talk more. I'll leave you to it, I wanted to write Gabe before it gets too late." She left him there, looking up at the dark starry sky.

CHAPTER 14

APRIL 5TH IN A PUB IN CANTERBURY

"We should have thought through this plan better. Sir." The last was not exactly grudging, but rather uncertain.

"Uncle Gabriel." Gabe was settled in a back booth in a pub in Canterbury called the Fox and Seven Stars, which had quite an interesting history, actually. Isobel looked like a suitable sort of niece, with her hair up in a tidy braid around the crown of her head. It made her look younger, certainly, though still an adult. Gabe was in tweeds, relaxed. "There we are." It was just past two, plenty of time for a casual meeting.

They'd talked through this as much as it was possible to talk through a plan like this. Gabe had found he had to run the thing on instinct, and that was the thing that couldn't be planned. He couldn't teach it either, he could just teach Isobel to trust her own intuition, if they were both lucky with it.

The long and short of it was that there were a number of groups making efforts, magically, in the war. Gabe sorted them roughly in his head into magical orders, fraternal orders, witches, eccentric ceremonialists, and downright batty. None of them had done anything terribly dangerous to anyone so far, but none of them had done anything obviously effective, either. Angelic visions aside.

He lifted his hand as the older man turned around, scanning the pub. Right on the first try, there was the single white rosebud in the lapel, matching the one in Gabe's own. Mistletoe was tricky to get at this time of year, for one thing. As the man came closer, Gabe nodded at the small gold tiepin in the shape of a sickle. "Good evening. Mister North, I presume?" He wore an older suit, made five or six years ago, but well-tended, and a worn wedding band on one hand, a signet of some kind on the other.

The older man nodded, then glanced at Isobel. Gabe offered his hand. "Gabriel Edgarton. I'm down near Maidstone. This is Isobel. I do appreciate your time, sir."

It got another grunt, then North settled into the other side of the booth, peering at them both. "Not what I expected." He was gruff, as Gabe judged it, and likely in some modest amount of pain from something like arthritis. It had the clipped sound.

"I hope you didn't have to come far? The weather gets my mother terribly this time of year. Me too, actually." It was a risk, but Gabe thought it a reasonable one. North's face hardened, then softened as Gabe moved his hand to brush the top of the cane resting beside him.

"The War?" North immediately clarified. "The Great War?" There being a current war on, of course.

Gabe shook his head. He wouldn't lie about it, not if he had any choice. "I turned eighteen in the spring of 1918. An injury then, before I could have enlisted. But it means I can't go to the fighting now, so I'm looking for a way to be a help."

"Ah." North weighed some information. "I asked around about you. Why'd you come up here, if you're from down Maidstone way? There's a lodge nearer there, too."

"I gather you've had a more forward approach to mutual aid." Here was where it got delicate. "Not just the usual sort of fete and games and knitting, though that's all important too, of course. I can do my bit there, but Isobel and I wanted to do a bit more, and we were given your name as the man to talk to."

It earned Gabe another grunt, and then he peered at Isobel. "We're a fraternal order, young man." To be fair, Gabe was some twenty years younger than North. Maybe more like thirty. And it wasn't as if Gabe would let that get in the way of his goal.

"I'm very keen, sir. Uncle Gabriel said that you—" She flushed, charmingly. "I mean, everyone has to do their bit, right? And there are the days of prayer, and those letters from London, but I wanted something a bit more direct." She glanced down at the table, then back up. "My mum's family is from up in Yorkshire, Granda was a cunning man."

"Ah." That got them both a thoughtful sound, a bit more than a grunt. "And you, Edgarton?"

"Well. I do have an eye to Isobel's safety. She's something of a niece by marriage. Meeting someone in a pub is one thing, but I'm glad to tag along and see her safely to whatever. I might have a bit of interest myself, though she's had more time to read up on the thing. But it's really not a thing you can just read up on, I'm sure." He kept his accent middle-brow, the sort of thing that a craftsman or businessman might manage. Educated, but not top-rank. "Need to get your hands in the dirt and all that."

North looked him up and down, but then he nodded

once. "I know a man. Do you have anywhere you need to be this evening? A bus to catch?"

Gabe shook his head. "Need to get along for the blackout, but we're good until six or so." That was nicely ambiguous.

"Right. Might have someone for you to meet. Let me toddle along and see if he's got time this afternoon. The darts game is usually decent if you want to join in."

Gabe nodded, agreeably. He wouldn't play darts. It was not the best of his skills, but there was enough in common between duelling and darts that his aim would be remarked on, and he didn't want to be noticed like that. He had learned the lesson about darts long ago in Scotland, though admittedly, he'd stuck out and been notable in Scotland for other reasons as well.

Instead, he and Isobel settled into agreeable conversation, nothing that would be a problem if it were overheard. Gabe had done a check-in at the home farm the day before, and so he could chat about chickens and the crops they were planning to put in. They were in public, so he minded his tongue talking about the pigs. The home farm was under Albion's guidelines, of course, not the War Ag proper. Magic, the fuel needed to work magic, meant bits of the restrictions ran by different rules. In this case, more support for pigs so they'd have more meat to send along to help support the Temple of Healing and those in magical service.

About an hour later, when Gabe was already well on the way to twitchy, Mister North came back in with a man. They went to the bar, and then North came over to them. "Give us a chance for a drink, then how about a walk outside? Take a right, down to the river, west along the river to Greyfriars Gardens."

"Sir." Gabe nodded, agreeably. They finished up their drinks and made their way out without looking rushed. Isobel was twitchy at this point too, and Gabe couldn't decide if it was on her own account, or because he was. Probably both. Once they were well away from other people, he cleared his throat. "Am I being too much?"

"Uncle." That had a definitely teasing note. "You were getting a tad obvious, fidgeting."

Gabe sighed. "It - well." Isobel knew why he was on edge. They didn't need to talk about it. And shouldn't, here, anyway. Rathna had been away for a month and four days. He missed her more every day, and he was sure Avigail did as well. For all he was the one at home, it wasn't helping.

He saw all the places Rathna should be and wasn't. No rides together, now the spring was coming in. No times when she was settled in the observation chairs in the salle, watching him duel or run through exercises on his own. No time in their sitting room, or the library, working on their own projects, but together. Certainly no teasing him about the amount of coffee he'd gone through. Absolutely no being there in bed, warm and soft and present.

It was a little tricky, too, socially. He'd escorted his mother, twice, to social events when Papa wasn't available, and there had been the predictable questions. "On war work, doing her bit," certainly covered a lot of ground, but people got curious. Gabe couldn't begrudge the curiosity, but he certainly couldn't indulge it in anyone else. Far too much risk for Rathna and everyone she was with.

But the work was going well, as much as Rathna had been able to tell so far. It was a faster process, what she was trying, but it was still a matter of weeks, even months, rather than days. They'd got the foundation work solidly established. She was making adjustments for the amount of water in the land. Ferdinand was being quite a help, and the rest of the party were settling into their roles well. They were taking all due care, and they were skilled professionals, but Gabe wasn't there and he wanted to be. He missed her, even though they'd been apart longer in their marriage before. He hadn't liked it much then, either.

He'd have gone spare without the journals, where at least they could check in as they could. At least he could wish her happy dreams, or tell her about whatever was on his mind. Often enough there was a flurry of brief notes that led to some brand new idea, and he'd have to come back and explain why he stopped writing.

"Sir?" That was Isobel clearing her throat. "They're coming." They'd found a bench in the park in the green in the centre of the Greyfriars Gardens. Gabe had been here, mostly with his father, a few times, when talking to the Thanets on what was more or less neutral ground. The gardens went with an ancient almshouse, for all it was in the centre of Canterbury proper, and the centre of their demesne lands.

Gabe stood as the two men approached. Mister North nodded. "Peter Douglas, Gabriel Edgarton and his niece, Isobel. I'll leave you to it." North turned around and made his way back toward the cathedral, more or less.

Douglas nodded once. "Why should I talk to you?" Gabe appreciated the bluntness.

"We've both heard a rumour here or there of people doing more direct work, on an esoteric level, to keep Hitler where he ought to be. Well, ideally out of power entirely, but one step at a time." Gabe was running on pure instinct again. He was reading in a dozen ways he'd never be able to explain - though he'd try later tonight - that this was no time to dance around the topic. Peter Douglas wasn't of

Albion, Gabe would have sworn it, besides the fact he had a decent idea of the local magical community. But he had a touch of something to him. Cunning folk, quite possibly. Interesting.

"Ah." Peter Douglas settled on the bench they'd been occupying, and Gabe let Isobel have the other seat, as was proper, standing beside the other arm. "Both of you?"

"I promised her parents I'd keep an eye out for her, but Isobel's quite able to make her own decisions." This was a delicate line. There were trends in the witchcraft groups they'd heard about, about younger women having more of an entry to the private rituals. Youth and beauty and all that, though not necessarily in a salacious way. Isobel was quite capable of protecting herself, magically and other-wise. She was better with a memory clouding charm than Gabe was, honestly.

"We are planning something for May first. I'd need to discuss, before sharing any details." He was carefully avoiding using names. That was interesting, but he was focused on Isobel. "Would there be a way to reach you for a meeting, Miss?"

"Certainly." Isobel pulled out a small card. "I can get letters there, quite promptly." She'd given the London drop. That would get sent along to their office in Trellech quickly if anything turned up.

"And do you have any experience with such things?" Douglas leaned back.

"My Granda, up in Yorkshire, was a cunning man. Mum picked up a few things, but - well. I'm staying with Uncle Gabriel at the moment." She was playing it up nicely. "And I do want to do my bit, and..." She glanced down, then back up. "I miss it. The little I knew. I'm eager to learn, sir."

That earned her a little harrumph but also a nod. Douglas considered. "What do you know then?"

It was tricky. Gabe had talked with Isobel about the options here, about how to play it. "Granda did a fine line in rheumatism cures, sir. Finding lost things. Dancing in a circle, at night."

Another grunt. "But you've not been brought in fully?"

"No, sir. Is that - would that be a problem?"

There was a long pause, as if Douglas was counting up numbers, weighing something. "Not for May. We need the energy, more than anything else." His gaze flicked over to Gabe. "Energy, yes. You can escort her to the meeting place, sir, if you wish, but no further."

Gabe nodded once. "And a meeting before?"

Douglas shook his head. "Probably not. I'll see what my lady says." A particular term of endearment, perhaps, or a title. "Look for a note next week. Likely Tuesday or Wednesday. You can get to Canterbury easily, even for something at night?"

"Sir. So long as it isn't terribly often. I can take the day for the first. Or I suppose overnight, from the thirtieth?"

It got her another approving nod. Gabe would be able to escort her that far, probably, but he'd have his own obligations for May Day. Papa could manage the land rites on his own. But they both preferred to ride the bounds fully if at all possible, and that went much faster with both of them.

There was a pause, neither of them speaking. Then, almost grudgingly, Douglas added. "I'll speak to my lady about you, as well, sir."

"Appreciated." Gabe left it at that. That would be even trickier, but if that was on offer, he'd make it work somehow.

"Right. Good to meet you. Look for a letter." Abruptly,

Douglas stood up and offered his hand. They both shook and then watched him turn and walk off.

"Well. Something worked him up a bit in there. I wonder what. Come along, we'll retreat and find our tea." Gabe wanted to think about the byplay there a great deal more. And write to Rathna about it, to sort it out in his own head and to get whatever ideas she might have.

CHAPTER 15
APRIL 9TH NEAR GRONINGEN

"Is it supposed to be doing that?" Ferdinand eyed the arch of the portal warily. It was not complete, yet. They still had a couple of weeks of work if everything went well, but it was beginning to draw in ambient magic, with little flickers and sparks.

Rathna grinned, running her hand through her hair to get the wisps out of her face. "It's a good sign. Don't touch it yet, though." She stretched, feeling one of her shoulders pop. "I'll want my working stones next. Let me warm my hands up a bit first."

To be honest, she was very pleased with their progress. She'd done this now four times, and each time it got easier. There was a song to a portal, or rather a class of songs. She got better and faster at refining the one for a particular portal each time. This one had a slightly melancholy mode to it, not a minor. Dorian, maybe, rolling through harmonies that echoed in ways not common in modern music. And by modern, she meant the last five hundred years or so.

The stones were all in place, though. They were

anchored sturdily, well into the ground beneath them. They didn't need to be touching bedrock, not for what they were doing, and that was good, because there was a fair bit of boggy earth beneath them. Trees wouldn't have done well, but they'd been able to find suitable stones from a ruined wall that were doing nicely. Nelis had even found a local mason to carve something for a keystone.

They'd placed that two days ago, with a mix of magic and scaffolding. The keystone had slotted into place perfectly, with a satisfying magical click. Ferdinand had looked at her, baffled. "You understand stone?"

She'd shrugged. She'd done more with it than most of the Portal Keepers, but they should all have the skills. "Carving it? I don't have the precision I'd like with stone, but we'll make sure you get time learning the basics. And the different woods, too." Though, to be fair, they tended toward a couple of trees for portals. Oak, yew, ash, most commonly, though she knew portals from two dozen other species. Water was a different trick. But learning how to understand the local water was a skill he needed.

She was still standing there, considering, when Beth, one of the Guards, came across. "Rathna? You want your journal. There's news. War, not personal." That was good. Well, not good, but Rathna's heart had stuttered at that. One of the Guards was always monitoring the journals for news of changes in the larger world that might affect them.

Rathna wheeled on her heel, going back to the hut for her journal, and flicking it open. She'd got access to the Guard news journal, which did regular updates, focusing on security implications. Because of Richard, she was quite sure. There was a new entry there, and she saw that the glowing notifiers that indicated messages from Alysoun and Gabe were both lit as well.

The Guard summary laid out that there were German attacks in progress on both Denmark and Norway, starting very early that morning. It looked like they might be successful, and quite quickly. Rathna wondered, suddenly, how many layers that had come through, and how that worked, for them to get the information so rapidly, it was only just past lunchtime.

Denmark, though. Denmark was not far away at all. Germany was between them, but if Germany were moving up north, would the Netherlands be far behind? They were running out of time, in a race that had always been short on it. Rathna made a prayer, for the safety of all who could find it, and repeated it two more times before she flipped first to Alysoun's entry.

It was, as she'd known it would be, all analysis. A very early one, yet, of course. Alysoun would be working from the same material as the Guard. But she'd added a few other comments from the newspaper and radio, and from an unnamed contact closer to Whitehall. Alysoun didn't think the Netherlands was under immediate threat, but she was exceedingly clear that Rathna should be alert to any sign of trouble coming closer.

Alysoun had never attempted to replace Rathna's own mother, nor had she attempted to fill Morah Avigail's seat. But there was something in the steady support that made a vast difference. Knowing that Alysoun was giving her all this attention for her safety. And on Rathna's own account, not just because of Gabe and their children. She hadn't ever expected to have a family like that, not in all her years between the age of eight and twenty-eight. And yet, here it was, and it still surprised and delighted her regularly.

She wrote a brief note back, to acknowledge the information. And then she added a question about whether there was any specific news of the form of the attacks, whether by land or sea or air. It could be all three, and knowing which might be a help. The land was flat enough here that they might well see any notable show of force near the German border. That was not terribly reassuring, especially with the portal still awakening.

Then she flipped to Gabe's note, which said, "You've seen the news. Keep safe," along with an annotation for a new warning enchantment, designed to trigger at a significant amount of metal, such as an automobile or tank. It could be placed a mile or two out, and alert them in the hut or the immediate area. Rathna shook her head. He must have only just come up with that one, or he'd have shared it sooner. But she took it right out to the Guards, to figure out how to implement it.

It meant sending Ferdinand on a quest for several dozen stones of similar origin that could be linked together. "Not halite, not any of the water-soluble ones. River stones would do, so long as they match." She hoped he'd find something that worked quickly enough. She didn't have enough suitable small stones on hand for this. They'd want to do rings, ideally, and to work within the range of the charm.

She peered at the notes again. Gabe had done something clever, even if she couldn't figure out what right now. It would probably turn up in her head at three in the morning. No time for that now. She wrote the briefest of notes back - "Working on it. Love you." - and went off to do her own preparation for that work.

No. She stopped and wrote one more note to all three of the children. "Still safe. Love you." Because there was never a time when saying it wouldn't be a help. It was a help to her, and a help to Avigail, in particular. Rowena and

Anthony would hear the news at their schools, almost certainly. Rathna trusted that Thesan and Isembard, at least, would check on Rowena at Schola, too. Having friends in varied places was a balm, considering. Even if it was also something she'd never expected.

She rubbed her hands together, turning to pluck the case with her working stones out of her bag from where it was sitting by the sofa. She came back out. "Right. Ferdinand?" He wasn't back yet, and she settled in to do one more scan of the portal stones, to find the places where they might be refined.

When he joined her again by the portal, she lowered her voice. The Guards would share the news around, but better to do this smaller and quieter for the moment. They could all talk through the more general implications over tea later. "They've passed along the news that Germany has invaded Denmark and Norway."

His face went white, and he took half a step back. "Both? When?"

"Starting at four this morning." Some of the early news suggested it had begun not with an attack but a meeting. Rathna felt that it was entirely uncivilised to have a meeting that early in the morning to launch an invasion. This was, perhaps, why she was not permitted anywhere near an army.

He took another step back, and Rathna caught his arm before he toppled over. She had been careful not to touch him more than the work required, because she wasn't at all sure what he felt about that. Now, though, it would do no good to have him go over in the grass and mud. "Steady."

"This feels more real." He said it cautiously, as if he were feeling out the words.

Rathna frowned at that, not upset with him, though she quickly added. "Thinking. Go on?"

"I knew about the other places. The Anschluss, Czechoslovakia, Poland. But this is different, somehow."

This was closer, for one thing. Rathna made sure Ferdinand was steady again and dropped her hand. "You're on the Continent, this time. Not too far from where you have kin. Albion's a different landmass, geologically speaking, as well as magically." She hesitated. "Well. Except for this strip of the Netherlands and northern Germany. It's possible you're more sensitive to the land magic here." Not Denmark, she knew that, and she didn't remember at the moment how Berlin - or more importantly, his mother's family home - fell. "Has anyone suggested you might be particularly attuned to the land magic that way?"

He blinked at her, unfocused. "No?"

Rathna would have liked to have spent ten minutes cursing Davis Fortnum out in Bengali, and she did not have the time. Near the first thing Morah Avigail had done with her was run her through a series of experiences to see what she sensed, then more formal testing to confirm it. Because Morah Avigail, very sensibly, wanted to work with the skills Rathna had, not force her into a shape that didn't fit. She'd assumed from the notes in Ferdinand's files that Davis had done the same, and no.

Not that they could do much about that now. For one thing, they did not have the leisure time for it, or the energy. For another, all of Ferdinand's experiences would have been shaped by his first years of training. She took a breath. "All right. Did you feel anything early this morning?" They were at least in the same time zone. That was a start.

Ferdinand frowned. "Nothing obvious, Mistress Rathna." Good. That was settling him down, giving him a structure. "But I woke up earlier than I meant to, and I don't remember my dreams."

"Do you, usually?" It wasn't something that was generally relevant to their work, not like some specialities. But she'd lived with Gabe and his dreams more than long enough to know that even the ones that weren't life-changingly prophetic mattered to his work.

"Often. But they're usually prosaic. A story of some kind, a narrative, or scenes from one." He looked up at her, blue eyes searching for some sort of reassurance.

"All right." She could be calm and in control here. "All right." That was repeating herself. She was not doing as well as she wanted to be. "First thing, we scan the portal again. You pay attention both to the readings I call out, and to whatever you feel. Tell me to stop if anything feels unusual. Then we'll want to talk about why I wanted those stones, with the Guards and the others."

Ferdinand bobbed his head. "May I ask, Mistress Rathna?"

Rathna smiled at that. "My husband sent me a love note, of sorts." Ferdinand blushed, rather shockingly red, and she went on. "A method of warding, that should tell us if there's anything large and metal coming our way. With a mile or two radius."

Ferdinand let out a low whistle, the first real sign of informality and immediate unfiltered reaction she'd got from him. Then he flushed darker again. "Pardon, Mistress. Do forgive me."

"I'd not have said it if I didn't think you should know. Both that we have that as an option - we'll see how to make it work - and because showing you how to be the kind of adult you want to be is also part of my work, the way I see it." She brushed her hands off. "Come on, let's to."

Ferdinand nodded, and went over to stand where she indicated, while she got out the working stones she needed. The conversation had helped her settle, honestly. And if it meant Ferdinand unbent a little more, that was excellent. He needed more flexibility, really.

CHAPTER 16
APRIL 20TH IN THE VERITAS LIBRARY

"April thirtieth. The night. Why couldn't they pick the full moon? Like tonight."

Gabe was pacing, for all the pacing was annoying him too. He couldn't be still, moving wasn't helping. Nothing was helping, honestly. His father was leaning back from his spot on the sofa, though Mama had gone off to soak in a long bath after supper. The weather hadn't been kind to Mama at all. It had been cold, stormy, with frost and snow showers on Monday, even halfway through April. Papa and Mama had been meant to go out to something tonight, and had cancelled, much as Mama hated to do that. It was admitting a weakness she'd still rather people didn't notice.

It meant Papa raised an eyebrow. "Because people have their ideas about the powerful days."

"But if I am there, I can't be here." That was what was driving Gabe spare. Well, that, his worry for Rathna, his need to keep calm about it for Avigail and the others, and the fact his own ankle disapproved loudly of the shifts in weather and pressure. The pacing certainly wasn't helping, but it was one of the days when sitting was even worse. He'd put on one of the wrap bandages when he went to bed, and he might go so far as a dose of one of the more emphatic potions.

Rathna had got him to promise, years ago, that he'd be honest about when he was taking the potions. Not because he was inclined to take them too often, the way some people might worry about. Rather the opposite, he took them only when there was no other choice. On the average day, he'd rather live with the known pain than worry about muting any of his other senses. He'd have to write her, and tell her. It would be one of those curious moments of proving he was taking care of himself in her absence by admitting he wasn't doing well.

It had made him feel better to know Uncle Gil had the same arrangement with Uncle Magni, to admit when nothing was touching the pain and discomfort. But he resented it, in a way he no longer resented the pain and ache itself. And he resented needing to think about it, perhaps even more.

He pivoted around to face his father. "I won't be back for the land rites." There were arrangements to put him - and Isobel - up in a pub's upstairs rooms, after whatever the ritual was. There was no way they'd be able to sneak out and get to a portal, and back to Veritas in time, especially not with curfew. It would look entirely too suspicious.

And he had missed only two May Days here since he became Heir. One, when he was still recovering from his ankle, and had just returned to school, and the back and forth was entirely too much. And while he had sworn he'd be up for riding the bounds, every single adult in his life had refused to let him try, some of them twice over. He could argue any one of them round, as a general, even

Mama and Papa, but not all of them when they were unified.

The other May Day, he'd missed because he and Rathna had been visiting her extended family in Calcutta for several months. That was a perfectly good reason not to be in Kent on a particular morning. The two points were rather far apart.

"And I am still entirely capable of performing them, Gabe. This is why you're the Heir, not the Lord. It's not as if it'll change anything for you." Papa sounded amused, at least, rather than annoyed. Not that Gabe ever pressed when Papa was remotely annoyed. It wasn't kind, for one thing. Not to Papa, and certainly not to Gabe himself.

"No. But I like them. I was looking forward to them." He was being petulant now, and he knew it. Papa knew it. And if Isobel didn't know it, she wasn't paying attention at all. Gabe glanced around the room, taking in the way she was half-perched on her chair, nominally pretending to look at a book.

"You'll be back for the village festivities later. I'll put word round that you're doing your own bit of war work. They understand, you know they do."

"It's not the same." Gabe pivoted again, having come close to the edge of the bookshelves. "Anthony?"

"We can make the arrangements for him to come back, certainly. Has he asked you?" Papa shifted, both feet on the ground now, stretching slightly. All the little movements that Gabe knew meant he was paying close attention now, the way he shifted his weight when duelling. They had near enough thirty years evaluating each other that way, so of course Gabe noticed.

"Hinted at it this morning. I said I'd check, so this is me, checking. Remembering to check." He kept feeling like he was losing pieces, no matter how many lists he made, but that was one thing he wouldn't forget. Gabe ran his hand through his hair. "He's doing well, though, and settling down to the necessary work, not just the interesting bits. Have I mentioned, Papa, how glad I am you didn't send me to tutoring school?"

The two-year schools were the ordinary way of things, for families of their background, and children who showed any kind of stronger magical potential. Two years, near enough in fostering, to meet others of similar background. Perhaps make a match, certainly enough time to begin to build alliances of use through their school years and into adulthood.

Gabe had not been sure about sending any of their three children, but Rathna, of all people, had argued it would be good for them. Coming from a mixed marriage, in a number of complicated ways, it was a means for the children to learn to balance the ways they differed from others, and the things they still had in common. And for others, quietly and not so quietly, to learn how competent their children were. She hadn't wanted to send any of them away, not exactly. But Rathna had wanted their children to have every advantage she hadn't.

And given both of them had their own demanding professions, it made a certain amount of sense. Both Gabe and Rathna could - even without the war - get called out at any time for an emergency. When Gabe and Charlotte had been growing up, Mama had been reliably around, with help from half a dozen others as their own schedules allowed. It had worked out well, but it had relied on her steady presence.

Charlotte had gone to tutoring school, mind, but she'd always preferred to be on her own in a small group. She had a handful of close friends, and for a while the whole family had thought she'd marry one of the boys from that time. They'd stayed close through their years at Schola. They were still, even if any hint of romance had gone sideways even before she got married.

Papa chuckled. "They'd have sent you home inside a week, I suspect. You were a terror at that age." He glanced over at Isobel, to see what she made of that.

"You say that, sir, like he's not a terror now." Isobel's voice came across quite clearly. "This is not, I admit, entirely what I expected when he suggested I move in, for all it's been more convenient."

Gabe raised an eyebrow at that and paused in the next round of his pacing. "I am not being nearly as much of a terror as I could be!" It was a point of pride. Honestly, he got no respect.

It made his father laugh, the long comfortable laugh that didn't happen nearly often enough, especially right now. It made Gabe glad. "It is a quiet evening, Gabe. Save the terror for some purpose." Then he waved his hand at Isobel. "It does make it easier to tell you stories of his youth. Or a year or two ago. Or last week, wasn't there something about fish?"

"A matter of testing to see if omens could be faked usefully given a few ordinary sorts of supplies, the kind of thing that could be carried in a pocket." Isobel had found the project delightful. The challenge was to figure out what could be added to a pool of water to encourage a reaction or cause a gleam of some shade or another. Nothing harmful to the fish or wildlife, of course, just specks of magic that did what was needed and dissipated.

They hadn't quite perfected it, yet, though. It had meant there were gleaming golden fish in the garden pond nearest the Guard Hall, who should more properly have been a coppery orange. Gabe waved a hand, wanting to get back on topic. Usually he was the one who went chasing after any digression on offer, he really was in a state. "We'll figure something out. This doesn't solve May."

"We'll make the arrangements for Anthony to come. And Rowena, too, it would do her good to see us. And you when you can." Papa made it sound easy, and to some extent it was. Notes to the schools, May Day was understood as a time when special arrangements might be made. "Cook's already making plans for an evening feast, assuming none of us are called away to duty."

Gabe sighed. "Why couldn't they do their ritual on the evening of the first? I know, I know, sunset is the powerful time, the evening before, the anticipation. I could quote you all the citations I had to learn for fourth year Ritual, still." He'd had to memorise a whole set. His professor hadn't believed him when he'd come up with the right answers without having appeared to have done any of the reading.

Reading wasn't everything, much as it was useful, which reminded him. "Isobel, did you get a chance to go through the notes about what sorts of things we might expect in the ritual?"

"Scattered references, and half of them are clearly not going to fit with the others. I can't tell what they're basing things on. Cunning man traditions, I think, more than anything else. I can work with that, well enough."

Gabe nodded. "I'll follow your lead, but write up a summary, if you would? I'm not sure what else I'm going to need to focus on in the next ten days. The reminder might be necessary."

Isobel settled back with another amused, "Sir."

"Does he do that often?" Papa had leaned forward now.

"Ask me for summaries? Yes, sir. I've learned how to write them so he doesn't come back with red ink." Isobel was teasing now, and they both knew it.

"I only did that twice, and only because they were getting kicked sideways." Gabe added to his father. "The Honourable Lucia Mackenzie." He gave the judge her full title, mostly because it would amuse Papa. She'd become more agreeable toward the family over the years, not least because Gabe was well-trained in giving her the information she wanted in the proper order.

"That's a useful skill, there." Papa nodded. "Half of the work, sometimes, is figuring out how to say the thing in the way someone will hear. So they'll give you permission to do what you think needs doing."

"And the rest of it is having confidence in what that is." Gabe followed it up as quick as he could. "Your summaries are excellent, Isobel. I look forward to this one."

Isobel glanced from Gabe to his father and back again. "Making a point, sir? Sirs?" That was a hair less certain.

Papa shrugged, another one of the deceptively casual ones. Gabe wasn't entirely sure why Papa had picked this moment for this particular lesson, but he'd long ago learned not to question Papa's judgement on this kind of thing. "Many people can learn the skills you've been learning. Not so many can figure out how to apply them deftly. And what you're going into, that takes deftness, both in when to watch and when to act. Do you feel comfortable getting yourself out of a bad situation?"

Isobel, to her credit, didn't rush her answer. Gabe was exceedingly proud of the fact she didn't dwell, either, just took the proper amount of time for reflection. "I believe so, sir. I've been doing my training with the Guardswoman that Captain Lefton recommended. I don't think much of my chance in a duel or outright fight, but I'm much better at the charms that help me slip away. I run well, and last week, Gabe walked by me for a good thirty seconds before noticing the keep-away working."

"Thirty seconds. My." Papa looked over and laughed. "What do you have to say for yourself?"

"I'd been reading a note from Rathna. And also I hadn't had any coffee yet." Gabe shrugged, agreeably.

It made Papa laugh all the more, before he waved a hand. "I'm going to go see how your mother's getting on. We'll let you know when the bath's free."

Gabe nodded as his father got up. He'd earned that, and he couldn't grudge either of his parents noticing that sort of thing. "Isobel, while we've got a few minutes, want to run through the cover story one more time?" Practice in this made perfect and smooth, as in many other things.

CHAPTER 17
APRIL 30TH NEAR GRONINGEN

"Right." Rathna let out her breath slowly. "I think we're as ready as we're going to be."

"Are you sure tonight is the time to try it?" Ferdinand was beside her, shoulders hunched a little under the cloak he wore against the chill. It was May Eve, Walpurgisnacht in Germany, and something similar here in the Netherlands. In other years, Rathna would have been home at Veritas, preparing for the land rites at dawn the next morning. Or rather, starting at dawn and continuing through the day, including a bit of time for Gabe to take her to bed to help the blessing on the land.

She shivered, missing him more in that moment than usual. He wasn't there missing her. He had his own work, for all he'd had to sort through his grumpiness about that. Grumpy was not a usual thing for Gabe, and she worried about that. Rathna shook her head. "It—" She frowned. She'd talked through this with a few people. Though to be honest, their various connections were not very clear on the practical details of how the land magic flowed here, what it meant to the Fatae.

CELIA LAKE

"We're ready. It's a night with power to it. And we are - we are working with the land, not against her." It was that which had decided Rathna, finally. And that argument which had been persuasive to Grietje and Nelis. She trusted their read on it more than anyone else's. She could see the faint glimmer of a bonfire in the direction of the nearest village. More to the point, she didn't want to put it off. If it worked tonight, they could start getting people out in the morning, however many they could. Every single one would likely be a miracle.

"Mistress Rathna." Rathna glanced at Ferdinand, the way he said it. He'd come to trust her over the last weeks, painstakingly, when she coaxed him through each new step. She'd pushed him, and she knew it. He knew it, too, because she'd told him when she was, and what she was looking for. That, apparently, had been so much of a novelty he'd had to make a circuit up to the bay and back to clear his head. From what she gathered, his entire training up to this point had been a matter of someone implying a thing, and Ferdinand doing it, usually quite competently.

Rathna knew perfectly well he'd had other training in his background. He'd had Thesan at Schola, of course, and Thesan was adamant about telling students what she expected. And she was insistent on spelling out the difference between rote competent work and brilliance. She marked assignments accordingly. But it was one more thing for Rathna to take up with the Guild when the opportunity presented, because this implication and innuendo had not been doing Ferdinand any favours.

A month of close work, however, had given him some reason to trust in her guidance. Or so she hoped, because she needed him for the next part. She'd been able to get a connection to Basel, which was close enough, but

Amsterdam was locked against her. Not at all unreasonable, with Germany on their borders, but no diplomatic plea had had any sway. Whoever made the decisions was convinced that this plan wouldn't work. There was no reason to weaken their protections to prove the point.

If they couldn't make the connection to the Heinrichs, there was no hope. There was no other portal close enough that either of them knew well enough to use as the anchor. Without that one German portal, remarkably in private hands rather than the government, this plan would fail. They'd have wasted a month or more of drainingly hard magical work, all the supplies, and more.

"Talk to me about the portal one more time. How it felt to you, what memories you have there." She had a purpose to asking. The more he felt a connection in his heart, the easier the magic should flow, the more gently the portal should remember him.

Ferdinand swallowed, finding a perch on the narrow wooden bench just behind them, starting at the stone arch in front of them. "It's well established, a signal favour to the family, back centuries. Family tales talk about it being drawn out of the ground, growing like a tree, but with arches of stone. It's a glacial valley, more or less, where the family Schloss is, cut out of the plateau, with forests, several rivers." He let his eyes half-close. Good. Excellent.

"Think about the land there, the way it spoke to you. A feeling, you do better with the feelings sometimes, the sensation of being on the land. What it felt like under your feet, how your magic answered it."

He took in a breath and let it out, then another, falling into a light trance. Rathna let him, talking him along, through each sense, one by one. She asked about the quality of the light, what birds and animals he knew lived there, the smells of the plants. What it had been like in the summer, as distinct from the winter, the one time he'd been there for Solstice and the holidays. Once he was well and truly caught up by the memories, she coaxed him gently into standing. She led him to the portal, so that he'd be able to reach out and touch it. She herself placed one hand on the stone, and one in his hands, and drew as deep on her magic as she could.

She had not understood, not for years, why they'd picked her out of the orphanage all those years ago. She hadn't grasped why they'd sent her off into a world made of magic and legends and things no one ever explained. Or at least things no one had explained until she'd met Gabe, who delighted in exploring what was obvious to everyone else. All she had known was that she was told she had a gift.

It served her well, here. She had what Gabe had finally described as a deep channel for this particular magic, capacity like the Thames or the Severn or another great river. Perhaps not so much as the Danube, but she'd not properly met the Danube yet. She rarely drew fully on that potential, only enough to dredge the channel periodically and keep the option open.

Now, though, she gave herself over to it, as fully as she could, trusting on the others to support them. Down went roots, deep into the core of the earth, and out they spread, touching into the lines of magic that traced the globe. She'd been reaching out beyond the immediate land, into the region. Things were more tenuous here. She didn't know them remotely as well as she did in Albion. There was no way to do that.

Once she had herself steady, she lifted Ferdinand's hand. "Hold the portal you treasure in your heart, stand on the land where we are, and reach out when you're ready." Then she drew his fingers to brush against the new portal stone.

His shoulders shuddered, twice in a row, hard and sharp and fast. She was terrified for a moment that he was seizing, that something had gone tremendously wrong. Then he exhaled sharply and spread his palm against the stone, then placed his other on the other side. Automatically, instinctively. She saw Beth, the Guard with a particular knack for steadiness, come up behind him, not touching, but close enough to offer a hand or a shoulder if he looked likely to collapse.

It was so difficult holding this place. She'd created portals before, and not just temporary ones. She'd had to be fierce and large enough after she made a tear in the world, in a measured way, so she could deliberately connect it somewhere else. It was one of the great magics, and every time she touched it, it changed her. As it should, really.

Today, tonight, she could feel it burning through her, like the tended flame of a great bonfire, and she drew on that, funnelling it all back into the work. She had to trust this was what it needed, all the ways she'd learned over the years. It was tenuous, though, too tenuous. Rathna could feel something flickering too much, as if it were smothered, or didn't have enough fuel.

She knew better than to offer everything she could. For one thing, it wouldn't work, and for another, that was an easy route to destroying herself, her magic, or both. Instead, she swallowed and tried to think of what to do. No, not think. That was too much made of air and intellect. She had to feel; she had to do what Gabe did, and let the flow of the necessity drive her.

It didn't come naturally to her. She was still too often

over-cautious. But she had learned something from seventeen years with Gabe, nearly that married, and raising three children. She remembered, like the flash of a fish in a pond, a conversation she'd had with Gabe. It must have been a decade ago, all about the trick of reflecting light into dark spaces, with a series of mirrors, aligning the mirrors to bounce the light from place to place, and how it amplified rather than dimmed the glow that allowed for vision.

Rathna could feel the land under her feet now. It wasn't anticipatory, the way Veritas would have been, leaning forward into the rites to come, knowing that she had her own particular part to play in them. It was more like a half-feral cat, a barn cat, who knew she might have a scrap of food, or a bit of a scratch. But a cat who also knew humans brought all sorts of unkind things.

She swallowed and tried to think about hope. About helping the people of the land who needed to be elsewhere, to be safe enough. About cherishing everyone of the land who'd been born there or chosen to make their home there. She could feel the curiosity there, in response, as if the land had been shaped in other ways.

But Rathna's logic was sound, or so she hoped, and after long moments, there was a greater willingness there. Whatever skittishness there had been had dropped away, making the whole tenuous connection much easier. That gave her enough to work with, to call the flow of the magic up into her hands, and to begin to shape mirror after mirror, along the way.

"Think of that portal. Know what it feels like." She spoke out loud again, and she felt Ferdinand shift his body a bit more, leaning his weight into the stones on both hands. There was a long pause, far too long. Her heart thumped a dozen times, then two, then three. It felt like nothing was happening at all.

All of a sudden, it crested, like water had been rising silently in a lock. It had lifted the boat they were floating in high enough to meet the higher water on the far side to join this place to that. As she was beginning to grasp that, she felt and heard Ferdinand gasp again, the shudder of his shoulders, and she immediately focused on him. "There you go. We're there, we're - just say hello to it. It doesn't need to open, it just needs to greet you."

English - and every other language she'd ever learned - didn't have words for this, for the feelings and sensations stone had. All she could do was gesture, and hope that everything they'd done together up until now was enough.

Nothing happened for ages. It was not terribly long, in absolute terms, but it felt like aeons. Finally, though, there was a glowing brightness from the other end, and then something snapped into place, perfectly secure. Ferdinand let out a grunt, his entire upper body shaking.

"Breathe with it. You're doing wonderfully. There we go. Breathe in, breathe out, again." She talked him through it for a good minute, not asking him to move, to leave the perfection of having made that connection work. Finally, slowly, the tension in him eased a little, and he pushed himself into a steadier position.

"Did it work?" His voice cracked in the middle of the last word, but she didn't laugh, she didn't dream of it.

"It did." Rathna kept her voice steady and gentle. "You can feel it, can't you? What did it feel like to you? You can move your hands when you're ready, and Beth, can someone fetch that bench and something bracing to drink?" She made the request in the same purely conversational tone she used for the rest of it, but someone immediately moved the bench just behind Ferdinand. He pulled one hand back a little, curving his fingers so the tips brushed the stone, then the other, then pulled back entirely. Rathna got one arm to guide him to sit on the bench before he toppled over.

"It felt...." He rubbed his face, and Rathna rummaged in her pocket for a clean handkerchief, pressing it silently into his hand. "It knew me. As family. They hadn't locked me out."

There might be no one there who knew how, not properly. Blood connections were tricky to ward out, and worse when it was the sort of magic no one in Germany admitted to knowing. "It worked. It worked very well. In a bit, we can open up a portal to somewhere sensible, and see how it goes, but I'm certain."

Ferdinand blinked up at her, his eyes still unfocused. "You're sure?"

"Absolutely. You did brilliantly, everything I could hope for." She wanted him to hold this moment in his head and his heart and his magic. Next time he made that reach, he would know what it felt like to succeed. "Now you need to eat and drink a little. You remember, I mentioned the potion that helps. And I need to do the same." She was more wobbly on her feet. And she needed to write to Gabe. He'd want to know.

Rathna settled down on the other half of the bench. She let the others bustle around, bringing what was needed, and an extra cloak for each of them, against the night's chill. The magic was burning away now, leaving no protection from the cold. It was enough for now. The rescuing could begin in the morning, a fine gift for the dawning May.

CHAPTER 18
APRIL 30TH IN KENT

Gabe had been a tad dubious about this ritual plan from the start. Not because he thought it would do any great harm, shatter the Pact, or hurt anyone. But, well. Because it wouldn't do anything at all.

In this case, it was decidedly a damp squib. The men and women they met in a secluded bit of woodland were all very well-meaning, that much was clear. He'd escorted Isobel to the meeting point, as instructed, and then turned back just long enough to cast half a dozen charms on himself. It wouldn't work if they got too close, but as long as he kept a bit of space, he could follow and see what happened.

Several older women had whisked Isobel into their circle when she arrived, glad to have someone young and strong to help with the final arrangements. The chatter as they went was all about other things they were doing for the war effort. From the snippets Gabe caught, that involved aggressively efficient gardening, the eternal knitting, and various more mystical pursuits. The men talked about the fire warden work, the on-again off-again discussions about some sort of Home Guard. And always the eternal question of where to get a decent cigarette these days. Nothing at all unusual there.

Isobel was, if not as capable of taking care of herself as Gabe was, entirely competent to manage in these circumstances. She wasn't a duellist; she didn't have his experience avoiding the things that ended in duelling. But she had a sharp eye for self-preservation, and for Gabe's preservation, for that matter. More than he did himself, at least a few times.

He was worrying over Rathna, of course, which didn't help. Especially not in the gap between escorting Isobel to her spot and waiting for the ritual to begin. He'd had to leave his journal locked up for the evening, in the room over the pub.

It was not a bad room as pub rooms went, clean enough and without any obvious leaks or mould. Not as nice as the inn where he'd met Rathna, though that might be a bit rosy in memory these days. He'd check in as soon as he could. He didn't use the word pray lightly. He wasn't a religious man so much as one aligned with the familial practices and traditions.

But he'd made his own offerings at the Ganesha shrine before leaving Veritas this morning, and at the family lararium. Then he'd spent a quarter hour standing by the pond, in one of the places he felt the land magic most strongly. That all would go well. That Rathna would continue to be safe. That her work would change the world, at least a little, for the best.

Here, well. He was less sure what it might do. There was a circle, and there was dancing to raise energy, but not the precise dances of the Council magics at Solstice or even what little he knew of the Fatae dances. It wasn't the energetic circle dances he'd learned in Ritual class, or the country dances of the village celebrations in their part of Kent. He didn't entirely know what to do with it.

No one had explained the particulars of the ritual, beyond what he directly needed to know, but Gabe had, of course, known what they were trying to do. Pool their magic, their energy, their desire and shape it and form it and send it out. They even had a simple enough focus, keep Hitler and all who were his on the far side of the Channel.

He and Isobel had talked about this. She'd been willing enough to share her vitality, the spark of her magic. The Penelopes were all trained in that, as Healers and nurses were, both to gather it up and to share it. There were times when a case would mean a Guard or Healer needed the help, and the Penelopes were there. And Gabe could see she was participating intently, concentrating on the dance and the chant and the shout that went up.

None of it did anything that Gabe could tell. Granted, he wasn't in the ritual, but he'd certainly observed plenty he wasn't directly involved in. All the Solstice dances at the Council Keep, for one, plus any number of others he'd been at. This was, well. Nothing. It fell flat. All that time and energy and fuss, all of him missing the May Day celebrations in the morning, and for nothing.

He took a breath as quietly as he could. They could learn from it. Learn where to focus next, who might actually be doing something that moved the needle a little. Winnowing out what wasn't working was helpful, all his training as a Penelope had been explicitly clear. But it felt like a failure. And a failure of his, for all he hadn't been the one designing or performing the ritual.

As they started to clean up what they'd put around the

circle, he withdrew, back to the spot where he was supposed to meet Isobel and Peter Douglas. They came along quietly, with a hooded lantern, about twenty minutes later, to find him on a suitable bit of log.

"Uncle." Isobel came and hugged him tightly. She took the excuse to murmur in his ear. "Keep up a good show, please."

He would have anyway, but he was curious about what she was up to. She talked easily with Douglas about the area, not about the ritual at all. Once they were back at the pub, the publican let them in the back door. They went up to their rooms. Gabe found a sandwich and a flask of more or less warm tea waiting. He sat on the bed with a thump, until Isobel knocked on the door.

"Come in." It made him push upright, and move to rest his hand on the doorframe, calling up the wards he'd placed when they arrived. There was a brief flare of luminescence.

Isobel raised an eyebrow. "Bit obvious for you, sir."

She was doing all right, then to be that tad bit cheeky. Gabe waved his hand. "How are you? Eat, you need to eat."

Isobel shrugged.

Gabe looked at her more closely. "Something put you off your food?"

"I feel queer in my stomach. Pass me the flask, though?" Gabe did so, then rummaged in his bag for the smaller flask of brandy. She nodded once and held the tea over for him to pour a bit in. She took a good swallow that seemed to help.

"From the ritual?" Gabe repositioned himself on the bed, then paused to unlace his boots and take them off. His bad ankle was complaining more than he wanted. It could be the weather, the rough ground, the fact he'd been not much use at all tonight. Probably all three. He rolled his toes, trying to figure out how much he needed to actually pay attention to the pain and how much he could go back to ignoring.

"The very tail end of it. How much did you see?" Isobel had settled on the end of the bed, one leg tucked up, facing him.

"Most of it, though I didn't hear all the chat after. I left about twenty minutes before you came along."

"They were talking about - one of them had been in touch with someone else. Somewhere else, they were careful not to let me hear the name. Some connection, and not in the ordinary sort of way?"

"One of the esoteric groups?" They'd both done their best to chart some of those out. The whole thing was the sort of unruly mess you'd expect if a dozen cats got some yarn, some ink, and a great deal of free rein. And that didn't even get into the more obscure connections. The things like who happened to be at the same party as someone else, or bumped into someone in the lane because they'd moved to the same village. Gabe knew of at least half a dozen of that latter form without trying.

Isobel nodded. "More than one, I think. They wanted me back, and I made all the proper noises about whether I could get away and all that. Implying some other possible war work, maybe not nearby." It was a good excuse, and one that no one could easily either argue with or check up on.

"Good, good." Gabe frowned at the rest of it. "That doesn't explain why you feel queer. What sort of feeling?"

Isobel took another long drink of tea and frowned. "Like it didn't do anything. But it wanted to. All of that balled up together, and it didn't go anywhere. Is that going to cause a problem for anything?"

"I suspect no one's going to have a good night's sleep, but that's not so different from otherwise for a lot of us, is it?" It was true enough. Everyone Gabe knew with any sense wasn't sleeping terribly well. The initial furor about the war and possible imminent invasion might have settled down among some parts of the larger population, but he knew too many people who had accurate information about what was going on. In some cases, it didn't matter much whether it came from a touch of espionage, divination, or simply having some idea of the patterns of history. "We could have a look tomorrow, before we get back."

"You want to get back to Veritas, though, sir. And I don't think there's too much to see, honestly. You'd want to do a proper thaumaturgical analysis, wouldn't you?"

"Can you find it on a map later? Though, no, we probably couldn't get a field team out fast enough." They, like every other bit of Albion, were low on people. "We'll sleep on it. How's that? See how useful you feel it would be in the morning. I have my kit."

"Sir." It was a more agreeable sound. "You're right nothing will change too much overnight." Isobel relaxed a little more. "What did you think?"

"I don't think it did much. Not for lack of earnest effort. But it didn't go anywhere useful. If you wanted a bit more blessing for a patch of Kent, sure, that's fine. Is it going to erect some great wall of protection? No."

"And we can't do that either." Isobel knew the theory, of course, but the hopefulness in her voice was so complicated.

"The land is living and breathing, and we can't make hard walls, not for a large space. A castle, at the outside. It would - it would suffocate. They've tried twice."

"The Armada and Napoleon, right? And we got - storms

and then weren't there other problems?" Isobel frowned. "That's a shakier bit of my history."

Gabe snorted, then sobered. "Famines and oppressive taxes and people who didn't have work. The Regency and George IV. Nothing good. There are some glimpses, if you look at the right records, of issues with the Pact. The Council was awfully active, visibly active." He'd never quite worked up the nerve to ask Alexander about it directly. It wasn't a period of Alexander's particular interest, even leaving aside the fact Alexander's grandfather had been on the French side of things.

Gabe knew enough to tell it had been bad, in complex ways. He was good at the patterns, and he could read some of the routine historical charts for them without even thinking about it. Some of those same things had started showing up already, even though other aspects wouldn't be fully reported for some time. The extremely unusual cold winter, for one.

Isobel was watching him when he looked up again. "And that's what we're here for. To figure out what's going on. And maybe help."

"We are." Gabe let out a long breath. "All right. We're not going to do more tonight. Can you eat a sandwich, or do I need to worry about that?"

Isobel grimaced. "I'll eat." She waved a hand. "When do you want me up, sir?"

Gabe considered, pulling out his pocket watch. "Half eight, is that too early downstairs? And we'll decide about the ritual site. We need to go part of the way there for the nearest portal, anyway."

Isobel nodded and took herself off. Gabe immediately pulled his journal over, forcing himself to write several notes related to their work of the evening before thumbing to Rathna's latest.

Finding out they'd made the portal work made everything better. It was tremendous news. He was up far too late writing back, thinking about what she'd told him, and reading into what she hadn't yet put into words.

CHAPTER 19
MAY 10TH NEAR GRONINGEN

"Up, everyone up. We need to get out." Lucas came down to the bedrooms at the end of the hut, banging on the walls. "Now! Up and out."

Rathna rubbed her face. She hadn't been asleep nearly long enough. They'd been up past midnight, getting another small group through the portal. Not enough. Never enough.

"What's happening?" she managed to get the words out as Grietje rolled out of her own narrow bed, pulling on boots.

"Invasion. News in the journals, but one of the warding stones just went off. Four miles, the village, but that's bad enough." Lucas turned his head. "We need to move. Bombs at the airstrip at Waalhaven, paratroopers since." He glanced at his watch. "It's barely four. More news coming in. We need to move." The last word was fierce and sharp. "Come on."

Rathna launched herself upright, her mind running fast. She'd kept her things packed tidily. They could hurl the trunks through, now, if they had to. No cart. "How much time do we have?"

Grietje grimaced. "It's an invasion. It's not as if they sent a calling card ahead. We're under two miles from an unprotected border, even if it's damp ground. You guess."

None of the possible guesses were good. Rathna shoved her feet into her boots after making sure the socks were straight - she didn't need them rubbing a bloody spot after an hour. Whatever today was, she needed to be able to keep going. Gabe had taught her how to think that through.

She couldn't write to him. He'd worry. Oh, he'd probably know soon, if he didn't already. But she couldn't take the time to write until she knew something that had meaning.

She shoved her last few items in the trunk, charmed it lighter, and hauled it out to by the portal. She could replace everything in it if she had to, but better if she didn't have to. Beth was out there, starting to tally up. "Trunk if we can?"

"Please. My bag's in the top, if we can't." She'd keyed Beth and Lucas as the senior guards into her trunk's warding on principle. If something had happened to her, even an ordinary injury, they might have needed to get in.

She was still rubbing her face when Ferdinand came up behind her, just carrying his smaller bag. "Mistress?"

"Ferdinand." She acknowledged him, sparing a moment for his personal logistics. "Not your trunk?"

"Nothing I can't replace easily." He nodded at hers. "Not like yours. I have my personal tools."

Rathna wasn't going to argue with him. "Make sure there's nothing identifying then, or make sure it's burned to ash inside." No point in leaving things that could mark out exactly who was here. "Do you know the charms? No, I'll have to do it." She raised her voice. "Anything that needs to be destroyed, make a pile by the bench."

She got a round of shouts of acknowledgement and sailed on. "Can we get anyone else out?"

"No one magical." Beth looked up from where she was calculating. "It'd break the Pact."

"We have enough potions for twenty." She cursed under her breath in Bengali. They couldn't send them to Amsterdam, nor to - was France safe? They couldn't get across the Channel. She'd been assuming, wrongly, that if they needed to get out, Belgium or somewhere closer would be an option. The Channel needed one of the Fatae portals, and besides, she was sure the portals were being locked to the Continent, or at least anywhere near them. "Switzerland. Can someone round up whoever can, drug them, and take them through to Switzerland, anyone who's willing for that?"

There was a shout from one of the other Guards, who went off at a run. Rathna settled into thinking about their options. They'd need somewhere to go, and she didn't want to end up in Switzerland. "Lucas, what do we know?"

"Very scattered information, a few reports, more scrying once they knew they needed to. You know how that is. But maybe the Netherlands, Luxembourg, Belgium."

You needed people who got a hook to work with. Albion had some, people who had family in all these places, who'd spent time there, who'd apprenticed in ways that made them part of that web. But not many. Not everywhere they needed.

"France?"

Lucas grimaced. "No idea."

Not Paris, then. Spain had likely locked its portals, such as they were. "Map, Ferdinand." The unadorned request could only be for the portal map. A moment later he was holding it up, casting a charm light to let her read it.

Her fingers traced along the map. Not Paris. They'd stand out anywhere, as new and foreign, but Paris portals were in the midst of the city, and cities could be dangerous in a panic. Not Brittany. Everything she'd ever heard about Brocéliande had made it clear turning up without an invitation would go exceedingly badly. The south of France might do, but they'd be cut off from anything. Her fingers ran down the northwest coast, in Aquitaine.

Aquitaine had ancient historic ties to Britain, and had had them for centuries. Nearly to the time of the Pact, in fact. She knew there were portals there. More to the point, she knew there were Fatae in the Pyrenees, and she knew someone who had at least spoken to them once or twice. If they had to negotiate, there might just be a chance there. If not, they were at least on the right coastline. And the portal there was outside the mountains, by a few miles. Not in the Fatae's own lands. Most of all, she knew it was active, but there shouldn't be anyone too nearby who'd have the skills to lock it against them quickly.

There were entirely too many ifs in that sentence for any sort of comfort. But it was the plan they had, with some options available. Land, sea, magic. That was as good as it was going to get.

"Ferdinand, first set for Basel, but then we'll want the coordinates for Dax. I'll work them out." It would be a stretch, with this portal, but - well. They'd stretch. It would work or it wouldn't.

That had taken enough time that the Guard who'd taken off at a run was back with one sole family from the next farm to the south. "They're willing. The others weren't. I explained we were getting farther away, to safety, but they couldn't know how we got there." He was speaking rapidly in English, and Rathna kept an eye out to make sure none of the little huddled group were tracking. They were shivering in the cold, each with a small bag or suitcase of whatever they could throw together.

"Are you willing to go with them?"

He nodded, with no hesitation. "I've picked up enough Dutch to manage. And I have some French." That and English would go a long way in Switzerland. "Go through with them. And anyone else who wants Switzerland."

That took a bit - first convincing each of them to take a little dropperful of potion, then setting them out where they could be carried through the portal. They'd have to open it for a good couple of minutes to get everyone through, but Rathna could do that.

Not without some strain, as it turned out. As they got the last through, two of their own party going with them, Rathna loosened her grip on the magic, and let the portal close. She immediately wobbled backwards, and she only avoided falling because of a hand on her back, then another. Grietje and Ferdinand both.

"Mistress?" That was his voice over her shoulder.

"We don't have long, do we?" She could feel it now. It hadn't been even an hour, she thought. She couldn't hear it, exactly. Wherever the planes were, the paratroopers, they weren't close to this isolated little spot on the coastline. But she could feel something in the land, the more she was listening for it.

The human boundaries were passing things to the land, they always had been. Though Albion itself was a bit different, being an island with more islands attached by a bit of string and chewing gum. But the land responded to what people thought about it. That was one of the anchors of the land magic at the most primal level. And the land knew this was an invasion.

Grietje shook her head, the motion just catching Rathna's attention. "What do we need to do before we leave?"

"I need to clear the hut. Not burn it, just - clear it. Of anything that can trace us. And burn the things we're not taking, anything personal."

"What do you need from us?" Grietje was fierce now, like a honed knife.

"Vitality." Rathna took a breath, checking her own stores. "A fair bit."

"Right. You prepare. We'll sort that out." There was a gentle push in her back, and Rathna took a step forward, then another, to the hut. She needed to summon anything that could be used to trace, hair or skin or fingerprints. Gabe called it blurring, and she wasn't supposed to know how to do it.

On the other hand, Richard knew she could. They'd spent a week's worth of winter storms arguing through the theory of it when she was home with Avigail as a babe at her breast. And if there was ever a time for it, it was now. The preparation wouldn't be draining, but the doing - well. That was a trick.

She leaned her back against the doorframe, Ferdinand still hovering. "What should I do?"

"Check one more time outside, make sure there's nothing anyone's touched - I'll have to try something different on the benches, the woodpile. And then. Well."

She sucked in a breath, and let herself begin to draw from the earth around her. From the watery earth, for all that was trickier, things kept moving and shifting. In one way, that was a help. Water cleansed all. On the other, making water go somewhere specific in a controlled fashion had made engineers curse since the Egyptians, if not before.

She drew up all her magic, all the way she could, like ink filling a fountain pen. Then, and only then, did she stretch out her hands, palms out, facing the far wall, and pulsed the magic forward around her, around them. Her fingers bent slightly and straightened, three times. She could feel the effort it took as she repeated three sharp syllables, far louder in her head than on her lips.

It was an ancient magic, and all kinds of problems to work, and she would use it for her people. And herself. She couldn't forget that. The world spun for a moment as she opened her eyes. That had taken more out of her than she'd hoped. A second later, there was a hand on her elbow. "Mistress? Vitality?"

Rathna turned to see the remaining people from their party. Lucas and Beth, Grietje and Nelis. "I need to clear the outside. And then what we're not taking. Then through the portal."

"To where, Mistress?" That was Beth.

"Aquitaine. I don't want to risk Paris, even if we could get there." She let out a breath. "Vitality, whoever's willing. Don't let me drain you. Keep enough to keep going for a few hours."

Lucas stepped forward first, his hands palm down. Rathna placed her hands under his, then brought them up, barely touching. She drew off some of their vitality, not wanting to take too much. Sleep, food, rest, would all restore it given a bit of time, but those might be luxuries they didn't have.

She shook her head at Grietje and Ferdinand's offer. "I might need a bit in a moment. Right. Let me clear outside, then deal with what we're not bringing with us, and then..."

Rathna felt the rumble, more than anything, but it made her suck in her breath. "We don't have much time."

The second charm was easier - outside, there was more for her to pull from. Burning the trunks to ash without causing a fire, that was harder work, a tight focus that demanded everything she had for an agonising minute. She counted out her heartbeats. When she let it ebb, there was a pile of dull grey ash, beginning to blow away in the winds, but she couldn't make her eyes focus.

A hand was under her elbow. "Now?" Grietje held out her hands, and Rathna nodded, placing her own again, and drawing out enough that the world wasn't spinning anymore.

"The portal."

"What do we need to do when we get there?" That was Lucas.

Before Rathna could say anything, Ferdinand spoke up. "French-speaking, a little away from the town, in a grove near the road. We should be all right to come out. It's still early in the morning. Move ten feet away or so, and wait for us to come through, yes, Magistra?"

"That." Rathna didn't waste words explaining or adding. "We'll hold the portal." Which left the challenge. "I don't—" This was the part she hadn't thought through. Not enough.

"What do you need?" That was Grietje, sharp as ever.

"I'd want to destroy it, but."

Nelis shrugged. "Tell me how." His chin came up, and he stared Grietje down. "I am safer in the country than you are. Go with them. Come back when you can."

Rathna suddenly suspected there was something much

deeper between them than she'd had any hint of in the month and more since they'd been here. Not romantic love, perhaps, but the kind of deeply rooted trust of shield brothers out of a saga. She saw Grietje nod out of the corner of her eye. "I'll come back when I can." Like it was an oath or promise. "Let's to."

Getting the portal to open was more effort than Rathna wanted to admit to. Holding it was harder. But she dug in her heels, set it for the portal at Dax, and through they went, one by one. Lucas went first, then Grietje and Beth taking her trunk between them.

Then it came down to Rathna and Ferdinand. He nodded once at her. "Go, Mistress. I'll be right after."

She went. The world went to the grey space between the places, with the shimmers of light that she saw and apparently few other people did. It was like the spark of light catching on minerals, for her. It had been since the first portal she'd ever taken.

At the other end, she stumbled out, taking three or four steps before she went to her knees in the soft grass. The portal was quiet behind her. Too quiet. For far too long. She glanced up to see the others gathered in the morning light, then twisted to look back at the portal and started counting, the way she'd learned as a child.

One Piccadilly. Two Piccadilly. Three Piccadilly. Four Piccadilly. Five Piccadilly. Six Piccadilly. Seven Piccadilly. Too long. Nine Piccadilly. Ten Piccadilly. Eleven Piccadilly. Twelve Piccadilly. Far too long. Fourteen Piccadilly. Fifteen Piccadilly.

Finally, the portal spluttered into life again, and Ferdinand stumbled through. He looked pale as a sheet, but he shook his head as she stood to offer a hand. "Minute." It came out as a croak.

He fell into a tumble on the ground, but they were - well. Safe was a relative term. They were not currently under attack. They'd brought the portable food and drink with them. They could figure it out from here.

She hoped. She hoped very much.

CHAPTER 20
MAY 10TH AT VERITAS

Gabe woke suddenly, reaching for the empty space on the other side of the bed automatically. It wasn't a dream this time; it was something else. His heart was pounding, and he didn't know why.

A moment later, there was a knock on the door. The bedroom door, which was extremely unusual. Gabe grimaced, rubbing his face, trying to focus his eyes. A bit before dawn, twenty or thirty minutes, maybe, by the light. "Yes?" It came out as a croak, like he'd shouted in his sleep. There were very few people who could knock on that door without waking him much earlier in the process.

"It's Magni." Uncle Magni. His voice sounded hollow. He only sounded like that if there was a problem, when all his decades in the Guard came crashing back together into a fearsome plan.

Gabe sat bolt upright. "What's wrong?" His heart was loud now, thumping. "Moment." He pitched that louder, hurling himself out of bed without bothering with his dressing gown, cane, or anything other than making sure his pyjama pants were still more or less in the right place.

He opened the door, blinking against the brighter light in the sitting room.

"Invasion. The Netherlands and Belgium, we think. Luxembourg, possibly. News is coming in, but just fragments." Uncle Magni looked grey and faded. "Gil was keeping an eye out. He was up in the night." Pain, then, probably, rather than a thread of prophecy, but at least a well-timed bit of pain. Other days, it might have been another hour or three before they knew.

Gabe swallowed against bile and worry and the way his stomach had gone in a knot. "Papa?"

"Gil's telling him." Uncle Magni waved a hand. Of course they'd split that work, they would. "Where will you be?"

There was only one answer for that, really. "The night nursery." With Avigail.

"We'll send up some food that can wait until you're ready. Coffee." Everyone but everyone in the house was aware of Gabe's habits there. And how it was better to provide coffee first. "And let you know, soon as we hear anything." Magni nodded once, then turned to make his way back out, down toward the library, most likely. Papa and probably Mama would join them there, and he was sure one of them would tell Isobel.

Gabe swallowed again, and then went to brush his teeth and rinse his mouth, in hopes of taking some of the awful taste away. He pulled on easy clothing - trousers, shirt, jumper, slippers - before he made his way upstairs, to the nursery rooms. Avigail had the night nursery entirely to herself, with her governess sleeping down at the end of the hall.

They'd redecorated when Anthony had moved downstairs last year. Now it was shades of teal and golden yellow, bold colours, much more than most people thought a child's room should be. There was a chair in the corner, for whichever of them might come up to read before bed. Gabe settled into it, tucking his journal beside him and making sure the sound charms were off. Except for Rathna. That one, he never turned off unless he was in the field and it was dangerous.

Avigail was asleep, her head and the dark braid of her hair barely visible beneath the lump of blankets. She was on her side, back facing her room, in the sort of trusting innocence about the safety of the world that Gabe was glad she had. There was a soft charmlight glowing, just enough for him to read by.

He flipped through the pages, to the notifications from the Guard journal that shared reliable intelligence and information about what was going on in the War, as much as such things existed. An attack on a Dutch airfield, and then there were comments of other attacks, scattered but increasing. There was not much news about ground movements, not yet.

Then he just sat. He almost never just sat. It wasn't in him.

He'd had a few periods of lethargy in his life. The awful days after he'd fallen from Invicta and broken his ankle. The hazy time before Uncle Gil had argued half a dozen healers into finding other options for potions. Then he'd been near insensible, unable to suggest anything like a change.

Twice, otherwise, he'd felt something like this. Both had been after the kind of immense magical work where utter exhaustion was the only sensible thing, like the time he'd been on the move for nearly twelve hours, between horse and his own feet and a fair bit more climbing than he'd intended. He'd finished it not with a duel, as he'd expected. That would have been fast. Instead he'd found himself needing to unpick a botched magical ritual, piece by piece. He'd known that any slip could have meant the end of him - and anyone who came looking for him. He'd collapsed after that for three full days.

The other, well, that had an easier explanation. He'd been sent to help with the Thames flood in '28. Every single person who could be spared and some who couldn't had pulled people from the water or held it back just a little longer. It had flattened him for two days, and led to half a dozen proposals about not doing that again in an emergency. Those plans were getting revived now, and Gabe hated that.

This felt the same, but without the physical exhaustion. His magic was there, but everything about him was focused on a single point, and that was being ready. Even his mind was remarkably quiet. Normally, it would be bouncing from point to point.

All he could do - all he wanted to do - was keep Avigail safe. He couldn't help Rathna, not directly. If he wrote, it might distract her. They'd discussed that, in fact, after Aunt Mason had reminded him they should talk through these things, not assume. She would write.

Or she wouldn't.

But no, he couldn't think that.

She would write. She would get somewhere safe, and she would write. His wife - his brilliant wife, doing magic no one had thought possible a few years ago - would come through this whole in heart and mind and body. There was no other possibility. No alternative. Gabe wouldn't have it. Couldn't have it.

He swallowed hard again. Having Rathna gone had been so hard. Much harder than he'd wanted to admit to anyone, including himself. His family had known. His parents hadn't teased, not once. Uncle Magni had let him work himself to exhaustion duelling at least once a week. Uncle Gil had laid out distractions of the more academic sort, to give him something to read and work through when his mind wouldn't settle. All of it helped, and none of it was enough.

Gabe had refused to stop her, even when people had made those too-quiet comments in his ear at one or another of her guild events. For one thing, he wasn't at all sure he could even if he'd wanted to. Not without cheating in the ways he'd always refused to do. Cheating in the ways that meant he wouldn't be able to face himself the next morning, or every day in whatever future he had.

And second, because Rathna should have every gift he could give her. If in this case, the gift in question was the chance to be brilliant, she should have that. Too many people had stood in her way in the past, because of her parents, her background, or who she knew or didn't know. He would not be like them.

It had taken Gabe a little way to work through all the ways that connected in her life, how she didn't expect to be handed something lovely or how she counted and tended even the smallest coins in her pocket. And there was the way she used every scrap of paper and how she darned socks to the end of their lifespan. Even now.

He was still tangled up in his thoughts when there was a sound from the bed, first a soft one, then a louder cry. Before Gabe thought it, he was on the bed, tugging Avigail into his arms. She was still young enough and small enough that he could fold her into his lap, hugging her tight. "Right here, love. Right here." He ended up with one foot tucked under him, the other off the bed, and that was going to hurt in a bit. He didn't care.

She whimpered against his shoulder, shaking.

"A nightmare?" He didn't want to put images in her mind, but if she'd picked anything up, if there was anything that mattered, he wanted to know. Needed to know, for all sorts of reasons.

It took her a moment to take a breath, to blink up at him in the growing light. "I don't know, Papa." She was a clever child, a far-seeing child, as one of Rathna's cousins had named her, every bit as sharp and determined as the woman she was named for. But she was not quick about saying things. She tested them, first, inside her head.

He had to wait. She needed him to wait. He would wait, even if his own mind was racing again, shooting out thoughts in a dozen directions, then a dozen more. Instead, he sat on the bed, refused to even twitch, and held his daughter.

Focusing on that was a help, until she said, half into his shoulder. "Something happened to Mama?"

Gabe swallowed hard. "We don't know much right now, Avigail, love. What was in your dream?"

"It was dark, and there were stones, and there were lights like the portal lights, the crystals in the rock." Her shoulders hitched against his arm. "It was scary." Just that, blunt and bare, and Gabe knew it to be true.

"It is scary. Not knowing what's going on. Do you want me to tell you what we know?"

She nodded once, and Gabe did his best to put it in something like order. "What we know right now is that there were attacks on the Netherlands, and we think on Belgium and Luxembourg as well. You know your map."

Avigail nodded solemnly and wriggled a bit more in his

lap. Gabe went on, carefully. "We don't know how close it is to where Mama is. Or if she's still there. I'm hoping some-time very soon she'll write and tell us she's all right." Putting your magic into words was something he'd been taught, over and over, from his earliest tutoring. You couldn't design an enchantment if you couldn't name what you wanted. In some ways, half of what he'd learned since then had been refining that concept.

"How would she know?" Avigail's voice was clear and sharp, cutting across Gabe's thoughts.

"Well, she has her journal. And the people with her have theirs. And you remember I said that I can read special information from the Guard, like Grandpapa can? She can read that too, and some of the people with her. So as soon as anyone knew about the attack, and said it there, she'd be able to see."

"When?" Which was the crux of it.

"Soon, I hope, love. Soon." Gabe hesitated, then went on with what he'd been thinking. "I'm worried too. But I - I hope I'd know if anything really bad had happened." He couldn't wish knowing into being, but oh, he wanted to. "The others are down in the library. Do you want to go down there?"

She didn't hesitate. "Stay here." The sort of stubborn she'd been - all three of the children had been - at three, at four, at five. Then they got better at words, and it was a different form of stubborn all together.

Gabe just did his best to sit and be steady. Being focused on it was a help, if not as much of one as he'd been hoping. He didn't want to talk much, and he was sure Avigail didn't need to hear the way his mind was popping from topic to topic. At least half of them were not of interest to someone who was eight.

They sat there for a fair bit. Long enough for Gabe's ankle to ache in earnest, long enough for the sun to start coming in, and Avigail's governess to appear at the door in her dressing gown. She'd been warned by one of the staff, fairly obviously, because she didn't say anything, just disappeared when Gabe shook his head once. Long enough for the sun to move and shine in more brightly and for the clock in the next room to chime eight.

Then there was the chime from his journal, and Gabe almost dropped Avigail in his hurry to lean and grab it. He thumbed through to the page, then hesitated. It was her writing. It had to be all right. "Do you want me to read first, Avigail, love?"

She was turning into a good reader, of course, but - well. He'd have wanted to know immediately, too. He opened the page and then read aloud the spare short sentences. "In France, near the Dax portal. Have rooms for tonight. More later." Twelve words and Gabe let out a whoop of delight, then hugged Avigail tight before letting her go. "Find your dressing gown, let's go down and tell everyone else." He let her scamper off to find it, levering himself up cautiously.

One step at a time. She was somewhere safer, far to the west of where she had been. They could work things out from there.

CHAPTER 21
MAY 14TH NEAR DAX, FRANCE

It took four days for Ferdinand to recover enough to be able to have a conversation. He'd stumbled through the portal, and it had been immediately obvious that he'd been caught in some snap of magical backlash. Lucas - who had better French - had gone off to find somewhere for them to be, and they'd ended up in a small magical enclave a mile or so away.

They'd been lucky, because the enclave had been remarkably kind to foreign strangers. Lucas had brought a man with a cart and an ox and a willingness to put the lot of them up in exchange for a modest sum of money. Rathna had made a show of counting out the coins from the purse tucked under her skirt, not letting on that there were more coins locked away in her trunk. She was glad she was wearing her engagement ring on a sturdy chain under her clothing, too, rather than having it show in a way that might tempt too much. That wasn't either kind or sensible.

The enclave wasn't really a village, more a farm and a collection of crafting buildings, along with homes for half a dozen closely connected families. All apparently named

Royer, so Rathna just applied "M'sieur" and "Madame" and "Mademoiselle" with the surname to everyone, based on age and how they wore their hair.

The five of them had been bustled up into two rooms above the stables, currently otherwise unoccupied. They were fitted out with narrow beds better suited for young men and women who had fewer aches and pains. There was at least indoor plumbing, though getting hot water was apparently a production. She was still getting used to the accent. Her French was competent for some things but nowhere near fluent. She gathered the stable rooms were kept for people coming in for festivals and for the harvest, extra labour.

This was the sort of situation Rathna had dreaded. Not quite as much as the more dangerous ones, but their place was tenuous, and she knew it. She was London's child. She knew a bit about horses, because of Gabe and his parents, but she knew very little about farming except that she respected the sheer amount of work it involved. More about the hops harvest, admittedly, but that was hard to escape in their bit of Kent. This was not in the best known wine-regions, but there were rows of grapes and fields of grain nearby.

Rathna certainly wasn't competent with most of the household tasks needed. She couldn't milk a cow or a goat, or get them to go anywhere useful. She was more or less able to feed chickens and gather eggs, but she also was not much good in a kitchen. Ordinary domestic matters for someone older than a child were not parts of her education anyone had thought should have a lot of time, one way and another. She was able to do darning and simple needle-work. Morah Avigail had considered that a necessary thing for any woman. But the Royers made intricate lace and wickerwork, far beyond the skills of her own fingers.

And, of course, they weren't about to trust her with the children. Rathna had skill and experience there, but they were strangers. And more to the point, strangers with unknown magical abilities. She'd seen more than a few gestures she was sure were wards against enchantment, curses, or raw bad luck. She'd ignored them; it was the only civil solution. No one had asked much about her background, once Lucas and Grietje had explained that the four of them were from Albion, and Grietje herself had connections there.

It had left Rathna to sit out on the terrace with a basket, sorting out the bean from the stones. As she was finishing up, Lucas came and waited for her to look up. "I think Ferdinand is waking properly. Will you come?"

In four days, he had only come awake for long enough for Lucas to get him to a chamberpot or for one of them to pour broth down him. He'd been muzzy, the kind of thing that would be taken for too much drink and a hangover if they hadn't known better. Certainly, he'd not been coherent enough for anything like a conversation. Rathna had kept watch over him, along with the others, paying attention to how he winced at any noise. A blinding headache, for certain. But the Royers had a well enough trained healer among them, who had determined there was nothing worse, at least nothing obvious.

By the time Rathna got upstairs in the stables, Ferdinand was bracing himself on one elbow, grimacing. The shutters were closed against the afternoon light, only a gentle charmlight in one of the hooded lanterns they'd brought along. "Lucas is getting you some coffee."

Ferdinand rubbed his face, tried to sit up more, and then toppled back onto one elbow. "Mistress, I."

"Don't be like that." Her voice cut through his visible uncertainty, but she kept it even and patient. "We're safe for the moment. You take the time you need to recover." She wasn't going to tut over him like one of her children, but he still deserved every bit of care she could offer. Not just because he'd taken a tremendous risk, but because she was responsible for him in that particular way. "Are you up for talking a little?"

Ferdinand started to nod and thought better of it. "I think so."

"How do you feel? As much of a proper report as you can manage." Rathna considered and then settled down on the chair beside his bed.

"A blinding headache. Better than it was. Is there a pain potion?" He went on before she could answer. "Aches everywhere. I don't want to think about magic, even something simple. But I don't feel as if anything's a problem there, specifically. I can feel it still, still there. Backlash?"

"Backlash. And you can have a pain potion once you have a little food or at least more broth. We're in a cluster of houses, a little magical community. We're up above their stables, a mile or so from the Dax portal." Well-managed stables, thankfully, and in this season the horses were mostly out in the near field, besides.

"The portal here." He grimaced, rubbing his nose, then adding too quickly. "Let me talk, please, Mistress Rathna."

She settled back in her chair. "As you wish."

"The one at Groningen collapsed behind me. This one, it was, it has not been tended well. Raw. Jagged. By the time I came through."

Rathna considered her own trip. "It's hard to tell with

the older Fatae portals. They're not maintained the same way here. By rote, with the rituals, not by touch." Not by the intimacy of the magic that Rathna knew and that Ferdinand was learning. Specifically, how the tending meant coming to the portal near enough as to a lover or an intimate friend, if it was done right. Or at least so Morah Avigail had taught, if not remotely in those sorts of terms.

Something of it must have shown on her face, because Ferdinand blinked at her owlishly in the dim light. "Mistress?"

"I was thinking about how I was trained. To touch the portal as a friend. Having a relationship with it, even if often that's borrowing the relationship we have with another portal. You know, you meet someone at a party, and then you compare who you were in school with, or who you're related to. You make a connection, and everyone's happier, knowing their place in the dance."

It made Ferdinand laugh, abruptly, before he winced and lowered himself carefully back onto the pillows.

"Pardon, I didn't mean to hurt you." Rathna watched him closely now.

He lifted one hand and let it drop. "Rather laugh than not." It reminded Rathna, in the moment, very much of both Alysoun and Gabe. She nodded, and at that point Lucas came in with a flask.

"Coffee. Milky, hope that's all right."

Ferdinand reached for it rather eagerly. "I'm sure it's grand. Thank them for me, please?" He took a long drink, sighing, then getting himself more upright against the headboard. "Who am I thanking?"

"An extended family, the Royers. There's a lot of agriculture, wine, grains, a lot of domestic livestock, mostly for their own food. You have missed me learning how to feed chickens." Rathna said the last with good humour.

"I am sure you are a quick learner, Mistress. I do, in fact, know what to do with a chicken, if it's helpful."

She raised an eyebrow at that. "Oh?"

"The home farm, when I was little. Mutti - Mama - thought it was good for me to have the fresh air. I can pluck a bird, too, that's from being at shoots." He glanced away. "What do they know about us?"

"That we're from Albion, our names, that we are trying to figure out what to do next. They have been kind, we have paid for our room and board, and can continue to do so." Rathna laid it out evenly, though there were a number of things she was not saying, and would not unless she was certain they were private. The kind of private that involved a large field with a clear view in all directions and a good few charms, to boot.

"Are you recovered, Mistress?"

It was thoughtful of him to ask, though also relevant. "A little drained, still, but doing better. If you need vitality, we can manage that."

He didn't quite shake his head, just the first hint of it, before he thought better of it. "Not yet, please. I don't think it would help much. I still feel raw, like perhaps a sunburn?" Not something he'd have had overmuch experience with, and not something Rathna worried much about.

"Which brings us back to the portal. Do you think this one's damaged permanently?" She hadn't gone to inspect it further. She hadn't wanted so much time away from Ferdinand or the others.

"Strained, certainly. Possibly strained through a sieve, like I feel." He was recovering a bit, to make a joke, if a weak one.

Rathna nodded. "Drink more of your coffee. It's helping. And then you can have some bread and broth and a potion." She considered. "When you're up to the walk or the cart, we'll go have a look. You needn't touch it, not yet, but I'd like your thoughts as I have a feel. If they'll let me."

"Let you, mistress?"

"Different country, different laws. And there's nothing like us on the Continent, you know that." It was part of why they'd got away with the plan for so long in the first place. The Dutch and French barely understood that there were people in Albion who tended the portals. Fewer actually believed that they made them, from time to time. "I think I can probably be convincing enough. It's more like a light-house, here, a public good, but normally they'd have to petition to the Fatae to tend it, and we're out of season for that. Not yet Solstice."

"And - and..." His voice trailed off. "Where are we going from here?"

"That, well. That is a very excellent question." Rathna settled back in her chair. At that point, Lucas knocked, bringing in a small tray with a bowl of broth with some thoroughly cooked vegetables, a soft roll, and some spread-able cheese. A reasonable meal for recovery. "Try that, a little at a time. Stop if it's too much. I'll fetch a potion, if you can keep handy for a minute, Lucas?"

He nodded, and she went across to her trunk in the other room, brushing her fingers to release a series of locks. First the obvious ones, then the blood lock, and finally the most obscure, one of Gabe's little tricks. She drew out the vial of potion, one of only a half-dozen they had of that strength, and was grateful they hadn't needed them in the Netherlands.

By the time she brought it back, Ferdinand had had

about half his food, and he was leaning back on the pillows again. "Try this, see if you can get better rest. If you feel up to it, you can come to supper on the terrace. Late supper. We are in France, after all."

That, as she'd hoped, got her a light chuckle. He drained the potion in two swallows, handed it back, and she could see when it took effect. His face relaxed, the way Gabe's sometimes did in such moments, as if it were a great wall of water, finally settling into its proper place without restraint.

She nodded at Lucas. "I'll see if I can make myself helpful. Back in a few hours."

CHAPTER 22
MAY 24TH AT YTENE

"There are two challenges - no, far more than two challenges. But two particular ones I am trying to sort out at the moment." Gabe had wanted to make the most of a chance to talk without Isobel listening this time. She was off on a ride with Rufus, getting a sense of how the land felt in the Forest at the moment.

Gabe was familiar with the library, of course. It was more common to have people to Veritas, to spare Mama the travel, but Geoffrey and Lizzie had hosted plenty of the occasional gatherings of their knot of people of like mind. Or their nest of specialists, as Geoffrey liked to put it. The mid-afternoon light shone through the window of the library, a gentle golden glow that was doing its best to lure Gabe outside into the open air. He had work to do.

"Besides all your others." Geoffrey's voice was amused. "I gather you've been all over the place."

"We've got connections with a dozen groups, one way or another, and goodness, do they have a lot of meetings and gatherings, even with a blackout. I've been in London two nights a week the last month, and there's a stubborn group in Cornwall we've been trying to get a meeting with. Isobel's mother is actually a wonder at some connections in Yorkshire. Too much travel, too much work remembering which name and persona I'm currently using."

Geoffrey had settled in his usual armchair, ankle propped apparently casually on his knee. Alexander had the chair beside him and was reaching for his glass. They both looked tired, but also more relaxed than Gabe would have thought. He ran his hand through his hair. They had plenty of time to talk, and for him to get back by sunset, because he was insistent on keeping Rathna's customs about Fridays if he could.

"We have a bit of our own news, though it's Rufus who heard it." Geoffrey flicked his fingers. "Pace, if you need to."

Gabe rolled himself upright, and would. Geoffrey had a knack for spotting when the need to be moving got too much. Though, from all Gabe heard from others, Gabe was not exactly subtle in that matter, not to anyone who knew him. He picked up his usual circuit, along the back of the sofa and chairs to the glass doors onto the garden, back to the shelves on the inside wall, and around. He'd made one full loop when Geoffrey spoke again.

"I know your ritual in Kent wasn't much. There was one here, on the full moon. Well, not here, obviously. It would have been a better designed ritual, if it were. Or at least differently designed."

"That sounds - well. Not promising." Gabe's chin came up, but he kept walking.

Geoffrey flipped his hand back and forth. "It did something. That was part of what Rufus wanted to look at, or at least see what to aim me at. Or Alexander."

Alexander grunted. "It's a fair ride, and I'm short on time, is part of it." Short on time was an understatement.

Gabe had only a fragment of an idea of what the Council was up to at the moment, if far more than most people did. And he was quite sure they were all working flat out, twenty-six hours a day, and extra at key astrological timings.

Geoffrey reached out casually to touch his fingers to Alexander's forearm. He barely had to lean to do it, they were sitting close enough. "I am glad to take on these little matters for you. And besides, I've the energy to spare at the moment."

Geoffrey was indeed near-glowing with the land magic. Gabe thought Papa was too, and Mama, but it had a different quality for them than it did for Geoffrey and Lizzie. Some of it rubbed off, perhaps, on Alexander, who looked tired, but not nearly as drawn as he might be.

Gabe had not inquired about what particular arrangements might be in place, other than the fact he knew Alexander had rooms here, and spent several nights a week in them whenever he was in the country and able. It wasn't like either of them would give him a straight answer if asked, anyway. Gabe had other, more directly relevant puzzles to crack. "The ritual?" He pivoted again, on his good heel, and set off in the other direction.

"Down in the southern part of the Forest, possibly at the Naked Man. They got into their head that a sacrifice was needed, from the bits I've heard."

Gabe pulled up short, his jaw dropping. "A what?"

"Oh, nothing like a penny dreadful. Or some of the old lore. Voluntary, of course." Geoffrey was speaking evenly enough, but Gabe knew how to listen for the thread of something too-tight in his voice. Gabe was, however, watching Alexander, to read whatever faint signals he might get there. Alexander was still, entirely attentive, but not tense. Curious.

"What happened?" Gabe turned to face them both, leaning slightly on the cane in his hand.

"Coldest night in May for many years, the ritual done naked, most of them with a protective layer of grease, bar the oldest member, who left it off. Hypothermia." Geoffrey wasn't giving anything away in his expression or his voice, not any part of how he felt about it, other than the clipped phrases.

Gabe rubbed his face, making himself take his time to think through this. He was glad, immediately, that Isobel wasn't here. That he didn't have to sort through both his reaction and hers at the same time. "Hypothermia's a kinder way to die than many." Truth, though, of course, not all of it. "But no blood shed on the ground." Alexander's barking laugh didn't startle Gabe, but it did grab his attention. "The way you think, Gabe. No, it's true. The blood matters. Blood always matters." He shifted in his chair. "We're not sure if it worked. But there are some rumours, tidbits."

"What sort of rumours? Believable? Helpful? Obscure?" Gabe picked up his circuit again, trusting that it would help him think.

"There's a family, used to live nearer Southampton. Two brothers and two sisters, it's a brother and sister we're concerned with. The other brother—" Alexander hesitated. "Ah, you'd have still been in school. The family he married into were suffragettes, socialists, and anti-war sorts." His voice gave away no part of how he felt about that, which was interesting information of its own, really. "The charges were that they made an attempt on Lloyd George's life in late 1916. Curare, of all things. It didn't work, of course."

Gabe tilted his head, pausing again by the table and picking up the glass of wine there. "Prime Minister?" He made it enough of a question. On average, he had quite enough to keep him busy with Albion's own politics. And, as Alexander said, he'd been in school. Third year, when his most compelling political concerns had to do with not getting in too much trouble with either his fellow students or his teachers. "Wasn't he fairly new at the thing in December of '16?"

"Brand new, yes. Finished up as Prime Minister in '22. Came up via the financial side, then Minister of Munitions, Secretary of State for War, then the PM." Alexander reeled it all off easily, and Gabe wondered - not for the first time - exactly what depth of information Alexander kept stored in his brain. A rather different set than Gabe himself, obviously. "At any rate, the rest of the family has a reputation for what some would call mind-control."

"Incantation, more or less." Gabe picked up his walking again, considering that. "To what purpose? Love? Wealth?"

"Most notably - so pub gossip has it from time to time - tales about the family holding back the Armada and Napoleon. Longstanding family in these parts. These days, the father was - I don't know. Some sort of chemist, I forget what kind. Not the apothecary sort. The current generation's bounced from the Theosophists to Co-Masonry to the Rosicrucians to I don't know what else."

"Much gossiped about, then." Gabe considered that. Village gossip was a key source of information. "But Southampton."

Geoffrey picked up. "Rather. And I don't have nearly the connections there. One of the sisters is in Christchurch, now, or near there."

"Worth seeing if we can pick up an acquaintance?

Isobel, maybe, they seem likely to take to her better. How old are the three we're interested in?"

"The oldest daughter's..." Geoffrey did maths in his head, visibly. "Near twenty years older than you. About my age. The brother's a few years younger, then the other sister."

"The name?" Gabe circled again, then moved to collapse in the chair.

Geoffrey got an expression on his face that boded ill for someone. Possibly Gabe. "Mason, of all things. No relation to ours."

It was a good thing Gabe had not actually taken a drink from his glass recently. He would have spit out, and that would have been a shame for the rug and the wine. "You're pulling my leg." He shook his head. "We should set her on them, only."

"Only, no. I would like the southern half of the Forest reasonably intact when this is done, if we can manage it." Geoffrey's voice had got a hair sharp, and Gabe immediately put his hands up in acquiescence.

"And none of them are magical by our standards? To be clear." Gabe ventured a sip of his drink.

Alexander shook his head. "I checked the records. Geoffrey checked the records." He spread his hands. "Do with the knowledge what you will."

"And were they involved in the - whatever they were doing?" Gabe pulled out his notebook and made a couple of notes.

"Likely. Though this came through the group Rufus has been talking with, and we don't know what has got altered in the retelling. Different set of people entirely."

"Never trust what people say," Gabe said, agreeably. "Key part of my job. One part in ten's accurate, a couple are a gesture at the right thing, and the rest you can't trust until you've proven it yourself." He let out a huff of breath. "Are they dangerous? To the land magic, to our goals here?"

"Probably not. But they might be more effective than some others, if only by accident. Or depending on how far they lean into those bits of family lore. You needed to know." Alexander stood, going to pour another thumb's width of brandy. "There are some rumblings about a - well, for lack of a better word, staged ritual. Near enough to Arundel and Garin and Livia, though in Ashford Forest, not the Arundel lands."

"That won't make them happy, will it?"

"It's only hints here and there." Geoffrey sounded mild. Deceptively mild. "My contact in Whitehall suggests it's far more a propaganda attempt than anything else. Likely for Lammastide."

"Well, that's appropriate for a sacrifice, isn't it, depending on your tradition?" Gabe sucked in a breath, and he saw both the other men flinch. Moving on, then. "All right."

"You mentioned two challenges?" Trust Alexander to remember that. But Gabe was ready for this one. Of course he was.

"First, the - well, this is an illustration of it. All the chaos of the different methods, varied goals, and who knows if any of it is doing any good, even as something more like prayer." Gabe shook his head. "No one seems to be doing tremendous harm to the land magic or to other people, but that's not a lot of reason to keep on with it."

"Do you think your project's no longer needed, then?" Alexander leaned forward, and all that intensity of purpose was focused on Gabe now. Like one of Geoffrey's falcons, or no. Some sharp-eyed canine, perhaps.

"That doesn't mean someone won't come up with a terrible idea tomorrow. Or stumble into one. No, it's more that I wish there were some way to, I don't know. Bring people together. Aim them. A unifying framework, as well as a unifying goal."

"And we all know that won't happen. An argument of esotericists, that should be the group noun. Often is. I mean, you've at least heard the stories of what was it, Crowley and Yeats and whatever the road was. Something with a B." Alexander shrugged. He flicked his fingers. "It's not as if we can send out a calling card, approved by some recognisable higher power. We certainly don't have one in our pocket."

Gabe shook his head. "And what would everyone believe in, enough? That's the question, isn't it? I'll keep thinking about it."

Alexander hesitated, and Gabe saw it. He waited, without jogging the moment. Alexander's gaze flicked to Geoffrey, who nodded just once. Something they'd already discussed, then.

"We're having the same problem on our side of things. A dozen, two dozen different ideas of how to protect Albion, many of them entirely contradictory. Somewhat more effective, on average, than what you're seeing, but that's not actually necessarily a help."

"Too many cooks and a spoiled broth." Gabe let out a huff of breath. "Thank you for trusting me with it. Is there a chance my asking about it would get some ideas you could use, then?"

Alexander nodded, just the once. "Do. Mabyn might have an idea or two, next time you're at the Keep. And she'd be flattered you asked." Alexander was about to say something else, but then there was a knock at the door.

Geoffrey called out, "Come," and in came Isobel in riding gear, along with Rufus. The conversation quickly went along to what they'd spotted, and to a surprisingly lavish tea. There were signs of some sort of effective ritual work near the Naked Man, and Alexander made arrangements to go out the next morning. Isobel also had several quite cogent comments about other spots they'd stopped at, and Gabe was delighted at both what she'd tested and how she made her report.

CHAPTER 23
MAY 27TH AT THE DAX PORTAL

" S till nothing?" Rathna frowned, and then tapped her tuning fork on a nearby entirely ordinary boulder, letting the sound resonate.

Ferdinand shook his head. "Not that I can sense. Are you sure you don't want to have a try?"

"In a minute. Let's take a break, I want to think through this." Coffee here, rather than tea, but that suited Ferdinand well, and Rathna could have hers with plenty of milk. Her nerves did not need the additional jitters.

Five minutes later, they were on a blanket some twenty feet from the portal. Lucas was keeping an eye out for them, Beth and Grietje were back at the enclave making themselves useful. Grietje knew how to deal with cows, among her other numerous skills.

Rathna let out a long breath. Ferdinand, bless him, gave her space for a bit, but eventually cleared his throat. "Mistress?"

"Yes?" She looked him up and down. "Before you ask whatever you're asking, how are you feeling?" He should be well over the backlash now, solidly recovering, but this was the first day he'd done much directly with the portal. Sometimes working with a portal involved with the backlash could rub barely healed places raw.

Gabe had a whole lecture about it. That was where she'd learned far more about backlash than she'd been taught. Morah Avigail's training had been heavy on 'don't do the things that cause it', which was fine in theory and less useful in extremis. Times of war were definitely in extremis.

The Penelopes, on the other hand, ran the risk of it - in themselves or in other people - on what seemed like a quarterly basis. Sometimes fortnightly. She had notes somewhere at home, and she'd sat through all of Gabe's lectures to all three of his apprentices on the topic. When he'd done it with Isobel, she'd had Aunt Mason leaning in her ear and telling her which stories to ask about. That had got them out of Gabe, who'd been grinning more and more broadly each time she asked.

Ferdinand shrugged. "My magic's a little sluggish, perhaps. But nothing hurts. All the exercises you had me do were fine." He sounded routine about it, like it was ordinary.

Rathna tilted her head, considering. "We're going to talk through that more tonight, then. So you understand why it matters. But as long as nothing hurts or feels wrong, you're all right."

Ferdinand didn't argue. She wasn't sure what to do with that, either. He'd been polite, deferential. Appropriate, that was the word. Now, there was something else in him, something watchful. She leaned back on one hand. "Go ahead and ask what you were asking?"

"Why are we here fixing the portal?" He glanced at it and coughed. "Trying to fix the portal? Why not a ship?"

Rathna let out a breath. She'd expected something of the kind. "For one thing, we had a part in breaking the portal. It's responsible to put it right if we can." That wasn't the whole answer, though, or even the biggest part of it.

Ferdinand seemed to realise that, because he frowned. "They don't expect us to."

"That is because they don't have a custom of Portal Keepers, official or otherwise. They're used to having to make a petition to the Fatae and hope one of them feels like doing something about it, eventually. But we have different expectations of ourselves." She then spread her hands. "No, it's not a sufficient reason. It matters, but the other reasons matter more. Can you think of either of them?"

Ferdinand looked down at the grass, thinking hard. She gave him the time for it. There was no reason to rush this. They both needed to rest a little magically. They might as well talk through something he needed to think about while they rested. After a good minute or two, he looked up. "You'd like to get more people out?"

"Yes. Though where we go to is a trick. Spain's already closed off their portals, though we might make arrangements to get one open. Portugal. And for that matter, I'd like to get this one to a point where it could be locked down if the local community wanted that. For safety."

He frowned. "They don't like you. Why do you want to help them?"

Ah. There it was. Rathna hadn't been sure how much of it he was picking up. Especially since he'd not been out and about for much of their first week on the estate or farm or enclave, whatever you called it. "They don't trust me. That's different from liking. And they have good reason."

"They, they seem to like Lucas and Beth more." Ferdinand kept poking at it, and Rathna cheered internally. That was good. This was what she'd wanted for him.

"The Royers know what to expect from Lucas and Beth. They don't have a Guard in the same way in France, but they have enough of an idea of what they do, what they can do. And Grietje has a number of useful skills, and that helps. Me, I do things with magic they don't understand, likely fear, and they don't know how I fit into anything. The Netherlands at least had plenty of trade with Asia."

"And me?"

Rathna shrugged. "What do you think?"

He let out a huff of breath. "I haven't talked about my family." He said it hesitantly, though.

"No. But you are, well. You are obviously from a certain sort of background. It's all over you, how you speak, how you stand, the clothes you're wearing, the assumptions you make. You've been polite, you've been courteous. The aristocracy's a complicated thing in France since the Terror, but they have their local nobility, one way or another, and you're close enough to that."

Ferdinand grimaced. "I didn't mean to."

"You can't help not." Rathna softened for a moment. This was a lesson she'd learned at six, at eight, at ten, at thirteen, and then again when she'd come into Gabe's orbit, and all his family. "Some things are written all over us. People make assumptions about me, even if some things I do confuse them. Because I am visibly Indian, not even Eurasian. Because I'm a woman with a substantial education, even if they don't understand what I'm educated in. Because much of my magic is quiet and takes a long time to become manifest." She shrugged. "There are quite a few people in your family's circles who won't give me the time of day."

Ferdinand flushed at that. "Some of them made comments. When it came out I wasn't with Master Fortnum. Over the winter holidays." He swallowed. "That's not all of it, though, Mistress. May I speak freely? Possibly also awkwardly?"

Rathna nodded. "Of course. Whatever you feel needs saying." She thought the 'possibly also awkwardly' was charming, honestly.

"Mutti - my mother - her family is well respected in Germany in magical circles. A very old family. We went through this talking about the portal."

Rathna nodded, but didn't expand on what she knew about them that Ferdinand hadn't told her directly. Perhaps he'd touch on that, perhaps he wouldn't. "Yes. Quite notable, to have a portal at the family home."

"All of them have their particular interests. Some of which tie rather well into the current, um. The current approved approaches. A return to the land, to the magical cycles of the land. That's what Mutti's mother and father are interested in, mostly." Decidedly the more reasonable sorts of things. Gabe's family were much the same, as were the Carillons, and to be honest, most of the Lords of the land who Rathna thought well of.

"Much like a number of people I know. Perhaps leaning a little harder on things like the fears in Walpurgisnacht rather than the passions of May Day?" Rathna suggested, gently. "Though bonfires go with both."

Ferdinand's mouth quirked up, torn between amusement and embarrassment. "Just so, Mistress. Mutti has two brothers, one older and one younger. Uncle Sepp, he rather likes magic for what it can give him. He's not very picky, I think. He doesn't exert himself much about it. Uncle Quirin, though. He's got into some things that he hints at. You know, the smirk? Or at least, last I saw him, a year ago. Before the war began properly."

It had begun sometime before that for Austria and Czechoslovakia, but Rathna supposed he had to count from somewhere. She nodded, encouragingly.

"There was a taste, maybe that's the right word, about his magic. Acrid, sharp, acid, I don't know the right words for it. Not in English, not in German." He hesitated. "He'd have been very curious about you, Mistress. I'm glad I wasn't your apprentice yet, for that reason."

"Oh?" Rathna kept herself calm and quiet, rushing this wouldn't do any good.

"There are quite a few in his circles, very taken with what's the word. Indo-Aryan connections. Arguing that the Aryan culture comes from India and connects to it. It honestly didn't make much sense to me, when Uncle Quirin tried to explain it, but he was a bit drunk at the time."

Rathna snorted at that. "Also, I suspect the logic has gaping holes in it. For one thing, you all in Albion, never mind Germany, talk about India like it's one place. And it's hundreds, thousands of different layers of culture and custom and landscape. Like saying Trellech and Glasgow are the same, only about twenty times more so." She didn't get into the more distressing parts of that line of theory, all caught up as it was with the Nazi ideas of a master race. This was not the time, they had other conversations needing to be had.

Ferdinand ducked his chin. "The other thing you should know is Mutti." He turned his hands palm up, making a cup shape. "She's always had a thing about the Grail. She came to Albion because of it. Some people think it came to France, what, southeast of us?" Still along the Pyrenees, Rathna knew that bit of lore. "But that's why she stayed in

Albion. And Papa needed to marry, and they get on well. He lets her have her interests."

Rathna nodded slowly. "That is, as an interest goes, a less distressing one to me than either of your uncles, to be fair." She said it as gently as she could. "I'm glad you told me a bit more." Ferdinand paused, looking away again as he asked, "May I ask more about your background, Mistress Rathna? Beyond what you shared that day after the museum?"

Rathna leaned back, pleased he'd asked. She wasn't entirely pleased to have this conversation here and now, where she wouldn't have any particular comfort to brace her tonight. She'd have dreams, almost certainly. She usually did when something brought her back to those moments. Possibly loud ones. She'd have to warn Grietje and Beth. That was only kind. "I was six. Baba was offered an opportunity on a long voyage, the kind of thing that would have changed our lives. We wouldn't have been wealthy, but we'd have been much more secure. Much less food running out before the end of the month."

It wasn't something he'd ever have known, though depending on how the war went, they all might be a lot more familiar with that. Rationing was already in play, had been since January, and she suspected it would only increase. She shrugged and went on. "He didn't come back. Ships are dangerous work, still, even when there isn't a war. Ma was working as a nanny, and she died of an illness when I was eight. The family kept me on as a playmate for their daughter, but then the father got posted to India, and they couldn't take me. I went to an orphanage in London."

"Not somewhere in Trellech? There has to be something?"

Rathna hesitated before saying as gently as she could.

"My parents weren't of Albion. They had no magic, not the way the Pact defines it. Certainly, they weren't sworn to it."

She waited, then for a dozen expressions to flow across his face, watching where he got stuck wrestling with the idea that she had known, strong magic, a kind particularly of use, and her parents hadn't. He opened his mouth, then closed it. He was choosing careful kindness, then, rather than asking the questions so obviously on his mind, hurtling around him. She had a very good idea what his family - all the various disparate bits of it - would think about that, and they would not approve, any of them.

When he'd settled into a wary uncertainty, she took pity on him and gave him more information. "Albion keeps an eye on the orphanages and children's homes for those with magical potential. That got me to Schola, though I'm still not quite sure how. I gather they couldn't decide what to make of my exam." She'd asked Thesan a few years ago, after one of the long discussions over supper and drinks about how the changes to the exam policies had been playing out.

"And then it was all right?" Oh, he was an innocent, in far too many ways.

"It was difficult, but in a different way. I had enough to eat, I had clean clothing. Fewer rats in my life. But I had no idea how to fit in with the other people in my house or my classes. They knew so many things I didn't know I didn't know. And I'd lost my family's customs, too, especially in the orphanage. But when I was in my second year, Morah Avigail came and looked for anyone who had the potential to become a Portal Keeper. She picked me out, and once she realised I was an orphan, she insisted I live with her during hols. Her people have very clear ideas about supporting widows and orphans."

"Oh." Ferdinand was still struggling with it. "You didn't have anyone?"

"Morah Avigail. Her family. She had great-grandchildren by then, and most of the family accepted she had taken me in, that I should be included. I'm not Jewish, and there was always a distance, an understandable one. But she - she gave me everything I could ever have asked for. Especially a chance to grow into myself. And then, not too long after I finished my apprenticeship, I met Gabe." She let out a long breath. "I've met my mother's family now, in India. Three times, as well as a few who've come to England. It's made a world of difference. And Gabe made it possible to go there."

Ferdinand frowned, looking away again. He didn't look back when he spoke again. "And you, um."

"I love him. I'd be an entirely different person without him. He'd be a different person without me, though his family did a lot to teach him how—" Oh, dear, she'd got tangled in this sentence. There was no way out of it but going on. "How not to be as obviously posh as you are. His parents have some interesting friends, including Grietje's Aunt Elizabeth. Now also our friends."

Ferdinand swallowed hard, but then he looked up. "Thank you, Mistress. I am learning a great deal with you, some of which I should have learned much earlier."

It made her smile broadly, despite their situation. "You are willing and interested in learning it. That makes up for a lot. And you learn fast. Both the portals and everything else I've seen so far." She brushed her hands off. "At any rate, the people here don't know what to make of me, and they don't trust that, and they're not wrong." She let out a huff of breath. "As to the ship..."

Ferdinand nodded, leaning back on one hand now, so

he could watch her. She weighed what to say next, because some of this had to do with alliances and friends and a web of trust. "Bluntly put, it is a time of war, and my family and I have friends whose lives were changed because of ships being sunk in the Channel. If we have to take a ship, we will, but it is a risk."

Again, she watched the expressions play over his face. "How common is it? I hadn't thought..."

"Most people don't, unless they pay particular attention to the shipping. Magical ships have a bit more protection, but even if we got to somewhere we could get one, a reliable one, that's a trick. We stand out anywhere, half a dozen ways. And I'm not terribly inclined to ask a stranger to risk his life - perhaps hers, but probably his - to get us to the other side of the Channel. They might not make it back." She hesitated, then added, "And there's that question of trust again. Whether they'd even make the attempt."

Ferdinand winced. "I have an, is the word, overly optimistic view of the world, Mistress. I am gathering." He swallowed again. "Is that something you learned from your family?"

"From my own experience. And Richard, Gabe's father, is in the Guard, Gabe is a Penelope, and Alysoun is absolutely in their league as far as paying attention to details and complications. Never mind that number of family friends." That was a tidy way to wrap up the lot of them. "I don't know that that's something you need to learn in general, but for getting through this, being a tad more suspicious probably won't hurt. We're safe enough for now. I'm thinking about the next step. We don't need to be hasty at the moment."

"If we did have to be hasty?"

Rathna let out a long breath. "I'd go into Basque country, the mountains, west of here. And I'd see about finding the Fatae. There are a number of risks there, both practical and magical, but if we have to, we have to. I'd rather get the portal working, and see where we can get to."

"What if we can't? Or we can open the portal but nothing's open to us?"

Rathna shook her head. "I don't have a plan for that yet. All the active portals in Albion that are old enough to serve will be locked to the Continent now, I'm sure, except maybe Switzerland and a well-guarded one or two in Spain or Portugal. And there aren't as many as all that. The Council Keep and Schola were both locked down tight, before the war even officially started." September of 1938, in fact, she'd been a witness to it. She kept thumbing through lists in her mind, thinking about options. "Certainly not Italy." That ship had long sailed, with the invasion of southern France.

"Are there portals in Albion that aren't active?" Ferdinand looked up at that, suddenly caught on something. "Of an appropriate age."

Rathna considered the question. "Nothing accessible. That's the point. A few of the ancient castles, but the three I know of are all walled off and have been for centuries." She flicked her fingers. "The caves below Tintagel - there was a cave in, I don't know a way through. Windsor Castle is impossible." For one thing, the United Kingdom's royal family lived there, which meant one could scarcely traipse in and out of the place. For another, she was fairly sure the portal was under the Round Tower, in the middle of everything, literally and figuratively.

"Oh." Ferdinand tilted his head. "Where's the other?"

"The Tower of London. But that portal hasn't been used

since the Pact." She frowned. "I'd have expected it to be warded against France, still. But I suppose that one, we could at least try to find out about it. It would depend on..." She tried to run through the dependencies in her head. Whether the portal could be reached physically. Whether it was active. If it was locked against them, or if it could be unlocked.

There were dozens of related questions. And of course, where there was anyone among the Portal Keepers who'd risk it. Whether they'd be permitted to open it, no matter how briefly. On the other hand, it was exactly the sort of challenge Gabe thrived on. Rathna had entirely got the sense in what he didn't say in the journals that it might be the right sort of distraction. Certainly Alysoun could make nice with people who might have influence if needed. "I'll ask."

Ferdinand nodded. "Mistress." It was agreement, more than that, acceptance that whatever she chose here would be suitable. "I think I'm ready to try again, if you are?"

"It's not going to change with us sitting here, is it? I'm wondering if we can try a variation on the technique of establishing one. Dredge the channels, as it were."

CHAPTER 24
MAY 28TH AT DOVER CASTLE

"Lord Thanet?" Gabe cleared his throat cautiously. The older man was standing on the top of the Great Tower, looking out over the water, across to Calais. Not that one could actually see either Calais or, more relevantly, Dunkirk at the moment. "Your man told me you were up here. Can I be of help?" He leaned slightly on his cane. His leg was complaining about the number of stairs up to this point.

Lord Vitruvius Thanet was of the generation between Gabe and his parents, but there were ways in which he hearkened to Gabe's grandmother's era in attitude. He'd left Isobel down with the car. No need to subject her to this particular conversation. It was delicate enough as it was; he didn't need to juggle the man's attitudes toward Isobel herself as well.

Papa and Lord Thanet were civil enough when it came to issues that touched them both. Or, more to the point, issues that touched the land magic. Kent was Kent. It did not care so much where the boundaries of who was responsible for which bit of the land's magic might be. But it was a touchy sort of civility, with something sharp boiling just under the surface. In older times, they'd probably have had a proper duel and sorted it out and been able to leave it. But Papa was a duellist, and Lord Thanet wasn't and had the sense to know it, and so it was like a dog that worried at a bone long past any usefulness.

Gabe had an even more tenuous place. Lord and Lady Thanet were civil to Gabe too, but it was a bare and scant sort of civility. No snub direction, but certainly no invitation to even the most general sort of casual conversation, even when they were next in line to each other at some procession or another.

It wasn't even about Rathna, which Gabe would have hated, but which would have made some sense. Or not sense, but which was common enough that Gabe had a reliable method for how to handle it. They'd been like that since Gabe had apprenticed. Before, a bit. And they weren't even the ones he'd doused with wine when he flipped a table over, entirely accidentally, when he was eleven.

He'd apologised for that, profusely, not that it had helped. Mama had told Gabe it wasn't a thing he could mend, he'd just have to work around it. He had, up until this point. Only now he couldn't leave the man alone. Some things mattered more than old aggravations.

Lord Thanet was also - as he'd learned from talking to Alexander and Cyrus and Mabyn - one of the ones who was being difficult about joining up when it came to shared protections. Kent was at the forefront of the worry there, along with Hampshire and the rest of the lands along the south coast.

Hampshire was fine, Geoffrey was sensible. He'd seen the last War up close, and he knew what they might be facing. West Sussex was held by the Fortiers, and Alexander was able to negotiate with Garin Fortier, at least. The Edgartons' edge of the coastline was well enough. But from east of Folkestone? That was another matter entirely.

Thanet and his lady wife were both given to alchemy and materia. They were fine magical arts, but not as focused on the protection of the land and her people as they might be. Worse, they didn't want to listen to expert advice. They wanted to keep with methods that had been outdated in the last war, if not well before. That was not today's problem, though it might well be tomorrow's or next week.

Right now, what mattered was a miracle. With any luck, some number of men would be coming across an ocean, threading through minefields and avoiding U-Boats and other disasters. Dover lay in the Thanet part of Kent, but not by so much as that.

Thanet looked him up and down, grunting once, before staring back out over the water. "What sort of help could you be?"

"For one, sir, I've access to the latest news from the journals, including the Guard reports. For another, I - and my apprentice, she's downstairs - are glad to lend whatever we can to the effort."

Another grunt. "Not your sort of problem, now is it? These are fighting men. Brave men, seen things you can't dream of."

Gabe didn't twitch. It was an old barb, one that Rathna had helped him defang years ago now. It still smarted, but Lord Thanet hadn't bothered to learn even the public truth. He just mocked Gabe as weak, for not having gone to the War in 1918.

Now, Gabe just shrugged. "Of course they have, sir. As you did in the last War." He'd fought, though mostly a safer sort of fighting, behind the trenches making decisions that got other men killed. Gabe had - on purpose - not dug into the specifics beyond that. If Lord Thanet had a part in the death of Gabe's village friends, or in Del's life-changing head injury, Gabe would have had to do something about it. And that would cause problems, even the more subtle forms of misery any trained Penelope could arrange without getting caught. Besides, Gabe in fact did have ethics.

Lord Thanet grunted one more time. He continued looking out to sea, not even acknowledging Gabe so far as that. "What do you think you can do, then?"

"Vitality, if you need it." Gabe led with that. He didn't much want to share his magic with this man. He could think of thousands of people he'd rather do that with. Possibly hundreds of thousands, by category. Every fishwife along the Thames, for example. "Relay communications. I've the Guard news access, as I said. Both Isobel and I are trained in emergency healing. We can get a few people to the portal, and on to Trellech, I brought our car." He inhaled, then added, "And whatever help I can be with the land magic."

"Your father?" Thanet looked over his shoulder at that. "He should be the one here."

"Coordinating the Guard response." Gabe half-closed his eyes, feeling for his father's magical signature. It was one of those things that worked far better on Kent's fair lands. "Down on the beach, there. With your permission, he'd like to do the rituals for Vortimer's Arm." Bones, buried a millennia and a half ago, to protect Albion from invasion.

He gestured, pointing out a knot of people laying out preparations, a dozen people in the Guard uniform. From here, it looked like just another of the aid battalions, all smart navy wool that would be battered and drenched within an hour or two.

Thanet grunted again. "And you're not?"

"I'm not in the Guard." Gabe shrugged. "Different skills."

"Scrying?" Thanet kept scanning the water.

"Some. Not much weather magic." Gabe hesitated, but the way the man kept looking made Gabe think he was right. "Are you looking for something specific, sir?"

That got him a sharp look. "Think you're clever, son?"

Not your son. And yes, Gabe did think he was clever. Or rather, he knew he was and didn't need to defend himself on that count. Water was wet, the sun shone above, Gabe was clever. They were simple realities. "I've a device with me, sir, that might be a help."

"Something bound to you?" Thanet leaned forward a hair, and Gabe knew he had a hit.

"I can set it for you, sir. It goes on your head, acts like a telescope, more or less. Magically focused, it's possible to use a charm to direct you toward a particular object if you can describe it using locational or sympathetic resonances."

"Let me have it, then." An order, not a request, but Gabe wasn't going to fight that battle. Not here, not now. And who knew, maybe being generous here would make something easier down the road. Gabe was doing this by feel, by thinking about what Rathna would tell him about restraint and patience and feeling for the magic of the earth and rock. Besides, Thanet hated his hastiness, his leaps of logic, the way his mind worked best. He'd have to hold back to have any hope of progress, no matter how tiring and hobbling that was.

Silently, Gabe opened the satchel over his shoulder, drawing out the broad shallow wood case. He set it on a wooden bench, fitting the lens to the strap carefully. He straightened up, holding it out in his hands. "I am glad to do the charm work if you let me know what you're looking for."

"The Ridgeway. Small vessel. There's someone on it, I hope." Someone else - near anyone else, Gabe would have asked who, if it were family or some particular connection. Here, he didn't. "What do you need to know?"

"Size, material, anything you know about when to expect her." Gabe used the feminine for ships, as one did. There was an interesting linguistic tendency there, a rabbit hole for him to chase some night when he couldn't sleep. The day after the day this evacuation was over, probably.

Thanet shook his head once, like shaking off a fly. "Wood, about thirty-foot, usually a fishing boat."

Gabe contemplated that for a couple of seconds, how to name that in the enchantment, then he put together a string of Latin, under his breath. Mason would be proud of him, and Witt would make him decline his nouns better, but it would work and that was what mattered. After five breaths, he held it out. "This strap over your head, tighten the others so it's steady, or I can do that for you, sir. Please don't touch the lens itself. It smudges very easily and takes a while to clean."

The man would not be helped, Gabe saw that at once, so he stepped back, folding his hands over the handle of the cane so he wouldn't fidget. He saw the moment when the effect kicked in, as Thanet took a staggering step back, and Gabe refused to admit he'd seen it. He kept his face steady and polite.

Thanet recovered quickly enough, beginning to scan the water. "What's the range?"

"A good few miles on that setting. Enough to cross the Channel near here."

"Do you know why the smoke?" Gabe hadn't had a look, but he knew why. The journals were a miracle of their own that way.

"The Luftwaffe bombed Dunkirk harbour." He cleared his throat, carefully. "Last I heard, they couldn't take the more direct route. They may be coming in more from the west. The ship it's set for, the Ridgeway, should be in sharp focus, everything else much less so."

It got him another grunt. Lord Thanet's mother clearly hadn't put the time into teaching him to be a charming conversationalist. Mama had drilled Gabe on that endlessly, though at least she'd made it interesting. They stood in mutual silence for a good five minutes before Thanet let out a long sigh. "I see her. Closer in than I expected."

"I'm glad, sir." Gabe didn't make a move. This was the delicate point, whether this had made any difference at all.

"Your father said you're working on a project to unite protections. I have no truck with that. We're lords of the land. We stand for the land and the people, and what suits him does not suit me." Thanet didn't look at Gabe, he kept watching the water. But his tone was a bit more conversational, not as rigid as earlier.

"I am, sir." Gabe hesitated, checking with himself, with the land, to see whether this was the time to launch himself. "Can I ask, sir, what might convince you?"

"A unanimous vote of the Council, and we all know you won't get that." Gabe could make that count, too. They had a solid majority for this, but not unanimity. "Or a sign from the Fatae, the sort of thing that can't be forged." Theoretically, the Council could arrange something like that, but whether they could in reality was an entirely different sort of question.

"Do you think the others would accept the same?" Gabe kept his voice even, the way he did when questioning someone in a case, letting them hear he wasn't making assumptions at all, just taking everything in.

Thanet moved his head slightly, winced, and went back to looking out over the water. "I think it would change the ground, certainly. If you produce such a thing, I'll cooperate, and tell everyone why. How's that?"

"Quite fair, sir." Gabe took a slightly easier position. The question was still impossible, the sort of thing he couldn't shift, no matter how clever he was. But he could take it to Alexander, to Geoffrey, and to Cyrus and Mabyn, and the others who were cooperating, and he could see what ideas they had.

After a moment, Thanet took the straps off. "I can see her getting close. I'll go down to the docks." He hesitated. "You mean it, about the help? Here and now?"

"In the service of the land all my days, and here, especially, right now. As long as I'm needed."

"Can you get yourself down to the ground level, somewhere I can find you again when I need you, and set up Thanet's Eighth?"

Gabe knew it, of course he knew it. Not his favourite of the supportive rituals for the land. But of course the Thanets would prefer it and use it, it had been their umpteenth great-grandfather who'd come up with it. "Of course, sir." He glanced over the edge of the tower. "I'm thinking there, when you want me again. I'll set my apprentice to running messages."

"Good." Thanet exhaled. "Having someone else to

anchor will be a help. Bring all our boys home safe, as many as we can."

"That is all I want at the moment, sir." Gabe leaned to put his device away, giving time for Thanet to lead the way down the stairs. They had work to be doing.

CHAPTER 25
JUNE 8TH NEAR DAX

Rathna brushed her hair back from her face as Lucas came barrelling into the clearing where they were working on the portal. Again, still, always, it seemed. She looked up, alarmed.

"News?"

"German Army's marching on Paris. Refugees are pouring out. Monsieur Dechamps wants to know how stable the portal is."

Rathna let out a puff of air. They'd been working round the clock the last week to encourage the portal along, and it was only barely stable again. Probably. "It's a risk." She hesitated. "Means we might not get out by portal after."

He took a half step back, looking at her. He wasn't arguing, but she could see him judging the choice she might make. If she went down one path, she'd lose his respect, and he was right about that. Likely, anyway. She'd lose all respect for herself, too.

"Give me a minute. Let me think it through. They're willing to have refugees here?" She knew he wanted to get people out. Rathna did too, but someone had to weigh the costs, and she'd apparently been elected, appointed, and touched with whatever divine madness picked leaders in times of chaos. She did not like it one bit. She was not born to this sort of leadership, and she certainly had not had anything like enough training. That was Richard, Gabe, Geoffrey, even Alexander and Isembard.

"They've got family in Paris, some of them. If they can get a portal here..." Lucas didn't need to finish that thought. He picked up with the rest of what she needed to know. "Beyond that, they think they can get people over the mountains to Spain. All the coordination's going by paired notebooks, though, so I'm needed back at the enclave soon as I can be."

The family estate had acquired half a dozen new guests in the last fortnight, all of whom were deeply connected to the local magical community, such as it was. It had been a hub of planning and coordination, or as much of both as information and resources allowed.

"Right. Let me think through the tolerances. Ferdinand?" She pitched her voice higher, gesturing to a pair of rocks they'd taken to using near the back of the little clearing that held the portal itself. He trotted over, meeting her as she found a place on the stone. "Did you hear that? What do you think of the portal?"

Ferdinand winced. "I had hoped to have more time."

"So had we all." Rathna frowned. "You could go now, before we take them in. Get out safely. You and whoever else. Portal to Spain, get a ship from there." She had to make the offer. She was responsible for him. For all he was a grown man, he was still a young man, and this particular part was not his sworn duty.

His chin came up, sharply. "Is that an order, Mistress?"

She lifted both hands, then turned them palm up. "I am looking at all our choices. Even the uncomfortable ones."

"Mistress?" His voice dropped in pitch and volume. "If you insist I go, you won't be able to hold the portal yourself. Not for long. Nor repair it."

"No, I won't." Rathna half-closed her eyes. This wasn't exact maths, none of it was, but she could make an informed estimate. "If we bring people through, in quantity, dozens, there's a two in three chance it will damage the portal right now. Probably."

"Probably." Ferdinand echoed the comment. "If I stay and help?"

"Two-thirds if you stay and help. Almost certain if you don't." Rathna opened her eyes again to watch him. She was proud he'd asked, whatever he decided.

"Of course I'm staying. Is there a chance we could patch it enough to use again if I do?" Ferdinand shifted, both feet now firmly on the ground, back straight.

"A better chance. I don't want to guess the odds. It's very likely we'll be stuck here, though. Or have to go across the mountains, and that has all sorts of risk."

"The mountains themselves. The Fatae. Animals. Other things we don't know yet." Ferdinand nodded slowly. "I have a little experience in mountains, but not nearly enough."

"It is times like this I wish Gabe were here. He is very good with a mountain, among his other skills." He would, in fact, be tremendously helpful right now. He was not an infinite pool of magical vitality, and he especially wouldn't be away from Albion. But he knew how to use his magic deftly, and most of all, he saw unusual solutions to problems. Near always. "But you're sure you want to stay."

"I am. My family might throw a fit at someone. I don't

225

care." The Howards had been attempting to exert pressure, she knew that. The Guild Master mostly had kept her out of it, but Alysoun had kept her updated on what she heard. Ferdinand was a younger son. He'd chosen what he wanted to do even if he'd had no idea what he was choosing at the time. But parents worried, and politics demanded certain things of them, apparently.

Rathna looked at him, sharply. "Make your peace with them, a note in the journal, whatever else you do. If this does all go wrong..." She swallowed hard. "That's not a loose end anyone should have to live with."

"Mistress." He subsided, at least for a moment. Then he looked up. "And you're staying, whatever the rest of us decide?"

She nodded once. Rathna could feel the pull in her, the way she was torn between going home to Albion, to stepping through the Veritas portal and knowing down to her bones where she was and what it meant. But she also knew she had to try. Some of it was professional bravado. If they could make this work, it was the kind of challenge others would rise to meet, and that could be wonderful.

But mostly, she wouldn't be able to look herself in the mirror if she didn't.

"Mistress?" Ferdinand's voice was tentative now. "May I ask why? I understood, a little, in the Netherlands. What you said about Magistra Levy's people?"

Rathna half-smiled at that. "Yes. But now?"

Ferdinand let out his breath in a rush. "You know how they look at you. How they talk, even if you don't know as much French? I've seen you, Mistress, when they won't let you near the little ones. Why stay?"

"People talk about me in Albion, too. I hear more of it, and it's not just because of the French." She shrugged. "I can't let other people tell me what I ought to do. I tried that. It was miserable. I was miserable. And I was raised better than to sink to that level." She looked off toward the portal stones. "Jewish teachings put a high value on life. Every life saved is a blessing. Whatever I can do that saves a life, that matters." She hesitated. "What's the verb tense for this? I wouldn't like the person I became if I left now. So I'll stay, as long as I might be able to help."

"Mistress." He subsided. "What will you do now? What can I do to help?"

"First," Rathna said. "I am writing to Gabe. He might have ideas. Next, you and I will - do you know Behenian's Eighth? Drawing vitality broadly from the local area? We need to be careful with it. We don't want to affect the crops or the livestock."

"I do." He frowned. "I learned a variant from the home farm steward. Can I write and confirm it?"

"Please. Whatever we do, I want to start in..." Rathna glanced up to track the line of the sun, then checked her watch for good measure. She still wasn't used to this latitude and what it meant for the light. "An hour. We'll both eat and refresh ourselves. I'll write to Gabe, take some measurements, and tell Lucas what we think we can do."

"Yes, Mistress." Ferdinand stood, made a slight bob of a bow in her direction. When she didn't say anything else, he went off at a near lope, first to Lucas and then to his own bag with his journal.

Rathna pulled out her own. Then she stared at the page. Dear Gabe, I might be stranded here. Dear Gabe, I love you. Kiss Avigail for me. Dear Gabe, how are you still sane? Dearest Gabe. Every life we save matters.

She stared at the page for a good three minutes, then she took a deep breath, writing carefully. *Dearest Gabe, I'm making a choice, and I hope it's the right one. We're going to open up the portal here for refugees from Paris for as long as we can. I don't know how long it will hold, or whether we'll be able to restore it afterwards, fast enough for whatever comes next. Whatever advice you can gather would be a help, what our options might be, especially for crossing the Pyrenees. I don't know what I need here. What we need.*

Rathna paused there, not sure how to say the rest of it. That she was taking a risk, a huge risk, they all were. Any number of things might go wrong with the portal. It could drain them all to the dregs and worse. Ferdinand was only recently recovered from the backlash. They could misjudge how long they had, and be trapped here.

Part of her wished they'd left as soon as they could, by whatever means. If they had to flee now, they'd be in the middle of a host of others, and that was another kind of risk. Especially when they were so clearly not French, not local, not connected to these places and these people by anything other than a thin thread of basic humanity. But that was not the choice they had, and it was foolish to bog down in things that weren't true, and that certainly weren't options now.

Rathna stood, taking her working stones to the portal. She made the measurements again, and they'd not changed since this morning. It might hold. It should hold. Maybe long enough. She came back to her journal and wrote out all the data she knew. Gabe could make sense of most of it, and if he couldn't, he'd know who to ask. He knew where she was. She'd sent him precise coordinates already, after confirming them with the stars the first clear night they'd been here.

It took three pages and nearly all the hour. As she was finishing up, Ferdinand appeared, silently holding out food and a flask of tea to her. She set the journal down after sending the message, then took the baguette and cheese, balancing it carefully on her knees. "Can you get Lucas over? And I'll need a couple of minutes to eat, but then we can start."

"I have the details on the variant, Mistress." He lifted one hand, and thirty seconds later, Lucas had joined them.

Rathna swallowed a bit of her lunch. "Tell them we'll do our best. I'm certain - assuming the portal at the other end holds - we can get groups through. Open for a couple of minutes, maybe five, maybe just two or three. I won't know how many until we do it, and we'll need four or six hours between them. It's more likely to close on the ends, rather than trap them wherever the middle travels. But it's a risk, and I don't know how to tell on this end when we reach that point for certain. Can you explain the risks to them?"

"I will." Lucas grimaced. "They'll take them, though. However risky it is, it's a chance."

"We'll get as many through as we can, and then we'll see what we have to work with." There were, fundamentally, only four ways this could go. This portal failed, the Paris side failed, they both failed simultaneously, or they both survived and kept working. "Can you ask if there's anyone who has any kind of relationship with the local Fatae? I'd—" She glanced back at the portal. "I'd like to make offerings, but I don't know what's proper or expected or entirely polite. I've asked a contact who might have ideas, but if there's anyone local, that would be better."

"We can't." Lucas looked as if she'd suggested swimming across the Atlantic. Something unfathomable, a mix of the utterly forbidden and the entirely impossible.

Rathna knew better. She'd had enough conversations with her Bengali family on their visits, but she had no idea how to translate any of that here. "We can. This is not Albion. We are not bound by the Pact in the ways we are at home. I do not know how best to do it, but I am certain it can be done. Enough for politeness, at the very least. And if we're very lucky, perhaps a bit of help. If there are people here who they are fond of."

Lucas gaped at her for a good twenty seconds, but then he just nodded. "If that's what you need, Magistra. Will you be here all afternoon?"

Rathna nodded. "We should be able to establish the connection late this afternoon, but I want to give us the best shot we can. Have someone come by at..." Another glance at her watch. "Five. With food we can eat on the fly, if you can. We'll likely have to sleep here."

"The tent, then, plenty of padding to sleep on, and a campfire. We'll sort that." He looked relieved to have a task that would keep him busy. "I'll send Grietje along as soon as I get back."

"Good." Or rather, none of this was good. But they had a plan, and having a plan would have to do for now.

CHAPTER 26
JUNE 14TH AT THE COUNCIL KEEP IN WALES

he first any of them knew that something was
unusually wrong was the wail of alarms from the
courtyard.

Gabe had been at the Council Keep for perhaps half an
hour in one of his increasingly regular meetings with
Smythe-Clive, Rolls, and whoever else had an interest that
particular day. Alexander had spent the duration lurking in
a chair in the corner, making an occasional brisk comment.
He was right, mind. But he was also sharper and sharper
each time he spoke. Smythe-Clive hadn't taken it person-
ally, which made Gabe respect him a bit more.

Then the alarm went. Gabe saw how Alexander waited
just a beat, as if to get some piece of information from the
pitch and duration that Gabe couldn't interpret. Then he
took off out the door, his robe flowing straight out behind
him. Gabe duelled the man regularly, and the way
Alexander could go from rest to full speed in an instant was
still a shock every time.

Smythe-Clive was standing, gone dead white, as

though he'd been hit with a tremendous blow. Then he was reaching for something from a shelf, a small box. Gabe held his hands up. "Should I wait here? Go?"

"That's the portal." Smythe-Clive looked upward, as if considering his options. "Come. Stay back. Don't touch anything unless you're told." He had no hesitation in the commands. The man had gravitas, as well as having the ultimate rule here. There was just an instant where Gabe felt the land react, the way it did to Gabe and his father on their own lands. He'd not felt that before here. Smythe-Clive was the Lord of this place - or if not that, the chosen steward. The land was making that clear.

Gabe - who was not, as a rule, inclined to follow an order just because it was an order - immediately decided to obey. He let Smythe-Clive go first, of course, following close behind while thinking through what he had on him. He had his wand, the better set of his working stones, and his satchel, with a few dozen bits of materia. Though he was sure if it came to that, that there was whatever he might need in the Keep itself, at least on that front.

He had a selection of potions in their padded case. There were the ones for wounds and for stamina and protection, a few vials of the one he took for his ankle, all the quotidian things he needed on the regular. And he had an evidence kit. He never left home without one.

He would hope that none of them were needed, but he'd seen Alexander's face. And Smythe-Clive's. Rolls was harder for Gabe to read, but his expression had held nothing promising at all.

He rounded the curve of the Keep a bare five paces behind Smythe-Clive, to find something that would have been a historic tableau, if this were a hundred years ago, and an artist had been handy to capture the moment. It was something out of a great battle painting, only stripped down to a few stark lines and shapes set against the unforgiving stone of the courtyard and walls of the Keep. Gabe rolled to a stop, a foot behind Smythe-Clive, taking it in, all his training shouting that here was danger of every magical kind.

Four bare steps from the portal was a figure. Garin Fortier knelt, his arms around a shape that Gabe couldn't make out at first, but that then resolved into Livia Fortier. His wife. His late wife. Gabe was sure from a look, but he knew the charms that would confirm it, and he called the knowledge to him before he thought better of it. It was as if they'd been painted in broad dark swaths of ink or paint, bleeding across the stone in shapes that would not quite focus. Magic was fair crackling off him, visible, but also sharp sparks against Gabe's own magic and protections.

Alexander had crossed most of the space, but he stopped five feet away. Far enough to have some warning of a sudden movement. Of course he'd think of that. He was focused entirely on Garin, but then looked to Gabe for just an instant. Gabe gave one slight nod. Alexander knew his skills, certainly well enough for this. And, for that matter, his impulses.

Smythe-Clive wasn't moving, wasn't saying anything, and Rolls peeled off, back to somewhere in the Keep, without a word or any sound beyond his shoes on the stone. Garin stayed bent over, rocking slightly, his voice rising, calling his wife's name. Always the triplicate liv-i-a, like it was an incantation that might mend a hole torn in the world.

"Garin, talk to me. What happened?"

Alexander's voice was curiously blunted. Not his teacher's voice, Gabe had heard that often enough. This was something made of bloody compassion that knew the only way through was to go forward, no matter how painful. Alexander had trained Garin before he'd trained Isembard. He'd known them both from their childhoods. He had the right, the way everyone in Albion counted it, to press on this point. Both as near enough kin, and as a colleague on the Council.

"We got most of it through to Trellech." What that was, he didn't say, but it obviously meant something to Alexander and Smythe-Clive both. "There was, it was like lightning, the moment before it strikes, in the entrance hall." He didn't look up, but his shoulders shuddered. Gabe could see now that both of them were smudged with smoke and blood and all the signs of a magical duel of great force and power. "She took two of them out. Then." He gasped and swallowed, his shoulders buckling.

"Did you seal the portal?" Alexander's question was sharper now, needing to know, an urgency that burned in Gabe's veins.

"I don't know. I don't care. Livia, please."

Alexander held up a hand, not looking away from Garin, as if Garin were a cobra who might strike at any moment. "Do you know how?"

Gabe was not supposed to know. He had never discussed what Rathna had taught him with anyone, not even his parents, though he was sure they'd guessed the rough measure of it. It was not precisely forbidden. She had taken no oath on it. She had thought, in her own particular view of the world, that he might need to know this thing, sometime. It was far easier to bar a portal than to open one up again. That was the thing.

He caught Smythe-Clive turning his head. "If you can, do it now. Temporary by preference, or something that can be undone with effort if you can't. Tell us if that's not an option." Another order, and one Gabe was willing to obey. He circled around, skirting the tableau, giving them as much space as he could. It was not remotely enough, he did not want to be behind Garin's back in this morning, not one bit.

Alexander was at least a little ahead of him. And so was Rolls. Gabe paused beside the portal stones, to take out the working stones he'd need for this. Rolls came back out, trailing an Indian woman and carrying a stretcher, two poles and a length of canvas. That was Vidya Archarya, a recent addition to the Council and also a Healer. Rathna approved of her. It meant Alexander could turn his attention to coaxing Garin to let them have a look at Livia, and Gabe could focus on the portal.

He began with observation, as Doyle and Witt had drilled into him. Instinct was all well and good - and his instincts were excellent - but rushing into a complex magical problem never ended well. He took a breath, as he'd been trained, then another. He had to find his own balance with the land, even if this particular bit of it was not his and he had no claim on it, beyond whatever claim anyone of Albion did. He was acting at the command of, for lack of a better term, its Lord, and it might know that. He let his senses float, like a bird gliding on the updrafts, without leaning into it. It was a time for seeing and hearing and sensing, not yet a time for doing.

Whatever had happened on the other end had done serious damage, the sort of damage that would take months to repair, if they even could. It wasn't just physical. Whatever Livia and the other fighting had done, it was something that ran down to bedrock. Not that he could tell too much from here. All the magics between the two were tangled and shorn and jagged messes. He wanted to trace each of them, to figure out what had happened, all his instincts screaming that he needed to understand this, to unweave the tangle the way he'd been made for. It was a wonder they'd made it back, honestly.

"Can you?" Alexander's voice was right behind his shoulder now, all of a sudden, and Gabe hadn't seen or heard him move. Gabe had near enough got lost in the stone, and that would have compounded the problem no end. For Gabe, as well as the portal. He knew better. He had known better for twenty-five years. There was no time for that now. Alexander needed an answer.

"Lock it to the continent, yes. With a little time and luck, I should be able to keep it open to Albion. Does Trel-lech need to lock down?"

"Yes. Check with them. You know who to ask. And then, when you're sure he can get through, write to Isembard. Tell him what he needs to know." Alexander looked suddenly ancient and exhausted. "I trust you. Do what you think is needed. Wait for us in the room we were in earlier. We'll be a bit." His chin jerked to one side. "We're taking her upstairs."

It meant something to Alexander, and Gabe wasn't going to ask for details. "It will take me at least an hour. Maybe longer. Probably."

"Whatever it takes." Then Alexander turned away abruptly, disappearing back across the courtyard without any further word. The instruction was clear enough.

Gabe gathered himself, taking a moment to lay out his tools where he could reach them easily, a flask of water in case he needed it. He wrote a bare six words to Isobel, "Busy. More later. Where I was." She'd know from that not to expect him, and what to say to his parents.

Then the note to Trellech, adding Smythe-Clive to the list, asking them on behalf of the Council to confirm that they'd locked their portals against France. The Guildmaster would be there, at least, or handy enough. That they'd have more to share later. He knew the language for that, at least, honed in making formal reports for the Courts, and from everything Mama had taught him.

Now, he set to seeing what he could do, so Isembard could get here quickly. So the rest of them could leave, if it came to that. There was nothing near the Keep, neither portal nor train stop or ferry dock. That was going to be a problem if Gabe was not very clever. If he didn't remember everything Rathna had told him.

Only then did he turn back to the portal, closing his eyes and sending a prayer to all those gods who removed obstacles, who blessed open doors, who understood how to balance on the head of a pin. It was mixing half a dozen cosmologies, and he didn't care at all so long as it worked. He placed a hand on each of the stone pillars at exactly the same moment, and he could feel the magic pulse and arch through him.

For a moment, he thought he'd made the worst of mistakes. That Alexander would find him here, burned to ash and spread in the wind, torn apart by ancient magics. This was a far older portal than any he'd ever worked with before. He'd only done much directly with the one at Veritas, which was a child by comparison. It was foreign, in a way he hadn't expected, but of course, it was Fatae made. One of the first of the Fatae portals, as the lore had it, was at least two thousand years old, possibly many more.

Gabe did the only thing he could think of to do and made himself vulnerable to it. There was no fighting a tidal wave, no ducking an earthquake. He could only ride through the storm swirling around him. He knew, deep in his heart, he would lose if he fought for even a moment. The power here could crush him, absolutely and impersonally, with the slightest twitch of a finger. Or a thought.

He hung there, willing himself to relax into it, to lean into it. It was perhaps the hardest thing he'd ever done. Stillness had never been his gift. Everyone who knew him teased him about being a perpetual motion device, always shifting. Here and now, he could only bring the focus he could gather to being here, in the moment, to making space for whatever was needed.

Gabe had no idea how much time passed. There was a moment where the enormous pressure was buffeting him, and then there was a moment where everything stopped. He had no idea if he'd passed into the eye of the storm, about to be tossed into the ferocious pull again any second, or if he had somehow come to a new place. He gathered his thoughts, and as clearly as he could, focused on his intention. Seal this portal against the Continent, leave open the paths within Albion. Please, for kin, for need, for duty, for the good of the land.

Something in those last phrases caught a scrap of fabric fluttering that unfurled into a heraldic banner. Gabe couldn't make out the symbols on the green field, nor form any sense from a flash of movement he caught, like a stag leaping away in the woods. Then it formed into something that was absolutely not a stag, a sinuous curve of iridescent green whose wings spread for just a second before disappearing into mist. But he knew, in that moment, what was needed, how to thread what Rathna had taught him with the reality of this singular portal.

The power released him blinking into the afternoon light, and he'd gone to his knees somewhere along the way.

Before he was thinking again, he had his tools in hand, working through the ritual of stone and affinity and measurement, over and over to lay out the trace work that would do what was needed.

Again, he lost track of time, but when he was done, he knew he'd succeeded. The portal hummed, and with harmony, not a singular note. He could hear Rathna's voice in the mix, dozens of other people he knew, with a richness that defied human song. Only then did he settle back on his heels, and summon his journal to his hands, writing to Isembard.

First, a bare warning, "You're needed at the Council Keep. Livia was killed, Garin brought her body back. Come as soon as you can." Too blunt, too sharp, and a moment later he wrote to Thesan, too. "Livia was killed in fighting in Paris. Garin brought her back to the Council Keep. Isembard's needed as soon as he can. Let someone know when he's coming."

It was only then that he took any notice of his other surroundings. The courtyard behind him was quiet, but as he shifted, there was a soft cough from his left. "It's Mabyn Teague. Can people get in and out?" Smythe-Clive's partner, and a Council Member in her own right for many years now.

Gabe shifted, grimacing as his ankle complained. "Yes. I've written Isembard. And Thesan." Who was, in fact, more likely to react to her journal promptly.

She looked strained, but she nodded. "I'll wait here. I can tell Isembard a bit more, before - well." Teague let out a long breath. "Cyrus will want to talk to you when he can."

"I'm not expected back. If I could." He could feel how his entire back was a band of strain, the ankle, a growing headache. "A bit of food and something to drink, so I can take a potion?"

"One of the staff is seeing to things. The room you were in earlier." He had to admire that Teague, at least, was careful not to assume what anyone had told him. Gabe nodded, leaning to put the working stones back in their case, smoothing his fingers instinctively over them. He'd need to properly cleanse and align them and, blast, the full moon wasn't for six days. He'd prefer that for timing. It would take twice as long to do it sooner, and it wasn't as if he had time to spare. Good thing he had the backup set.

Then, carefully, he leaned to grab his cane, and levered himself up. The ankle held, and at least he'd worn ankle boots today under his trousers. It was a help. He repacked things in his satchel, making sure the potion he'd want immediately was handy.

Once he was standing, Mabyn nodded once at him, and he made his way with as much grace as he could back into the Keep. It had an ominous sort of silence to it, as if all the attention was far away. Gabe didn't see anyone but the one member of staff who brought him coffee - Alexander's preferred mode of it - and sandwiches. Gabe took the vial he'd pulled out, which didn't so much conquer the headache and aches of his body as hold them back. He pulled out a second. He'd take that in a bit.

It was at least another hour before anyone else appeared, as Gabe peered periodically at the clock across the room from him, or counted the chimes for the quarter hours. He kept himself busy enough by laying out arguments for what should be done next. Even though it was not remotely his call, and likely no one would ask.

Just after five, there was a knock on the door, and Alexander came in, followed by Smythe-Clive. "Isembard's with him." There was something beyond the moment there, like there had been some great decision, shivered sideways, and Gabe had no idea how to measure it. "Talk to us, Gabe. What's the status?"

It was Alexander as he must have been in the last War, at his height, before Perry's death and how everything had shattered for him. He had a sharpness and focus Gabe had seen when duelling him, but also a purpose that Alexander rarely let surface. Everything in his world was divided into what mattered in this moment and what did not.

Smythe-Clive settled down heavily, reaching for the tray of sandwiches and a plate. He clearly knew what to expect from the food. He'd done this often enough to know how to eat when what mattered was getting some food eaten. He didn't say anything, visibly deferring to Alexander.

"Whatever happened in Paris tore up the portals and surrounding magic no end. I don't know if it's repairable without the touch of the Fatae." That was, arguably, France's problem, for all they had much more immediate ones at the moment and by the thousands.

He went on, as well-ordered as he could manage, though Doyle would mark him down on several points. "The portal here is locked against the Continent. I tested it. I wrote Isembard, obviously. You should get someone up from the Guild to confirm it. I'd recommend Fortnum, though he might be difficult. But he's got the most experience with that right now." Gabe tracked the Portal Keeper guild politics as routinely as he tracked a number of other groups, if with more attention to detail, because of what it meant for Rathna.

"How sure are you? I don't ..." Alexander rubbed his

face, suddenly sinking into himself and going a sallow yellow-grey.

Gabe stood, without thinking of it, barely cursing his ankle in his head. He grabbed the potion vial he hadn't taken yet and a cup of coffee, going to one knee and holding them out. "Take it. Witt's make." It was a stamina potion, and Gabe could get another at home.

Alexander snorted once, but he downed the vial and then took a long swig from the coffee, as the colour came back into his face. Gabe leaned back a little, only then glancing at Smythe-Clive again. "Did I overstep, sir?"

Smythe-Clive considered for a moment. "I think, on the whole, we might be considered to be on first-name terms, if you wish. We owe you." No name, on the end of that, letting Gabe make the choice. That was frank, and at least it gave Gabe some idea of the implications.

Gabe stood again, feeling ungainly for a moment. He claimed his chair again before he spoke. It was easier to be dignified that way. "Cyrus." He was trying it out, carefully. It wasn't just that the man was head of the Council, tied into magics Gabe had no real idea about. It was what he knew about how Alexander had distrusted him, then trusted him, and whatever they were now, it was solid. "Please, the same. Gabe, by preference." Gabriel was a different kind of formality.

"Gabe." Cyrus rubbed his face. "They were getting treasures out of Paris, ahead of the invasion. From what Garin said, nearly everything we'd hoped for, irreplaceable gifts. What we know is that Livia and Garin - though Livia was in front - duelled at least four trained mages, skilled in combat. There were others converging, hoping to force the portal. She called down a final strike, delaying it just long enough to let them get through the portal. Vidya thinks she

died near instantly, for whatever mercy that was. Garin is
—" He paused. "I am exceedingly glad Isembard could
come so quickly."

Gabe knew the theory, of course, all of them did. Livia
had traded all of her vitality, every single last scrap of it, for
that magic, like lightning pouring down from the heavens.
She'd called on one of the great magics, the miracle she
needed, when no one could know if it would work until it
was tried. Every single time was something out of legend.
The previous one he could remember right now had been
back in America in 1780 or so. He almost missed Alexander's comment, his head twitching as he got himself to
focus again.

"As am I. Garin is, in a word, an unstable magical point.
Besides his grief, which is - I do not know how to describe
it. Won't, for some time." Alexander picked up evenly
enough, though the weight of the words began to fall like
blows of a hammer on an anvil. "How much may we share
with others on the Council about what you did?"

That was Alexander all over, figuring out how to hit the
question square on. "Rathna swore no oaths against
teaching me. But it would cause her some difficulty if it
came out in public." If she came home, but of course she'd
come home, of course they'd have a future in which what
he'd done might be a potential problem to her reputation.

"We will see it does not, then, not beyond those who
need to know. Likely all twenty-o." He caught himself.
"Twenty of us." Alexander looked at Cyrus. "We'll need to
as soon as we can."

"I know." That sounded weary of the world, a deep
exhaustion that was going to chase the man for weeks and
months and cycles. They'd need challengers for Livia's
Council seat, and sooner than later, Alexander was correct

there. Though it would be a few months, at least, they needed to give people time to prepare, whatever the preparations involved.

"Can I be of any other help?" Gabe was not entirely sure what to do here. They had a desperate need for food and a snatched moment before they went back into the fray of what this all meant. Gabe could only provide the moment, not help with any of the rest of it.

Then, something moved him to say words he hadn't expected. "I didn't care for Livia. You know why, Alexander, how she was about Rathna." Bigoted, provincial, and snobbish, in all the most destructive ways, all three of them. "But I respect what she did. Her skill and her bravery. If it's any help to share that with either of the Fortiers, please do."

Alexander nodded just once. "Will you be at home tonight if we think of something else?"

"Yes. I'll keep my journal handy. And tomorrow's currently not scheduled with much, though that will probably change by suppertime." Gabe took that as his cue. "May I show myself out?"

"Mabyn's still at the portal. We have people coming in, everyone who can." Cyrus nodded. "We'll talk more soon. Will you send along a report on what we didn't discuss today, about your work, when you get a moment?"

Gabe nodded. He'd write that up tonight. He could do it while waiting to do the cleansing and realignment work for his stones. He stood and gathered his things without further comment. By the time he was outside again, he had begun to think about what it meant for Livia Fortier to make that kind of sacrifice, and how she'd done it wholeheartedly. There was something there that caught at him, and what that sacrifice meant, in the ripples it made out from her, over and over again. How some of them wouldn't be known for years or perhaps even decades.

He nodded to Mabyn Teague, opened the portal, and stepped through to Veritas. Now, he just had to figure out what to say to Isobel and his family.

CHAPTER 27
JUNE 15TH NEAR DAX

Rathna woke late with the sun pouring in on her face. The Paris portal had vanished from the world sometime around one the previous afternoon. They'd been down to panicked groups when it happened. Then they'd managed to make and hold a connection to Rennes well past dawn, when the Dax portal had finally spluttered out.

She had been exhausted, on the edge of backlash herself. She didn't remember any part of them bundling her into a cart and back to the enclave or pouring her into bed. Her eyes felt filled with sand, and her mouth was dry as cotton wool. They'd been working near enough flat out since the ninth, near a week of eating, sleeping, and going to the portal, leaving just enough time for the portal to recharge a bit. She'd downed more stamina potions than ever before in her life, and she'd drawn vitality from dozens of people.

She sprawled back on the bed for a moment before she sat up, entirely too fast as it turned out, which made the room swim for a moment. Before she could get a grip again, there was a voice. "Water, first." Grietje was right there, holding out a mug of it. It was clear and cool and the best thing Rathna had ever tasted.

She had enough sense not to down the mug all at once. She drank half of it. "Ferdinand?"

"Stirring, not awake yet. Your journal chimed." Grietje nodded at the trunk at the end of the bed. She'd written to Gabe, what? Two days ago? Three days for anything meaningful, though she'd written a quick note to the children and to Gabe yesterday morning before they began again. It felt like months ago.

Rathna handed the mug back. "Food in a little?"

"Lunch at one. There's some bread and cheese for you if you want it before then. They're—" Grietje's voice shifted, and Rathna peered, blinking to find the other woman looking amused.

"What happened?"

"I got a rather thorough interrogation by one of them about what foods you preferred. One of the grandmothers, I think she caught that you'd been making do a bit, and she is having none of it. I explained, she's familiar enough with kosher cooking. I didn't ask why. Cassoulet for us, something else for you and anyone else who doesn't eat pork, apparently."

Rathna shook her head. "I manage. And - this is not the point for a Talmudic discussion about the priority on saving lives, anyway. Besides, I'm not remotely qualified for that debate. I manage."

"You need to build your strength. You were—" Grietje hesitated. "We were worried last night."

Rathna opened her mouth, wanting to dismiss it. She

took a careful inventory of her body, her head, and her magic. "Thank you. It's going to take me a bit to sort things out."

"The portal?" Grietje jerked her chin. "Or is it done for good?"

"Let me tell everyone at once. We might manage, but you should investigate the mountain routes. Continue to, I mean. Either way, we're going to need to decide soon. A week or three, at most." No one, not in all her education, had ever adequately explained the timing of an invasion to her. Or, more to the point, how to make decisions when she didn't know how fast she'd have to move.

Grietje nodded. "Paris is an open city, they're calling it. No resistance. The rest of France, that is still a question." She let out a long breath. "Do you want to wash up before you eat? I can get the bath going."

That idea sounded fabulous. It would be putting people out, but not too much. They'd set up a copper tub in the next room over, which drained behind the barn, and the water came from a well. "Please. I need - well. A number of things." The loo, first, and then her journal. "Give me a hand up, make sure I don't fall on my face?"

Five minutes later, she was back on the end of her bed, pulling her journal open. She had several messages from Gabe and from Alysoun, but all Gabe had said was to write when she had a few minutes. From the way both he and his mother worded those brief requests, she was sure something had happened, but there were none of the code words that meant it was the immediate family at risk.

She took a deep breath and wrote back. The reply was almost instantaneous, as if Gabe had had his book open, waiting for any sound from her. He began with a single sentence, that all in the family were well, not to worry there, and then there was a flood of words. He'd written it up, clearly, and copied it into his journal in a single swath of information.

He'd organised it, at least, laying out in bare sparse words that Livia Fortier was dead, that she'd died after calling down a potent magical strike in the Grand Salle des Portes in Paris. Which explained quite a lot on Rathna's end, and she was suddenly shivering. It could have been so much worse if they'd had a portal open at the time. For anyone who did. She didn't even know how to ask anyone elsewhere in France. She pulled a plain notebook over and made a list of things she'd have to figure out how to convey to the guild and to whoever should know in France.

Then she went back to Gabe's words. She saw Alysoun's hand in how he'd laid it out, but she wasn't sure if he'd directly consulted his mother or just used her reports as a model. It was hard to tell at the best of times. She added half a dozen other things to the list as she read, including the fact the conversation with her Guild was about to get more delicate.

She agreed with Gabe's recommendation for Fortnum. However poorly he'd handled Ferdinand's training, he knew his own work, and he was one of the most experienced with the Trellech portals. And he was as familiar with the Council portal as anyone. He'd be difficult about Gabe having done what he did, but that couldn't be helped. They hadn't exactly had time to send for anyone else, and it wasn't as if the portal had been working until Gabe had thrown himself into it.

She went back up to the top and read through again, looking for all the little tells that Gabe and Alysoun had taught her to look for. And several of their other circle, too. The way he was choosing words, that was telling. It had shaken him more than he was admitting to himself. She noticed several particular verbal tics that came up in the aftermath of him following his impulses.

Rathna considered and began with three declarative sentences. "Alexander and Smythe-Clive were glad of your work. Praised it. You know Alexander wouldn't, if you'd overstepped." She went on from there, working her way through each point as deliberately as she did calculations and measurements for a portal. It took her two pages. She was just finishing up when there was a knock on the door.

"Yes?"

Grietje peered around. "Bath water's hot."

Rathna wanted to focus on the words again, but she needed a bath. Her skin was itchy and increasingly unpleasant, and she'd think better when she was clean. She wrote a note to that effect, then a quick one to each of her children, that she was well, she'd write more later.

The bath was not as restorative as she'd hoped, but it was something. By the time she'd charm-dried her hair, they'd sorted out more hot water for Ferdinand, and she passed him in the narrow hallway as someone was refilling the tub. He nodded once, and she immediately said, "Debrief after dejeuner." He looked relieved.

The next hour and a half was filled with people wanting to thank her. It was yet another thing no one had trained her for. Rathna was used to doing her work and having it be ignored. No one noticed when a portal worked properly. They only noticed when it didn't.

She had the respect of her colleagues, because her work was reliable and she was not tedious to collaborate with.

Her family valued what she did, even the children. Maybe especially the children, who had somehow kept a childlike wonder at the idea of what a portal was, stepping from one place to another as easily as going down a flight of stairs.

But here, once she came down to the main courtyard, there was an endless row of people. There were grandmothers and grandfathers, young women and men, children clinging to their skirts or trousers. All of them thanking her, and one of the women translating when the accent got too thick for Rathna to make sense of. Then she was firmly escorted to a seat at the head table, with the local elders proudly presented with a large bowl of fragrant soup. Fish-based, she could tell that, and there was a spark of something peppery that delighted her.

"What is this?" she asked, carefully. "I do not know the name for it?"

"Tioro." That was what it sounded like, but a moment later, one of the little girls spelled it out, ttoro. An older woman, definitely one of the grandmothers, bobbed, and explained in careful French what was in it. Five kinds of fish, she couldn't quite work out which ones, but not shellfish, she knew the words for that. And there were herbs, white wine, onions, tomato, and pepper, both sweet and the Espelette peppers that had turned up once or twice in previous meals.

Rathna smiled and nodded and then took a sip when it was clear everyone was waiting for that. She let the taste roll around in her mouth. Not nearly so biting a pepper as some of the dishes she'd had with her family in Calcutta, but kin. She beamed and said, "My mother's family has something a little like this. It is very good. Thank you. I am so glad to have a chance to eat it."

It was, in fact, fabulous. Whoever had made it had a deft hand with the layering of flavours, the way herbs came through, then onion, then the different tastes of each fish, the textures. Nothing was over-cooked, nothing was chewy. It was, in a word, restorative, in a way Rathna hadn't known she needed. She ate, periodically smiling at the people around her, and accepted a second serving gratefully when it was clear there was plenty left. Along with it, they offered plenty of fresh bread and butter, and, of course, wine.

As she finished, there was a slight rustle, and then a small child - perhaps a year younger than Avigail - appeared at her side. She had Avigail's dark hair, too, but much lighter skin, and Rathna was caught for the moment by the comparison.

She turned a little, glancing at the people seated near her, but no one stopped her, no one pulled the child away. There was a rapid flurry of French, and Rathna couldn't make out more than a few words - 'merci', and 'papa' and a few others that anyone might spot.

Behind her, Grietje's voice cut clearly across the rest of the chat. "She is thanking you for making sure her papa could get home."

Rathna nodded once. "I am glad I could help. I have a little girl, perhaps a little older than you? She just turned eight."

Again, a flurry, shorter, and Grietje's translation. "She wonders why you are here and not with her."

"I live in Albion, but her father is with her and his parents. I am here so I could help. I wanted to help keep people safer." Her ability to put things simply fled. There was a moment's hesitation, as Grietje translated back into French, and then the little girl was hugging her tightly, without any further pause or distance. Rathna hugged her back instinctively. "Your name?"

"Katherine." She gave it the French emphasis, and Rathna repeated it, before the girl darted off again. The conversation picked up around them as the meal took its own time. She appreciated that, here, that no matter how dire the situation, while they could take a proper pause for lunch, they did.

Eventually, everyone filtered off to their afternoon work. But a number of the mothers and grandmothers had paused to speak to her, whether or not she understood them. One of them had asked her to hold a baby for a moment while she rearranged what she was carrying. Something had shifted, definitively and absolutely. What-ever else she was now, she was trusted that far.

Their small group found a space in the grass to one side of the main house, with Lucas spreading out a blanket to sit on. Rathna lowered herself, then took in Ferdinand's posture and expression. "How are you?"

"Exhausted, Mistress, but recovering. I need a day or two before we try anything again that's effort."

"Me as well." Rathna let out a long breath. "All right. I don't know if we can get this portal working again. I won't be able to try until tomorrow or maybe the day after. It depends how I sleep." She considered. "This isn't public yet. It will be in a day or two, perhaps. The Grand Salle des Portes is, if not destroyed, seriously damaged."

"You're sure?" That was Lucas, quick as he could be.

"Quite." She let the one sharp syllable fall. "A massive magical battle, I gather. News via Gabe." And Gabe had a wide variety of sources, no need to mention how direct this one had been in practice. "So we need to figure out where to go from here. One option is over the mountains. If we can get the portal working, where do we go with it?"

There was silence. They knew the map as well as she did at this point. "We'd need a contact in Spain, to go there. Not impossible, but it will take time. And we don't have it." Beth laid it out, little flicks of her fingers gesturing at the geography.

"Is there any place in Albion that might open to us?" That was Grietje. "Even briefly?"

Rathna let out a long breath. "Ferdinand asked the same question, not long after we got here. It would need to be an ancient portal, and one not locked against France. One no one's had access to for years, centuries, most likely. The Tintagel portal's behind a cave-in. Windsor Castle, obviously not available." That one was not locked against France, in specific, but it was behind layer and layer of other warding and illusion work. "And the Tower of London, but I haven't heard of that one being used since England lost Aquitaine in the 1450s, before the Pact. Not that I have all the records here."

"Can you - is there even anyone to ask?" Grietje spread her hands.

"When we're done here, I'll write to people who can find out. We should at least make informed decisions, if we can, about what our options actually are." There was a round of tired, amused sounds. It was true enough. "And if we need to go across the mountains?"

"The mountains are - there are Fatae in the mountains." Grietje was suddenly hesitant.

"Do you know how to get their attention, politely? Does someone around here? I need to do that, no matter what we decide. To explain about Paris, what I know about it. More than will be public." Rathna didn't know what that would shake loose. But somewhere between Gabe's note and the bath, she'd come to the decision that it needed to happen, apparently. The intuitive tug. She couldn't ignore that.

Grietje grimaced. "You don't ask for much, do you?" But they both knew that in not too long, if no invasion swept this way first, they'd be doing what they could about that.

CHAPTER 28
JUNE 18TH IN ALEXANDER'S TOWNHOUSE, TRELLECH

"Port?" Alexander had gone immediately to the drinks cabinet in the corner of his library. Gabe sank into a chair, gratefully. The three of them - Alexander, Gabe, and Geoffrey - had spent much of the afternoon at Livia's funeral, a formal affair in the public rooms of the Council Keep. The Council had, uniformly, gone their different ways as soon as the guests were leaving, bar Cyrus and Mabyn. It had been formal, brief, and attended by all the people who needed to be there, but not more than that.

Gabe had volunteered to go in lieu of his parents. Papa was on call for all manner of things, and Mama was having one of her worse weeks. Funerals involved, along with all the other strains, quite a lot of standing around for uncertain amounts of time. Besides, Gabe felt an obligation to attend, having been there when Garin Fortier brought her back, given the glimpses he'd had then.

All three of them were in formal black suits, but they'd all near simultaneously abandoned the black silk ritual over-robes and the relevant formal marks of rank on the hooks in the hallway. Geoffrey had what was clearly his particular chair, and he was staring at a point on the bookshelves, deep in thought.

"How much time do you have?" Gabe leaned back, trying to find a position that didn't make his ankle ache.

"I said I'd be at Arundel by supper time, to help spell Isembard. It's a gift that he doesn't have to juggle being at Schola, but we can't go on like we are, any of us. Who knows what we're going to do then?"

Gabe wasn't sure about how to ask about that. Geoffrey nudged a footstool in his direction with one foot and stepped into the fray. "How badly off is Garin?" Gabe didn't know how he'd have felt if something happened to Rathna, much less like that. Except he knew his world would have broken into the tiniest shards, and nothing would have made sense.

Alexander didn't answer immediately. He brought them both glasses of port, going back for his own before he claimed his own chair and settled in it with a tired grunt. "Not like any of us expected, including him. Including Livia, I'm sure." He rubbed his face. "There are a couple of friends, in as much as Garin has actual friends. Montgomery Worth, his wife Alicia, what was the name? Helling. Anthony Helling. But none of them are, shall we say, up to dealing with Garin if he actually decides to be difficult. Isembard wouldn't have managed, for a long time."

Which was to say, Gabe could interpret, violent or lashing out. The man had skills and strong magic to draw on, and he had been visibly only barely controlled during the funeral and its aftermath. He paused and asked something he'd never have thought to ask a decade or two ago. "How are you, Alexander?"

Geoffrey and Alexander exchanged one of their lightning quick looks, before Alexander snorted, but he also relaxed a hair. "Conflicted, but that's my average Tuesday. Livia was, well, we usually say, challenging. I don't think any of us had realised how much Garin leaned into that challenge, knowing it would absolutely be there. What it means now that she isn't. And it's something that's going to keep hitting him, over and over again." He flicked his fingers. "And I, well. Liking's the wrong word entirely. But she gave herself wholly to her work once she agreed it needing doing, and I'm old enough to know how rare that is."

Before Gabe could say anything in reply, Alexander went on. "May I speak freely about Friday?" He inclined his head at Geoffrey to make the query entirely clear. Not that Gabe hadn't already known that. Alexander was right he was feeling complicated, if he were being that unsubtle.

Gabe gave the question a sensible amount of consideration. "You know your oaths far better than I do, sir. And you must have questions, beyond what we talked about then."

"And not much time to ask them in." Alexander agreed. "Did you have anything in particular?"

"Yes, but it's very much Council business, though it touches on demesne lands. Rather thoroughly." Which meant Geoffrey had some useful input.

"There, Geoffrey, you can stay, Lord of the Ladder." The epithet clearly meant something to Geoffrey, who seemed entirely amused and at home. "Tell me about your experience on Friday."

Gabe raised an eyebrow. "I'd say I was not expecting a viva voce, but I do know you, Alexander. I've already given my report to Mason and Witt, of course. In summary, at least. There were, in fact, matters they decided they wanted to disclaim knowledge of for the moment."

"Start there." The comment was brisk, then Alexander took a long sip from his port.

"In brief, I was on your land, your particular land. I saw your reaction, and then Smy - Cyrus's. I didn't know what it meant, exactly, but of course I knew how serious it was." Gabe considered. "To be honest, my instincts drove me as much as my training, but both in tandem. A two horse carriage, both used to working together, pulling the weight either, neither shirking."

"Shirking is, to be fair, not an adjective I have ever applied to you." Alexander nodded once to accompany that moment of praise. "We'll come back to that. And?"

Gabe shrugged. "I could do something. I knew I could. And you needed it. No one's argued with that at all, even the Portal Keeper's Guild. They did drag me in yesterday for an explanation, mind you."

"Trouble?" Geoffrey leaned forward at that.

"Not any longer. For either me or Rathna. Not that they can get at her to lecture her at the moment." Gabe let out a long breath. "She has a question, though, separate from the others. I put it to Geoffrey, Saturday morning."

Alexander considered that, but did not get distracted from the original topic. "Come back to that. What did you, no. Let me ask a different question. Why did you act as you did?"

"Who am I answering this question for?" Gabe parried back just as quickly.

"Myself, in all my parts, Gabe." Alexander shook his head. "I cannot untangle them, especially not this week, for all you might actually be able to do it."

Gabe smiled at that. "I do like having my skills appreciated. I worked hard for a number of them." It made the other two men laugh, and they all needed that. Gabe spread his hands. "I did what I do. I saw something that was needed, that I could do. I was near certain no one else there could. There was the dual problem: to keep invasion from Paris from coming to the Keep, and to preserve the portal for travel within Albion. You're in an awfully awkward location for anything by land or sea."

"Intentionally, yes, but it does have limitations." Alexander considered. "Tell me what you did, from when the alarm went, would you? What you sensed."

It had come to that, then. Gabe had thought it might, though he was, perhaps, a tad surprised that it was Geoffrey here and not Cyrus. Easier for him. Honestly, he trusted Geoffrey, solidly and securely. And he knew the man was as focused on getting things handled as any Penelope might like, rather than getting stuck in protocol.

"The alarm went. I noticed how you waited a second to confirm. That the pitch told you something, I think. I saw Cyrus go white, and I suspect, in hindsight, that it was when he knew Livia was dead. I don't know how you all are tied together, magically, but I do assume there's some sort of enchantment."

"Cyrus as the centre hub, all of us as spokes, more or less." Alexander flipped his palm up. "I had a feeling of something being wrong. Unsettled. Moving, there's the word. But not what, not until just before the alarm. Garin, I think, more than Livia."

"I wondered." Gabe offered after a moment. "You taught him, before Isembard. That makes a bond, even if it's been years."

"You are kind not to count them." Alexander lifted his glass. "Go on."

"I got to the courtyard a few steps behind Cyrus, and I called the charm immediately. I can't not, you understand?

Not easily. It's the first thing we're taught about arriving at a scene where there's magical damage. Who is alive, who is dead, who might be dead momentarily."

Alexander grunted. "I am familiar with the problem, yes. I was sure you'd done your own evaluation. The confirmation was a help, though. You know as well as I some of it can trick the mind. Wishing for something different." That was more of an admission than Gabe had expected to hear, in all honesty, but he appreciated it.

"And then you asked if I could do something about the portal." He swallowed. "I didn't tell the Guild this. We might later, Rathna and I need to talk it out, when we get a chance, in person." He was holding fast to the thought that they would, that they'd get her home from France, and sooner than later. That she'd be in a fit state to have that conversation, which seemed a tad more tenuous than Gabe could stand to think of. "I near enough got lost in it. Pulled into it. I've never worked with a portal that old, almost no one has. Half a dozen of the Portal Keepers, not even all of them. And not when what it had just been connected to was what's the word. Enflamed."

"Almost, but didn't." Geoffrey's voice cut across Gabe's own thoughts suddenly, dropping ripples into the pool. "What was it like?"

"Ancient. Foreign. Like being dropped back into a world where people spoke ancient Greek in its many dialects, all making sense of it, rather than the fragments that survived. And - I haven't exactly had time for an extended discussion with Rathna. But she thinks it is as if layers of years were stripped off the portal, that it had, in a word, gone back to thinking in something spoken by the ancient Britons. It made sense, more or less, but it was foreign in ways I don't have words for at all." He let out a rough breath, almost a cough. "And then I knew I couldn't fight it, I could only yield to it. Be vulnerable to it." He glanced at Alexander now, watching the expressions attentively.

"What had you expected to do?" Of course Alexander would ask the question Gabe didn't know how to answer.

"Not that." He frowned. "Stillness is not my gift. You both know that."

"Mabyn thought it quite compelling, for the record." Alexander dropped his own pebble in the pond. Gabe was sure the two older men were coordinating in some way he couldn't quite see. "She had some interesting comments."

"And you're not going to tell me." Gabe knew how that went.

"You are doomed to disappointment, yes, at least for the time being, though when we can catch our breath more, I do have a few things to talk about. She noted, however, that you understood the risk, the scope of the risk, but that you gave it your all, unstintingly. And she has enough skill of her own to understand how you were, how did she put it. Oh yes, distilling a gas at the same time you were spinning three plates in the air and juggling a flaming torch or two. I have considered commissioning a caricature to mark the occasion."

Alexander said it absolutely straight-faced, so it took a moment to register. Then Gabe was setting down his port, and laughing like he hadn't in weeks, bent over and shaking. The others joined him, somewhat less enthusiastically. When Gabe finally caught his breath, he said, "Please do. I would love a copy to give Mama for Winter Solstice."

It led to another round of chuckles, then Alexander shrugged. "These small things are within my power, I will let you know. She was impressed. As was I, to be honest. It is one thing to know intellectually of your skills, the range of them, and another to see them in action outside the duelling salle."

Gabe acknowledged that praise with a simple nod. He didn't need to demur, and he didn't need to make the praise louder. After a moment, Geoffrey cleared his throat. "That brings us to the other two questions, doesn't it? The one you raised with me, first, or your other?"

"The one I brought to you. In short, Alexander, Rathna wonders if the portal under the Tower of London is still potentially active. It was shut off with the fall of Aquitaine in 1453. From what I could find yesterday, Richard III had intended to open it, and - that never happened. It's down in the depths of the White Tower, walled off."

"So you need what? No, wait. Physical access, which Geoffrey might, in fact, just be able to arrange. And the Council's blessing?"

"Both. It being a matter of national benefit. No one else would know it's active, and we could lock it down near immediately."

Alexander steepled his fingers. "What's your other request? You can draw on quite a favour at the moment, but I don't know how you want to spend it."

"This is personal. I want my wife home, and we don't know how long that might—" Gabe stopped short. "Her situation might change quite rapidly." It came out tight and prim, but both Alexander and Geoffrey understood. "The other is decidedly a Council matter, and related to my current work."

Geoffrey shifted a little at that, reaching for his glass again. "Should I give you a moment?"

"Not on my account." Gabe waited for Alexander to focus on him again. "It was Lord Thanet who gave me the idea, though I'd touched on it with you earlier, Alexander. That dream and the green dragon."

"Ah." There were volumes in that, and Gabe was suddenly certain Alexander had had more dreams, just as inchoate as Gabe himself had.

"What would happen if we could get a token? The sort of thing no one could argue with, to align Albion behind a shared approach to the protection work, and that might also carry weight with those outside Albion. Lord Thanet said he'd accept a unanimous vote of the Council - unlikely, even now - or a token that could only come from the Fatae."

Alexander let out a sharp whistle, startled into a visible reaction. "You certainly do follow my namesake's approach to the Gordian knot, don't you? My. Give me a minute. Not so much unweaving there as moving the entire loom to another plane entirely. And I'm quite sure Caliburn's unavailable, or Excalibur, or whatever we're calling it."

"I have no desire to be king." Gabe said it to Alexander's back as the older man stood, moving to circle along one row of bookshelves, then making a loop. Geoffrey watched him intently, reading something there that Gabe couldn't spot, some hint of either tension or the line of his thinking. Geoffrey wasn't particularly worried, Gabe thought, but there was nothing in his world but what Alexander was doing at that moment.

It took several minutes for Alexander to alight again. "Is that how you want to spend your favour, then? A petition to the Fatae? We'll have to be quick about the planning. Solstice is Friday. So we'd need to decide by..."

Then his shoulders went tight, and he swore, in Arabic, then added a comment that must be a prayer and in ancient Egyptian, his family language. The room went entirely still for a minute, more than a minute. Finally, Alexander nodded once. "Of course it would be Solstice." He said it as if were one of those pieces that fell into place, no matter how everyone might want to avoid them. "If you're sure. What do you need from me?"

"Permission from the Council. And then the wording, of course. I don't know how long it would take you to put together a ritual petition. I assume faster than I could. I do have some drafts." Gabe leaned back a bit now. Alexander hadn't dismissed the idea out of hand.

He grunted again, and pulled his journal over. "Can you be at the Keep at ten tomorrow?"

"I will make myself available, yes. Not a full meeting?"

"You need to convince Cyrus, at least. Bring your best arguments. And your drafts. You seek a token, something that anyone of Albion would know, and ideally something that others would recognise. That's a trick, isn't it? The language and what you might be handed. What are you willing to give for it?"

That was a harder question. "Quite a lot. I won't know my limit until I'm asked, I suspect." Gabe shrugged, once. "I didn't on Friday. I hope to rise to the occasion and not fail."

Something in that brought Alexander's chin up, a sudden fierce stare like some great predator making a judgement. "You might just manage it, at that." For all there were a dozen other things in Gabe's head right now, he caught a thread there, something to follow through. It had the same weight and shiver as that first conversation about taking on this work in all its forms and seeing the magical protections properly tended. Something about the idea of Livia's sacrifice unsettled Alexander, it was a thing he could not get his head around. That was rare indeed, given Alexander's breadth and depth and reach of knowledge and experience.

Alexander went on, his head tilted, and Gabe brought himself back to focus. "What made you decide on this?"

"We need some solution. If I can manage this, Thanet will have to assent. Concede. And he'll bring quite a few with him. Leverage, as you said. Movement. It won't be enough, by itself. We'll still have to do the protection work."

"It never is enough to make the glorious gesture, is it? The world would be quite a lot different if it were. Geoffrey?"

Geoffrey set his drink down with a quiet little clunk. "It is outside what has been done. That doesn't mean it isn't needed. And the terms of the Pact allow for such negotiations, even if you haven't for a very long time. You know we've wondered about the Armada, in particular."

"You and your history." Alexander half-smiled. "Cyrus will know better, when. All right, Gabe. Off with you. I need to write a number of notes and do my own research."

Not at all subtle, now. Gabe stood. "Tomorrow at ten. Let me know if there's anything else I should bring besides myself and my notes, to be gone through with red ink."

Alexander shook his head, but stood to come let Gabe out of the warding. At the door, quietly, he added two sentences. "We were all grateful, Friday, and extremely impressed when we had a chance to catch our breaths. I don't know if you realise how much."

Gabe didn't remotely know what to say to that, so he just nodded once, went out the door, and down the street.

CHAPTER 29
JUNE 19TH NEAR DAX

"Ready?"

Ferdinand nodded, closing his journal. He looked distracted, but he didn't say anything, and Rathna was not going to press. On the way back, perhaps. They were borrowing a cart large enough to take four of them to a point in the woods, to go up to a cave in the foothills of the mountains where one of the grandmothers was willing to make a petition.

None of the folk from Albion had language for this. It wasn't a thing people did. It was a matter for the Council, if anyone was going to. Grietje was a bit more sanguine about it. The Fatae weren't beings one talked to in the Low Countries, but the idea of petitioning them for help wasn't entirely unheard of.

Rathna was working on instinct here - instinct and need. She'd talked it through with Gabe, as best she could in the journal, and with pauses between every comment. She kept coming back to something they'd discussed early in their relationship, before they were even betrothed. Rathna had argued, rather compellingly, that the magics in

Albion were a wall, but also a container. She went through it one more time in her head, trying to peer into every crevice of logic, to see if she was, in fact, missing anything.

Richard III had made the Pact with the Fatae in 1484. It had been a mutual agreement, both sides benefiting. The Fatae had places to retreat to, where no human could come. They could build their homes in safety, not to be meddled with. There had been some particular concessions about specific locations, but none that were too much of a reach, as it turned out.

In exchange, they had given three great gifts. The gift of the Silence, which bound all of Albion, all those with magic, to silence about magic around those without it. It was arguably a chain, too, but it had, over and over, kept people safer. Rathna knew enough of the history, both in Albion and in other places. Related, the Fatae kept from meddling with people who had made that pledge, and that had saved no end of trouble.

More directly useful, the Fatae had given mortals the gift of making portals. Or at least those few, like Rathna and her guildmates, who could learn the knack. It meant that portals now dotted the landscape of Albion, easing trade and travel, rather than being in Fatae hands, or only in places the Fatae cared about.

And third, they'd given other gifts of magic, advances in healing and alchemy and materia that had allowed Albion to shoot forward in a number of ways, and keep Albion's people that much safer. There were plenty of times the measure of that safety was small. But a farmer of Albion died less often of small cuts. Minor infections stayed minor and healed. The milk stayed sweet longer, leaving more to be sold on or made into cheese or butter. Animals and plants were less prone to illness or blight. Fewer women died in childbirth, fewer children died of the diseases of youth, more people survived the plague or cholera or whatever epidemic sprung up like fire.

It hadn't been the same outside of Albion. There was tale after tale of the Fatae having their way with the world - angry, joyful, specific, general. Gabe had been doing research, as had several others they knew, about the sightings of the Wild Hunt in Albion since the Pact. And about how many more were reported in France, in Germany, into Spain, through the rest of Europe. It was hard to tease some of the tales apart, of course, as always.

Rathna at least had a little space where she had explored the idea that gods and naga and all manner of Fatae walked among the villages and cities of India. Her aunts in Calcutta had not only told her stories, on their second and third visits, but they had taken her to several of the temples and taught her a little of the way to make offerings. Some things were cultural, some things were negotiated, but gifts and politeness and caution braided together seemed universal. Don't make promises you can't keep, gifts imply obligations, and some Fatae have well and truly earned their reputation as tricksters.

These thoughts took them a fair way down the road. Grietje and the grandmother, Miren, were chattering away in French. Rathna followed half a sentence here or there, but she was still tired enough that keeping track of the conversation was far more effort than it should be. Instead, she folded her hands in her lap and looked out at the scenery. It moved from fields and trellises into the foothills of the mountains, with taller trees and rocky ledges.

It took the better part of three hours, but eventually the cart pulled up in a small copse of trees, and they piled out. They had talked, with translation running several directions, about how to do this. Rathna would make a petition of a physical offering, a bit of her magic, and the words in English. Grietje would translate them into French, and Miren would translate them into Basque. It was only polite to talk to the Fatae in their own local language. Rathna wasn't actually sure how that worked. Did they have their own and just borrow local human languages for the occasion?

She had not been able to figure out if Alexander had even spoken directly to the Fatae. By the time the answer was particularly relevant, it was clear he was working flat out. Whatever she asked would take him away from two dozen things that needed his attention. It wasn't likely to be the thing that decided the matter, anyway.

Rathna had asked for a few phrases, how to give her name, how to express her appreciation. Not thanks, directly, that could be touchy in a number of cultures. Not an obligation, either. Simply, "I am glad that you have listened." More or less. Miren led them not toward the more obvious cave mouth, but sideways, curving around a bit of stone, with them moving left. Then she slipped into an opening in the rock that barely appeared to be there.

Once inside, Grietje called a charmlight, illuminating the cave, and Rathna stopped dead. The ceilings, from about waist height upwards, were filled with figures. There were dozens of horses, not the sleek and angular horses she'd come to know well thanks to Gabe and his parents. These were rounded beasts that made her think fondly of Verity, the dun Highland pony she'd ridden in Scotland when she'd met Gabe.

There were giant aurochs there, tremendous deer with massive antlers, an enormous bear, and what seemed likely to be a lion. There were other markings - both carved and painted - that were some sort of symbolic pattern, or so she had to assume.

And the whole place was made for ritual. Rathna could feel that, for all the blessings or protections or warding or whatever one properly called it was nothing like what she knew. Or mostly not like what she knew. It had a feel, if she peered at it out of the corner of her eye so as not to scare the faint sensation, of the container of the eruv.

Before she could pursue that further, something in the cave shifted. It wasn't a sense of presence, but it had a weight to it, like some of the oldest portals. Places that had stood through wind and weather, the rise and fall of empires, the reshaping of mountains and canyons. Rathna inhaled and then gave herself over to just experiencing it, not trying to analyse it. She let herself fall into the beauty of it, the reds and ochres and umbers, but also the deep blacks she could see, the white from kaolin clay. Mostly the black and the red ochre here, but splashes of the others.

Along one side was a small flat table, near enough an altar, though it was currently bare. Miren bowed respect-fully before it, then took a step back and to the right, gesturing for Rathna to do the same. Rathna took a deep breath, then she stepped forward. She had made offerings thousands of times by now, and she placed what she had brought on the altar.

She had given careful thought to this. She'd chosen gems from her set of working stones, but they needed to be ones she wouldn't need for the work on the portal. Two stones from that, and she had pried the aquamarine out of her Guild pendant. That stone she'd worn since her third year at Schola, when Morah Avigail had presented her with a proper stone for her House necklace.

Rathna had so many other gifts from her, she could give

this one as a token of her truth. She knew it was the right thing. The other two, though, were easier to put down. First the good quality piece of jade, then a pearl, then finally the aquamarine.

"I give you greetings, ancient ones full of magic." She waited for the dual translation, the sound bouncing and echoing in the cave. "I know the smallest touch of your magic. I bring these offerings." She went on, pausing after each sentence. "The great net of portals in Paris has been damaged. I will gladly tell you what I know of how that happened. We also seek your help to return home. Please, if you are willing to speak, send some sign." She had to come to this as a competent professional, seeking to give information to those who deserved to have it, by right and nature.

They stood there in the flickering of the light. Rathna counted her heartbeats. Gabe had taught her that one. Don't make any assumptions for at least the count of twenty-one. Three times seven, the magical numbers. The number of the Council. The number of completion, in some systems. If you ask a question, allow the terrifying magical being time to answer.

She got up to seventeen before anything changed. There was a flicker of light, entirely separate from the charmlight, then the entire cavern lit up in a soft glow like the last hour before twilight, golden and perfect. The offerings on the altar disappeared entirely in the blink of an eye, and then four charcoal marks appeared, one after another.

Rathna blinked, and glanced at Miren, who counted off on her fingers, and said something in French about St. John's Day. The solstice, in two days' time.

"Four days from now?" Rathna asked, to confirm. The lights dimmed and rose again, as if in agreement, like a great figure far above nodding, changing the angle of the light.

"We will return in four days." Again, the light dimmed. At least that held some promise that when they did, Rathna might be able to speak for herself. Then, the light faded slowly, and they were alone in the cave again. Surrounded by figures and echoes and the weight of centuries. None of them moved for rather longer than twenty-one heartbeats. Finally, Rathna made one final bow. "I am glad to have been heard." Then she retreated, backing up the way they had come, until she was well into the neck of the cave entrance.

The others followed, one by one, to come out blinking in the sunlight. The sun had moved significantly. They had got here before noon, with the sun overhead, and now it must be closer to three or four. Plenty of time to return to the farm enclave, given the long hours of sunlight, but Rathna would have said they'd been inside only a few minutes.

Ferdinand wobbled once, and she put out a hand immediately to steady him. "All right?" She kept her voice quiet. She couldn't imagine speaking loudly yet.

He shook his head, the negative, but she gave him time for a few breaths. Grietje went to the cart, where the cart horse was nibbling amiably on the last bits of grass he could reach from where they'd tethered him. She brought back a flask of water, and then brought out the smaller one of the alcohol she carried. Ferdinand eyed them both, then nodded, taking a swig from the brandy before chasing it with a bit of water. Rathna didn't hesitate before doing the same.

Once they'd done that, they could at least set off for their current home. Grietje drove along in silence, while Miren watched them carefully, as if that had not gone as she'd expected. Rathna had had that impression, but how did one ask about that? There were so many underlying principles and assumptions that might be the same between them and others that might be entirely different.

It wasn't until they were a good way back, perhaps two hours, that Ferdinand cleared his throat. "Mistress Rathna. I learned this morning that Mama had been interned. Taken to a camp, with others who aren't...." He didn't have to finish the sentence. 'Enemy aliens' was the phrase used. Rathna had caught some of the discussion about it from her journal. People had been classified months ago, but most had been allowed to keep having their lives. Now, though, well. Things were changing, and terribly fast.

"I'm so sorry." Rathna reached out, almost without thinking about it, though Ferdinand was, in general, not someone who welcomed touch easily. This time, he turned his hand so she could take it in his without twisting. "Do you know how she's doing or where she is?"

"She's not permitted her journal, just letters, but my father and brothers have visited her. They didn't want to worry me, but then they realised I'd write to her. And not hear back." From the expression on his face, it had taken them long enough he had worried, indeed.

She had not pressed for more about his family. It had been so clear from what he'd shared already that he loved his mother, even when her interests made him uncomfortable. Rathna just held his hand. "If you'd like to talk about it, when we get back, you let me know. And I hope, very much, we will find our own way home soon. And you can go see her."

"It's allowed?" He said it warily. "I'm an apprentice. In a sensitive line of work."

Rathna let out a long breath. "And we know people who

can do the truth enchantments. Richard, for one, Geoffrey for another. They'd be glad to recommend half a dozen people who don't know you and don't like me much if you want something more neutral. For my part, I think you should get to see your mother and I will do everything I can to make that possible. Starting with getting us home and going on from there."

It came out fiercer and sharper than she'd meant to. Her own desire to get home was rising higher and threatening to breach the narrow banks she'd nudged it into. But that was not to the bad here. The other two women in the cart didn't comment, didn't even look up, but she suspected they entirely understood.

Ferdinand fell silent again, but he didn't let go of her hand, not until they were turning up the road toward the enclave itself.

CHAPTER 30
JUNE 20 AT AN ANCIENT STONE IN KENT

Gabe waited as patiently as he could. He was alone by the great sarsen stone that marked an ancient barrow in the fading light after a long day. It was half nine, and the sun would come up again at half four tomorrow, for the longest day. He waited, dressed for what might come in solid tweeds, breeches, and tall boots.

He had the cane in his hand that could be magically folded and tucked away if needed, and a flask of hard cider slung on a strap over his shoulder. And in his pockets, there were half a dozen options for offerings. He'd laid out the honey cakes and a cunning little wooden cup of cider already, as a starting token.

Mama and Papa were back at Veritas with Isobel, and with all three children. They had not forbidden him to do this. They hadn't even made a gesture at suggesting it, but he knew how worried they were. Alexander was also deeply worried, parked in the library with the rest of them. He suspected at least three of them would have paced a hole in the carpet by morning. Of course, the family also helped tend the fire outside, with clean bones and carefully chosen woods. There were people up all through the short night to keep watch and celebrate and call the blessings in.

It had been a challenge, figuring out where to be. The lore suggested the deep woods, a stone circle, a place with a particular tinge of myth. But Gabe knew - as well as anyone did - that the lore was changeable, as changeable as the Fatae. He'd wanted to do this on the land he loved in Kent. It wasn't much, but it was a small gift, somewhere, that gave him a scrap of hope this idea might work.

When they'd pulled out the ordnance maps for scrying, he'd held what he wanted in his head, as best he could. They'd watched as his wedding ring, the weight they were using for the pendulum, swung back and forth, then settled with a rolling spin around White Horse Stone. It was just barely in the Edgarton half of Kent, miles from any place Gabe knew particularly well, but it was still land he loved. It hummed and sang to him, just at the edge of his hearing, as if it were some music far away, drifting through the wind.

Something here held his attention, though. It was easier to keep from fidgeting or distraction than he'd expected. Of course, he knew the risks. He'd discussed them with Rathna through the journal, he'd talked through them with Mama and Papa and Mason and Witt. He'd even talked it through with Charlotte, who'd had her own bout with a particular snare of enchantment once upon a time. All he could do was hold fast to what he was doing, why he was doing it, and who he was.

The music grew louder, all of a sudden, as if the musicians had stepped from a half mile away to just beside him. He could make out the melodies now, but they were nothing he knew. None of the country dances, none of the folk songs of the area, but something akin. After a phrase or two of music, he could feel the hair on the back of his neck rise, the prickle of magic. He settled his weight steady as he could between his feet, a dueller's stance to move with whatever might come.

He'd expected the Hunt to come with baying hounds and the undeniable thuds of galloping hooves. Gabe had planned on shouts and cries of a hunt in full chase that had a line on their prey. Fierceness and power, tinged with anger and pain. Those were the dominant tales of the Wild Hunt, in many of the legends he'd looked at.

First, the light changed. Gabe had had the chance to see the aurora more than a few times, and this had all of that magic. It was as if there was a veil brushing everything everywhere, a whisper of undeniable and entirely intangible enchantment. Gabe thought his heart stopped beating, not because he was unwell, but because time itself had come to rest between one beat and another.

There was nothing, and then there was everything, forming out of a glowing silver light around and above the stone. There were horses, dozens of them, each with a rider. Gabe blinked twice to clear his vision, and the riders took sharper shape.

All of them he could see were women, but women of every shape and age and seeming. Some had pale skin, some darker skin like Rathna's, a few of deep black unlike any human he'd ever seen. Each and every one of them had a luminous pearlescence to them, a shimmer that defied description but moved with them, lit them and flowed around them.

They were in flowing skirts but riding astride, hair loose and unbound. All of it, the silks and skirts and trailing hair, moved like it was blown in a wind, though the air around him had gone still. He could hear laughter and chatter. One of the women eased her mount to where she could scoop up the honey cake and cider, breaking a piece off and handing it to the woman beside her.

Heads thrown back, they enjoyed it, whole-hearted and joyful. Then the two focused on him. On Gabe, standing there. He bowed as smoothly as he could, lowering his eyes for only a moment before he straightened. When he stood tall again, they'd pulled their horses into a loose curve, watching him. The music and breeze had dropped away, leaving a soft background sound and only the slightest rustle.

Gabe held his tongue. He'd been told how to do this, and Cyrus and Alexander had been extremely clear. He pulled out a ring from his pocket, tossing it up in a graceful arc in the air, toward the woman who'd first taken the cake. "I would parley, lady, in keeping with terms of the Pact."

She snatched it out of the air, quick as a peregrine taking a bird in flight or a cobra striking. Gabe did not flinch. He'd expected that, and he was focused on her eyes. She'd barely glanced away, as if knowing the metal would come to her hand. "Yes?"

No encouragement, but they had not gone on their way. One of the horses tossed her head, a tad impatiently, and the rider patted the mare's withers, once, calming. Whatever else they were, they respected their mounts, and Gabe could work with that. This was, though, where it got tricky. Trickier.

"I come to you to seek aid only you can give, should you choose. You, who are born of the stars and the green earth, who dwell in the hidden places, and who ride out in blessing and judgement, I ask for you to hear me." They had worked out the text, the praise and anchoring, as Alexander had put it, painstakingly. It wasn't the language the Council used, but it couldn't be, not quite. Gabe was coming as petitioner, not as diplomat.

The landscape shifted, then, and here was the eerie hint of the Wild Hunt. Gabe did not hear hounds or a pack in full fury, but suddenly the shadows beyond the group were darker. He could see a twist of a great iridescent green coil, as if it were circling them all, always moving and catching the light anew. Here, now, was that woodland he'd dreamed, months ago, and had not known, and they were no longer entirely on mortal land.

He took a breath to steady himself, waiting patiently because waiting was the only thing he could do. It was like that moment with the portal, the same terrifying demand for stillness, for waiting, for making himself a shape for what was needed. A time when he had to rise to the challenge of doing what was hardest for him.

The great lady at the centre nodded once, her voice now full of bells. "Speak what you wish, Gabriel Anthony Edgarton, who holds the magic of this land deep in his blood and bones, ancestor to ancestor." Well, that answered one question, whether they knew who he was. Then the lady's mouth twitched just once. "We have places to be." Amused, he thought, not irritated, but how on earth would he be able to tell?

Gabe permitted himself a quick flash of a smile before settling to the work. He was no ritualist, not the way Alexander and Geoffrey and Cyrus were, but he knew how to do the thing properly. "We fear invasion. We of Albion, we of all who live in England's green land, and the hills and valleys of Wales, and all of Scotland's crags and lochs and everything in between. And we humans, we scrabble, thinking each of us, each group, has the right of what to do.

I come to you, to the Fatae, to ask for some token that might offer a cause for unity. Something all might recognise as a symbol, a sign."

There was another flash in her expression, one he could not read at all. Then she raised her hand, fingers flicking in what must be some silent language. She didn't look away from him, didn't look to see what message might be returned. Just that steady, even stare. As the mist and starlight had settled, cloaking them rather than dancing around them, he could see the lady's hair was dark, with twists of vines and flowers pinned in it. She wore a dress of deep green, the sort of green that sang of enchantments and of those great coils that still twisted behind them.

"What will you give us for such a thing?" She flicked her fingers. "It is quite a boon."

They'd talked about this. What he could offer. What he had the right to offer. Taken one way, all he could offer was himself. But sacrificing your life was an offer you could make once and only once, at least if it were accepted. It certainly wasn't the thing to lead the negotiations with, unless he were determined it would be his only gift. But she'd given him a hint, at least.

"You know me, lady, my name and my blood. You know of my parents and my children, and my wife, away across the Channel." Gabe couldn't help the way his heart skipped at that, at even the thought of Rathna.

"Our kin have heard her, and are considering her own request. A less direct one, at the moment." The lady on the horse shrugged once, a very human gesture to cut across the stillness she'd had til then. "I do know your measure." Before she spoke again, the ranks of horses parted, making an aisle, and one of the women rode up, a riderless horse's reins in her hand. "Will you ride with us?"

Gabe blinked. Riding was not the problem. Or at least, he expected not. They were horses, after all, and he knew horses. Even if these were obviously magical, they were still visibly like horses. They stood and stamped and were in every way a horse. "Yes, lady, in hopes of an answer. And a safe dismount at the end?" He made the last a clear question.

She laughed, the sound like bells and the deep beat of a large drum tumbling over each other. "Mount, adjust your stirrups, and we shall ride." It was no direct answer, but it was what he was offered. The mare with no rider was enough the shape of his beloved Invicta, but also not the same horse at all. She had fine shapely ears, a light build, a curving neck, and excellent legs for a hunter.

It might be the last thing Gabe ever did, the last thing he remembered of his life, but he could not have turned down the chance for anything in the world. "May I give her a treat, lady, to make friends?"

That got all of them laughing, the sound echoing around the clearing, but when the world got quiet again, their leader was quick to add, "Please, do. You may call her Apple." A use name, clearly, whatever others the mare answered to.

Gabe fished the little apple and oat biscuit out of the bottom of his jacket. He'd not expected to need it, not tonight, but he generally had one there, just in case. He held his palm out, thumb tucked neatly to the side, as he took the reins from the woman who was holding them. Apple whuffled at his hand eagerly enough, and it gave him a chance to get a better measure of her. Well-built, with an elegance and sturdiness that suggested some ancient breeding line. Her hooves were tidily trimmed, and recently.

He put the reins over her head. "A moment, if you please?" He took the time to circle her, getting her to pick up one foot, then the other. He checked the girth as he went down the curve of her barrel, adjusting the stirrup automatically to the length of his arm. Then he reversed, doing the same again on the other side. The women murmured, something he didn't understand, but it seemed amused as well, rather than impatient. There were no stones. The girth was snug, and the mare did not object to his check.

By the time he'd got back around to her left side, the women had spread out in an easy arc again, giving him plenty of room to mount. By preference, he'd have mounted from the right, but he knew it would cause comment, and he could manage. Would manage. One bounce, then two, his ankle complaining a bit, before he swung up and into the saddle. He gathered up the reins, squeezing lightly with his calves, testing the mare's responsiveness. Apple moved forward two steps, then halted again when he sank into the saddle and rocked his hips to hold her between hands and his seat.

"Ready?" The lady glanced over at him.

"As you will." Which was a dangerous thing to say, but here he was on a horse, and who knew what the evening would hold.

Without a word, the lady signalled her own mare, who picked up a canter, neat and tidy as any pavo mount. Apple was eager to follow, falling into place among the others. She had a glorious gait, smooth as Mama's own mares always had, a rolling pace that covered ground easily. It was the kind of canter that could go on for ages, even without magic. The group turned down a long track; the horses spread out, people rode in twos or threes. It was only as they got going that he realised the horses never quite touched the ground. They took a turn, leaping over a fence, and Gabe felt Apple's haunches bunch up for the jump, taking it entirely in stride.

He could do this part. He had no fears here, beyond the ordinary cautions of a horse. They were moving at speed, but if they never quite touched the ground, he didn't have to worry Apple would stumble or find some hidden hole or tree root. All he had to do was keep an eye out for his own head, and stay with them.

They rode for what could have been hours, except that the sky did not change so much as all that, circling in a long path through fields and woodlands. They crossed streams, even a river, once, in places Gabe recognised and places he'd never seen.

They trotted along the edge of villages and grand estates, and circled around a castle once. Here and there, the lady would pause, and one of her court would toss something down. Whatever it was, it was glowing white, and it floated, like flower petals or feathers or both. They had more weight, though, rather than drifting in the air, they slipped down to land. They always moved on before Gabe could see what effect that brush of magic had, but whatever it was, they were deliberate about who was touched and who was not.

Gabe didn't ask. He couldn't, for one thing. The women around him had picked up conversations, but they were in some language he'd never heard. He knew enough Welsh and Scots that it wasn't either of those, though it might have been a related language, or an ancient version of the tongue. While they might well also speak modern English, he wasn't going to interrupt.

He would ride, he would pay attention, and he would, whatever else, enjoy this moment as wholeheartedly as he could manage. It might be a gift that came with unexpected fangs. But until they showed, he would make the most of a wonderful horse, a gorgeous night, and a moment of respite in the midst of war.

Eventually, they came to a pause, having found a stone circle somewhere high atop a hill, from which they could see all the surrounding land. There was no one there, no bonefire, nor wakefire, nor solstice bonfire, just the ring of stones shining in the moonlight. The ladies all pulled their horses into a loose ring again, and their leader pivoted hers to face Gabe and Apple.

"You ride well, Gabriel."

The praise first made him a little wary, but he nodded once. The trick was to appreciate the compliment without implying obligation. No one knew for sure what did that, but thanks were generally a bad idea. "I have loved to ride from the time I was tiny, lady, and I am glad of the chance. Apple is a grand mount, and I only wish to do her justice."

It brought them to laughing again, laughing and a murmur of chatter.

"Do you have questions, Gabriel?" This had a more serious tone, a slight edge to it.

"Many, lady, but none I will ask. I am sure you will tell me what you wish, and not one morsel more. This is your time, your night, your steeds, and your hunt. It is not mine to question, much as I am, on an ordinary day, made of questions."

"And on extraordinary days, as well." She drew the words out with a purr. Now she was laughing again, her eyes gleaming. He wasn't close enough to see the colour, but he thought they must be more like golden yellow than like human eyes, the way the flashes of colour caught. "What will you do with a token if we give you one?"

"Do my best, lady, to unify our work, in keeping this land safe, and all who dwell on it. Human, magical and not. Animal. And whatever we might offer to the Fatae who dwell here as well, though I do not know what that might be." He did not ask for himself, after all. That wasn't what he was here for.

There was a tiny pause, as if he had said something she had not quite expected. "Well said, Gabriel." Her fingers flicked once in another one of those silent communications. "We will give you the gift you seek. There are three things you must do. First, ride with us the rest of the night. Second, do as you have said, doing your best to bring together those who would stand and defend the land. We will know if you shirk or falter, but we know that you can cajole, not command." Then she paused. "Last, when you are asked a question you wish to refuse, say yes. You will know which one when that time comes."

The first two were - well, not easy. The riding was a joy, and if the rest of the evening was the same, it was no great demand. The second, well, he'd already committed to doing that, and they had made it clear they understood the limits of what he could do. The third, though. Of course it was three things. It was going to be either three or seven. That was how it went. And the last always had the sharp bite.

But he nodded, just once. "As you say, lady. I trust you know your work, as well as I know mine."

It made her laugh again, head thrown back. She picked up the reins again before the sound trailed off. "The petals we drop are gifts, blessing those who have left particular offerings, or who have need of a touch of lightness. Nothing that breaks the Pact, of course, just a wish on the wind. A moment of belief in things beyond the seen and heard."

Gabe inclined his head once, acknowledging that. A

particular line of lore, that, but it was perhaps to be expected. There were tales out of Germany and Scandinavia, the northern isles, about the Wild Hunt led by women being one that shared gifts, rather than a trooping of the graveless dead, or a mass of hunters after prey. Before he was done, the lady had wheeled her horse, and they were off and away again.

In this second half of the night, Gabe found he could relax a hair, watching the landscape change and shift around him. They circled, leapt fences, caught a sett of badgers frolicking by a hedgerow, a pair of foxes and kits in a field. Gabe heard the murmuring of twilight nightjars in a pause, caught a flash of a star hare. And then, deep in woods he thought might well be the New Forest, a flash of a white hart.

He didn't think they'd circled very far north, but he wasn't sure. The places he knew best were Kent or the New Forest, but it wasn't as if he knew Cornwall or Wiltshire or Cumbria near as well. Once, he was sure they'd come up to Norfolk, near where he'd spent a week on a case. But it seemed they were there for only an instant before they were away again.

As the light began to glow again, they pulled up, and suddenly he was home. There was Veritas, and they had come up on the pond side. The lights were still bright in the library, though they were well down the hill toward the salle. The lady drew her mare up and nodded once, holding out a hand. One of the others placed something in it, and the lady rode closer, so they were knee to knee. "Your hand."

He gathered the reins in his left hand, holding out his right, uncertain what she meant to do. She took his fingers in hers, turning his palm down, and slipping a ring on his fourth finger, mirroring where he wore the wedding ring on his left. It glinted in the moonlight and then sparkled with its own internal light, a flash of green that was all the same magic as the insistent dragon.

"May I ask what I should know about showing it to others, lady?" He didn't know how to put the question better than that.

"You will see." Right. He wasn't getting answers. Gabe hadn't really expected them. "It has been a fine ride with you. It is good to know that some respect the old agreements, and have good manners. You may find your family." That was a clear dismissal.

Before he moved to dismount, though, Gabe cleared his throat. "May I offer your mounts - or you ladies - any refreshment? Fresh water, oats, whatever I might get from our kitchens or cellars?"

That got another laugh. "We are well, Gabriel, we are well. But if you were to leave a plate of honey cakes and a flask of cider out somewhere private near here tonight, we would gladly feast then."

"I will see it done." Gabe swallowed. "I will do as I have said in all things tonight, to the best of my ability. May all your rides be blessed in all the ways you wish."

That said, he dismounted, feeling solid ground underneath his feet for the first time in hours. His ankle jarred for a moment, but before he could wobble, the horses and their riders swirled up, disappearing like scattering leaves. Gabe stood alone in the grass, the ring on his finger to prove that it had not all been some enchantment or dream only in his head.

Then he unfolded the cane again, and walked up toward the house, the glass windows that looked out on the lawn, hoping he didn't scare them too much.

CHAPTER 31
SUMMER SOLSTICE NEAR DAX

Everyone had made the best of the solstice festival, though there was a looming shadow over the whole thing. There had been a feast, and dancing, and people telling stories. Rathna's French had improved, of course it had, but she still wasn't fluent enough to catch the wordplay or innuendo, even with Grietje murmuring in her ear.

After a bit, she'd gone off to sit a bit further from the circle of people sharing tales and songs and dances to find a bench where she could observe. The little ones hadn't exactly gone to sleep, but they were in little piles on blankets and cloaks, curled up against a mother's leg or a father's.

Five minutes later, Ferdinand joined her. "Are you all right, Mistress?"

Rathna grimaced, rubbing her face. "That obvious?" She let out a long breath. "I was thinking what it would be like, at home. Worrying a bit less this morning than I was last night."

"You had said your husband was." He stalled and tried

again. "There was something?" Ferdinand was tentative, exceedingly tentative.

Thinking back, she hadn't said much about what Gabe was up to. She hadn't wanted to talk about it if it didn't work. And now that it had, she wasn't sure how to talk about it at all, though it was, in fact, relevant to their next few days. "Ah. Last night, my husband made a petition of the Fatae, and it was answered. Or at least, he got what he asked for. It remains to be seen how that plays out."

"Mistress?" Ferdinand pulled back, blinking at her. "But he's..."

"He had the Council's permission. For something he's working on with them. But he's the one who did the asking." She shook her head, feeling the long braid down her back rock, the weight of it. "I don't know all the details yet. Some things defy writing about. But it went well. He's hopeful. We're hopeful." She let out a puff of breath. "That it went well for him. I hope it means it will go well with us too. Though we're not asking quite the same thing."

"No, Mistress." Ferdinand coughed. "What are we doing, then?"

"You are observing, we very much hope. Helping carry the offerings, but I will do all the talking, or with the help of our translators. It is not entirely clear to me how the Fatae manage the variety of human languages."

Ferdinand smiled a little at that. "And we have rather a lot, don't we? You said your French was better, so is mine."

"And you're fluent in German, which I hope we won't need." If they did get caught up by the advancing German army, there was a slim chance he'd be able to talk them out of trouble, but a very slim one. She did not want to rely on that fragile a hope. "And I'm reasonably fluent in Bengali, though that's not much use here. A little Hindi, but mostly ordinary needs, nothing complex. And Latin, of course. A bit of Hebrew and Yiddish, but again, either for ritual or very practical. That's plenty to keep me busy."

If she'd had a different childhood entirely, she might also have picked up Sanskrit, for ritual use. But that would have meant a different family, a different upbringing, parents from a different caste and background.

Ferdinand nodded. "What do you expect when we go back to the cave?"

She took a breath and laid it out for him. Her goal, first and foremost, was to pass on what she knew about what had damaged the Paris portals, and whether it would impact any of the others. Gabe, bless and keep him, had been informative at length about what he'd got from the Council. Mostly from Alexander, if she was reading between the lines correctly.

If so, Alexander was being unusually informative, perhaps because of a touch of guilt on some front or another. Thesan had shared a few more notes, snatches she'd picked up from the conversations her husband had had with his brother. The two of them at least knew what might matter, and she'd make more offerings of thanks for that when she could.

When she got home. Which brought her to, "I was sitting alone because I was thinking of what I'd usually be doing. There would be the bonfire on the estate, solstice eve. The day itself, of course, we've obligations at the Council Keep for the offerings, and usually some small gathering after, with friends. And then, tomorrow, the whole next week, we'd be at the Midsummer Faire."

It was still happening this year, even with the war, because the harvest mattered, the harvest rituals mattered, and this was the beginning of them. Muted, of course, with many people fighting or in war work, but food was essential. Solstice was the promise of harvest, as Geoffrey had put it once. It was the pause in the agricultural cycle where you could wipe your brow and take a short rest between planting and gathering in. No matter what else happened in the world, that needed to happen for them to make it through the winter. "And I miss my children."

Ferdinand cleared his throat carefully at that. "Not like my family. Though," he sighed, "I suppose Mutti misses me."

She was sure they had one of the more distant sorts of families, with the children trotted out when clean and scrubbed for a few minutes. Not how Gabe had grown up, or his sister Charlotte, nor the way they'd brought up their three. But it was quite common in the First Families. Not at all good for them, if anyone asked Rathna, but no one did, generally. "I am sure she does, whatever else. With any luck, we'll make it home safely soon, and you can see her."

He looked up at her, blinking several times. Then he nodded and quickly excused himself to go have a cigarette while leaning against one of the ancient trees, looking out across the vineyard trellises.

Two days later, they made the long trek by cart, through the winding roads and up into the foothills of the mountains, back to the cave. Rathna was dressed as well as she could manage at this point. She wore the one of her dresses that had taken the least damage over the past months, in a vibrant green that at least felt suitable to the height of the summer growth. They had a basket of items to offer, pastries and good bread and wine, as well as some of the berries and early fruits, a quarter wheel of one of the best cheeses. And a bit more of the same for food when they were done. Offer your best, that was the rule, but always what you would gladly eat yourself.

This time, Rathna went first, with Ferdinand carrying the basket of offerings. Miren and Grietje followed behind. None of them was sure how this would work. The other two carried two lanterns each, enough to illuminate the cave properly, at least where they expected to be. Rathna moved to take her place in front of the flat stone they'd made the offerings on. Before she could decide what to do, there was a pop, like the pressure before a thunder crack or a bolt of lightning. There had been no one there, and now there was.

Before them stood a woman. Her hair was pulled back and covered by a net of silver and sparkling beads, closely framing a rounded face with a broad forehead, high cheek-bones, and a generous mouth. It was a face that would not be out of place on any modern city street, and yet it was ageless. Rathna had no sense of how old she was, but she didn't even have much sense of what age meant on such a face. The woman before her might have been any age between the youngest adulthood and that point where she visibly aged, well into her later years. She wore a gown of deep green, darker than Rathna's, but very much of the same intensity.

There was nothing immediately that marked her as being one of the Fatae or of being anything other than entirely human. Her skin was pale, about the shade of Ferdinand's, but it did not glow with unearthly light. Her ears were not visible, but the shape of the netted hood suggested they were not unduly pointed. There were five fingers on each hand, not the sixth finger that some lore ascribed to those of witchblood. But there was something about the speed of her gestures, the slow flow of them, that was not at all like any human Rathna had ever met, as if she were dancing to an entirely different drumbeat than a human heart.

Rathna inclined her head and made the sort of bob she had learned to make when making the offerings during the Council rites. It was not entirely a curtsey, as she understood it, but it was a reverence and a sign of respect. When she straightened up, the woman was watching her intently now, and that was more than a little uncomfortable.

"How may I call you?" Ah, that was something she'd been warned to expect. The giving of a true name had power, of course, but at the same time, she would need to establish her credentials, such as they were.

"I am called Rathna. I am of Albion." It was terribly hard to know how to begin, what was enough, what was too much.

"You come from..." And then a pause. "You are from many places and many peoples. How is that?"

It was a question Rathna had heard far too often, and she could not quite restrain the slight sigh at it even here. No one ever thought she belonged where she did, apparently. Even the Fatae. It was almost a moment of feeling anchored in the normal expectations of the world.

"I am a child of Bengal, born among London's dockside tenements. I am family to a people without a home for many years. I am woven with an ancient line of Albion by marriage. All these things are true, and I call the magic of the portals to my hand and it comes." The last came out not sharp - she was doing her best to avoid that - but with a hint of frustration that she had to keep proving herself.

The woman shifted, like wind blowing through clothing hung outside to dry, a long length of silk or cotton moving, then it settled. "Peace, keeper of Albion. Your magic is not what I expected."

Well, that wasn't any more reassuring, but at least it was a different sort of confusing puzzle than the usual. Rathna let out a breath. "Lady. I do tend the portals of Albion."

That got a nod, perhaps approving. "Your husband is Gabriel, yes?"

Rathna blinked. "Yes, mistress of magics, he is." She had a flash back to the moment before she'd met him, where that name had sounded like a woman's to her. Even more so in this Fatae woman's accent, the lilt of the local French and Basque underlying everything.

"My sisters across the sea have met him and spoken well of him." The woman inclined her head, once in acknowledgement. "You may call me Urdin." Rathna had picked up that much Basque from Miren. It was a colour word, one of those that meant blue, green, grey, the shades of water and other depths. A potent use name for this sort of meeting, then.

"Is there a proper form of respect I might use? I do not know what is polite."

There was a laugh, cascading off the walls of the cave, joyfully scattering like the sound of bells. In almost any other situation, Rathna might have read it as a half-mocking laugh of her naivety or youth. Here, that did not matter. Chances were good this woman was hundreds, thousands of years old. If the question amused her, well, all to the good. "We do not need titles between us, do we? Whatever would we do with them?"

Rathna suspected that near any of the Council, confronted with this question, would have their formalities shattered into pieces. The framing, though, made her ask, "May I ask, then, do you know Alexander Landry? He would have stayed in these parts thirty years or so ago."

It brought forth another peal. "What makes you ask that, then? Oh, yes, we remember him, quite well. He made, how do you say, an impression. A generally good one."

"He is a friend to my family, and family to our close friends. A recent one, a handful of years, but a welcome one." Without his aid, she'd never have known how to make the original offering as properly as she had. Clearly, she'd done something right, given how this was going. "He sends his good wishes and asked me to say something." She then repeated the phrase in Basque he'd shared with her, which Miren had refused to translate, which made Rathna fairly sure it was about magic or ritual or both. She'd practised it carefully.

Urdin arched one eyebrow, then nodded once. "We are glad to be remembered so." Approving, whatever else she was, Rathna was reasonably sure of that. Or, possibly, entirely wrong, and all of them would be turned into frogs or snakes or something else out of a fairy tale at any moment. Then she glanced around the cave. "You had information to bring to us, and also a request. The portals, in Paris." It was very much as if she were in a conversation with her fellows of the guild, or another of the most powerful guilds, treating her as an acknowledged mistress of her art. Not, as Gabe had described, being decidedly a petitioner. Rathna filed that away for contemplating later.

The information first, obviously. Rathna took a breath. "Yes, mistress of magics. You must know, I am sure, that the Grand Salle des Portes in Paris, as we call it, has been badly damaged, possibly destroyed. I know something of how it came to be so, and I wished to share it with you, in case it was a help in the mending."

"Did you." That was calculating, all of a sudden. "How do you come to know this?"

"My husband was present when first anyone was told what happened. Others, friends of the family, have told him more in the last few days."

"And you do not bargain with this information?" Urdin seemed taller now, certainly more impressive. Ferdinand was still a foot or two behind her, but she rather thought Miren and Grietje had stepped back.

"Some things are not for a bargain, lady. Some things are shared because it is right to do so." She had her own ethics, whatever anyone else in Albion might have done. "I speak on my own behalf, judging that you have a right to the knowledge. That I would want to know, if a door I had tended might be mended better, by the knowing."

"We might not mend it at all." There was a sudden sharp sorrow there. As if it were one straw too many, one stone that caused an avalanche. Urdin looked away, up to the corner of the cave for a long moment. "Go on."

"As I understand it, two of the Council Members of Albion were in Paris, getting those last magical treasures out of the Paris library and museums before the German army took the city. Many are now safe in Albion, to be protected and guarded until they may be properly returned." Rathna could only hope that would happen. The alternatives did not bear thinking about.

"That is," there was a slight catch there, before Urdin continued. "It is better than not, though we feel the wound of their absence. But that would not destroy the portals." Urdin's voice was no less musical now, but it had something of the open octaves and spaces of someone playing on a great pipe organ, something that reverberated uncomfortably through body and bone.

"I am glad to take a message back, for those who might answer." Rathna wasn't at all sure how that would go over,

297

but she could try. And she did, in fact, know Alexander, who had his own opinions about a country's magical heritage being away from home.

Urdin nodded once. "Go on, what happened?"

"They were pursued to the portals by fighters, mages and magicians, duellists, seeking to stop them. As told to me, Livia Fortier, born to an ancient line and married into an equally ancient one that stems from France herself, called down a final strike, spending her life to drive them back. She sought to prevent them from taking the last of the treasures and wanted to seal the portals. Her husband mourns her greatly." All of that was true, without editorialising. One did not do that when conveying what must be said. "I have information about the portal readings when they came through, in my notes."

"I wish that, yes. And you have been tending the portal at Dax." That seemed more neutral. At least if Rathna were reading Urdin's expressions at all accurately, and she had no idea. She had been warned, more than once, that the Fatae might look human, but they were not human at all. Their priorities and reactions were based on entirely different lines of thought.

"To the best of my ability, yes. We did all we could to keep it open for those fleeing Paris, then from Rennes. It is, pardon, I do not quite know how to describe it outside the terms we use with each other. It is a frayed cloth, still, but we have been mending it, weaving in new strength as best we can."

"A serviceable gown." That had a moment of amusement again. "A fair description. And you have something you need?"

Rathna had had a fine speech ready for this, and now, in the moment, she could not bring herself to make it. "Mistress of magic, if it pleases you and your sisters and your brothers and your kin, I wish to go home. We wish to go home, we of Albion, and those who have ties there." She gestured slightly behind her, where Grietje was. "We have done as much as we can here, and I fear we will be a burden if we stay much longer."

"A burden and at great risk." That had a sharpness to it, like the bite of a tart apple, the flavour of it bursting in Rathna's mind like Urdin had placed it there with her words.

"Both of those, lady."

There was a slight nod and a long pause. Rathna did not speak. Jogging the elbow of the immortal power who might do you a favour was never a good idea. In fact, the whole thing was making her deeply suspicious about the truth of certain myths and tales she'd learned from her mother. Though, she supposed, some people would be eternally foolish when presented with this particular challenge, no matter what the cost.

The silence went on, well beyond comfort. Finally, Urdin nodded once. "You must open a door to somewhere that we know. An ancient portal, one not locked against us. Your school, your keep, your city, none of them will do."

Rathna swallowed. "We are still working on arrangements, but we believe the portal in the Tower of London may yet open to your call."

Urdin's chin jerked up. "That would do." It was something made up of praise and just a hint of surprise. "You will need to strengthen the portal here, to have the reach. Across the ocean is a challenge, and that path has been asleep for many years."

"Near enough five hundred, lady." Rathna spread her hands out slightly, the way she did when she was pointing out something to her seniors in the guild. "Is there any specific rite we should tend to?"

"Give me your hands, if you would learn. You will, I think, know what to do."

Rathna swallowed hard. Gabe had told her about climbing onto a horse's back, and this was like that, reaching out without knowing what might come. It could destroy her, it could change her utterly, it could swing her life in some new direction. She could only trust she was making the right choice. She lifted her hands, palm up, in the supplicant gesture. A moment later, Urdin reached her hands, palm to palm, then fingers brushing Rathna's wrists, resting right at the pulse point.

The knowledge swirled into her head. She'd have gone to her knees except that there was an arm there behind her, holding her up at the waist, giving her something to brace against. She swallowed twice, grabbing for any sense of self in a torrent of understanding. It washed over her like an ocean, going from the coastal waters into something deep and full of dangers she didn't begin to understand. Best she could, she stood her ground. She let it soak in; she did not fight any of it. Morah Avigail had taught her this, built it from the bedrock up, how to be present and feel and know and listen.

Slowly, steadily, she made enough sense of it to let it flow better. It turned, somehow, from a downpour to a soaking rain, filling her up, seeping into crevices and hollows she'd never known she had. The magic had flavours to it, tastes she'd had and loved, of chocolate and pastry and smoked fish, of wine and coffee and ripe cheese. The bright and melded spices of India. It had flowers in it, the ones that were the height of summer here, in Albion, in India, all tangled together. There was honey there, fresh from the hive, and made into sweets. And then there was the pure crystal water, cold as if from some deep well underground, ageless and perfect.

She didn't know how long she stood there, but when she finally began to come out of it, her knees were trembling. She kept standing through sheer force of will, as she felt Urdin's fingers brush one last time, then part. It left a gaping hole in her magic, in her palms, and she could not think about stemming that void, not yet.

Instead, Rathna forced herself to focus on Urdin's face. Now, the other woman glowed, with an unearthly light, like the moon distilled into silver. It made the cave shine brightly, enough that Rathna had to blink against it. "Leave your notes. And you will need this back." Urdin twisted her wrist, and then she held up the single aquamarine stone that Rathna had left a few days before.

Morah Avigail's aquamarine. Rathna's aquamarine. She could have wept, and she couldn't, not yet. Rathna simply held out her hand, feeling the weight of it drop into her palm. Then, between one of her too-rapid heartbeats and the next, Urdin was gone, taking all the light but the two dim lanterns with her, and leaving them all in an echoing silence.

In a story, in a novel, the heroine would have pluckily turned to her companions and said something like, "That went well!" If people wrote novels about something like this, which they didn't. All Rathna could do was breathe. Breathe, and try not to collapse. She could feel the sweat pooling in the small of her back, the dampness of it and the way the cloth was sticking. Her feet ached as if she'd walked a dozen miles or more, her knees were throbbing, and her head was about to join them.

Ferdinand's arm was still at her back. He hadn't moved.

She swallowed. "First things. My notes." Her voice cracked audibly, and she didn't try to speak again, just reaching into the small pouch over her shoulder for the folded paper. Five steps brought her to the flat altar space. She left the sheets on the top, adding a stone from the ground to hold them in place as a precaution.

She finally turned to look at the rest of them. "I—" Then she took in their faces. "Pardon?"

"Mistress? Did it go well? We - I saw you react to things several times, but I could not hear anything, or see anything." Ferdinand was hesitant.

Ah. Well. A very personal visit, then. Right. She'd have to recalibrate that later. With any luck, with Gabe's help. He would at least understand. "It went well. We need to do some additional work on the portal. We need to find one willing to open to us on the other end. But there is hope. And they were, I think, pleased I could give them more information about the Paris portals." Then her knees threatened to give way. "Can I have your arm, please, back to the cart? And a rest before we go back?"

She wondered, for a moment, if Miren had seen a tad bit more than the others. The older woman kept looking at Rathna curiously, as if she couldn't believe whatever she'd glimpsed. It wasn't fear, though; it was more like awe or wonder, the same way Rathna had felt, to be honest.

Rathna had expected some catch. There likely would still be one. That was how this went. It was worth it, or so she hoped. And telling them about Paris had been the right thing. They could only go forward as best they could.

CHAPTER 32
JUNE 28TH AT YTENE

This time, it was Gabe who was pacing. They were in the library at Ytene. To be fair, it was made for pacing, given it was a large room, with the furniture in a ring, well away from the shelves. Gabe made a loop, pausing by the doors for a heartbeat or two, then set off again. Alexander was settled in his chair, fingers steepled, mostly staring out the French doors onto the terrace when Gabe wasn't blocking the way.

And there wasn't anything to fill the next quarter of an hour, most likely. They were waiting to meet someone who could get into the White Tower, in the heart of the Tower of London, to see if he were willing to make it happen. Someone Geoffrey knew well, Gabe knew that, but Geoffrey had not explained the details. And then the man had written to say he was running late. Geoffrey had gone off to meet him, leaving Gabe and Alexander to wait. Uselessly.

It did not make Gabe feel any better that he'd been the one who'd kept meetings waiting twice in the last three days, despite all his best efforts. Or that he'd been unable to get to sleep last night until he'd finally given in and taken half a potion dose.

Gabe didn't have words for how he felt. He might have worked it through with Rathna right there, able to see all the subtle, tiny things she reliably noticed. But they'd tried and failed - three times, before calling it quits - in the journals. He might have asked Mama, but he was, to be honest, unsure what she'd say. Same thing with Mason and Witt.

He was not at his best. That was a way to put it, for certain. The rush of the Wild Hunt, of that night's ride through hill and dale, however he wanted to put it, had been exhilarating. The crash that evening, the next days, had been entirely the opposite. He'd ached, physically. He'd not spent so many hours on horseback with no break in years. But he'd also ached somewhere deep in his magic, in his sense of self.

He hadn't snapped at any of the staff, or at any of his family. But it had been a near thing, a dozen times, and that wasn't like him at all. Getting up on Meliora had been an effort, for all she was a splendid horse. And for all he'd wanted to be out riding with his children. All three of his children, home from Schola and tutoring school. He'd had to take a few days before he went back to the work of trying to gather people up, along with Isobel and the other staff working with them, because he hadn't trusted himself. Urgent as the need was, he couldn't mess it up.

The inside of him itched, like clothes binding and fitting too tightly. The outside of him itched, as if something were rubbing against his skin in all the worst places. He couldn't settle. He could work himself to exhaustion and fall into bed, and he'd been doing that, steadily. Last night, he'd swum in the lake until he could barely move his arms. Another man would have gone running, but his ankle wouldn't hold up to exhaustion, and duelling drills could only take him so far.

And he hadn't dared ask someone to duel him. Gabe didn't trust his instincts right now. It was as if everything had been shaken loose. He might have trusted Isembard or Alexander, but both of them had been working flat out since Livia's death, entirely tangled in far more important things than Gabe's moodiness. Alexander moved a foot, and Gabe twitched toward the sound.

There was a silence before Alexander spoke. His voice was far more careful than Gabe had ever heard him. It wasn't the clarity of high expectations made audible, but something new. "You've been changed. What you're feeling is normal, if anything is normal after that."

Gabe stopped, pivoting on his heel to look at Alexander. No use trying to hide his reaction. Alexander would have seen it from the first twitch. And Alexander was an ally, a friend, and he had been remarkably honest, considering everything. Gabe shouldn't have to hide. That was the theory. Most of the time, in practice, he covered over a great deal of what was in his head with other things.

"Oh?" It was not the most suave reply Gabe had made in his life, but it would have to do. Not that he started walking again.

"Whatever you did a week ago, it worked. Sufficient unto the purpose. Making the request, that is, obviously we still need to see what the ripples do in the world." He leaned forward, intent. "But it changed you. This is, of course, why we have the Pact. On both sides. We change each other, we and the Fatae, when we interact." Alexander hesitated. That wasn't like him. "May I ask how long you were with them?"

"Sunset, near enough, to dawn. I got back into the

house right at quarter to five. You were there for that part. Seven and a half hours?" Gabe had written down what he could remember, before anything else, once he'd let his family know he was home, but it was in flashing fragments in his mind. He'd get a glimpse of a place they stopped, a line of ancient trees lining a road, a manor house towering up in the landscape, and ancient yews and oaks and fallen ruins.

Alexander blinked. Something in that had discomfited him, made him rearrange his thoughts. Visibly. That was worrisome. Alexander was not a man who let that sort of thing show. "That is, for the record, rather longer than anyone has spent in their company than I know of, in at least a century. Perhaps two or three. I am not asking what you did."

They - Alexander, Cyrus, the other Council members he'd spoken with directly - had made it clear they wouldn't. Gabe didn't know if they'd made oath on it, or whether they felt it was distasteful, some sort of taboo, or something else. It wasn't as if he could ask, and that had nagged at him too.

Gabe was used to the collaboration of the Penelopes, and the way that had filtered in to every conversation at home, with his parents, with Rathna, with their children, with their apprentices. Apparently, by now, also with Ferdinand, from what she'd said a few weeks ago. The Council, though, seemed not to talk to each other nearly enough, certainly not the way Gabe thought they should. He was arrogant, yes, but in this case, he thought he was also experienced enough with the world to rightfully think he knew how to do things better.

Not that he'd say so now. Even if he was right - and he was right - pressing Alexander about it here and now wouldn't help the upcoming meeting. It was possible, Gabe thought, that Geoffrey would agree with Gabe on this point. If so, they might mutually manage some leverage. Later. Sometime after, after everything.

Now, he had to figure out what else to say. Longer than Alexander knew of. Gabe wasn't sure what to do with that information at all. It hadn't felt that long, but of course time and the Fatae were long known to be on imprecise terms with each other. "To be honest, I am waiting for the other shoe to drop. Not today, probably. Sometime." A younger Gabe might have shared the last requirement they'd placed on him, and Gabe now did not. He wanted to think about it more. It felt like the kind of thing to protect until it was time. Though he'd talk it out with Rathna if, when, once she was home.

That was the moment, though, where there was a noise outside the door, and then Geoffrey opening it, gesturing someone in. A man, near enough Geoffrey's age, in a good but indeterminate suit that would be entirely ordinary in Whitehall. "Lap, you know Alexander, and this is Gabriel Edgarton. Gabe, this is Lapidoth Manse." He nudged the door closed and brought up the warding. Gabe could feel it rise and prickle against his own magic. Then Geoffrey added, "My handler, senior in MI6 these days. Well-connected in Whitehall, and willing to hear you out."

Gabe nodded, settling himself evenly on both feet, hands behind his back, where he could fidget with one of his rings without it showing, spinning it on his finger. "Sir." He waited while Geoffrey saw to drinks, and then went on once Geoffrey nodded to him. "In short, sir, we know there is a portal in the depths of the Tower of London. We believe it will be easy for someone with suitable magical skills to unseal the entrance, and to open the portal to entrance from France. Dax, in Aquitaine, to be specific." He gave the old name for it. That was the one that mattered here.

"That is quite a favour." Lap was a sharply precise man, the sort that Aunt Witt and Doyle would entirely approve of. He crossed one leg over the other, pulling out a small notebook to jot down something. "Why?"

That was the crux of it. On the surface, it was an entirely personal favour. The sort that was made of nepotism and borrowing power, taking what was wanted because it was possible. But it wasn't that simple. "Bordeaux's been occupied, or likely will be by tonight. My wife and several other experts - her apprentice, several of the Guard, and a few others who have key intelligence information - are in Aquitaine. They can get the portal working, and they likely have a few days before anyone investigates in detail. But they are running out of options." Gabe held up a hand. "Even the mountains."

"And she thinks this will work." Manse's voice was flat.

"She is a Portal Keeper. She knows her work as well as I know mine. And she has other reasons to think the portal will open to her, if we can get her out on the other end."

Manse nodded slowly. "What do you know about this side of it?"

"She says - and I agree, as do the other experts we've consulted - that it must connect to one of the Fatae portals here. One that it knows. Cross-channel portals are a trick that way. Schola, Trellech, the Council Keep are obviously all out. So is Dover, and so is Windsor Castle."

That made Manse wince. "Rather, yes. I don't know how we'd begin to explain even if there was time to unravel all the warding. And the other ancient portals, similarly a problem, yes. But no one thinks the one in the Tower is at all accessible. It hasn't been since, what?"

"1453. When the English lost Aquitaine. As it turns out. There are some references that Richard III intended to open it up, and that never happened." Gabe had those details fully at hand, in the front of his mind.

"And you're sure it hasn't been disturbed?" This was the tricky part, because Gabe wasn't at all sure. It wasn't as if he could go wandering around the Tower to check. They frowned on that sort of thing.

"I can find out if you can get me in there without an audience watching. Matter of a few minutes for me. A bit longer to open it up." Gabe swallowed. "Ground floor level of the White Tower, middle of the south wall, just past where some stairs come down from the chapel." He took two steps forward, snagging a copy from his notes and handing it over. "There. It was walled over, but this information here suggests we can open it up with a few charms. Not a load-bearing wall."

Manse rummaged for reading glasses, tucked in his breast pocket, then perched them on his nose. "Of course it's there." He glanced up and handed it to Geoffrey.

Gabe raised an eyebrow. "I know the lore about finding the princes in the tower. About three feet east, as I understand it, for the record. And whether or not they were, that's another question. There's a Healer we sometimes consult with about bones, but of course no one was going to let her near them. Not in, what was it, '33, when they had a look again?"

The idea that bones could be informative was scarcely new to any Penelope, though on the whole their work involved the messier side of things, when anatomical investigations were done. Gabe added, after a moment, "There was a lot of discussion about whether they might have been some sort of anchoring sacrifice. Rathna thinks not, for the record. As do I. No real evidence supporting the idea, and not in that location, so far as I can tell."

Manse peered up over his glasses. "I can't recruit you. You're entirely too unique." It came out crisply, but as a certain form of praise. Geoffrey, mind, was grinning broadly.

"Also entirely too occupied with my own work, thank you." Gabe crossed his arms. "Can we? If you can't, I need to figure out another option."

Manse glanced at the paper. "When?"

"They need a day or so for the final adjustments on their end. I'll need to get access to the site with one of the Portal Keepers. Rathna's first apprentice is willing to help, and we think he can do the work brilliantly. A couple of people to hold bits and bobs and make sure we aren't interrupted. Can you?"

"It's the twenty-eighth now." Manse counted. "It will take me a day or two at least to get the permissions. A day or two more to make the actual arrangements. Can she hold on that long?"

"If needed. Not much longer. They might need to camp by the portal, ward it to the heavens. There's only so long that can hold." Gabe let out a cautious breath. "Three or four days. You'll make the attempt?"

Manse nodded slowly. "Geoffrey said you had other reasons that might make the argument more compelling."

"I do." Gabe drew out the summaries. "Intelligence from multiple sources, including the fall of Paris, in exchange for refuge for a handful of allies, with skills we can use. Rathna and Ferdinand's own skills." It would speak for itself, really. Mama had done a fine job writing it up in the way that administrators could hear.

"Excellent." Manse hesitated. "May I have a walk in

your garden, Geoffrey, before we get on with the rest of it? You mentioned you had a few more things for Penelope Edgarton."

Geoffrey nodded and went to let Manse out of the French doors, opening the warding again. When he closed the doors behind the other man, he said, "Lap's not much for chitchat, I should have mentioned."

Gabe sank into one of the chairs for a moment. "None of us are at the moment. I've been rather horrid company all round. I'll get out of your hair in a minute, of course."

"Never a bother. Or rather, we understand." Geoffrey glanced at Alexander, then looked back at Gabe steadily. "What can we do on your end?"

"We're working on putting the word round to the various magical parties. The ring's a tad compelling, it turns out, when handled properly." He held up his right hand, though he didn't do anything to trigger the effect. It was not a compulsion, exactly, but it drew on the truth the way the courtroom magics did, some of the oldest magic of Albion. It made people understand when something true had been said. "We've talked to the Guard, the Healers, and a dozen experts. The Council next Wednesday, and a collection of obstreperous Lords the day after."

"That gets you to, what, first week of July? The other reason for wanting Rathna back home before then?"

Gabe nodded. "Rather." He let out a sharp breath. "Any luck on the non-magical side?"

"Rufus thinks he has an introduction. He only got it last night. It'll take some more time to sort out. And there are these rumours about something in Ashdown Forest, too near Arundel for comfort right now. We're keeping an eye on that." We, clearly encompassing Alexander, as well.

"Let me know, then." Gabe rubbed his face. "I've got to

get back to Trellech. You know where to find me." He suddenly needed desperately to be at home, to do something with his hope that this near-impossible scheme might actually work. Everything else was rubbing him raw and doing no good, and he was out of patience to deal with the irritation. The least he could do is not inflict it on friends.

Geoffrey opened his mouth, then just nodded, standing to walk Gabe out to Ytene's portal in silence.

CHAPTER 33

JULY 2ND IN THE DEPTHS OF THE WHITE TOWER, LONDON

N ow, all Gabe could do was wait. Isobel was on the other side of the portal arch, helping to monitor it, and Gabe could feel the touch of her magic against his, all springtime potential. He could feel Alexander, behind him, a heat and intensity that Gabe never wanted aimed at him in anger.

Rathna's former apprentice, Petrus, was a few steps back, the peak of a triangle between Gabe and Isobel. Petrus had quietly taken his place, observing and ready to assist, without much chatter. Gabe hadn't seen him for months, and it was good to see he was as steady as he had been when he'd been working with Rathna. More so, as if the recent work had honed him into more of himself.

Manse had stepped back to divert anyone who might interrupt them. His help had, it turned out, been critical. He'd got them all in here two evenings ago, so Gabe could find the right spot and figure out how to get through the wall and undo the warding. That had taken most of the next thirty-six hours.

It had required the combined efforts of half a dozen

Penelopes. Also Kate Lefton's knowledge of preferences in warding enchantments during the Wars of the Roses, Uncle Gil's ability to decipher much altered architectural drawings, and lashings of coffee and tea. It was all capped off with Mama's knack with eyeing a comment in bad Latin and figuring out what the person must have meant.

Rowena had even been a help. Anthony had, with incredible patience, kept Avigail cheerfully entertained. Rowena, though, had not only run copies from person to person, as needed, but she'd twice had an eye for something in the portal information, making a connection that proved useful. Gabe was tremendously proud of her, and he was certain Rathna would be even more so.

Now, though, it was Gabe and an ancient portal, and he felt like he'd done this particular dance far too recently for anyone's comfort, even his. Especially his. All he could do was wait and hope that everything worked up to this point. He did not like having it out of his control, as much as he trusted Rathna like his other self, because she was.

Gabe also had to restrain himself from checking his watch. It would take the time it took. Manse was in charge of alerting them if they were getting close to time. Fortunately or unfortunately, Manse's orders from above had given them quite a lot of breathing space. Somehow. He kept his hand on the stone, hoping he'd feel the first hint of the portal humming to activity.

There was nothing. There continued to be nothing. The portal was alive, though they'd not dared open it to anywhere else. If everything went well, they'd take it to Veritas, all of them except Manse and Alexander, who'd cover the visible retreat. If things went wrong, they'd have a more complicated exit. Or at least, he hoped that was the case, that they'd need to make a complicated exit. There was a tiny chance, so small no one had actually talked about it, that they could do something drastic to the Tower itself, despite it having stood for century upon century. At least if they did, Gabe wouldn't have to explain the problem.

The distraction, as pitiful as it was, actually worked. Gabe felt it before he heard it, the tiny flick, subtle as a cat's inaudible purr, just the vibration making it clear the portal was preparing to open. Isobel was watching just as closely when he glanced at her. Before he could comment, the portal flared open, a burst of magic filling the space like a wave, then almost illuminating it.

Out came a woman who must be Grietje, then the Guards. Gabe had met those. They were followed by four people - three men, one woman - who looked tired and drawn, and also rather surprised. Then Ferdinand, stumbling through, and immediately turning back, looking worried. He didn't quite reach back through the portal. It wouldn't have worked, but he looked like he wanted to.

Gabe shifted, because he could count, and if this worked, it would be Rathna next. He didn't crowd the portal. He knew better than that, especially if it were less than stable. There were half a dozen heartbeats before he started really counting, then another ten, an impossibly long time, before Rathna stepped through. She looked exhausted. Her clothes were hanging on her, and there was dust in her hair, but she was home, and she was real.

He held out his arms as soon as she got clear. She came right to him, hugging him tightly, as if he'd been as much a figment of hope as she had been to him. Gabe just held her and held her, burying his face against her hair, heedless of the dust and whatever else she'd walked through, metaphysically speaking. Someone moved behind her, and the portal closed.

Everyone gave them perhaps thirty seconds of silence, before there was a comment - that must indeed be Grietje. She sounded like Mason, though with a Dutch accent to her English. "Such a welcoming party. May I ask how we get the dancing started?"

It made Alexander snort. Gabe knew that sound anywhere by now. It also brought up a bit of chatter, as people introduced themselves, or made it clear who they were. Gabe ignored it for the moment, before Rathna finally pulled away to look at him and cup his cheek. "Missed you too, beloved." Her fingers traced. "Do we try the portal again?"

"Isn't that for you to say? Nothing alarming here, other than the wait." Gabe let his hands slip from her back, giving her more space. She nodded, and then took in the alcove where the portal was placed, where Ferdinand was standing.

"Isobel, may I borrow your hands for the moment? Hold this, would you?" Rathna's voice was clear, orderly, entirely in control. But Gabe knew how she'd been trembling, how she still was, and he could hear the edge in her voice even if no one else did. "What enchantments are on the room, please?"

Gabe listed them out, with Alexander adding two comments about this level of the Tower itself, folding the information into a tidy package. Rathna nodded a couple of times at particular points, then handed the case with her working stones to Isobel to hold, plucking out several to try an attunement. The first selection didn't work, somehow, and she grimaced.

"Need mine?" Gabe was quick to offer.

"The pearl, if you would. And your, hmm. Do you have your fluorite? It's a better cleavage than mine."

Gabe nobly refrained from commenting on her cleavage, given how much he'd missed it. This was neither the time nor place. They would have those in a bit. At that point, he might properly indulge in both cleavage and puns. He pulled his own stone case out and handed over the fluorite first, then the pearl.

Neither worked, and Rathna grimaced, trying half a dozen more with equal amounts of success, which was to say, none. When she reached for another, Gabe cleared his throat. "You're looking for a resonance?"

"Of course." There was a note in her voice that others might have read at annoyance at Gabe. He didn't, because - while he'd heard it very seldom, considering how much he could be sometimes - that wasn't it. It was annoyance at herself that she hadn't solved the problem yet.

"You could try a lodestone. But I'd try, hmm. You want something solar." Gabe waved his free hand, almost toppling his case, and stopped. Grietje moved to hold out her hands, and Gabe set the case there. "Ruby's classic, but it doesn't feel right here." For all there were rather a lot of rubies, stored not very far from here at all in ordinary times. His mind went whirring through the range of what he had, what Rathna had, which resonances might work best here.

Rathna shook her head, then tilted it, the posture she took when she was thinking hard. The others hadn't interrupted, at least, though Manse must have all sorts of comments. And worries. Certainly there were plenty of worries to go around. "Lay out your reasoning, Gabe, while I think."

"There are all the legends about it being a solar alignment, a temple of some sort, before the Conqueror. Something here must respond to something there. And we might as well draw on the light of whatever it is we're trying to do. Bar the portal against the Continent, open a door to Veritas, making sure everything runs smoothly in the middle before we go through?"

Alexander snorted. "Not the most ept ritual statement I've heard, but in the circumstances, it will do."

Gabe didn't bother to look over his shoulder. He kept focused on Rathna, who considered. "We have four, yes? Isobel, you have yours?"

"Ma'am." Isobel spoke right up. "Shall I?"

"We want the stability, yes." Rathna considered. "Ferdinand, where's your amber from?"

The younger man blinked. "Hungary, mistress. Is that a problem?"

"We'll have to compensate. Our three are from the same piece, originally." She held up her hand. "I know you're willing, Petrus, but would you keep an eye? Let me know. I trust your sense of it." Rathna was running a dozen calculations in her head now. Gabe left her to it, taking out a small piece from his own set and placing it in Rathna's hand, automatically.

"Calcite." Not that she needed him to say that, but the others probably did. It was from the Veritas demesne lands, and it would help balance things out, by force of identity of place, or whatever the proper term was. Rathna absently nodded before gesturing them into places and handing the calcite to Ferdinand.

"We want to anchor the portal here, remind it where it is, specifically. Do you have calculations?"

Alexander had those and handed them over. "Thesan did them, so you don't need to trust my maths. Besides, she wanted a hand in getting you home. Schola and Veritas, like you asked. And Ytene, if you need a third." Rathna's lips twitched slightly at that. Then she was running through them, along with the implications she saw near-instantly and Gabe had to work for with pencil and scratch paper.

"Right. Compass?" Petrus held one of those out, and Rathna promptly aligned them, this way and that, making the angles as precise as any ritualist might like. They were playing off the connections, the similarities and differences, of the stones, of themselves, of the space.

Rathna positioned herself where she was half in front of the portal, one hand on it. Ferdinand took his place on the other side, with Gabe on the far side from her, tucked into the corner, and Isobel next to Rathna. A particular form of polarity, drawing on Gabe and Rathna's relationship, across one axis, and the apprentice relationship across the square. Hopefully, they'd all make it work, even if Ferdinand and Isobel were not close. And for that matter Gabe did not know Ferdinand nearly as well as he expected he would in a few more months.

"Stand back, everyone, please, and give us a moment before any panicking." Rathna's voice was clear. "It may have some unusual effects." The others stepped back, obligingly, and Rathna looked over at Ferdinand. "Ready?"

"Mistress." Gabe wanted to know, rather a lot, what had changed for them, in their time on the Continent. Ferdinand had not been grudging, not since that day at the Natural History Museum, but what they had developed was visibly running far cleaner than it had. A deep river that could carry all sorts of things, rather than something silted up or dependent on the finicky coordination of locks and dams. The man just nodded and waited.

"Isobel?" She didn't bother to ask Gabe, who just nodded and grinned, as Isobel nodded too. He could feel her, attuned enough to her magic to not need the outward cues. Nervous, but willing, which was all he could hope for. It wasn't always possible to do much about the nerves, just about whether what needed to get done happened despite them.

Before he could get too tangled up in possibilities, Rathna went for it. She called the portal open, a flash of iridescent light flashing half a dozen colours and shades, before she did something that began to steady it. Gabe could feel her calling on all their magic to do it, building up a container, coaxing it like a potter would. Where he had put himself in the eye of the tumult, she stood, letting it shape around her. His mind flickered to the implications of lost wax casting, what it might mean as a magical metaphor. Also the question of how irritated Mama would be if he found somewhere to set up a kiln on the property.

All the while, he was holding as steady as he could. These were the trickiest workings for him, the ones where he didn't need his whole focus on the work, but had to avoid too many obvious distractions. Just feeling Rathna there, nearly close enough to touch if he wanted, was a help. He'd fall into that, for seconds at a time, weighing out what was new and changed, what was steady and known.

It took longer than he expected, but then something shifted, as if she'd built up enough of a shape. The magic steadied, turning from a wave beating on the sand over and over into an increasing still pond, the ripples fading out quickly. The light grew steady too, more like stained glass than a shimmering prism that moved.

Only then did she let out a long breath, as if wishing with all her heart that nothing would shift. When nothing changed, she cleared her throat. "The portal's locked to the

Continent. Usual precautions. Petrus, can we leave you here to confirm it?"

"Ma'am." That was gently teasing. "Of course. I'll go out with Magister Manse and the Council Member and the others. I do need to get back to my work, but I can snag the, mmm. Southwark portal. Talk to you when you have a chance?"

"In a few days, likely, I'll be in touch." She pulled away from the portal to give him a proper hug, then kissed his cheek before she turned back. "Everyone else through first. Even you, Gabe."

He wasn't going to argue. For one thing, he was tired, bone tired. For another, arguing wouldn't actually help anything. Rathna brushed her fingers against the stone, the way she touched him, when they were private, like there was nothing else in the world but what her fingers knew. Then she opened the portal again. Gabe went first, if he had to go, and that way he could meet people on the other side.

He stepped out into the twilight of Veritas at her most beautiful. Mama and Papa were waiting, and the children. He grinned at them, held up one finger, and then waited for the others to come through, one by one. Last of all, though not much after Ferdinand, came Rathna. As soon as she was through, Gabe caught her up in his arms, swirling her around, then kissed her soundly.

Behind him, he could hear Papa formally welcoming Ferdinand to Veritas as a friend and trusted guest. Rathna had explained that his mother was interned, his father had gone into active service, and if he went home, there'd be no one there but the staff. They had room; they had people, and - well. She hadn't needed to ask, just lay out the situation. He'd be tucked into a nice suite in the guest hall within half an hour.

"Baths all round, for everyone who needs one. We have a cold collation in the breakfast room after that." Mama was sounding terribly relieved.

Rathna finally pulled back from Gabe. She bent to pick up Avigail with a grunt, then got swarmed by Rowena and Anthony, none of them shy about showing how they felt.

There. That was proper. That was how things ought to be. If only they'd stay that way, but Gabe had a feeling, deep in his heart, that it wasn't going to be that easy.

CHAPTER 34
THAT EVENING AT VERITAS

Rathna finally closed the door to Avigail's room, as gently as she could. It had taken a tremendously long time for Avigail to go to sleep. She'd kept checking her Mama was there, over and over. To be fair, Rathna hadn't wanted to move either. She'd promised she'd be there for breakfast in the morning, whatever else was in the day, and breakfast came after sleeping.

She hadn't quite known what to expect from her return. It wasn't as if she hadn't had other times when she was away from the household, anywhere from days, weeks, even two months or so. She'd thought she knew how it felt to be gone and to come back. She did, and she didn't. This was the same, and it was different. Or, more accurately, she was different. She wasn't sure how to put words to a lot of it. Some of it was for Gabe to hear first, and some of it she'd likely never talk about.

They had customs, though. First, she had the Roman bath to herself to scrub off the travel, as Alysoun often said. Gabe had given her the space for it, for all he had visibly wanted to be touching her every chance he got. She blessed her marriage frequently, but his knack for seeing when something would tangle or untangle the situation gave her gift after gift. He'd made sure she had all the little luxuries she might want, and then left her to it.

By the time she emerged in clean clothing she hadn't been wearing in rotation for months, everyone else had gathered in the breakfast room. Ferdinand and Grietje were already eating. Rathna was starving. It wasn't just the length of the day or the fact all of them had been too nervous to eat much at luncheon, the transit itself had been a drain even before Rathna's work on the portal.

The cold collation was easy to eat while talking or listening, with plenty of roast chicken, for Rathna's benefit, and beef for the others. Ferdinand had quietly let her know he'd been well taken care of. It wouldn't be the surprise it had been for Isobel. She'd been startled several times on her early visits by the way a large house ran, even in these days. But Veritas was a demesne estate, and they felt different, down to the bedrock, to someone attuned to the portals. After the meal itself, Gil and Magni had taken the apprentices and Grietje off to chat quietly and make sure they had everything they needed.

The immediate family had retired to the library, where they tended to be when there was any choice. Rathna had had all three children leaning on her. Rowena was on the floor against her legs, Anthony on one side, Avigail tucked between Rathna and Gabe, and Gabe's arm around her. None of them could bear not to be touching her. Richard and Alysoun hadn't pressed for details, and Rathna was terribly grateful for that. Gabe hadn't either, though it meant that his conversation bobbled. He'd get an idea in his head, and set it aside, over and over again.

Instead, she got the children talking about the tail of

the school year, particularly about what Anthony was considering for his first-year courses at Schola. And, of course, there was plenty of conversation about what all of them had been reading. None of it was urgent, none of it had to be discussed that night, of all nights. But it was comfortable and that was what she needed more than anything else.

Then it was time to put Avigail to bed, and she'd been reluctant, of course. Rathna found herself lingering in the hallway, not sure if she wanted to hear some noise and check, or not. When the time stretched out and out, she finally went back down to their rooms, wondering why she was so unsure of what to do.

They were empty. She glanced at the charmlights along the top of the door, and Gabe was - actually, she wasn't sure how to read that. The light kept flickering. Some glitch in the charmwork, maybe, unless he was doing an unusual amount of pacing in the garden. Rathna stared at it for a moment, but staring wouldn't change anything. Instead, she went to wash her face and brush her hair into a tidy braid, and change into her dressing gown.

Somewhere in there, she started crying. She had no idea how long she was in the bath, leaning on the sink, letting water run on her hands as if that would help, which it didn't. It wasn't sobbing; it wasn't loud. Just tears down her cheeks, sometime around the point where she opened the door from the bath again. Rathna wasn't looking at anything. Her eyes wouldn't focus, and she didn't need to. She was home; she knew what she needed. She crossed to the bed, avoiding the furniture by long habit.

She'd just sat on the bed when it moved, and Gabe's hand immediately touched hers. "Shoulder?" She'd barely nodded and he was right there, curling his arms around her now, and she could bury her face. This wasn't like her. It was ridiculous. She was home and safe and her family was safe, and why on earth had she turned into a fountain? She could feel herself shaking, the tears running into shivers. Gabe leaned in a little, holding her steady, until it sputtered out. Not unlike too many portals recently, which set her off again.

Rathna had no idea how long it had been when she finally lifted her head. Gabe's shoulder was decidedly damp. She was sniffling, and she had a crick in her shoulder that was aching now. "Sorry."

"Hey." Gabe sounded very gentle. "It's a lot. It's been a lot. It's probably going to continue to be a lot."

The way he put it made her snort. "Six impossible things before breakfast. That's the tradition."

"Believing them is a trifle different from doing them." He pulled back, watching her carefully now. "What parts shouldn't I ask about?" He then half-smiled. "I know. That's impossible to answer sensibly."

"It is." She sucked in a breath. "Can we curl up? Maybe I can talk about some of this in the dark."

Gabe nodded, going to make sure the curtains were drawn and the last things were tended to. She stripped out of her dressing gown, sliding into clean crisp sheets as he did the same and claimed his side of the bed. Sides of the bed, that was new again, going to be new for both of them, likely. "Did you sprawl while I was gone?"

"Some sprawling. Some sharing my bed with books. Not nearly as comfortable, I'd entirely forgotten how to not roll over on one in the night." When she nodded, Gabe turned out the lights, then immediately offered his shoulder for her to curl up against. She lay there for a good dozen breaths, just feeling him, smelling him, hearing all the small quiet sounds.

"Why aren't you bouncing off the walls?" As soon as she named it, she realised what had been bothering her. Or, well, one of a list of things that had been bothering her.

She felt him shrug the other shoulder, the way it carried through his collarbone to her current bit of pillow. "The Wild Hunt changes a person. I knew that going in. Don't worry, I've been doing plenty of pacing before and since. And thinking. But I don't know. Rather a lot of me is still caught up thinking about it. You know how I get when I'm thinking."

"Hmm." She did. And this was like that, and different from that, but it was a matter of flavour. Different proportions of spices in the curry, rather than an entirely different category of food. Or, as Morah Avigail would have put it, the same theory applied to chicken soup. "I owe Alexander a very large favour or gift of thanks, or some such. For the record. My own - I suppose we could start there."

"You told me most of getting out of Groningen, I think. Reading between the lines a bit." His hand shifted, then he brought his fingers to stroke along her shoulder. "I missed you a great deal. I'd say horribly, which is true on one hand. But I want to be clear I was extremely competent at missing you. I put a lot of time and attention into it."

It made Rathna snort, reflexively. "I missed you. And your way of putting things. Ferdinand is coming along well, and Grietje has a wicked sense of humour, like you'd expect. But neither of them is you." She nestled a little closer. "All right. The cave."

"I'm still not entirely sure what I think of both of us talking to the Fatae within a couple of days of each other."

He nuzzled at her hair. "I keep waiting for the other shoe to drop. You?"

She considered that particular question, letting her fingers shift to his arm, feeling the warmth there. "Mine was much more - certainly not as equals. But I had information they needed, thanks to you. And what we needed in turn was, I mean. They'd want to fix it, anyway. I did not get the sense of a trickster, in our case, particularly. Though I allow as how that's generally very hard to tell if they're actively trying to trick you." She hesitated. "I got the impression Alexander was feeling a tad guilty over something, which I didn't expect."

Rathna couldn't see Gabe's face, the room was entirely too dark for that. But she could feel the little shift of tension. "It isn't as if he's explained properly. He never does." She took that to mean that Gabe had guesses, that he wasn't going to talk about his guesses now, and she'd have to trust that. Right.

She went on, because that was the only thing to do. "Asking to come to the Tower surprised her, I think." Rathna was feeling her way through it. "She was pleased, though."

"Urdin." Gabe considered the name. "Blue. There's power in a colour, isn't there? And not a native pigment, when it comes to paints." He was circling around whatever else he was thinking about. "But we could get to the Tower, into it. And it worked."

She nodded. "It worked." Then she hugged him tightly, because she was overwhelmed again. His hand stroked her back, waiting until the wave of it passed. "Sorry. Going to do that a bit, I suspect."

"I'd worry if you didn't." Gabe's voice was quieter now. "I was talking to Lizzie, last time I was out at Ytene, we were waiting on Geoffrey. Coming back is, it's a whole series of stages. They have little rituals for it, because he will go off and do something dangerous now and again. Not as often as he used to, though that may change. Probably will."

Rathna swallowed. "I'll go have a talk with her, when I can get a little time. How's that?"

"She'd like to see you. And I think it'd be good for you. Thesan's still caught up with matters at Arundel, or at least making lists so Isembard can keep things sorted. I said we could have their two out here, sometime, maybe for a couple of days."

"Good." She shifted the angle of her chin. "How are they? All three of ours?"

"They've been wonderful. All three in their ways. Anthony's stepped right up to keep Avigail entertained, and he's got a touch for it. Papa said, two nights ago, that if he wants to go into the Guard when all's said and done, that will do him a surprising amount of good. Being steady, knowing what he's aiming at, not rushing it. And his duelling's coming along nicely, though it's mostly been Uncle Magni there, so far this summer." Being retired certainly meant he was the one in the household with more reliable spare time.

"And Avigail?" Her voice cracked there. She couldn't help it.

"Missed you, like we all did, and less experience with being away from you." Gabe kissed her shoulder. "She was very brave, all through. Steadfast. A few bad dreams, especially the morning of the invasion, but I was with her for that." He let out a long breath. "Knowing - having the Guard journal to read - was a huge help. I can't imagine what it was like in the last war, when you had no idea what was going on."

"Or if I'd been there and stuck just using my own wits and whatever we could arrange." Rathna had frankly had her own nightmares about that. "We'd be on a boat out of Spain, probably, with all those risks."

"Don't dwell. We - mostly you - did amazing work. You and Ferdinand and everyone with you. There'll be some debriefing to do, whatever information they can get, but Geoffrey and Manse are arranging that, so it shouldn't be unpleasant. Just thorough."

"On the whole, I'd prefer thorough competence to slap-dash incompetence." Rathna agreed. Then she yawned, suddenly. "Do you - I'm suddenly terribly tired."

Gabe half-laughed. "I have a number of things I would like to do with you, bright lady, but the more carnal ones can wait. The morning, if we get a chance, and if not, I am sure we'll find a time."

It made her smile, then shift to find a more comfortable position to sleep. The dark took her almost immediately, as if her mind and body had finally decided she was safe now.

CHAPTER 35
JULY 3RD AT VERITAS

No one woke her the next morning. Not Grietje or Beth, not noise in the hallway, not the sound of cows outside the window or sheep or the rooster. There were roosters, mind, just not very near the main house. Rathna rolled over, sometime, to find Gabe lying there, reading, and buried her head again. He didn't move, or at least not more than the finger or two required for the book.

When she finally roused, the clock on the bedside table said it was well past nine and she was starving. Gabe was still there, reading, though he'd got rather farther. "Why didn't you get up?" She sounded grumpy. It came out all wrong. She didn't actually feel like that. Probably.

He shrugged, agreeably. "Wanted to be with you. How are you feeling?"

Rathna stretched cautiously, taking her time to figure out how to answer that question. Achy, she'd expected that, given the amount of work she'd had to do on two portals. Plus an entirely different sort of bed and all the accumulated exhaustion finally beginning to ebb. It left fatigue poisons. She knew the basic theory of that. "Better for having some food. Why are you still here, Gabe?"

It wasn't that she wanted him to go. She didn't. But she didn't know how to sort out what she did now. He must have caught something in her expression. He was watching her closely enough. "You know what I'm like after a case, love. You've the same thing. All at loose ends. I have some reading I need to do, catching up on all the analysis of what's in public. But I can take the morning. How do you feel about breakfast, swarmed by children, followed by a ride?"

The thought of a ride made her grimace, but she missed being on horseback. "Just us?"

"If you'd rather." There was a flicker of something in his expression now, and she filed it away, for when there was more information. "And then I can do my reading, and you all can do whatever you think best. You'll have to make reports and all that, but no one's going to bother you for them today. Start them tomorrow."

Rathna let out a slow breath. "Riding breeches, then." She could do that. It simplified the clothing choices, anyway. And it'd give her a good reason for a bath after, and a hearty lunch. Then she pushed herself up on one elbow, kissed Gabe on the cheek, and rolled out of the huge bed to get ready. It wasn't his fault she was cranky. By the time she came back in jodhpurs to put on her low riding boots, Gabe was dressed himself in tall boots and breeches, as he preferred.

Breakfast was predictably loud, with half a dozen people talking at once. Avigail kept snagging a bit of her potatoes and then looking up and giggling. Rathna rumpled her hair and asked Anthony what he was up to, and Rowena wanted to ask Uncle Magni about something. All well and good. Rathna let herself coast along with it, agreeably enough.

It wasn't until they got out to the stables that she caught another hint of something just a little off. Gabe was a ferociously talented rider. His parents were, their children all were - even Avigail was, despite her age. And there was a moment, just a flicker of one, where Gabe hesitated before mounting Meliora.

He never had before. She wondered, now, if he had the first time he'd got on Invicta after his terrible fall, the one that had changed the arc of his life in a dozen ways. Though that would have been obvious to his parents, at least. She'd ask them, maybe, if she got a moment this afternoon when Gabe wasn't around. Or, well, Alysoun. Richard had apparently been gone nearly at dawn. There were bombs being dropped over South Wales.

She'd been told, over and over, that Trellech was probably safe enough. For the Luftwaffe themselves, the non-magical wouldn't know there was a city there. Those who did were not as likely to be up in the planes, or at least not in quantity. If someone did try, there were precautions and magical warding that should help. But of course, it wasn't the sort of thing one could actually test reliably. Whatever else, Richard would be needed to coordinate relief efforts, both among the folk of Albion and the non-magical folk, however they could. That line of thought wasn't going to end anywhere good.

Instead, she swung up on her own mare, reminding herself how it felt to have a horse between her legs. Rathna guided the mare a step or two forward, halted her, checking everything was as it should be. "You take the lead?"

Again, there was a tiny flicker of something, but then Gabe led the way out of the stable yard. Predictably enough, he turned right, to the path that would take them through the woods, curving along the stream, back on the far side of the home farm. A pleasant hour's ride, depending on how fast they went.

The ride itself was lovely, enough that she began to relax and not be quite so afraid of some other shoe dropping. Gabe relaxed as well, and once they were in the woods, he pointed out several things that were new since last she'd been out. A badger sett there, a curious vixen and her kits a little further along. By the time they turned back into the stable yard, Rathna wasn't sure if her eyes had deceived her, or not.

By the time she was done with a long soak in the Roman baths, Gabe had had his own upstairs. He'd disappeared into his work in the small office he used when he wanted privacy, with Isobel, who at least was at less of a loose end now. Ferdinand had joined her at lunch - he'd already eaten.

She was worried about him, too. He was quiet, rather withdrawn. Understandably so, given all the chaos and the additional worries about his family. He earnestly had reassured her, the sort of reassurance that wasn't really, that Isobel had shown him around all the public parts of the house. She'd taken care to make him feel welcome. And they'd had a pleasant conversation with Alysoun before lunch.

Something in the way he put that made Rathna tilt her head. "Not much like your mother, then?"

"Yes and no, Mistress." They'd claimed a bit of the library, by that point, but apparently everyone else was leaving them to it. "She wanted to know what would make me feel welcome."

Rathna smiled, leaning back in the chair. "She's very

good at that. I didn't expect it when Gabe brought me to meet his parents." She nodded. "You let any of us know if there's anything you need. And you truly are welcome to stay as long as you like. No reason you shouldn't."

"My family," Ferdinand stopped, then started again, "They won't like it. They'll say I should stay with my cousins or something."

"Do your cousins really want you coming and going at all hours? We will probably be, for the record. A few days to recover and write our reports, maybe a week or two, but then we'll need to get back to work. You've learned a tremendous amount, the past months, and we can pick up some of the load. Testing, if not repair." She waved a hand. "This household is used to it. They have been since Richard and Alysoun married, near enough."

Ferdinand tilted his head. "Oh." There. She'd given him a good few dozen new calculations to work on. That should be a help for a bit.

"And you ask Alysoun how to finesse your cousins, if you need to, or aunts or uncles or whoever it is. She doesn't go out much, but that doesn't mean she doesn't know who's who." Ferdinand nodded again. Rathna took pity on him, settling into talking about what the reports would need to include, and what the debriefing would probably be like. That part, she was less worried about. She had a pretty good idea what they wanted and needed to know.

The rest of the afternoon and into the evening were full of the ordinariness of family life. Gabe and Isobel reappeared in good time for tea. They took a walk with the children before supper. Then there was a delightful, complex, dance of tucking everyone into bed in sequence and relearning how the routines went right now.

Avigail wanted two chapters of her book, of course, and

both her Mama and Papa there. Anthony wanted to hear about what it had been like to be away for so long. Not about the war, which she'd half-expected, between his age and the way the world was going. Just the places. She got on to talking about some of the food in Dax, and then about the cave, and his eyes lit up.

Rowena was a little trickier. She was watchful, making a dozen evaluations as they talked. Very like her father that way, and even more like Alysoun. Rathna had wanted to talk through the rest of her school year, all the things that hadn't made it into the journals. Instead, she asked about what Gabe had told her while they were out riding, about spotting a couple of things in the notes. Rowena looked away, flushing. "I remembered what you said about the patterns? And I looked for the patterns."

"Papa was very proud of you. Me too. When we get a chance, let's talk through it properly, shall we? And if you want, if I can get a little time, I can show you a bit about the portal here."

Rowena blinked. "Mama?"

Rathna had not expected to have this conversation right this moment, but no time like the present. "Your Papa thinks - and I agree - you maybe show a knack for the portal magic. If you'd like, we can try a few things and find out more." Finding out more was a family habit, and perhaps less scary than all the larger decisions that might come later.

The Guild had long run on family connections, since the gift for the portal magic tended to pool in particular families. It would, in fact, be possible for Rowena to apprentice with Rathna if she wanted. Or they could find her someone else. Rathna wasn't entirely sure which she'd rather. Not a decision she had to make tonight, whatever else. Figuring out if Rowena wanted to learn more would do for now, and even for the next year or two.

While she was still thinking, she was startled by arms around her, a tight hug, before Rowena pulled back. "I'm very glad you're back, Mama. It wasn't easy on Papa. Or any of us."

"I know, love. And - well." She wouldn't be going anywhere from here, she was quite sure of that. Too much risk, not enough benefit, even those places she might have considered early this spring. "I'll be here. And we'll see about sorting out what else would be helpful."

Rowena nodded, and then wriggled into bed, half-reaching for her book. "You should go to Papa."

Rathna half-laughed, and bent to kiss Rowena's head. "I'll do that. You sleep well, love."

That meant it was time to find Gabe. She found him, curiously enough, in their bedroom on the sofa, draped over it as he often was. As soon as he heard the door, he sat up more or less properly. "All good?"

"We have some entirely amazing children. Had you noticed recently?" She turned away to take off her watch and pendant, setting them neatly on the dressing table. When she turned back, he was leaning forward, elbows on his knees.

"They are. Entirely due to an amazing mother." He tilted his head. "Though Mama and Papa help. And Uncle Gil and Uncle Magni. They've been a wonder, keeping steady. Uncle Magni's been drilling Anthony a bit. No charms, just the physical. If Isembard gets a chance, they'll do a bit more this summer, when they can contain things fully."

"If we all get a bit of a breather." She glanced at the

lights over the doorframe and gestured. "Richard's not back yet, then."

Gabe shook his head. "Likely sleeping in Trellech tonight. I'll have to go in tomorrow, at least." Again, that tiny catch.

Rathna considered her options, feeling along with them, the way she felt along the connections of a portal. "Something happened to you. More than one thing, or no. Wait." She held up one hand. "You're thinking about something, deep and hard - and don't make that face at me. I didn't mean the innuendo. Yet."

That at least made him laugh. Gabe stood, coming to slip his arms around her and nuzzle at her neck. "I'd like that too, tonight, if you're up for it. I missed you." Then she heard the catch of his breath. "And I have been thinking about something. Are you all right talking about it tonight? It's a heavy topic."

"Time-sensitive?" She asked it for information, but also because how he reacted would be telling. She could feel a slight flinch, the tension there, and answered her own question. "That's the sort of thing we need to talk about tonight, yes. Meet you in bed?"

He kissed her neck, then the spot just in front of her ear, before letting go and padding into the bathroom to wash up. She focused on braiding her hair, wrapping a ribbon in the last inch or two and tying it off to keep it tidy. Then Gabe was wandering out, kissing her on the way by, and she took her turn. By the time she was done, he was lounging in bed, looking like something out of a Roman mosaic, lying on his side propped up on his elbow.

"You look suspiciously still, love." She settled in, facing him for a moment, then twisted onto her back, where she could watch him but let her shoulders begin to relax a little.

"Figures, that's what you'd catch. What else?" She'd have to prod him into conversation then, but it was a reasonable enough question. Gabe would want to know what gave him away.

"Half a dozen things. Particularly that you hesitated this morning, before getting on Meliora. And then things like this." She wriggled a finger. "A little too quiet, a little too still, not your usual ratio of pacing."

He grunted. "Fair." Then he took a breath. "I'm not trying to be difficult. I just don't know how to start this conversation at all."

"If you had to pick one word, what would it be?" She might as well try that.

What she hadn't expected was the face he made, like she'd cut through to the heart of it, tunnelling through every defence he had. "Sacrifice." Immediately, Gabe held up one hand. "That's where it gets complicated." Her heart was pounding now in her chest, she could hear every beat.

"Start somewhere and go on until you've covered everything." It was the only way forward. However, she fumbled with her hand, reaching for his free one, and her heart only slowed a little when she did. She was being entirely too rational for that word and the way he'd said it. Some part of her knew that was her fear, all her worry suddenly having a place to roost.

Gabe nodded once. "This is out of order when it comes to time, but I think it makes more sense this way. At the end of the Wild Hunt, the Fatae set three things as the payment for the ring." He'd explained that part and that he'd agreed, but not the requirements. Some things were better not written down, and they both knew it. "Two of them were easy. Riding with them for the night and doing my best to bring everyone together. I was already doing both. We're making some progress, and more to come. People are listening, at least. The ring does something. Not a compulsion, we tested for that, but an openness. A sincerity? Though that's the oddest thing to accuse a Fatae ring of, isn't it?"

"There are the legends about how truth telling is a gift or curse they bestow." Rathna pointed out. "And the third?"

"That's the hard one." Gabe let out a long breath. "To quote, 'when you are asked a question you wish to refuse, say yes. You will know which one when that time comes.'" He looked at her, suddenly seeming very young and unsure. "I said yes, and I should have asked you first."

Rathna squeezed his hand, unable to find words for the moment. Her mind was racing. She could see, or at least begin to see, why he'd got the thought about sacrifice. But she was reasoning ahead of the actual information. "Tell me why that brings you to sacrifice?"

"Two things." Gabe lowered himself to the bed, dropping her hand so he could slide an arm around her and set his head on her shoulder. Permitting himself the closeness, that was good. Giving it back to her was even better. She needed it rather desperately. "Livia Fortier's death. My fall." He hesitated. "And there's that death in the ritual in the New Forest, the hypothermia."

She could more or less see how that fit. "All right. Go on? You've been thinking about it - well, one of them for decades now, and the first since it happened."

Gabe swallowed. He, who was usually so glib, was struggling for words here, and that was telling. "I didn't like her. I certainly didn't trust her, except in the most formally bound circumstances. And I know what she thought about you." That sort of gossip got back to them sometimes, the rants and nastiness. "But she had as good a death as anyone like her might want. Doing something that made a difference, going out fighting." His fingers closed, knuckles brushing against her skin before he straightened them again. "Turns out I respect that."

"You're your father's son. And the long line before you. You appreciate a death in battle." His family history was littered with it, even if it wasn't recent. "That doesn't mean you have to. And you're not a fighter, Gabe, not like that. Duellist, yes, but you've other uses."

"That's the thing. I can't get it out of my head that this is what the land magic saved me for when I was eighteen. When it twisted and caught me and shattered me." He'd had the pain in his ankle ever since, for all the damage had theoretically healed. Until they'd met, he'd also carried a tremendous amount of shame about it, not that he'd ever talked about that with anyone.

Rathna didn't know how to think through this sensibly. "Do you really think this is it?"

He let out a long sigh, curling up against her far more deliberately, the way all the children had burrowed into her today. "I don't know." It came out muffled. "Do I feel like this because I'm fighting it? Because it's right? Because you weren't here? Because I agreed without talking to you about it?"

Ah, that'd be part of the knot, certainly. She let her fingers trace along his shoulder, up far enough for the length of his hair, feeling the strands against her skin. The smell of him, of grass and summer flowers and the herbs of his shampoo and the smell that was all him. "We both knew we'd have to make choices we couldn't consult about. I did, half a dozen times. When to stay, when to leave. It all worked out, but there were so many places it could have gone wrong."

Gabe let out a shuddering breath. "Not angry?"

"No. We'll see it through. Whatever's needed." It made him twist his head to peer at her. "Don't you do anything more reckless than usual, mind. If you don't need to sacrifice yourself, if it's not what you're asked, don't. Can you promise me that?"

He nodded immediately, then something in him relaxed, despite the way his body was arranged. "It doesn't bind, in my oaths. That helps, love. Rather a lot."

"Good. We'll keep talking about it, then. Tomorrow, you've got to be in Trellech. I have reports and the first part of the debriefing. London, for us, apparently, one of the inns the Ministry keeps."

"Home for supper?"

"I entirely expect so." They talked through the practical parts of it, the timing of it, if they'd both be home for tea. Once they'd done something that felt absurdly, joyfully normal, she brushed her fingers against his neck, the spot she knew he found a particular sort of arousing. "I missed you entirely as much as I should. And we did get to bed very early."

He pushed up on his elbow and smiled. "May I exhaust you properly, my brilliant wife? Praising you as I go?"

It made her laugh, shaking loose the fragments of what they'd talked through. "Sate me." Before she could say anything else, his hand was sweeping up her hip to her breast, easy and deft. Like he was when he was on a horse, flying to take a fence and completely free. She could feel him rock against her as she spread her legs slightly, to give him space to rearrange.

"I learned a new charm or three while you were gone. An application of something I was researching. Never tried it on anyone, of course."

"You are single-minded about me, love. I am entirely sure of that."

From that point, there was not much talking, at least not on her end. On his, he managed to keep up a long string, through her first climax, into her second. He drew it out, like beads on a necklace, praising every bit of brilliance she'd shown that he knew about since she left, all in order. The praise still could make her shudder all on its own. Hearing him lay it out as perfectly and completely as he did shattered her in all the best ways. She knew how hard he'd worked to put it all in order in his head and keep it that way, storing it up for this particular moment.

When they were finally both sated and thoroughly exhausted, she took a long breath, snuggling up against him as they drifted off to sleep.

CHAPTER 36
JULY 17TH AT YTENE

G abe ran his hand through his hair. "It's not enough."

They were in the library at Ytene. Gabe, Isobel, Alexander, Geoffrey, all arrayed around the room. They had a meeting at the Council Keep that afternoon, and Gabe was still trying to figure out what he was going to say. What he could say, because he certainly didn't want to give voice to his increasing certainty that some sacrifice was going to be asked of him. He couldn't feel the shape of it, but he could feel the cool shadow reaching out towards him or flowing towards him, or something of the kind. The elderly man at the ritual he had been investigating, the one who had died of hypothermia, then Livia, and things came in threes or sevens, and the last one bit hardest.

"Lay it out one more time. Please." Geoffrey leaned forward, casually snagging a stool with one properly shod toe, and pulled it closer.

Gabe shrugged and gestured at Isobel. "You start."

She cleared her throat. "We've made overtures to all the Albion pieces of the puzzle, so far, and it has been, if not

344

glowingly successful, certainly sufficient. There is, however, a general feeling that Lammastide is the proper time for a combined rite, to anchor into the land magics, rather than the full moon."

Geoffrey, who was fully anchored in that particular cycle himself, nodded. "It's easier. On two fronts. First, we're used to doing a ritual then, most of Albion, of some kind. May Day, Summer Solstice, Lammastide, Winter Solstice. Sometimes other times, but it varies more. But we all agree on the need for a harvest."

"That's the problem, though. What exactly are we harvesting?" Gabe felt his shoulder twitch. The other men didn't comment on it, but he knew they noticed. Of course they noticed. Gabe was not gifted with subtlety at the best of times, and he'd been struggling with it more and more in the last weeks. Even Rathna coming home hadn't settled him. Oh, it was better, certainly, but better and settled were two entirely different things.

"So you have agreement from the Ministry, from the Lords and Ladies - that one, you sorted after Solstice, I know." Alexander kept moving forward. They'd all had to come together for the Council rites, and Gabe had been able to be exhaustingly persuasive over and over again. He'd approached Lord Thanet privately, of course. No point in making more of an enemy by adding a bit of public shame to the mix. Papa and Uncle Magni had taught him better tactics than that by the time he was eight.

"Yes. And support from the Guilds, and of course the Penelopes agree, at this point, that what we propose is sensible." That one got a grin from him. "Mind, it took three days of arguing about it, but that's quite short for us, really. More about how than whether, in any case."

"And where the Penelopes go - and your father and Kate

- so too the Guard. The Courts?" Geoffrey asked, and Gabe realised Alexander must not have had a chance to fill him in in the last few days, or at least not about this.

"The Courts were easier to persuade than most anyone else, interestingly. Not that they explained why, though there is a reasonable amount of precedent to draw on. Both since the Pact and before, a few long sieges and such. And the goals are to preserve the oaths of justice in Albion, and in the lands of Britain, so." Gabe had found that a surprisingly simple argument. They'd wanted to make sure he'd seen to all the details, or that someone had, which had been a mite tedious but entirely achievable. Witt had set up most of that, and she knew just what they'd need. Gabe sighed and reached for his coffee, nodding for Isobel to go on.

"And today is sorting out the practical details of the Council. Seeing as how this began as your project. Do you see any particular problems there, sir?" Isobel put it directly to Alexander. She hadn't yet learned that he rarely answered questions like that.

Alexander shrugged, the sort of movement that made Gabe immediately take notice. It was just a titch too casual, like a cloak hiding the shape of the hands beneath it. "We're making our way. Losing Livia left a hole in more ways than we'd realised, and Garin's, well." He paused, now visibly choosing his words carefully. "Not sure what to make of himself, and arguing out of habit."

Gabe winced. "Will he be there today?"

"Not in the afternoon. There's your incentive to be done and get out of the place before half-six and our usual meeting time." Alexander lifted a hand. "His first meeting back, and there is some business we need to tend to that involves him. The Challenge for Livia's seat."

"When?" Gabe asked it idly, more than anything,

though it would be good to know how much of their attention would be focused there and when.

"That's part of the discussion, but likely October, maybe November. Some of it depends on what the timing looks like, some on particular candidates." Alexander flicked his fingers. "Livia's seat has often been held by a potent duellist, and I suspect we'll have several want to make a go of it."

Geoffrey snorted. "And it would be preferred if you were not the only one on the Council with that skill. I still wonder if that's how the reputation developed, that you need at least one."

Alexander snorted. "Not having that debate now, nekheny, we have other matters to tend to." He went on without missing a beat. "There's a fair number of theories around the timing, but the lunar cycles are good, the equinoxes, if we can."

"And then too near Solstice, you all have other obligations than - whatever the results are."

"Also, Cyrus would prefer to have someone seated before the Solstice rites. Not impossible, we've had gaps of, oh, I think the longest was six years, before? But not something we'd choose if we have an option."

"Not before October, Alexander?" Geoffrey asked it almost idly, but Gabe was suddenly suspicious of the reason. Not that Alexander was giving any hint, just taking a sip from his own coffee.

"We want to put forward as compelling a selection as we can. For one thing, the chance we'll need to fill another seat, sooner than later, that's always a consideration. Especially if the air raids pick up and someone's in the right place at the wrong time, lending a hand. And that means giving people time to make decisions and prepare. But with a hope some of them might again, next time we need to."

Gabe flinched. "Rather." They were all expecting more of the bombing, it was looming quite literally over them. The New Forest proper was sheltered by trees, the middle of Kent was likely safe from direct attack, at least an intentional one. But London and Dover - well. Any fool with a map could draw the correct and worrying conclusions.

"All right. What's going on the other side of things?" Alexander waved them on. Gabe was sure it was to keep them from lingering on more delicate questions.

Isobel cleared her throat and picked up. "The most recent letter from the Society of Inner Light's a reasonable example of the thing, sir. Let's see." She rummaged in her notes, and quoted, "If we as a nation make ourselves a channel of cosmic law through realisation of the spiritual nature of the struggle we are waging, we become the channel for the manifestation of the power of God, and the stars in their courses will literally fight for us, as they did in the weather conditions attending the evacuation of the B.E.F. from Dunkirk, when the storm and the calm fell exactly as needed and even the military authorities talked of a miracle."

"Does the letter propose a means for creating miracles? Though, to be fair, it was." Geoffrey's voice had gone sharply dry, the kind of change in tone that made Gabe blink at him.

"She goes on to talk about 'subversive telepathy' being used to influence the souls of nations. And we've had some evidence of that." Isobel peered at the paper. "She goes on to talk about the need for courage and loyalty. And for the sure protection being, let's see, 'spiritual principles, clearly realised ideals, and dedication to them, even unto death.'"

Gabe had expected to feel that shuddering ache, what children called someone walking over your grave, at that. He knew it was coming. He'd read through Isobel's notes. And it wasn't, even hearing her say it out loud. Curious. He'd have to prod at that more. Later. Now he steepled his fingers. "We need a connection to a group that might have some cohesion and ideally a bit of power behind them. Courage."

"Rufus has a lead. Not just to the folk he's been talking to, someone else. As I mentioned before, well, all of it." Geoffrey uncrossed his legs and then crossed them the other way. "He thought he could set up a meeting this week, if you're willing. How are things going with the people in Kent?"

"The half dozen groups we've met with have been willing enough. We're not asking them to change their practices. It's hard to tell, though, what effect the ring has. They're willing to hear us out, is more or less my guess. I've not analysed it. I have more sense in this case."

Alexander's laugh came out as a bark. "Possibly the only time you haven't broken something down to first principles, and it's on your finger."

"Don't remind me." Gabe let out a huff of a breath. "But no. Because I agreed to take it on. They'll hear us out, they'll maybe talk a little about what they have in mind. Lammas is as good as we're going to get for a date, I think, though a couple of groups have been doing full moons."

Isobel chimed in with a "My family's been talking to people up in Yorkshire. They've put us on to a few people. And we think we can get a fair bit of a 'Do an extra prayer, why not' in a number of places."

That had been her idea. She had a better feel for how things went in the non-magical villages, it turned out. A gentler touch with it. That was the way to put it. She could suggest something and ten minutes later they'd think it was entirely their idea, where Gabe had to be a lot more heavy-handed to get the same result.

"So what's your goal here, then?" Alexander brought them back on topic.

Gabe shrugged one shoulder. "They seem a bit more effective about it than the others. Join in with them if we can, and use that to direct and anchor what we have. We've given people tokens to link the rituals, Mason ran up a whole set in the workshop. Paint on stones, using minerals for the pigments that will link, sealing the pigment properly. All designs with the symbols we need embedded. They came out rather well, really."

"That's something. So you can connect all of that." Geoffrey considered. "Your ritual skills are up to it?"

"I'm not as good as either of you, but not that many are. I've more experience working collaboratively in that kind of thing, I suspect, I've done it for the Penelopes often enough when we need to. Renewals on our own warding, all that." He waved a hand. "And I know that's different, but it's not as if you've got a better candidate."

"You and Isobel, both?" Geoffrey leaned forward now.

"If we can. Me, if we can't, but that may be the harder sell. Youth and beauty turn out to be motivating factors for invitations. I can't pull out my more usual incentives of who I am and who I know." Gabe gave up on sitting then, and rolled up onto his feet, to circle the library.

There was a silence while they contemplated. "Can you show us the ritual form? In the workroom here?" That was Alexander, though Gabe noticed he didn't ask Geoffrey for permission or consent or whatever it was that might apply here. Just assumed or had already arranged the workroom would be available.

"With you both? I can work through the model. We have a couple of spare stones."

"Let's, then. I could use a nice bit of ritual theory to soothe me before we go up to the Keep. And I'd like to see your style." Alexander's voice had that too-casual note again. Gabe was getting better at hearing it. Or better at fancying he was hearing it. Quite possibly both.

"Sure." He stretched, hearing several of his joints pop. "Probably do me some good. I have a couple of the stones with me, we'll need some sort of flame, I need my potion set, Isobel, and, hmm. A bit of earth from outside, the usual small pot will do."

"I'll see to the earth, then. You go along and set up, Alexander." Geoffrey stood, without looking back to see if Alexander agreed, as if they were entirely used to dividing this sort of task that way.

At least it would be a chance to spend a bit of time in Ytene's workroom, not a place he usually saw on his visits. And the opportunity to talk through the ritual in detail with both of them wasn't to be sneezed at. They really did know their work as well as Gabe knew his, and he would cheerfully acknowledge that truth as needed.

CHAPTER 37
JULY 20TH IN TRELLECH

"What were your plans for the afternoon, Mistress?" They'd just come through the Trellech portal, and Rathna was considering that exact question. She stepped out of the way and Ferdinand kept pace with her, right at her side. They'd spent the last few hours working with the Schola portal, as one of the oldest of the active portals that was not in heavy daily use.

"I'd like you to have a chance with one of the portals here, preferably Caeruleus." The Trellech portals, the seven public ones, all had colour names in Latin to distinguish them, a custom that had started well back before the Pact. Everywhere else - even the portal the banks used and the one the Guard used - there was only the one in a given place.

"Why Caeruleus, Mistress?" There was a cluster of people going through, rather noisily, and a cart. Rathna waited for the noise to clear a bit. "It's that one, there, nearest on our left?"

"It is." She smiled at him. "You studied last night, I gather? If we wait around until mid-evening tonight, we can probably arrange to have an hour or two. Say, half-eight?"

"Don't you want to get home, Mistress?" Ferdinand leaned forward, a little worried.

"Rowena and Anthony are visiting with friends. Avigail's off for a treat with her Uncle Gil - he's doing a bit of research that mostly involves walking around a garden right now. And Gabe's got to work late. They have a meeting this evening. We could have supper with him and Isobel, though, if you wanted company."

"As you prefer, Mistress." He hesitated for a moment. "I'm curious about the Trellech portals, of course. And working with Schola, this afternoon was—"

"It's very old. One of the oldest. That one, the Council Keep, they're the two most ancient. But they're also the most heavily warded of the current active portals, of course." No one wanted an imminent invasion at a school attended by the finest flower of the Great Families, and of course the Council Keep had to hold against all threats. "These are late 13th century. The Tower of London's between them, and Dover, and Windsor. There's an assignment for you. Write them all out in chronological order, as well as your observations about each. It'll take you a bit to visit everything. I recommend a notebook with a page for each one."

Ferdinand snorted, then blinked as it became clear she was serious. "Something you've done, Mistress?"

"Oh, yes. And recopied twice now. Better leave yourself two pages per portal. You'll need two notebooks." It was, in fact, one of her most used resources. He'd seen her current working copy several times today.

"Um. Yes." He hesitated. "Could we perhaps stop by a

stationer's shop this afternoon, then?" Ferdinand was at least rather more adaptable than he had been.

Rathna beamed at him. "Excellent idea. Now, then a little research at the townhouse, then we can meet up with Gabe and Isobel, and make sure they've had a reasonable meal this evening."

They were about to set off again, down toward Rathna's preferred shop, when Ferdinand stopped dead. It took Rathna a moment to realise it, so she went a step further before she wheeled around. There was a man, perhaps ten years older, who looked remarkably like Ferdinand, his hand on Ferdinand's shoulder. Ferdinand looked almost stuck in amber.

Then he swallowed. "Magistra Edgarton, my oldest brother, Maximilian Howard." Rathna was sure he was making a particular point of etiquette - well, several. But as she was the woman in this equation, as well as of greater magical rank, it was not as obvious as it might have been in other situations. She had, in fact, studied the orders of precedence intensely for a bit, not that it had really helped. Gabe - or his mother - whispering in her ear at the events where it mattered continued to be far more useful.

Maximilian Howard was of an age to be fighting, and he was in nothing like a uniform. He wore a sharply tailored suit. Last year's cut, but it still emphasised broad shoulders, a properly manly figure. Gabe had tried one on and promptly collapsed laughing. She remembered it and had to force herself not to smile at the memory. Instead, she extended her hand. "Master Howard."

He took her hand, back of it up, and made the more continental brush of a kiss in the air above it, a slight bow over it. "Magistra, I have heard a great deal about you these last months."

Rathna nodded. She could not say the same. Bar the basic outline of the family and a mention every fortnight or so, Ferdinand had barely mentioned his family outside his mother. Now she had to figure out how to finesse this. Did Ferdinand want a few minutes to speak to his brother? Or would he rather a rapid excuse for an escape? "I do hope you've been well? We have been very glad to be back on Albion's soil again."

That was a decided hit. For all he was a Howard, Maximilian was not up to his uncle's standards in concealing his emotions. Rathna had found Lord Howard entirely intimidating for the level of control he exerted on himself, last time she'd seen him at the Winter Solstice offerings for the Council. "The family is quite glad Ferdinand is back. We were rather distressed when we found out the scope of the work." Maximilian hesitated. "Perhaps we might step aside, Magistra? The park, just here?" There was one tucked away, just up past the Scali Bank.

It was not raining; the weather was not unpleasant. Rathna glanced at Ferdinand, and he was impressively unreadable. At least now she had plenty of experience with that sort of expression from him, and could tell he was not happy with this, but was not disagreeing. "Of course. Shall we?" She kept her voice brisk and cheerful, then pivoted on her heel to lead the way, letting the men fall in behind her like trailing ducklings. Ferdinand would likely find it amusing. She suspected his brother would be peeved. All to the good.

Once in the park, Rathna glanced around before moving to claim a seat on the stonework surrounding a small fountain. Water was not her best affinity when it came to magic. She did far better with stone, but she could still amuse herself with ideas about accidental splashes if the conversation got dire. Ferdinand stood, evenly balanced between both feet, while his brother sat, twisting uncomfortably to face her. "You understand, Magistra, that the family has some concerns. We had hoped to arrange a supper in the next week or two, but seeing you today, well."

Ah. There were a number of reasons they might have concerns, some far more legitimate than others. "I do hope your mother is well? We were hoping to make arrangements for Ferdinand to visit her, now that we're back and settled again. Necessary obligations have taken much of the last few weeks."

It put Maximilian off balance, as she'd hoped. He looked up at Ferdinand, then back at Rathna. "Beg pardon?"

"Of course, he wishes to see that she has whatever comforts are available, including a lack of worry about him. And as a mother myself, I entirely understand and approve of the impulse. Don't you think it's far better to have some fondness and care than a lack?" She made it sound utterly conversational, while she knew perfectly likely that he would consider fondness a particular sort of weakness, never to be admitted to.

Maximilian coughed. "Magistra." He considered. "The family did come across some information about your family that was a bit of a concern. We did not realise until you and Ferdinand were already overseas."

Ah, indeed. They had been slacking, then. In any decently competent investigative family, they'd have had a precis of her, down to commentary from her teachers at Schola, a month in at the latest. Though perhaps her own family set an exceptionally high bar on the investigative skills front. Which meant she got to decide how to play this.

If she'd had her choice of anything in all the world, it would have been to have this conversation when Gabe and

Alysoun, at the very least, were able to enjoy the show. Richard would smile, perhaps in the wrong place, but he'd do it for all the right reasons. Alas, such gifts were not on offer today. Instead, she settled back, not glancing at Ferdinand. If he didn't know what he was going to get from her by now, he really hadn't been paying any attention.

"How curious, the different customs of families. Surely, if you'd had any concerns, much earlier in the apprenticeship would have been a far better time to address them. Before we made the binding oaths, for example." There was nothing this man could do to her that would harm her. A social snub, perhaps, but it wasn't as if the Howards, any of them, had been inclined to be close personal friends. Ferdinand was entirely of age, his apprenticeship was signed over. He could call it off if he wished, but she was sure now he wouldn't. He had the portal magic bubbling inside him, and there was only one real way to keep that going. Then she tilted her head, the precise tilt she'd practised for months early in her marriage. "May I ask what concerned you?"

Maximilian coughed. "There is no history of your people in Albion."

"Well, of course not. Both my mother and father were born in Calcutta." She gave a string of Bengali that was, in fact, their particular heritage. It sounded deeply impressive, even though what was given was a list of names and occupations - mostly stone and gem cutters. Respectable craftsmen, in terms of caste, but not nearly the rank the Howards would want. Of course, since it was in Bengali, she was quite sure it was entirely opaque to him. Though to be honest, she had her suspicions that ancestral tendency to stone work was part of how she'd come by her particular magical gifts.

357

And then, to top it off, she added, "And then, of course, I apprenticed with Magistra Avigail Levy, of a long-standing family with deep ties to the Portal Keeper's Guild." This one she could do the names all properly in Hebrew. She'd practised it. Likely even more opaque to him. By the time she was done, it was as if she'd dropped the entire catalogue of begets and begats from the Mabinogion on his head. Or perhaps all the ships from the Iliad, name by name adding weight upon weight.

Then she smiled. She'd learned that from Alysoun. It made people unsure what to do with you, and it worked nearly as well for Rathna as it did for Alysoun or Charlotte, Gabe's sister. It was not a gift that depended on fair skin, like so many. And she waited. That one she'd learned from Richard. Pauses unsettled people. Not rushing to fill a pause wrong-footed them surprisingly often.

There was a silence. Ferdinand had learned many things in the months they'd been working together, including how to let those silences sit. It took a good thirty seconds before Maximilian cleared his throat. "No one was claiming you aren't properly of the Guild, Magistra. I hope I have not given any offence?"

She shrugged, just the once. What she wanted here was to make it clear that while he could make his own situation decidedly worse, in several ways, none of it would trouble her. "I do like to be clear about the standards I uphold. Ferdinand has been exceedingly helpful. I gather there's some conversation about a formal commendation for war services being contemplated."

Rathna hadn't mentioned that to Ferdinand, yet, and she saw him straighten, just a hair more formal. They'd bloody well earned one, even if the portal design didn't have direct military applications. And if - when, the bombing raids were making that all but certain - one of the established portals went down, they'd need every bit of those skills here in Albion too.

"Oh." There. She'd entirely discomfited Maximilian. That was excellent.

She took the smallest amount of pity. "Ferdinand is doing exceedingly well with his apprenticeship. We have a long one, of course, and for excellent reason. Just like the Healers or the Guard, there's far too much risk if any short-cuts are taken. I do not expect we will be going abroad again. Though it's quite likely we'll be travelling a fair bit in Albion in the coming weeks, depending on what is needed. Not much time for social calls, but there is a war on."

Maximilian hesitated. "Well, yes. Ferdinand, you do look surprisingly well. We were quite worried about conditions wherever it was you were."

Ferdinand inclined his head. "I could not be specific, of course. Magistra Edgarton was very clear about how important it was not to share information, besides the oaths about what could be shared in the journals. Isn't the phrase that's going around 'Be like Dad, Keep Mum'?" His voice had an edge to it now, Rathna could hear it like shouting. It was an entirely different register than Ferdinand preferred, a statement of complicated preference and loyalty she was sure his brother would not entirely uncypher.

"Pardon?" Then Maximilian cleared his throat. "Should I perhaps let Father know we spoke, and mention that you'll write? I am sure Mother would be pleased to see you. Father can best arrange it, of course." There, he was fleeing the field.

"We'd both appreciate that. I do hope we'll see you and the family at some point. Depending on our obligations, of course." Rathna did not stand as Maximilian did, just offered her hand one more time. He gave it a quick pat and bow, and then murmured further excuses. So sorry, an urgent purple rhinoceros to see to. Or whatever nonsense fit in that space. She didn't much care what it was.

She waited until he was well and truly out of the garden, then gestured at the bench. "Have a seat. We'll wait a bit for him to be well gone. Are you all right?"

Ferdinand had learned to deal with the fact she would ask questions like that, rather than assuming that all she would get was a polite demurral and a stiff upper lip. He'd also learned that she expected some sort of answer. He did take a couple of breaths first, this time. "That did not go at all as he'd played it out in his head, Mistress."

"No, it did not. Delightful, wasn't it? I assume it won't cause you too many problems?"

Ferdinand considered that, playing through it in his head, most likely. "You were very polite, really. And I'm now quite sure you had thoroughly investigated the family before we first spoke."

"Well, yes. I wanted a good idea what I was getting into. Shoddy of them, though. If they were going to throw a fit, they should have done so months ago. Months and months."

"They have never much known what to do with me." Those months ago, it would have been apologetic, a recognition that he did not measure up to whatever proper standard they chose. Now Ferdinand shrugged. "I find I don't care much. As you said, the apprenticeship agreement is settled, there isn't much they can do. I have a stipend. Thanks to your hospitality, and that of Lord Richard and Lady Alysoun, I have a most comfortable set of rooms in which to make my home. I learn more from you every day.

And I suppose we do have a liminal position in society, in several ways." He smiled, a little hesitantly, at the pun, making it clear it was deliberate.

"We do." She let her praise show in the warmth of her voice. "Thank you for giving me my head. I do wish Gabe, or particularly Alysoun, had been here. She'd have liked the show a great deal. She's the one who taught me most of it, one way or another." She considered. "If I have any blessing to give you, it is that if and when you marry, that you are every bit as fortunate in your in-laws as I have been in mine."

There was a flash of a smile on his face, and then he flushed. "I wish so too, Mistress. But they also have a great deal to feel fortunate in, I think. Perhaps you might write and let them know there will be a story later tonight for everyone to enjoy."

"That is a fine idea. Let me write that, then we will go find you a notebook or two, and then go see about the rest of the day's plans."

Ferdinand nodded, folding his hands in his lap while she wrote the note in her journal. She added a note to Gabe for good measure, and prepared to brave the streets again.

CHAPTER 38

JULY 26TH AT A PUB IN THE NEW FOREST

"There." Gabe nodded at Isobel, spotting the two people in a quiet corner of the pub's lounge. They'd gathered up their drinks, both because that was entirely proper and to give them a chance to get the lay of the land. He was not entirely sure what to make of the fact the pub was named the Green Dragon. It smacked entirely too much of an omen for Gabe's comfort. It was not terribly far from Ytene, though; the parties involved had suggested meeting there, and Gabe would make the best of it. Omen or no.

The two waiting at the table looked rather ordinary. Deliberately so, Gabe expected. He and Isobel looked the same. She was wearing a blouse and tweed skirt with a cardigan jumper over it, and he was in country tweeds. Rufus had been clear that this lot was on the upper end of the educated middle class, give or take. Certainly, they ran to the intellectually focused. The two of them had left the pony and carriage in the yard, with the pony glad to take a break, rather than ride.

Gabe was a decent judge of age in many circumstances,

it was something of a professional advantage. These two both looked to be in their early fifties. Neither had made the Pact, he could tell that thanks to the trick Alexander had taught him of reading the oaths. Reading the oath of the Pact was the simplest one to read. He could draw on the resonance of his own to spot the shimmer. They both had a something about them that wasn't entirely ordinary.

The man was on the tall side, and a bit angular, especially around the face. When he moved his hands, Gabe could see dark smudges on them. Silver nitrate, maybe, though it was hard to tell at a glance. Decidedly not of Albion, to have his hair that short if not obligated to. He had glasses tucked in his breast pocket, the way men did if they needed them fairly often, but not for a casual conversation. His suit was well made, but a few years old, with a single red rosebud in the lapel.

The woman was perhaps a year or two older, neatly dressed in country clothes, a tweed skirt and jacket set, but nothing that caught the eye. She had shorter hair too, or at least Gabe thought those were carefully managed waves and curls, not a mass of hair pinned up at the back like Isobel's.

He approached, nodding once, tapping the book in his hand against the other. "Pardon, I gather you know an acquaintance, a man named Pride?" It was a common name in the New Forest, though none of them but his immediate family were related to Rufus, not anymore.

"Rufus? Interesting man. Do have a seat? A friend of ours chats folklore with him, quite often. She's been delighted. Not all of those with long roots here have the time to chat."

Gabe half-smiled at that. "He's proud of his family's history here, for certain." He nodded at Isobel. "This is

Isobel, and I'm Gabriel." They'd discussed using a pseudonym, but it wasn't as if either of them would be terribly easy to trace back by non-magical records, not by first name only. And there was always the risk of not answering to it.

"Call me George." Clearly not his actual name. "And this is Theano."

"George, Theano." That one, Gabe thought, was a name that the woman used more regularly, like it fit her comfortably. Gabe inclined his head again. "Rufus mentioned your interest in folklore." This was the delicate part. You couldn't just come out and say 'what ho, good chap, are you by chance having a witchcraft ritual in a week?' For one thing, witchcraft was on the books as illegal, at least for those not of Albion. For another, they'd only just met. Anyone sensible would be skittish, and anyone who wasn't, well, Gabe wasn't sure about getting entangled with them.

Fortunately, he and Isobel had discussed this, and she spoke up, brightly. "I'd so much love to learn a bit more. We were chatting with some people in Kent, near where Uncle Gabriel lives. Some of the lore about Napoleon, the Armada even. Being on the coast, that's such a thing. We were helping out at Dover during the evacuation, of course. Pitching in every way we could."

"Ah, now, there's quite a lot of lore about that, isn't there now?" George spread his hands, settling into his topic. Bless Isobel, for figuring out how to get that started with quite a bit of elegance. "We've some tales about that. In my family, even, about people getting together, using their will to keep Napoleon across the channel."

"Really?" Isobel wasn't laying it on too thick, just enough earnest curiosity to be appealing. "I grew up in Yorkshire. There's different sorts of traditions up there, and of course, not so near the Channel by a long shot." She chattered on for a minute or two, about her granda, the cunning man. Isobel made a point tossing in various of the little folk traditions the family had kept that wouldn't remotely break the Pact because just about everyone did them.

"Now, I've heard Rufus has a touch of a gift with a horse. More than one cantankerous sort he's handled and calmed. Like magic, some would say." George added that after Isobel made a comment about breaking charms on livestock.

Gabe grinned. "Ah, well. If you ask some, they'll say he's got the Horseman's Word, and I've never heard him deny it. But the treats he keeps in his pocket are a fair bit of help. And he's kind with a horse, and they know it."

Theano inclined her head at that. "Kindness goes far, doesn't it?" She had been keeping an eye on the room around them. "You take the lore seriously, then, both of you? Ever explored any of it yourself?"

This was where it was going to get tricky, to thread the needle between truth and lie, Pact and what they could say. "Not as much as what we've been talking about as I'd like. But if there were a magic to keep the coast safer, I'd be all for that. My family takes the obligations to the land seriously. All the customs - hodening, in Kent, of course. The traditions around the hops harvest. All sorts of songs and chants and dances, and they mean something, don't they?"

It must have struck the right note. More to the point, he could feel the ring on his finger warming to the work, quite literally. It had never burned him, but he'd learned the feeling of it coming more alive, exerting itself. It wasn't that it forced a decision. Perhaps the Fatae had known that if they'd tried that, he'd have pitched the thing into the deepest bit of water he could get at with a bit of cold iron to weight it. The Bolton Strid, perhaps, where the waterfalls would pull it down immediately.

"And you think that's got some weight, then? There are plenty who'd laugh - and a few who'd go tell the constabulary that witchcraft is still on the books."

Gabe was familiar enough with the laws, Papa made sure of that, the ways that it interacted. Among magical folk, it was one more reason to keep to the terms of the Pact, if the oath on the Silence wasn't enough. He spread his hands. "The prosecutions I know about for it either have to do with fraud - and we all know there's some of that about. Spiritualists turning their hand to separating the grieving from their money, and nothing else. Or a bit of card reading as an excuse for someone else to pickpocket. But the problem there's not the magic or the lore. It's what people use it to cover." Then he shrugged one shoulder. "At the moment, the constabulary's got other things to keep up with."

George snorted. "Fair enough."

"Tell me a bit more about what you've done, in terms of exploring your interests." Theano was, he thought, a tad sharper and more cynical in a particular way than George was. George liked the lure of the magic. He might have been right on the line of making the Pact, honestly. Gabe had come across a few like that. It was where some of the cunningman tales came from. Somehow, their magic worked. It just wasn't of Albion. Theano, though, seemed more like a ritualist, someone who leaned into the incantation to shape the ritual, deliberate as a theatrical performance and when it worked, just as transformative.

Gabe decided it was time to put his cards on the table, or at least the ones he was willing to play. "I've seen more than enough things in my days that could only be magic walking in the world." Or riding a few inches above the ground, his mind reminded him rather loudly. "I don't know what I think about the Society of Inner Light bits about a vast astral castle, all those rooms that seem so empty." Though there was something about that, as he said it, that was like the Council Keep, how people moved cautiously there. He shrugged once more. "I'd rather turn toward magic, in whatever form. Wonder. Possibility. And there's something about the tales, isn't there, about doing the thing together."

He could feel Isobel's foot against his, under the table, pressing on the good side, then her fingers tapping something on his leg, to let her take the next bit. He signalled his own agreement and waited for their response.

"What would you give for it?" Theano, again, and sharply. "For the chance?"

He had to answer that, at least to start. "I've already made promises a plenty in my life, adding more's a trick. But I am - well. When I was young and a good bit more foolish than I am now, I swore to the land, and to keeping it thriving." All true, though, that wasn't a fraction of the oath he'd made.

Isobel picked up. "We're in a position where so long as it's not doing something in the middle of the town square, all public, there's not much others could do to harm us. We're not dependent on the goodwill of our near neighbours to put food on the table, or anything like that."

"And your neighbours aren't near here, either." George nodded once, and then his eyes half-focused, as if he were trying to do something specific. Gabe had seen Alexander take on the same sort of expression when he was reading oaths in the lines of magic. And he'd seen Cyrus do much the same when considering which line of action to take, like reading currents in the water that carried the bobbing ship of each person and their soul along. That was probably fanciful, but Gabe hadn't been able to shake the image since he'd had it months ago.

Gabe held himself still. He trusted that his own magical training wouldn't let anything slip that he didn't intend. At this point, he trusted Isobel's to hold as well. She'd come through Schola well, and that had taught her how to navigate scrutiny half a dozen ways before breakfast. There was silence at the table for a good minute before Theano lifted her glass, took a sip, and set it down.

Theano and George exchanged glances. Then she leaned forward. "We might know some people gathering to do something. If you're in earnest, willing to give your all, and respect the privacy of all those involved."

Those three words, 'give your all', echoed for him, but of course that was, in the circumstances, a quite reasonable thing to say. He held still, he couldn't let his personal take on that show, not here and now, the hollowness of the certainty of it. The privacy was easy enough to swear to, at least. Gabe was actually quite sure they weren't going to get introduced by name at such a thing. "No names, or chosen names, all that?" he asked, because why not make it clear?

"It does make it easier to keep the agreement." Theano produced a small notebook from somewhere and wrote a few words - perhaps a dozen - with a stub of pencil tucked into it. "Can you get there, just before sunset, on the first?"

Gabe glanced down at the paper, then nodded. "We'll need to ride and leave the horses, but we can do that." The Naked Man. It was a reasonable site, all told - clear, a bit away from the more likely places the Army had people stationed, not near a pub or other activity.

"Ask Pride where you should leave them, then." She

dismissed it as entirely not her problem. Not a horse-woman, he guessed, but the horses they'd borrow would be fine. If all else failed, Rufus or one of the stable lads could ride down with them and meet them in the morning, spending the night in a pub's loft nearby. All in a bit of war effort, or something like that.

"Sunset, then. Anything we should wear or bring?"

The 'wear' made her snort. "You know the answer to that, surely. Trust to your lore. Though you shouldn't need the bear grease."

Gabe could interpret that easily enough. "May I ask if this is a rite that's been done before?" It felt clumsy to say it like that, but he wanted a bit more information, or confirmation of what Rufus had got, rather.

"The full moons, starting in May. We had it suggested Lammas night might do well. We were looking for a few more to see what it helped." She kept her voice soft. "There you go."

The conversation was clearly over. Gabe inclined his head and waited for Isobel to stand before he scooted out of his own chair. He'd forgone the cane for this, no reason to raise that question, but of course now his ankle had stiffened up. Isobel immediately took his arm on the left side, which helped him cover for it.

It wasn't until they were a good half mile up the road, well away from anyone who might overhear, that she cleared her throat. "Does that mean naked for the ritual, then?"

"Oh, I expect so. There are reasons for it, even in our lore. Ask Alexander sometime, when he needs a bit of a distraction, you'll get a good twenty or thirty minutes even if he's being brief." Gabe flicked his fingers. "Me, I'd rather a robe, but robes are identifying, unless you're quite careful about it. Marks of status, of money, not just what they're made of but how well they're made. When it's skin, everyone has what they were born with."

"No boots, either?" Ah, that was sharp of her.

"That, I don't know. I'll wrap my ankle, put a bit of an illusion charm on it. You can do the same with your feet, keep them from getting cut up. I think Mama's still got some charmed linen suitable for it. If not, we can snag something from the stable that's suitable." Gabe let out a long breath. "All right with doing this?"

"If you are. I've done odder things so far."

"That, well. That's true enough. The time with the doe, the interior hall, and the hunting horn, for one."

"And the black hound, neither black nor a hound." Isobel agreed. "And I know you have a plan, sir."

"Several." Gabe clucked at the pony to pick up a trot. "Let's get back to Ytene and talk it through."

CHAPTER 39
AUGUST 1ST AT YTENE

Rathna was doing her utmost not to fuss. Fussing would not do any good, it would not change anything. It would distract Gabe, who did not need to deal with that nonsense, and it would worry everyone else. This did not make any of it easier.

They were assembled in the courtyard at Ytene, waiting while Gabe and Isobel checked their mounts over, looking at the hooves, the tack, all the necessities. Rufus was set to ride out with them, and he knew someone with a suitable barn where they could spend the night. Rufus, to be fair, seemed to know half the Forest these days, and Geoffrey knew the other half.

She tucked her hands behind her back so she'd stop fidgeting. Alysoun had not made the trip. She, Uncle Magni, and Uncle Gil were entertaining the children back at Veritas. Richard was at the Guard Hall in Trellech.

That left the people who lived here. Geoffrey stood further back with his wife, Lizzie, next to Alexander. The children of the house were off staying with Thesan and Isembard, and Rufus and Ferry's little ones were off with some of Ferry's cousins. What no one had spelled out - no one had had to - was better to have them out of the way if there was an urgent problem. Readily available, if need be, but not right on top of everything.

It wasn't as if Gabe were going into an actual battle. It wasn't even as if he were going off on a mythical ride with the Fatae. He'd done that one already. These were ordinary human people, with a touch of magic to them. Gabe had a pretty good idea what the ritual would involve. They'd talked it through enough with Alexander and Geoffrey and a few others.

Raising power, that was how the phrase went, making it swirl and aiming it. It was impossible to tell the form precisely until Gabe and Isobel were in the midst, but Rathna trusted they'd be able to manage. A great deal of what the Penelopes trained for was evaluating a new approach to magic on the fly. They were made into tools for measuring what it could do and what it mustn't be allowed to do.

Tucking her hands behind her back wasn't working, and she folded her arms. That didn't help either, but at least was a different strain on her shoulders. Gabe was checking the packs one more time - his travel kit, wrapped food and drink, restorative and healing potions, a spare folding cane tucked behind the saddle. He knew what he was doing.

Finally, he left the mare he'd be riding with Isobel and came back over toward Rathna, holding out his hands. "Harder when you're here, isn't it, love?"

She sighed, then leaned her forehead on his shoulder as he held her. "It is." It came out muffled. "And I can't go down with you."

"No. Even with Rufus. You wait here. We'll have our

journals. Rufus knows where we'll be, and he'll keep an eye out. We know the land around there, there's nothing that unusual. Not even bogs very nearby."

"If there were bogs, Rufus would be a particular help. Ex-bogs." Rathna tried to make a joke, and it fell flat. Rufus was, in fact, strong enough magically to convince a bog it was solid earth for a little. Not that it was kind to the animals and plants there, exactly.

Gabe kissed her cheek. "One night. We've both done much more terrifying things, and recently."

"What if we're wrong about that? You said yourself..." Rathna swallowed, catching herself. She hadn't been able to get that conversation out of her head, the one about sacrifice. They'd circled back to it, a couple of times in the days since, with no more resolution. Gabe hadn't been able to expand on why he thought it might be the thing asked of him. Rathna hadn't been able to put into words the gaping hole that she felt whenever they touched on it.

She had a family now. They loved her for her own self, not just on Gabe's account. If sacrifice was called for, Gabe's sacrifice, she'd had years and years with him. Not nearly enough, the century mark wouldn't be enough. But a great deal more than many people got, including her own parents. And none of that began to fill the space in her life that was Gabe. That she wanted to have Gabe for decades and decades more.

Rathna hugged him tighter. It wasn't helpful, not to either of them. In a minute, she'd have to let him go, and the Carillons would see she'd teared up, and that was going to be awkward. Gabe kissed her cheek again. "We'll write when we leave Rufus with the horses. He knows what to watch for. And I won't say yes to anything unless I'm sure it's needed."

"No promises you can't keep." Rathna agreed, sniffling a little now.

"No." Another tight little hug. "And either way, it'll be over tomorrow."

There was that. "Not like when I was on the Continent, and we had no idea how long. However did you manage?" It was enough to get her to pull back a little.

"I kept very very busy and annoyed everyone who loves me in strict rotation." Gabe was teasing, but only a little. He had, too, both the annoyance and the rotation. He was considerate about that point. "Charlotte threw me out of her house twice." That said quite a lot. His sister was in many ways calmer and more even-tempered than Richard.

She considered for a moment, then kissed his nose. "Tell me that one tomorrow."

"If it is within my gift, I will." His eyes were shining now. "This is just going to get worse the longer we wait."

Rathna swallowed. He was right. They both knew it. She just nodded. "Just. Do what's needed. Don't do what isn't."

That got a quick smile, a quirk of one, and he stepped back to make a bow. "As my beloved wishes. Wise words to guide my choices."

She had to laugh, it was the only answer. "Take a hand-kerchief with you, as a favour, if you're going to be like that. Even if it just stays in your pocket."

"I won't have pockets for some of this, I'm quite sure. But I'll keep it with me, so much as I can." She fished out a clean handkerchief from the sleeve of her jumper and handed it over. Properly embroidered with the emerald-green R that made it clear it was hers. He kissed it, folding it into his breast pocket, and then leaned to kiss her one last lingering time. When he pulled back, she nodded once, and he turned and went back to the horses.

She stood there without moving, just watching them, until they were past the turn in the road, past where the dust from the hooves could be seen or the clip-clop sound heard. She stood there until Geoffrey came up beside her. "They're off the immediate property now." He'd know, of course he'd know. He knew the bounds of his own lands as well as Gabe knew Veritas.

Rathna nodded once, unable to bring herself to speak. Lizzie came up on the other side, tsking. "Geoffrey, why don't you and Alexander make sure we're set up in the library? Ferdinand, too, if you would?" It wasn't at all phrased as an order, but Rathna was sure Geoffrey heard it as one.

He murmured a simple comment, "Of course, Domina." Then he called out, pitching it just right. "Ferdinand, we had a book we thought would interest you. Come along, they'll be in in a bit."

Rathna could tell she was being managed. She didn't have the force of will to argue. Lizzie waited until the men had all gone inside - Benton, as well, of course. Lizzie didn't reach to touch her, just waited. "You have something to say?" Rathna's voice cracked on the last word.

"Not platitudes. You know what he's doing. What might happen. Is there something you're particularly worried about?" Lizzie half-turned to her. "I know you're closer to Thesan, some ways. She's nearer your age, of course. And there are the professional pleasures."

Rathna shifted, twisting her shoulders to face Lizzie better as she blinked. "Is that what you think?" She swallowed. This was certainly diverting, as a topic, if also a challenging one. She let out a sharp breath, then saw a slight shift in Lizzie's expression. "You are deliberate."

"I suspected I wasn't going to fool you for long. Would you rather sit, or walk in the garden, or go watch the mares and foals?"

"You want a conversation, just us, where we won't be overheard." And she wasn't going to fuss over it. "The foals." She could see gardens at a number of places, and while Ytene's were flourishing, they were in much the same style as Veritas. And sitting, well, they could do that inside. But Veritas didn't breed most of their own horses - in fact, they often came from Geoffrey's stable these days. All three of the children's current mounts had been born here.

Lizzie didn't say anything further as they circled round, through the aisle between the courtyard and the stable yard, with its long L of stalls, off to the right. They went along past the nearer paddock, off to the further one, where three mares and foals were grazing. Lizzie gestured at the mares. "Lean on the fence? Bench?"

"Leaning." Rathna felt fidgety. It'd be easier if they weren't sitting. Then she turned her head, peering at Lizzie. "What are you up to?"

"It's not easy letting them go off, is it?" Lizzie shrugged, wriggling the hand off toward the house. "Geoffrey in Germany." Rathna had known about that while it was happening, the trips that had brought Geoffrey and Alexander into orbiting each other like a tight little system of stars. Triple, arguably, or more complicated.

Rathna had come to the decision that the Carillons and their various others were more like the Ursa Major Moving Group than a binary or even triple or quadruple system, though they'd come to that from different places. The metaphor didn't hold up at all well. She'd ask Thesan about it sometime, when they both needed a laugh.

Rathna brought herself back to the current conversation with a start. "I am not at my best right now. Do explain?"

Lizzie laughed, but it was a cheerful laugh, not a mocking one. "He went off to do something important, and he came back and the world changed. His. Ours. And he could have got quite badly hurt, in the process. He almost did."

"That part was not entirely clear at the time, besides the dangers from the espionage itself. Which were there, yes, but - different?" Rathna didn't know how to put that. She was used to her work being aboveboard. Or when it wasn't, it was more about privacy than secrecy. Gabe was the same way. Rathna knew he could keep things private when he had to, but she also knew he hated it, he wasn't made for not sharing what he'd learned with someone. Enjoying the learning, that was a good way to put it.

Lizzie snorted. "Well, it wasn't supposed to be that obvious. And we did explain after, when we invited you and Gabe to size up Alexander for yourselves."

Rathna smiled at the memory, the way Gabe had immediately offered a duel. And then fought Alexander to a draw, which Alexander absolutely hadn't expected. She looked back out at the horses, cleared her throat, and did her part in this conversation. "I don't even know what I'm scared of. Or I do, but it's not like most of it's new. Penelopes don't have the safest line of work. And it's not as if I haven't been taking risk after risk."

"There's something different about this one, perhaps? You know the patterns. This is outside of them." Lizzie laid it out evenly, without any hint of judgement.

"Something like that. Gabe and I talked it through. The range of possibilities. I don't know. That there's something in here that will change everything."

"Like falling in love, but you're not at all sure it will be nearly that pleasant?" Rathna glanced over, and Lizzie was half-smiling. "This is nothing like I expected my life to be, and I still find myself thinking it most days. You either, I'm sure."

"No. There's a way we're more alike than Thesan and I. She at least is doing what she expected to be doing from the time she was sixteen or so, in the place where she expected to be doing it. Though she'll admit the marriage was a bit of a startlement."

"I can't decide if it's better to know a lot of what our husbands get up to, or to have to send them off and not know. I feel for everyone left at home, having no idea what their men are up to. Especially anyone without a journal. Or where their loved ones can't have it with them. We, at least, we know when we should be more or less worried?"

"More. Currently more." Rathna let out a long breath. "I - it's not mine to talk about. But I appreciate you're wanting to make space for it."

"Fair. And we're well used to people not talking about things around here. Geoffrey's better than he used to be, but Alexander? Still king of not saying things he doesn't mean to." That was entirely affectionate. "We'll give you space, and all three of us pulled out books you might like. And Ferdinand, of course."

Rathna ducked her chin. "I appreciate you having him out here. He's rather at loose ends."

"That would be the other reason we should stay out here for a few minutes. Geoffrey wants to get him thinking about some of the interconnections a bit differently.

Between what you do and ritual magic, in particular. He and Alexander have been looking for a chance for weeks, I gather."

"Am I going to regret that? No, of course I will, and I won't. Do I get the teacher's notes so I can keep a step ahead of him?"

"Annotated bibliography and a couple of copies of the relevant books, waiting on the desk in your room. And a copy of Geoffrey and Alexander's working notes." Lizzie grinned impishly now. "We do try to provide exceptional hospitality."

Rathna laughed. "Certainly unique. Can I get twenty minutes up there to look at it, without attracting too much attention?"

"Oh, at least that. It's the question of how soon you want your tea. I could come up with you, read companionably?"

Rathna nodded. "I'd like that." Then she swallowed. "Thank you. For understanding."

"If we don't, who's going to? Besides your family. But we're here and they're not."

Rathna let out a slower breath now. "And Gabe will come home, and we'll see what we do then."

"Just so." Lizzie gestured back toward the house. "Shall we?"

They walked back, chatting idly of the late summer plans for the property. They talked over when the figs might ripen, the tomatoes in the kitchen garden, and how things were coming along for the harvest fair. Pretending everything was ordinary.

CHAPTER 40
AUGUST IST, DEEP IN THE NEW FOREST

Gabe and Isobel arrived at the indicated clearing right on time, an hour before sunset. They had a knapsack between them, shaded lanterns - it was blackout, of course. And they had themselves. Gabe had tucked the most condensed of his canes into the knapsack, folded up so it was no more than a foot long. But he'd also worn the boots that made it less necessary. They'd been warned it might be a bit of a walk, and Gabe had correctly translated that as "miles, plural".

He didn't expect he'd be able to keep the boots on, so he'd also wrapped his ankle with a charmed bandage, for support. It was enchanted further to be entirely invisible to those who didn't know it was there. Isobel had watched him, as he'd done it, without comment other than "What should I know, sir?"

She knew where the potions case was, that he might need something from there before they could make their way home. If it came to that. What he'd said was, "Know where your journal is, know how to get back to Rufus, all the small landmarks, tell them to me as we go. And we'll see what happens."

Gabe had no idea what the night would bring, but he'd taken no chances. He'd left a pile of letters and notes on his desk at home, the one he knew Rathna wouldn't look at unless he didn't return, or didn't return alive. Aunt Witt would be shocked.

For the first time in his life, all his case notes and reports and commentary on Isobel's apprenticeship were entirely up to date. He'd left letters for everyone he loved, pages of them, that he'd been writing on and off over the past few days, his pen skittering across the pages. Everything he wanted to make sure he'd said, if he couldn't later.

And if they weren't needed tonight, well, they'd be on record. Maybe someone would find them amusing eighty years from now, after he'd died from old age. He hoped that would be the case, but the rumoured deaths from this group earlier bothered him. He was not elderly now, and it was not a season that called for insulating bear grease, but there was no telling what magic would demand.

If a sacrifice were demanded of him, at least Gabe had the training to answer that challenge fully and properly. He didn't know about anyone else. Isobel was not fully trained, and had an entire life ahead of her. George - or whatever his name was - had power in him, and Theano, as well, but he was quite sure they had different skills than Gabe's own.

The one thing Gabe knew was that magic had infinite forms. He could feel it warring in him, the need for caution and preparation, and the knowledge that there were things that could never be planned for. His mind had caught - obsessively, he was quite aware of that - on the risks here. That might be because there was a real risk.

More likely it was that he had been terribly worried about Rathna. He continued terribly worried about the war, about the planes flying overhead and the bombs dropping in increasing numbers. Never mind whatever the ride with the Wild Hunt, with the terrifying glory of the Fatae riders, might have changed for him that he couldn't begin to unravel.

Worrying about one solitary ritual, no matter how potent, was a lot more manageable than worrying about everything. Rathna and Mama had been very tolerant about it, so much so that he'd done his best to stop fixating on the worries. That had only worked so far, but at least they'd had other, far better conversations in the last few days.

Someone was waiting for them there - George, in a hooded coat. He nodded once at them and said. "It's a mile or two." Without comment, he went on further into the forest, through the trees, into a clearing. They had no way to leave word for Rufus. They'd have to rely on location charms and landmarks.

The walk was three miles as Gabe counted it, winding on paths and dirt roads deeper and deeper into the trees. A vast swath of oaks, proper English oaks, with others here and there. Gabe caught the murmuring of a nightjar, the flick of a fleeing tail of a deer, the little rustles in the under-brush of smaller wildlife. He didn't stop and try to spot them. This was not the time.

Finally, they came into a clearing, and Gabe knew exactly where they were, coming into the realm of the Knightwood Oak. He and Isobel had been here in, what was it, March? Yes. The day they'd come back from the Naked Man. They were in the southern part of the Forest, still, not Geoffrey's own lands, but that was better. Likely better.

There were a dozen people in the clearing now, each taking up a place in a large loose circle just south of the massive oak. The tree must have been two dozen feet round, give or take, a true queen of the forest. They ringed a circle, the same circumference as the tree that had been marked out in brushwood. The centre had five candles in little metal cans, but no one stood inside the brush, not yet.

Gabe hesitated, then glanced at George. "May I pay my respects?" He nodded once at the tree, to make his intention clear.

"Do. And then I will take you to do the same to our Rose of the wood."

Gabe set off, nodding agreeably without focusing on anyone too closely, with Isobel at his side. Those assembled were on the older side. Gabe himself was, so far as he could tell, one of the youngest there, and that made Isobel near two decades younger at the least. Four people stood together, near each other, two men, two women.

The women must both be in their seventies, both with the sort of deceptively innocent matronly demeanours that one ignored at one's peril. Not at all like Mama, but Mama would get one glimpse and veer toward them in any room as the most interesting companions. The men were an intriguing contrast to each other. One was leaning into the conversation, the other looked almost bored. The interested one had the look Gabe suspected others saw on his face all the time, of repressing a dozen comments and interjections, knowing that wouldn't go over well. He had a rather chaotic goatee, from what Gabe could see from this angle, and enough hair for it to be a tad wild.

Gabe walked over to the tree, made a slight bow, and then pressed his hands to the bark. This wasn't his specialty. Normally he didn't do well with trees. They moved in a pace he found tremendously challenging to match for more than a few breaths. Even so, he'd learned enough from Rathna how to listen to them better.

This one was ancient indeed, old enough to have had solid roots when the Pact was made, though she'd still been quite young then, barely out of saplinghood. She recognised him, the way trees often recognised those who had particular attention for the land magic. Gabe sent a little of his own magic out into her, a brush of gratitude and acknowledgement.

Isobel came up and as Gabe removed his hands, she did the same little gesture, the same press of palms against bark. When she pulled away, Gabe offered his arm, and George was waiting to bring them to the little group of four. When they came over, George cleared his throat. "Lady, as I promised, a little youthful vigour."

The elder woman inclined her head slightly, secure in her place here. "We welcome all willing aid. Follow what we do, and you will do well." It had an echo to it, some instruction or blessing from an older text, the sort Alexander or Geoffrey would be able to put their finger on immediately. Gabe inclined his head without speaking, and after a moment George led them to take their place in the circle.

Time passed, perhaps half an hour, until there were fifteen, sixteen, seventeen people standing in a loose circle. A few more men, and the group was about even men and women. Isobel was still the youngest by far. There was no man here but Gabe who was of an age to enlist, and only one other woman near his age.

At some sign from the eldest, most of the others began to strip their clothing off, piece by piece, leaving their clothes folded in a neat pile by whatever bag they'd brought. Gabe did not hesitate at the clothing, though as he had told Isobel he much preferred ritual robes. He did pause at the boots, before deciding he would deal with what would come and go barefoot. At least his ankle was wrapped, he'd have a little support there.

That done, they were each guided to an entrance in the brush, met by someone with a smoky incense and a bowl of fragrant water to dip their hands. Gabe murmured the prayers he'd learned at Mama's coaxing, back when he was tiny. They were about purity of heart, nobleness of spirit, and washing away all that did not serve.

He took up a place to the northwest, as someone lit the candles in the centre, setting them to flickering. Then three hooded lanterns in the southeast, where Hitler must be, the direction they were loosing their arrows. A bare minimum of light, one didn't want the Home Guard or air-raid wardens, or, for that matter, the Luftwaffe to spot anything. At least the tree cover overhead would be a help with the last.

Someone walked around the boundary three times, scattering some sort of powder. Gabe could smell the light, almost citrus note of the vervain, a hint of lavender, a touch of mint, and something he couldn't quite identify under the more obvious scents. At least four herbs in the mix, quite possibly more.

The eldest woman processed into the centre of the circle, standing before the candles in their tins, somehow bringing every mote of attention into her hands, despite the oddity of the setting and tools. This was no workroom, as Gabe was used to. And it was certainly nothing like the Temple of Healing or the ritual room at Schola, or any of the other places he had done rituals in the past.

Somehow, she made this be a place of power, as if she were calling it into being like Rathna coaxed a portal to life.

It was not an order by sheer force of will. It was not a fantasy made of wisps of illusion and enchantment. It was something far more solid than Gabe had realised was likely, outside the boundary of the Pact.

When the woman spoke, her voice had power behind it, a harmonic ring much like a harp. "Join hands. We will dance. As we dance, think only 'You cannot cross the sea, you cannot come'. Follow my lead, or the lead of my maiden, as it builds." She indicated Theano, who stepped forward from halfway across the circle, nearer to Gabe and Isobel.

Then her voice grew deeper, a vibrating resonance. "Listen to the words of the Great mother, who of old was also called among men Artemis, Astarte, Dione, Melusine, Aphrodite, and by many other names. At mine altars the youth of Lacedaemon in Sparta made due sacrifice." She paused, as if normally the rite had some other word or phrase there, then continued, "For I have come to sweep away the bad, the men of evil, all will I destroy!"

The last word almost had thunder to it. Brief though the speech had been, Gabe could see the power of it resonating. They were all there, wherever they came from, because they wanted to do this one thing, with everything they had. As one, they stepped, moving sunwise, motion by motion. It began slowly.

In Albion, there would have been a ritual drummer, almost certainly. There would have been a floor, one of the ancient great halls, where you could hear the steps, the deliberate stomps, the way the stone or wood became part of the music. Here, there was only the rustle of steps in the grass, the slight noise of skin on skin, then someone clapped with hollowed hands, and others picked it up. This was also not Gabe's great gift, building a rhythm piece by piece, so he kept to the anchoring beat. To his right, he heard Isobel pick up something more complex and syncopated.

They circled and circled, murmuring at first. "You cannot cross the sea. You cannot cross the sea. You cannot cross the sea. You cannot come. You cannot come. You cannot come." Many of the others - though not all - seemed to know how this went, as if they'd done it before and not just once. Six or seven of the seventeen, perhaps. Others, like Gabe and Isobel, were simply picking it up as they went.

That was the thing. Gabe could feel the magic being coiled up. Not as Alexander would do, not as Cyrus did in the Council dances now. Not as Gabe himself might do, certainly, for all this kind of ritual wasn't his usual line of magical work. Entirely too many people, for one thing, for his sorts of workings. But whoever was guiding it, that eldest woman, was competent. She was making a glorious orb of it, twining and living, being given shape and form just as was needed.

It built and built, the steps moving faster and faster, until Gabe's heart was pounding in beat with the throb in his ankle. Somewhere in there, the woman to his left reached out to take his hand. He reached for Isobel's. They were circling then with no sound but the chant; voices getting rougher with strain. Gabe had no thought for anything now but the rising power, nothing but the goal, the burning need to keep the harm away on the far side of the water. You shall not come. You cannot come. You cannot cross the sea.

Then, all of them answering the same signal, the dance changed from circling to rushing inwards toward the light at the centre, hands raised. Then they fell back, like a great wave. It was a tidal wave made human, formed by bodies dripping with sweat, heaving for breath, drawing every last ounce they could to send their will into the world.

Somewhere in there, Gabe gave himself over to it utterly. He had not been asked a question, not the way the Fatae had meant, and it did not matter. He was here. His heart was beating with the land, for the land, twining with the deep, far-ranging roots of the tree, the connection from branch to leaf to branch to root that ran through the forest, all out through the lands of Albion.

He could feel the sparkles of the stones held by other groups, the way he knew where he was in relationship to the one in the pocket of his folded clothes. They spread out behind his eyelids like stars in their constellations. Each one slotted into place across the south of England, then spreading out west through Wales, and north, even a few up into Scotland.

The arms rose, they fell. They rushed in and drew back. Over and over, endlessly, what felt like hours and hours. Gabe had gone far beyond counting, far beyond any sense of his body, as if he were riding again with the Wild Hunt. His feet felt like they barely touched the ground, his limbs moved without his will. All that mattered was the dance and the thought. He drew on that memory, as much as he could, what their magic and power had felt like.

Something rushed through him, answering that call as nothing else he'd felt in his life had. It seemed that the land herself had been waiting for the moment. All the desire for growth and flourishing greenness had been waiting to explode through the door he made into the world. He could only make a doorway, make a portal as Rathna made portals, and do his best not to get in the way. This was wild magic, and it was magic of people who had lived and loved and chosen this land over and over and over again, through millennia.

Everything went black, then everything went quiet. There was nothing, just the dark and the void and the stillness. He didn't know how long he was there, in that umbral space beyond desire or meaning. He could barely think, just drift there, as if everything had rushed through him and left him a shell. If this was it, if this was what sacrifice felt like, at least right now, he didn't hurt.

He hung there in that liminal space, not moving, not thinking, barely breathing. Somewhere in there, he was aware he was still himself, that there was a him who could consider and measure the pain he was or wasn't feeling. He couldn't move, though, he certainly couldn't bring himself to any sort of action, even inside his own head. Everything kept spinning away, beautiful, fragile, and entirely insubstantial.

When he remembered how to move again, everything changed. All of him was in pain. His ankle, most of all, but everything else, too. Something hard was under his hip, something else bumped an elbow that felt bruised, every muscle in his legs and back and arms complained at the slightest twitch. There was some sort of cloth over him, with a warming charm, but he shivered despite that.

Something in the movement changed the world around him. There was a hand, very lightly resting on his shoulder. "It's morning. Well past dawn. They're all gone." Isobel's voice, quiet. "Rufus is on his way. Potion?"

Gabe could only nod once, before even that effort was too much. There was the click of his potions case, the sound of two vials being moved, then Isobel was pressing one into his hand. He didn't try to look at it, just drained it. Then the other. The first was a painkiller. He'd regret the effects in a few hours, but that should allow him to get home. The second was a stamina restorative, the aftertaste on that always took a moment to announce itself.

"How long?"

He didn't even know whether he was asking how long until Rufus would meet them, or how long he'd been unconscious. Isobel answered both of them. "Ten or fifteen minutes, maybe. The last of them only left half an hour ago. And you've been out a good few hours. Three others collapsed, fully." She hesitated, then added, "There was some joking about how young folks don't have the stamina they used to."

Gabe half-rolled onto his back, and regretted that too, but it let him blink at her. "You all right?" He should have asked immediately.

Isobel sounded amused. "I've already taken my potions, sir. You took the brunt of it, or - no, that's not the word. You made yourself into the brunt of it. I think the priestess knew, but I don't know who else figured it out. No one asked me. Just checked to see if you needed anything, and didn't bother us. I cast a look-away charm once they'd gone. I didn't know if we'd have ramblers or what out."

"Good." His voice cracked on the last part, then he let his head roll back. "Wake me up when there's a horse."

CHAPTER 41
AUGUST 2ND AT YTENE AND VERITAS

Rathna was near enough climbing the walls by the time Gabe, Isobel, and Rufus returned. Lizzie and Geoffrey had been exceedingly considerate, but none of it had helped.

Isobel had written right around dawn, when Gabe hadn't yet woken. Now it was getting on for eight, and they were finally turning into the courtyard. Gabe was riding upright on his own, but she was certain it was only sheer bloody-mindedness and force of habit that was keeping him there.

As soon as the horses stopped, she was at his leg. "Come here, love." He blinked at her, owlishly, as Rufus came over with one of the stable lads. Strong, broad-shouldered men, both of them.

"Here, mistress, or would it be better to get him back to Veritas?"

That was a trick to sort out. Only it wasn't. He'd be better on his own land, even if he wasn't going to be any good for the rites today. "Veritas, please." She turned over her shoulder to nod at Lizzie and Geoffrey, Alexander standing beside them. "We'll let you know?"

It got a silent nod, a half-salute from Geoffrey, and then Rathna was consumed in getting everyone home. Isobel, thankfully, was in better shape, and Ferdinand was glad to carry the satchel and lend an arm. Twenty minutes later, Gabe was tucked into bed in their rooms. Rathna had checked in with the children and Alysoun and Richard, before they went off to the village for the various festivities. Those were both about the wheat and about the bread.

She stayed and waited, hour on hour. She nibbled at sandwiches the staff had left; she drank tea from what seemed like an endless pot, and she flicked through pages in her book before going back to read them again, a dozen times. Around noon, she dared leave him for long enough to go downstairs to the stillroom and the potions cabinet, and pull out half a dozen options from the stores there.

It wasn't until nearly three that Gabe made much noise. He normally moved around in his sleep without being restless. Today he slept like the dead. He wasn't. She kept checking that he was breathing.

It wasn't a nightmare that woke him. Gabe didn't have nearly as many of those as he probably should, given his work. This time, it was him waking and reaching for something, his hand closing on the air, before he pulled his hand back toward his chest, curling around it.

She cleared her throat. Rathna had talked with others about it - Thesan and Lizzie, mostly. Their husbands had fought in the War, in ways they didn't ever talk about, that stalked them in dreams. Thesan had been pragmatic about it, that she never got between Isembard and his magic, never between him and the door. She'd made it a habit, and Rathna didn't have the knack of it.

All she could do was make a noise and wait. Gabe took far longer than usual to figure out what was going on, to blink at her and push up on one elbow before he fell onto his back. "Come here?"

She went, of course she did, settling on the bed with her foot tucked up, one hand resting on his shoulder. "Potion? Your choice of the pain potion you'll probably take, the one you'll resist but I have to try, the one I will make you take tonight if you don't now, or a restorative. Or if you insist, a stamina potion or that one that makes you ignore everything your body is shouting at you."

Gabe's eyes wrinkled up at the list, at least a sign of his humour being largely intact. "The first and the restorative. We'll see about the others." He pushed up on an elbow as she reached for those two from the bedside table, his hand shifting to rest on the curve of her hip. He drained them and handed the empty bottles back. "Isobel?"

"Tucked into bed, one of the staff was checking on her regularly. In better shape than you are, from what I gather." Her glance flicked up to the little lights. "Everyone else is still out, though I expect them back in an hour or two."

Gabe nodded once, flopping onto his back, reaching for her fingers with his other hand. "You?"

"Not my favourite means of passing the time." She hesitated. "Do you think it's the sort of thing you'll be taking up regularly?"

"Rituals with unknown groups all night? Four of us, I think, to the point of collapse? I have no idea. I don't know how well it worked."

"Well. Even if Hitler dropped dead of a heart attack, it would take a little to be sure of it. And that's not what you were doing, was it?"

"Goodness, no. He's got his own protections. That sort

of frontal assault ends badly. Basic tactics. Ask Isembard or Alexander for the potted lecture." Gabe blinked up at her. "Did I not explain that bit?"

"Only in snippets." Rathna said. "To be fair, I was rather occupied at the time." She let out a slow breath. "What do I need to know, then?"

There was a long silence, a time where Gabe didn't say anything. He let his thumb brush against her skin in no particular rhythm or pattern, his eyes half closed. Finally, without opening them, he said, "I gave it my all. I don't think she expected that. Any of the three that pronoun might apply to." He stopped. "No. Two of the three didn't. I think."

"Define your terms, please? Or your personages." Rathna was not entirely following, but she wasn't expecting that at this stage. Gabe, in the midst of working through a problem, only glancingly made sense to anyone outside his head. Aunt Mason had slightly better odds sometimes, but only because she and Gabe shared a whole language of references strung together by tremendous leaps of logic.

"One, the land herself. That one's known." Gabe opened his eyes, watching her again. "Two, the Knightwood Oak. That's where we were. I want to go back and take readings, actually, but..." He pushed up on an elbow. "Tomorrow." He considered. "Maybe tomorrow."

"Ask Geoffrey to go. You know you can trust his work." Rathna kept watching. Something was still odd. Out of place, maybe out of season. She didn't begin to have the language for this.

Gabe shrugged once. "We'll see." That listlessness worried her more and more.

Now she leaned back. "Talk to me, Gabe." It was not her

habit to press. For one thing, she didn't usually need to. Gabe, on average, moved at a dizzying speed.

He grimaced, rubbing his face with his free hand. "What am I for, then? There wasn't a question there, not anywhere. I gave and gave, and it was welcome. But it wasn't - whatever the Fatae expected, it wasn't that. No questions at all, not to say yes or no to."

"You said three. The land, the tree, and..."

"The tree's glorious. She dates back to just before the Pact, I'm sure of it. There's a study for you. Your Guild, too, maybe. Which trees date before the Pact, what that means for materia. I'm sure there's an article on it somewhere." He rubbed his face again. "Yews. Lots of yews. Some bones. Animals, I mean, not people. People would be very rude."

That last bit at least sounded more like Gabe should. "The third, Gabe?" He was decidedly more scattered than usual, as if every guide he usually funnelled his thoughts through had disappeared in a puff of wind.

"The, I don't know. Priestess. Priestess is a good word. She was in her seventies, and I think I surprised her? I mean, I have manners. Mama made very sure of it. I wasn't going to try to take over." Now he just sounded indignant. That was also a good sign, honestly.

"Did you find out any more about her? Any of them?"

Gabe tilted his head. "There are connections between some of them. More than others. I think she was married to one of the men, the one who looked rather bored. But friends, close friends, with two of the women. The one who met us at the pub, Theano, was close to one of the other men. Most of them were older, though. A couple of them might have been siblings? The one who called himself George. Cousins, at least, they looked alike, as well as the, um. Magical bits."

"So people who knew each other, but also people who weren't as close? How did the priestess work with all of that?"

"It was really very simple as rituals went. I expected a lot more fuss and mysticism and I don't know, all the drawings and designs. Though of course, it's hard to do those on grass and leaves, it's not like a working room floor or a temple or whatever." There was a moment at the end of that when something caught at his attention. It wasn't a catch in his breath, it wasn't nearly that long, just a slight gap. "She announced it, said something that some of them had obviously heard before. Isobel wrote it down, she said. And then we got to it. Very simple. Quite long, dancing around, then in and out. I wasn't the only one who collapsed."

Then he flushed. Rathna leaned forward and kissed his forehead. "You were going at it rather differently than they were, several ways round. How do you feel now?"

Gabe shrugged one shoulder. "Barely warmed over. I should probably soak in the baths."

"Soak in the baths and not talk about something some more?" Rathna raised an eyebrow.

He grimaced. "Come soak with me, and I'll do my best to talk? I should soak. I must smell awful."

"Not your best self at the moment, no. Come on." She spent a minute or two getting him into a dressing gown and handing over his cane. Then she checked with one of the housemaids for a change of bedding and to let the other staff know they'd be in the baths, and that they'd want a solid tea after. Most of the staff would be off in the village, still, but there would be a couple here.

It wasn't until Gabe was neck-deep in hot water that he

spoke again. "I think I'm haunted by it. If this wasn't what the Fatae meant, what is?"

"Do we need to figure it out immediately, do you think?" Rathna leaned back, letting Gabe settle a bit against her shoulder.

"Sooner than later. It has a, I don't know. It feels like it's ticking. A time pressure." Gabe lifted his hand out of the water, twisting it sideways, like he was reaching for something again. "I can't find the words for it. Very annoying."

"You have had rather a day of it." This was true. It was also not exactly helpful. "Talk it out with people, and see what comes to you? Go for a ride, teach Isobel something entirely different. Explode something in the workroom."

The last one made him snort. "You are very patient, bright lady." His lips brushed against her ear. "However do you put up with me?"

"You have a number of virtues." It came out a tad prim before she smiled at him. "Quite a few."

He was quiet again for a couple of minutes, then he asked, "What do you intend to do this week? Fortnight. Month, I don't know."

"Ferdinand has a visit with his mother scheduled for Wednesday. Other than that, we're picking up taking care of the older portals. Schola, the Keep, and figuring out a rota for Trellech."

"How annoyed is Fortnum?" He could be exceedingly prickly about his prerogatives.

"Working on Dover and several of the other ports. He's finding the challenge interesting, actually. Ferdinand ran into him in the Guild library. When was it? Tuesday. I think Fortnum's not really happy with an apprentice, and he's glad to be freed up to be obtuse on his own. He does know his work. Ferdinand came and told me after, and he's rather pleased to be with me. I apparently explain things better."

"Well, of course you do. To begin with, you explain them in the first place, and you certainly didn't get that from me."

It made Rathna laugh. "You keep a lot close to your chest, love, but you also talk about all manner of things. Some of them are even explanations. Anyway. We're getting on well enough. We can base ourselves here as easily as anywhere else. Though I've made sure there's a room ready for Ferdinand in the Trellech townhouse in case we need to be there overnight. Everything else is, I don't know. There's a war. Things keep changing, but it's steady enough."

Gabe nodded once, but didn't say anything. This time, Rathna did not press him to. Whatever it was in his mind that was nagging at him, it would take time to grow into words.

CHAPTER 42
AUGUST 12TH IN THE DUELLING SALLE AT VERITAS

"Yield?" Gabe held his wand and staff. The staff was anchored against the ground, a foundation to launch from if he needed it, while Gabe could feel the magic coiling up his wrist, ready to pounce. He was in excellent form today, fully recovered from the previous week, and he'd had Alexander fighting for every inch of ground from the beginning of the bout.

Alexander promptly raised his hands, signalling that he did. He took a breath before speaking. "Yield. Take a breather, then the last bout?"

Gabe grinned. "You need to get out more. Too much time behind a desk the last few months."

The older man snorted. "Keep telling yourself that. No, it's that you're vibrating with the summer. And we're on your land." They were indeed in the salle behind Veritas. None of the staff would come down here, not without Papa or Uncle Magni's permission. Everyone else was out. Mama and Papa had a do in Trellech that night. Rathna and Ferdinand were off at a portal until at least supper time. Isobel

399

had begged the day to go see her family, since they had a bit of work to do on the Saturday.

Gabe had, in fact, been enjoying taking a bit of the afternoon for himself. It was a rare treat. When Alexander had offered the duel, he'd been glad of it. Now, though, he cocked his head as they made their way to the observation seats. Gabe pulled out a bottle for himself, then raised an eyebrow. "Ginger beer? Lemonade?"

"Ginger, please." Alexander lowered himself into a chair, sticking his feet to rest his heels on the ground in a decided sprawl. Gabe lifted his bottle in a toast as he passed the other over.

As he sat, Gabe shrugged. "You want to talk about something. At least one thing." He considered what he'd spotted so far. "Three or four."

Alexander snorted once, lifting his own bottle. "Most people wouldn't spot it." He wriggled his other hand. "And you're not most people. That's the point, actually. First, how do you feel about the way your bit of work on the first went? Now there's been time for it to settle."

"Hard to tell, isn't it? It's not as if Hitler dropped dead on the night, and even if he had, there'd likely still be a war, at least for right now. Nothing so obvious changed that we know of. On the other hand, there's no sign of a mounting attack across the Channel by sea. By air, though, that's another thing." It was a relief to be talking to Alexander, who had access to all the information Gabe had and likely a good bit more, in a well-warded space.

He let out a breath and went on. "The air attacks though, that worries me. Last night wasn't terrible, not nearly as much as it could have been, but..." Another shrug. "We're back to dreams, really. Eagles, which is really not subtle of my subconscious at all." Not given the German fondness for 'adler', the eagle, as a symbol.

"Just eagles?" Alexander asked it almost casually.

"Also dragons. Or rather, I keep seeing a flicker of emerald, something that's more a wing than anything else." Gabe half-closed his eyes. "Mind, my sleep hasn't been the most reliable this summer, one way and another."

"That's true of us all, I suspect. Anything in particular?" The question was almost guileless, except that Gabe absolutely knew better. He could demur, and Alexander would probably let him get away with it.

"Between Rathna being away, Solstice night, Lammastide.... My dreams have quite a lot to work with. Nothing obvious. Nothing I'd write down in my reports. Even to you." Gabe spread out his free hand. "And I've never been much of a diviner. Not my skill set at all."

"Fair." Alexander nodded. "Did you get any sense of anything Fatae touched, over Lammas?"

"How much is everything?" Gabe couldn't help but laugh at that. "I feel the greenness more than I used to. And I used to feel it a fair bit. Being there, under the oak, knowing she went back to before the Pact, that did something. I could feel the earth rise to me. Not coming to my call like horse or hound or hawk, but I don't know. There. Watching me."

Before he could go on, Alexander interrupted. "No dragons?"

Gabe shook his head, a tad irritable now, still rubbed raw by the whole thing. "Not that I saw. It was bloody dark." Then he went on, before Alexander could say anything else. "In any case, they seemed to be seeing if I had sensible ideas. I have no idea what that'll mean next month, or over the winter, or after, mind you."

Alexander grunted. "None of us does. Just hints and whispers and hopes." He tapped his fingers on the arm of the chair, and Gabe could tell he was still circling around some other topic. "Your work for the Council?"

"My report's not due until Wednesday afternoon. It is Monday. Ergo, I have not finished writing it up yet." First year Trivium, also honestly, how long had they known each other now? "Besides, I have some interviews tomorrow that need to go into it, whatever they produce."

"I am the one who has repeatedly told the rest of our lot to let you work at your own pace. For the record." Alexander flicked his fingers. "Overall, though? Is it worth continuing?"

"There's not as much talk about building up to a partic- ular working. And—" Gabe hesitated. "One of the inter- views is in Christchurch. There's one death there, and another man poorly. It's not as if I got a good look at every- one's faces, but." Gabe stopped there.

"But something makes you think there's a connection. That's an unsustainable magical act for you." Alexander grimaced. "And the Society of Inner Light folks?"

"I haven't looked at this week's yet, it's on my desk. But last week's, I quote, said 'England stands alone and happy'."

It made Alexander crack into a bitter laugh. "We are alone. Though you'd think she could have a thought for Wales and Scotland, at the very least. Even if Ireland is a tad complex in those particular esoteric circles." He shook his head. "All right." He looked up, his eyes half-lidded. "Four."

"Four." Gabe was instantly on alert. Alexander hadn't moved a muscle, not except for his eyes, but that didn't matter. Gabe could read the shift as swiftly as he had when they'd been duelling. Not perfectly, never that. Alexander was highly competent and just as lethal, and he'd been at his work since before Gabe had been born. One of the very first lessons Gabe had ever been taught that he could remember was the danger of underestimating someone.

"Keep the new moon in November free, please? That day and the next. You might want the following three or four, and the day or two before, if possible."

Gabe blinked once. Just the once. "Why?" He flicked through the calendar in his head. "The twenty-ninth."

"Yes." Which was not at all informative, and Gabe was sure Alexander was doing it on purpose. He usually was.

"Not until you tell me why." Two could play at that game, and if Alexander wanted to be the unmovable object, Gabe could be something else. Wind and rain wore down rock, eventually. Vines broke it open. As the repairs on the west wing from the ivy had been proving, this year and last. Gabe let his attention widen a hair, to see what else he could pick up.

Alexander set the bottle he was holding down, casually. "You know why. We have an open seat that must be filled."

"No." Gabe let it out in a rush. "I said no, eighteen years ago." There was something prodding at him now, and he turned his back on it mentally. The snare had not closed, not yet. Not that he couldn't feel it lurking. But Alexander had not actually asked that question, the one Gabe wanted to say no to.

"Times change. Needs change. And—" This got a brittle cough of a laugh. "The particular objections that Livia had to Rathna are no longer in play. Your wife gets on well with Vidya. We're bringing Isembard in more firmly as an affiliate. You'd have allies. Besides me."

"Come on, Alexander." Gabe stood, suddenly, pushing himself away from the chair, up, moving, vaulting to balance for an instant on the top of the hip-height wall that separated the observation area from the salle. Then he tucked and flung himself at the ground, using the momentum and the height to fling himself into a hand-spring and a flip. He landed on his good foot, facing where he'd been sitting a few moments ago, but now a good dozen feet into the salle.

Alexander was still standing up, but he came to the wall. "A tad excessive, Gabe, don't you think?" He'd told the truth when he'd said he hadn't seen the dragon, but now he did, a great green sinuous curve forming behind Alexander, the arch of the wing curving as if in blessing or warding or some unnameable gift. It was a distraction, and Gabe was resolutely determined to ignore it. He settled himself into a duelling stance automatically. "Why, Alexander?"

"We need you to make the attempt. We're not the ones who decide. But we need you to make the challenge. You, three or four others. Give the land a choice, the magic, whatever name you want to give her."

"Why?" Gabe could feel his skin near to itching. He wanted to fling himself into more flips and handsprings, but his ankle wouldn't take much more, not if they were going to duel again. And besides, running wouldn't actually help. Not with the promise he'd made, not with Alexander. Not with the oncoming weight of everything it meant.

"Come on, Gabe. Did you think you could reach into an ancient portal and not have us notice enough of what you were doing? Ride with the Fatae, a whole night? Or Lammas night. Threes, Gabe."

"Where do we begin to count?" Gabe pointed out. "I've done any number of other things so far. And I have a profession I—" His breath caught. "I can't give it up."

"We're not asking you to." Alexander leaned his hands

on the wall, considered, and then bounced once before pressing up on his hands, sliding his legs to Gabe's side of the wall before he perched on top of it. "Besides, you're getting ahead of yourself."

"Either I'm taking this - whatever you call it - seriously, or I'm not. If I'm taking it seriously, I have to think of the consequences."

"You don't have to make your life all about the Council. It might change which cases you take, but maybe not. Or at least not forever, if we somehow win this war and go back to ordinary time, as it were."

Gabe grunted. Still, he could run the numbers on the Penelopes, how many they had, how many they didn't, how the specialities ran. More than that, the way the politics ran, it had been ages and ages since a Penelope had been on the Council, nearly as long for a Guard. Both were bound by oaths that sat poorly with what the Council had to do.

More to the point, he had a set of skills - more than one set - they couldn't fill easily. All of them did, really. "What would be..." He cut off the words. He didn't want to say the words 'ask' or 'expect' or anything like that. "How would that work?"

"Meetings, as you're doing now, near enough. Projects. Advising Cyrus. In time, whoever replaces him. The rest of us. Taking on what you felt you could do well." Alexander spread his hands, but Gabe didn't fall into the trap of assuming that this was over. It was only barely begun.

"End of November." It came out sharper than Gabe had meant.

"Yes. Will you make the challenge, Gabe?" Alexander's voice was now absolutely neutral.

There it was, brutal and blunt, and yet so politely phrased. The question he wanted to say no to, and he had to say yes. He'd promised. His magic was pulsing, not just inside his head, but in his heart, his fingers, his toes, every bit of him.

Gabe lifted his chin, taking as deep a breath as he could, then Alexander flicked his fingers, his eyes darting. Gabe had seen him read oaths, and it had looked like that and not at all like that, as if Alexander had no idea what script or language he'd just read. "No. Don't answer me now."

Gabe could guess at what Alexander had seen, at least, and spare a half a thought to be amused that he did not know what to make of it. He nodded once, then offered, as something of a buffer, "I will consider it. Thoroughly. Give you my answer one way or another by the end of the month."

Alexander returned the nod, briskly and respectfully. Not pushing, and of all the things in this conversation, that was perhaps the most unsettling. It was not the most unsettling thing this summer. But as Alexander himself had said only minutes ago, it had been a summer full of unsettling and arcane hours.

There was a silence then. Alexander was giving him time. Gabe's thoughts were whirling. He'd need to talk to Rathna, of course. His parents. Mason and Witt, who could help him sort through the implications for the Penelopes as a whole, for his place among them, for what it might mean for Isobel's training.

He'd heard stories, of course, of what the Challenge might involve. Many people went in bristling to the teeth with magical protections, dozens of potions, charmed cloaks or even armour. Gabe knew his own worth. He knew there were precious few human duellists who could best him, but he wasn't so foolish as to think he could outfight anything and everything.

On the other hand, most people came out of the Challenge chamber alive. Changed, and they certainly never spoke of the details. Alexander had never spoken of it more than in passing. Not speaking of it, that reminded Gabe of things that bothered him about the Council once more. He was far too used to the easy, rapid collaboration of the Penelopes, the way he brought that home, to talk with Rathna and Mama and Papa and his chosen aunts and uncles.

His hands clenched, then he made himself relax them. He did not need to answer now, in this moment. Not even when he himself knew what the answer was going to be, what it had to be. He could - contrary to all his usual inclinations - step back, take his time, confer.

It wasn't the question of deciding. Ah, here he was, on far more solid ground, riding a mount he knew far better. It wasn't deciding whether or not to challenge. That had been decided already. It was how he was going to take the fence, ride the course. It was something like riding a point to point, galloping across country, as he'd done a fair few times. This was a race not just against the other horses and riders, but against the challenges of the land. Brush fences, wood fences, streams, up and down hills.

Not whether he raced, but how he rode the course. His heart settled, and his breath, before he looked up. "What may I ask you about?"

Alexander tilted his head, as if he had expected that question. Sensible of him, Gabe was made of questions. Of course he'd see what he could get. "That's a matter for some negotiation. But I will freely share what advice is already public. Geoffrey's alchemist has some potions going, the best of the usual run people want to take in with them. If you don't want them, it's not as if they'll go to waste."

Gabe snorted at that. "But I get first dibs, if I choose. All right. And less public information?"

"We'll see." Alexander held up his hand, forestalling further comment. "I mean it. We don't talk about much of it, and I am trying to sort through what is permitted but never done, versus what is not permitted and for good reason." He grimaced. "I have been trying to sort through that, for the record, since the day Garin brought Livia home."

Gabe blinked once. "You and who else?"

That made Alexander's lips quirk into a smile. "Cyrus and Mabyn. They left the timing of asking you up to me."

Gabe nodded once more. "All right." Then he took two steps back. "Will you duel me again?" Did Alexander dare, with this between them, that was an interesting question for the moment. Would Alexander press to find his limits, or let Gabe have a moment of riding his own competence? Both, probably, because this was, after all, Alexander.

Alexander looked him up and down, then hopped off the wall. "Same limitations?"

Gabe nodded once, retreating to his proper end of the salle. Maybe, just maybe, it would let his mind settle. Alexander could take care of himself in a duel. And perhaps some part of Gabe needed to prove it, before he could take another step forward into what everything meant.

If you enjoyed *Old As The Hills* and would like to read more of this series, please sign up for my mailing list to get all the latest news and fun extras. *Upon A Summer's Day* (a direct sequel to this book) will be out June 21st, 2023.

Your reviews (on whatever review site you use) are much appreciated, too! Read on for more historical details about this book.

AUTHOR'S NOTES

Thank you so much for joining me on the first half of this particular journey with Gabe and Rathna.

I know this book leaves you on more of an unanswered question than I usually do. You can get *Upon A Summer's Day* here (out June 21st 2023, available on pre-order until then). My great thanks to my editor, Kiya Nicoll, to all my early readers, and all the people who let me talk their ear off about this one.

This book is also new in another way. It's far more tied into specific real-world events than I have done in the past, and so this author's note is going to be on the longer side. I want to share my sources, and let you know which bits are historical, which are part of the historical record (but sometimes from some unreliable narrators or sources), and generally take a dive into esoteric history of the period.

Let's start with everything that isn't about witchcraft, ritual, and various esoteric and occult groups.

If you're curious about Geoffrey, Alexander, and the Heinrichs, there is more of interest in *Best Foot Forward*.

Chapter 1 : One of the challenges of any book anchored in history is figuring out not just what happened, but what people knew at the time about what was going on. In the first chapter, Ferdinand mentions a recent **white paper** from the British government that made it clear they had some understanding of the Nazi treatment of concentration camp prisoners. Rathna, with her long-term connections to the Jewish community, was certainly aware of it (and Ferdinand was due to his mother's background.) I've used anti-semitism here as the modern preferred spelling, which was also in use at the time.

Chapter 7 : **White feathers** were given to shame young men who were not in uniform, both during the Great War and during the Second World War. There are some reports of women deliberately forming groups of the kind in this chapter, though mostly informal (and often ill-considered, since as Rathna points out, there were a number of reasons someone might not be in uniform.)

Unlike the Great War, there was an explicit list of **reserved occupations** in the Second World War. This was meant to make suer that people with specific key skills were not sent off as infantry or some other purpose that wasted their skills and training. Reserved occupations included teaching, a number of skilled trades, and key industries to keep the country going.

Chapter 12 : **The Naked Man**, as Gabe notes, is in fact a tree. In more recent years, it's suffered from weather and some vandalism, and there is barely a stump left. In the 1940s, it was a notable landmark in the New Forest. It was also quite close to Brockhurst, which was a significant centre for Army placements during the War, including possibly some radio signalling intended to mislead the enemy. (You may imagine our unnamed party in this scene as from that unit.)

Chapter 16 : The **weather** throughout is as accurate as I can make it, which in this period is "quite", thanks to the archived and digitised daily records of the Met Office. That late April into May were exceptionally cold in many parts of the UK.

Chapter 18 : There were discussions in progress about forming something like the **Home Guard** from 1939 into early 1940. It was not officially formed until May 14th, until after the invasion of France, Belgium, and the Netherlands.

Chapter 24 : The evacuation at Dunkirk was pretty much as described in this chapter - absolutely a miracle of getting many people out of there, many on tiny fishing vessels and other small ships pressed into service. They did have to zig-zag quite some extra distance due to mines and other threats in the Channel. Dover was a key coordination point, both for its location and its existing infrastructure.

Chapter 29 and 31 : The **caves** Rathna and the others visit are largely real, with an addition where she meets Urdin. They're known as the Grotto de Pape, the artwork in the main caves is as described in the chapter. I was quite taken with a carved image from these caves, known as the Venus of Brassempouy, a woman with a net over her hair, who Urdin rather resembles.

Chapter 34 : **"Six impossible things** before breakfast" is indeed an *Alice in Wonderland* quote. (It's said by the Queen of Hearts.)

Chapter 37 : There was in fact a campaign with the tag line **"Be Like Dad, Keep Mum"** in this period. I couldn't find a more precise date than 1940, so I may have taken a liberty with this showing up a few months early. It was just too perfect (in that "awful propaganda phrasing" sense) not to use.

Chapter 42 : The last day of this book is August 12th. August 13th is known as **Adlertag**, when a series of more intense bombing raids began. These ramped up rapidly toward the Blitz, which is generally dated as beginning in September 1940.

Now that we've got through the other history, you might want a cup of tea (or your drink of choice) as we dive into the esoteric history. There's quite a lot here to explore. I did my best to tread lightly with historical figures, but I do want to share my sources and how I handled some details.

The late 1800s and early 1900s saw a huge surge in interest in a variety of esoteric and occult topics, as well as an interest in folklore and mythology. Ronald Hutton's *The Triumph of the Moon* gives a good overview of many of the different threads of this period. A number of people came together, formed groups, schismed, formed new groups, and tried a wide range of things.

For some of the (brief) details that Gabe and others discuss at various points about magic in Germany, I drew on Eric Kurlander's *Hitler's Monsters: A Supernatural History of the Third Reich*. It discusses a number of the changes in attitude around various esoteric topics, the different strands (exemplified in part by the varying interests of the Heinrichs), and the way fields like astrology were treated at different points. As well as, of course, a wide range of upsetting biases and actions based on them.

Some of this information was widely shared. The comments from the **Society of Inner Light** are taken from the collection of letters written by Dion Fortune and collected in a volume edited by Gareth Knight, *The Magical Battle of Britain: The War Letters of Dion Fortune*. These letters (as noted below) were circulated starting at the beginning of the Second World War.

I'd already been familiar with a fair bit of this history when I started the research for this book, but I needed to dig into a lot of details to make sure the names, dates, and known or documented information lined up with (or at least didn't conflict with) the events of the book. As I kept joking while I was writing, it appears that you couldn't walk through the New Forest in the period without tripping over an esoteric group of some kind. And not just the ones people who've done some reading about this period have heard of, either!

I was hoping that I'd be able to bring my plot to intersect with a particular event. That would be the **Lammas night** working to keep Hitler on the other side of the Channel (purportedly) done by a coven of witches in the New Forest in August 1940.

I've been intrigued by this bit of lore since reading Katherine Kurtz's *Lammas Night* at an impressionable age and fairly regularly since. She's mostly dealing with a different line of ritual and magic, much of which does not apply in my Albion. However, there are a lot of ways in which *Old As The Hills* is very much in conversation with her book about the nature of sacrifice, what it means, and what it is good for.

For details around the **New Forest coven**, I relied heavily on two books: Michael Howard's *Modern Wicca: A History From Gerald Gardner to the Present*, published in 2010. Howard was the longtime editor of a significant British magical magazine (*The Cauldron*), and knew many of the people he was writing about. The other key book was Philip Heselton's *In Search of the New Forest Coven* which came out in 2020. It explores the possible members and origin of the New Forest coven in a great deal of detail.

This group was, to the degree we know about it, made up mostly of middle class, educated, older adults. While most of the names are guesswork to some degree (due to privacy and secrecy considerations), we can make some suppositions about some of them. Several were actively involved in known esoteric groups in the general area, such as the Rosicrucian Theatre based in Christchurch, on the Hampshire coast immediately south of the New Forest.

The complication, of course, is that some people are unreliable narrators. Much of what we have about this event and direct reports of the group comes from **Gerald Gardner**, founder of modern Wicca. He commented in several places, years later, that he was part of that ritual and coven. The problem is that some of the information Gardner gives is contradictory, some doesn't fit in other ways, and a lot of it is really rather vague.

After I took quite a lot of notes from various sources, I was left with some commentary about what the ritual involved, that there were 17 people there (possibly), and a lot of vagueness. As an author, this is actually quite helpful.

While various sources have suggested lists of who was involved, there's only substantial overlap for about 10 of them. This made inserting Gabe and Isobel as participants a lot more feasible.

Chapter 3 and 10 : As noted above, **Dion Fortune and the Society of Inner Light** circulated regular letters among members of the organisation. Some people met at the building in London that the Society used, but other members around the country would join in the shared meditation at the same time. The idea was to build that focus with particular goals and intentions. Gareth Knight's collection usefully includes notes on ongoing events of the war as linked

The Wild Hunt has a long and storied history, but interestingly, reported sightings of them drop off dramatically post-Pact (1480s) in England, but continue in continental Europe. There are several ways they manifest in these sightings: a hunting pack baying after particular prey, the trooping dead, and a group of otherworldly women, much as appear later in the book. I've taken a few liberties with the descriptions, but Claude Leconteux's *Phantom Armies of the Night: The Wild Hunt and the Ghostly Processions of the Undead* was tremendously useful and includes a lot of the extant historical reports.

The **angels** described at the beginning of chapter 10 (as quoted) are drawn directly from the letter of the previous week. The image was entirely too amusing not to play with. This may be my favourite opening of a chapter ever. Of course, those not of Albion don't know about Schola or wrap it into their mental image of the British Isles.

Depending on which sources you believe, there were quite a few small **witchcraft groups** active around England in particular. It's less clear exactly what any one of them meant by witchcraft, what their practices included, or how they came together. While the New Forest Coven (discussed later) had one mode, there are references to the group that Rufus connects with. They're described as being more mixed in class and background, and including crafters and skilled agricultural workers who'd have a familiarity with the Horseman's Word.

Chapters 18 and 22 : During this summer, Howard mentions a number of groups (outside the New Forest) doing rituals, and I drew on that for the **ritual in Kent over May eve**. There are few details, but the mentions are consistent enough Gabe brings them up.

There are also various mentions about the New Forest Coven doing rituals all through that summer. As usual, there's some vagueness and contradictory information, but the full moons in May, June, and July seem plausible from the information we have. As noted in the book, May eve was one of the coldest in decades, and the rumour of someone dying from hypothermia is persistent in this bit of lore through several tellings. (As Gabe and Alexander note, blood being shed on the ground is a fairly constant approach to ritual deaths in a number of cultures.)

Here, we get the introductions of one of the things Heselton dug into. **Ernie Mason and his two sisters** were involved in quite a wide range of esoteric groups over time, and Heselton includes much of a conversation he had with someone who knew Ernie Mason well as an esotericist and teacher.

As discussed, their brother Alfred married Alice Wheeldon's daughter, Winnie. Many of that family were active in anti-war politics as well as other progressive to radical causes. They were known to be sheltering men trying to escape conscription. In 1916, Alice, her daughters, and Alfred were accused of a conspiracy to murder Lloyd George, who had just become Prime Minister. Three of them - Alice, Winnie, and Alfred - were sentenced to prison. Recent review in 2022 suggests that the convictions would be likely overturned if they went before the Court of Appeals.

The Battle of Blythe Road is a real event, where the rivalry between William Butler Yeats and Aleister Crowley turned into a magical duel, or at least a public disagreement at the headquarters of the Golden Dawn in London. (The Golden Dawn was at the time one of the preeminent esoteric/occultic groups in the UK.) They shouted spells at each other, but the actual end of the event involved Yeats tripping Crowley, Crowley falling down the stairs, and Yeats calling the police to make sure Crowley wouldn't return. The name stuck, though.

Chapter 38 : We have here our first actual direct appearance of known historical people, drawing on information in *In Search of the New Forest Coven*. As I mentioned, I did my best to tread lightly, but meetings of this general kind were (and still are) a way to feel out mutual interests in the witchcraft and other marginalised communities. You can read these two as fictional, but I was thinking of historical people when I wrote them. George, in this scene, is the pseudonym of **Ernie Mason**. I picked George as a pseudonym because it was both his father's name and the name of the founder of the New Forest Rosicrucian Theatre, where Ernie was involved for some time.

Theano was the name that **Edith Woodford-Grimes**, often known in this bit of history as Dafo, had a particular fondness for. She played the role of Theano (wife or student of Pythagoras) in a play at the Rosicrucian Theatre, and also named one of her homes Theano.

Chapter 40 : In the various discussions about the location of the Lammas Night ritual, sources give a couple of different possible location. Gardner mentions the location as involving either the **Rufus Stone** or the **Naked Man**, but he also mentions they were starting points before going deeper into the New Forest. The Rufus Stone is on Geoffrey's lands (and I wanted to avoid that) while the Naked Man was rather too near existing spaces in use by the Army.

I stared a lot at maps of the New Forest and realised that the **Knightwood Oak** was a substantial but manageable walk from both locations (forming a triangle with them). At this time, it was part of a large enclosure of ancient oaks, not near any particular settlements or current Army or military use, and suitably private. As well as having a very interesting tree. (Current research seems to suggest that Gabe's estimate of the age is about right. Gabe knows his trees.)

The **four figures Gabe sees** standing together are arguably Rosamund Sabine, her husband George, Katherine Oldmeadow, and Gerald Gardner (identifiable by his goatee). Again, *In Search of the New Forest Coven* is what got me to focus on them. Though, as you see, they could be also other people, given those descriptions. What is notable is that all of them are on the older side. At this time, Rosamund Sabine and Katherine Oldmeadow are in their 70s, George Sabine was in his late 60s. Gardner, Dafo, and the Masons were in their 50s. Gabe and Isobel (at 40 and early 20s) are decidedly youthful by comparison.

On the other hand, if you'd like to assume they're other people, feel free to do that too.

The text of the Charge that the priestess makes is taken from the oldest version of the **Charge of the Goddess** in Gardner's writing, dating to before 1948. The first part is taken from Charles Leland's *Aradia*, as is the last sentence. The middle bit, "At mine Altars the youth of Lacedaemon in Sparta made due sacrifice" was removed in later versions (Doreen Valiente's, etc.) perhaps because it's both geographically confused, and because there are later lines in the text about not needing sacrifices. Even if they are very much on Gabe's mind at this point.

The actual **shape of the ritual** is drawn from comments Gardner made about it at various points. These include that the circle was marked out by brushwood, with a fire lit as candles in lanterns in the direction of the object of the rite (i.e. Hitler). They danced around the circle until enough power had been raised, then rushed in and out toward the light, shouting their desires. The text - "You cannot cross the sea, you cannot come" - is also as given by Gardner. The ritual was kept up until they were exhausted or someone passed out from exhaustion. Gardner explicitly doesn't talk about the mechanics of the energy work (as we might use the term these days), but is explicit that it relied on the life forces of the participants.

∿

I do hope you'll join me for Gabe's answer to Alexander's question in *Upon A Summer's Day* as soon as you can. Being Gabe, the interesting part, of course, isn't the answer by itself, it's how he's going to go at it. That book has six point of view characters, so you get to see a bit of how Gabe,

Rathna, Alexander, Geoffrey, Richard, and Alysoun fare through the second half of 1940.

My newsletter is always the best place to find out what's coming out soon, and to get more historical tidbits, answers to questions, and extras! (I have quite a few in mind for this book.) If you'd like ways to make more connections with other books I've written, my authorial wiki at bit.ly/celia-lake-wiki has all sorts of ways to link characters, places, and events together.

Happiest of reading to you!

ALSO BY CELIA LAKE

Best Foot Forward

Nocturnal Quarry

Old As The Hills

Upon A Summer's Day

Other stories

Complementary

Winter's Charms

Forged in Combat

Learn more about the world of Albion and future books at my website, celialake.com. Additional information linking characters, places, and timelines is available at bit.ly/celia-lake-wiki

Sign up for my newsletter to be the first to hear about future books and learn about fascinating bits of research. Happy reading!

www.ingramcontent.com/pod-product-compliance
Lightning Source LLC
Chambersburg PA
CBHW020830030726
47496CB00001B/174